Barbara Morris

ROAD WITHOUT SIGNPOSTS

CACTUS RAIN
PUBLISHING

Arizona USA

ROAD WITHOUT SIGNPOSTS

Published by Cactus Rain Publishing, LLC
San Tan Valley, Arizona, USA
www.CactusRainPublishing.com

ISBN 978-0-9962812-1-8

Cover Design by Cactus Rain Publishing, LLC
Photo Credit: Barbara Morris, Gardens of Dunvegan Castle, Skye, Scotland, 2013

Published June 1, 2016
Published in the United States of America

Barbara Morris

ROAD WITHOUT SIGNPOSTS

DEDICATION

This book is dedicated to everyone
who knew and loved Rhuraidh Morris
and to the uniquely wonderful RHM himself.

Son, the privilege was all ours.

ACKNOWLEDGMENTS

Thank you to Cath Stanley of the Huntingdon's Disease Association for her help and assurance, to all of my family, friends, and readers for their continued encouragement, to Runrig for their music and to their wonderful fans for the interest and support. Thank you, Alan, for the author photo!

Thank you to Skye Batiks for their ability to clothe me, inspire me and deck my home in colour, but mainly for supporting my writing efforts and making the Skye experience feel extra special each time.

My eternal thanks (in traditional alphabetical order) to Emma, Jake, Jayne, Jill, Kate, Monica, Morag, Rachel, Rowan and Sally - amazing ladies, who have always been keen to express their ideas and opinions during the writing days, and have made it such an easy task to put pen to paper.

Nadine Laman, Judith McKee and Cactus Rain Publishing, thank you. Thanks for seeing the potential and working with me to polish and refine the story – it has been a complete pleasure.

Finally, thanks to Geoff, for everything.

《●》《●》《●》

PART I

November 1993

CHAPTER 1

Saturday, 20th November 1993

Nervous energy, or its close relative anticipation, should definitely be made use of. It could help a person focus the brain, and if you soaked yourself in the situation of the moment for a short, intense period, you might come out of it feeling assured, if not elated.

It was this thought which accompanied Kate Wilder as she wandered around Camastianavaig Bay on an unseasonably bright November Saturday. The thought that when her family finally came around to accepting her 'outrageous' plans for her future, the end result would more than make up for this painful period of disapproval. She would be able to release and enjoy the love she felt inside, without further condemnation. But how long was it going to take?

The Isle of Raasay lay flat on Kate's horizon, partially bathed in areas of fluid sunshine, while the crags of Ben Tianavaig stood as sentries before her, protecting the cottage where her family were, no doubt, talking about her yet again. Honestly, how many more times could they accuse her of being insensitive and out of her mind? Her older sister, Hazel, had used the word 'certifiable', although Kate had a suspicion that Hazel had heard it on the telly the day before. Hazel rarely used such words, when wild gesticulations would do.

Kate settled herself at one of the picnic tables next to the gorse hedge, and listened as the water rippled and lapped a few yards from her feet. After two months in Canada, this place's familiarity was both comforting and upsetting. It was from this spot that she had watched her mother wander aimlessly in their garden, trying to spend 'every moment left to her' out-of-doors, where the scenery soothed her puffy eyes. Kate could hardly believe that only ten months ago her mother's illness had not yet been diagnosed; that their family had pottered about in that one-storey cottage, contentedly trying to find a way through life which suited each of them, totally ignorant of what was to come.

Ignorant of the speed at which the cancer would take Fiona's life, tearing her apart from the inside out, and unaware of the stagnant pool of depression that was about to close over them. In an attempt to prevent them from drowning in that foul-smelling grief, Fiona had astounded everyone by inviting her estranged husband into their home and asking him to keep the family together.

Kate now frowned, aware that in this area, she had systematically demolished every bridge the man had worked hard to build. In the two manic months since her mother's passing, Kate had divided their family even further, when he had tried so hard to keep it united.

As she sat twirling a white shirt button between her fingers, Kate felt the heat of the sun finally seep through her fleece and begin to caress her shoulders. Was it the sun? She had been outside for over half an hour, and yet it had only begun to affect her, as she watched the tiny piece of thread disengage itself from the button. The heat was spreading; over her collar bones and down her chest, settling on her stomach. It was a welcome sensation, one which she had learned to conjure by thinking of the button's owner.

David, tall with worker's arms, his face rarely clean shaven, was her love. Kate had barely touched the man's body, but regularly enjoyed picturing his skin through the gap from the missing button on his shirt. Thank God no one could read her mind, or her thoughts, too, would be condemned.

"Thank God," Kate repeated, and pressed the button against her flushed face.

Two weeks since she had left David in Canada. Two weeks since she had waved goodbye to his green eyes and bewildered face. Kate had not minded his dazed expression, because it had meant there was hope for them. Hope that he might allow her to love him, however much of a surprise it had been. And, relief that he had not immediately cut her out of his life. That was all anyone truly wanted, wasn't it? The chance to realise a dream with the person you needed the most? The hope that those closest to you would be as happy as you were? A cool breeze lifted the front of Kate's fringe.

All around her were the greens and browns of late autumn; the shrivelled hedges, dead bracken and bare trees; even the sea took part, showing off the same tones in seaweed and kelp. A solid block of red appeared in her eye-line, bumping its way up their drive. Kate was suddenly on her feet, furious at her own lack of concentration for the reason she was there. She cursed loudly as she ran, scattering the sheep who patrolled the road and startling the crows from the trees. How had she failed to notice the Royal Mail van's arrival?

Kate managed to maintain her speed as the road banked upwards, but as her trainers hit the gravel of the driveway, she saw the van driver hand the post to Hazel, and she skidded to a frustrated halt. Through her shallow breathing, Kate watched her sister laugh with the man, agree that the weather was a welcome respite from the gusts of yesterday and then accept his pat on the arm.

Apparently, when your mother passed away, folks felt that patting your arm helped in some way. Kate bit her lip at her own cynicism and waved as he pulled out of their gate, heading up the hill in a rev of purple fumes.

Hazel was standing motionless in the doorway, arms folded and devoid of humour now that they were alone. Equally, Kate was in no mood to toe the line.

"Anything for me?" she shouted, moving once more, but Hazel had already returned inside, the door closing behind her. That nervous shimmer which Kate had been so happy to entertain now formed a weapon and wounded her with panic. If David had replied to her letter, a letter where she had been amazed by her own eloquence, then it was private and for her eyes alone.

The first thing which struck Kate as she entered the kitchen was the smell of baking. The second was the look on her sister's face.

"What are you playing at?" began Hazel, her long, dark hair a spinning skirt of strands as she turned away from Kate. "You're spoiling everything – and you know it, which is the very worst thing about it. Why?"

"Would you like to give me my letters, please?" It was no effort for Kate to match the flint in her sister's voice as she held out her hand. They had not shared a soft word in nearly a fortnight.

"No," replied Hazel, as Beth appeared, making her way to the oven in pretence of not interfering; as their aunt, it was an act the older lady had perfected over the years. "No, you're not getting it. It's his writing and it's, it's not fair."

"Is it my name on the envelope? I'm pretty sure it's illegal for you–"

"Do you think I care? Grow up, for God's sake!"

Before the heat crawling up Kate's throat had a chance to erupt out loud, Beth stepped between them, her oven gloves giving the impression that she was ready to fight in someone's corner. With both nieces looking at her, wearing matching indignant 'I'm-right-about-this' expressions, Beth momentarily wished she could take the entire tray of shortbread and retire to the top of the Ben.

"Are those my photos?" said Kate looking at the package in her sister's hand, her voice rising before her aunt could say a word. "They're mine. I took them and paid for them."

"Come on, now," Beth tried to soothe, "Let's just take this back a step."

"Not while she's holding my post," stated Kate. "Give it to me," she said, extending her hand firmly toward Hazel.

There was a time Hazel might have turned to persuasion at this point, pouting in a way she thought endearing and citing her mother's dying wishes to make an impression upon her sister. But Kate's present crime did not permit this. Hazel, at three years her senior, had been injured more than any other by Kate's 'insane' declaration of love and intention. This was not a time for compromise.

"God knows what you said to him to get him to write back," began Hazel, her voice burning the air around them, "But you had no right. He's my–"

"So you think you're the only one with rights?" Kate felt her nose itch, a sure sign of nearby tears. She shook the itch away. "I've told you how I feel about him. I'll tell you again, if it'll make any difference."

Hazel looked hopelessly at Beth. "Are you listening to this?"

The two envelopes, both of which Kate had longed for almost as much as the touch of David's lips, were so close. If she could just bring this present fight to an end, she could be lying on her bed, precious sheets of paper in her hand and a pamphlet of Canadian photos by her side.

A week ago, when Beth had asked David to stop phoning the house, Kate had dared to hope that he might write instead. Since then, she had been waiting daily to intercept the post, and had only missed out today because she had let her mind meander through her feelings. Kate extended her hand further now, absolutely sure that she was on the right and proper side of this.

"I could ask him to write again, but I'd have to say why. Shall I tell him everything you've called me? Called him?"

This time Hazel did not move a muscle. Her face seemed to close down instead, as if someone had unplugged her, and her eyes which normally matched her name were black marbles in her head. Beth seemed to have stopped breathing. At any other time, Kate may have marvelled at the hostility in the room, but all that mattered now was that people should take her seriously and listen to her.

Hazel gently laid both envelopes on the table.

"Here then. Thank God Mum isn't here to see what you've turned into," she said. Not wishing to witness Kate's relief, she headed outside.

When Kate had her treasures in her hand, she was surprised to see one tear fall and land on her name, where the ink ran and the thick paper discoloured immediately. Hazel still had the power to slip beneath her skin and apply pressure to her nerve endings. Perhaps Beth wished that Kate would go back to acting for the greater good, as she had done for most of her life. Perhaps they should all try to understand her feelings better, instead of condemning her. Love was love, after all.

"Is it definitely from him?" asked Beth, sliding off the gloves.

Kate nodded and then dared to smile. The potential of this particular love affair was enormous. How was it possible that no one else in this house could see this? Not Hazel, Beth, or even Kenny, Beth's constantly unflappable partner. Did they really think that she deserved less than the best, after the revelations of the last year? When her entire existence, from conception to the present bereavement, had been the subject of discussion and opinion? Kate had changed, had been changed, and yet they assumed she would not react to any of it. She had reacted by grabbing relief, excitement and happiness where she found it, in the most unconventional of places. Yet it was only unconventional to others; to Kate, it made perfect sense, and she was almost positive that David loved her in return. He had told her so.

"Do you mind if–?" Kate asked, edging towards the hallway. Beth waved her away, as she hoped she would. Within a minute, Kate was lying on her bed staring at the ceiling, enjoying the shimmer once more, this time purely of anticipation. Whatever he had written had come from him and no one else. He would speak to her again as soon as she opened the envelope.

Inside the paper was lined, ripped from a notebook as if at speed. Kate smiled, trying to imagine David hunting for an envelope, concentration on his face, wishing to reply to her honesty as quickly as possible.

Dear Kate,

I'm sure I've never written a letter to anybody in years, but you make it look so easy. I can't promise that I'll be able to fill as many pages as you, but it feels good that what I write down, you will read. It seems a long time since we spoke to each other. The phone was okay while it lasted, but I miss talking to you face-to-face. You made me laugh. You made me take part, which was unexpected in itself, and it was great. How is Hazel? I need to know that she is okay ...

As Kate heard David's voice in her head, she tried to picture him twiddling his pen. She had known him only for a short while, but in that time had committed his whole self to her memory. She could not imagine he found the intimacy of writing easy, no matter how tall or handsome he was. She had seen a variety of emotions appear in his eyes, a range of expressions run across his face before he managed to conceal them, but knew that spontaneity was far too dangerous a concept for him. Oh yes, Kate knew how he worked, knew more about him than any other man on earth and knew that, at this moment, when one life had ended, she had the ability to save two in return. She wanted to do that more than anything. She would do it.

However, whilst trawling through her photos, sorting them fondly into those with people and those of the sights of a small Canadian town, Kate's confidence in her abilities began to dip. She caught hold of it quickly and, in an attempt to keep it from plummeting downhill, began to rearrange the items on her dresser. With that completed to her satisfaction, she lined her boots and shoes neatly in the bottom of the wardrobe and went to find a cloth to clean the bedroom window.

Her mother's vacated room had become hers in the aftermath of the fighting, and although a double bed felt strange, there had been some comfort in the space. Fiona sometimes floated in to say hello.

But as hard as she rubbed at the panes of glass, poking the cloth into the corners of the frames and peeling off the loose flakes of paint, her mind kept returning to David's letter and his concern for Hazel.

There Hazel was outside, wandering the garden as their mother had done, in just such a frustrated state. Never had they argued like this about anything, least of all over who had first claims on the heart of a man.

David was worried about Hazel, and Beth was fading away, fretting about everybody.

Kate sighed. If she was going to enjoy reading his letter again, she had to make some sort of effort to pacify her sister.

The kitchen clock seemed louder than usual as Kate poured tea into two mugs. She felt like telling it to keep the noise down, that she was about to go and speak to her sister and that pointing out the passing of time was not helping. She would not be rushed. It appeared to listen and allowed Kate to construct an opening sentence as she shoved two chocolate biscuits into her pocket and the pamphlet of photos under her arm. She found Hazel at the picnic table, her face flat on the wooden slats, eyes closed.

"Hey, H." It was all she had.

Kate placed one of the mugs three inches from Hazel's face and watched as her eyes opened, focussed, and closed again. She took the bench opposite the slouched figure and tried to slot her legs under the table without making contact. At this stage, baby steps were required. She sipped her tea and waited. After a moment, Hazel mumbled a few words.

"Sorry?" Kate said.

"I said, I'm not drinking that."

"That's not a problem," Kate replied, and brought out the biscuits. She heard Hazel sigh loudly, then, "I hate you sometimes."

"Do you want a Kit-Kat?"

At last Hazel levered herself off the table, two parallel lines now etched onto her cheek. She regarded Kate for a second, recognising a hint of regret in her eyes, and reminded herself that the girl had been through a lot and that surely, in time, she would outgrow this astounding infatuation. Hazel looked at the treat on offer, and picked up the packet of photographs instead.

"Go on, then," said Kate, and steeled for the next phase.

Holiday photographs. It was traditional that a person should comment on every single one of them, even if there were over fifty in number and not all of them contained a person or a spectacular view. However, this particular 'holiday' was in no way conventional and only warranted the term because it had involved both Hazel and Kate being removed from their island home and transported across the ocean to a new and exciting location. Hazel had come home after a fortnight, Kate remaining for an extra month, both of them returning with more knowledge, emotion and altered perceptions than they could ever have imagined.

Kate watched as Hazel waded through the pile of photographs, careful to ensure that they stayed in order; a habit they learned from their mother that they would take to their own graves.

Hazel remained mute throughout the viewing, even when the scenery on show was beyond anything they had seen before. When the first photo of Hazel and David himself came into view, Hazel let out a jagged breath, holding the image close to her face and marvelling at the fact that they had been so happy together. He had been everything Hazel hoped he would be, but now her experiences were tainted, and she felt her resentment threatening her again. Kate allowed her time to study the photo before handing over the next few landscapes, sensing that any words she spoke would jump-start the criticism and disbelief once again.

The first few days in Canada showed photos of Hazel in various poses, leaving the airport, outside the huge house they had called home for the duration and standing next to many of the town's weird landmarks. Then David had begun to feature more and more, usually with his arm slung along Hazel's shoulder, both of them beaming. Indeed, because Kate was less likely to drop the camera in a puddle or leave it in a cafe, she only featured in one photo. Hazel stared at this particular image now. It showed David and Kate by Lake Cowichan, the sun behind them and the slightly squint horizon proving that the photographer had indeed been Hazel. However, in spite of the poor composition, she guessed that this one was Kate's favourite of them all.

"Forgot to say," Kate's voice was determined to cut through the thickening atmosphere. "It snowed before I came away. I know you were hoping to see it, so if you look at the last few ..."

Hazel wordlessly viewed the sparkling pathways, the laden trees and the brilliance of the blue sky against each subject. The sights were beautiful and would normally have had her gasping with delight, but she knew her voice would have sounded hollow, so she said nothing at all. The final picture showed a pair of spectacularly carved wooden gateposts, over eight feet tall and composed of interconnecting Celtic knots. At last, Hazel trusted her voice.

"I'm glad you took a photo of those," she acknowledged. "They really were a work of art. Thanks for showing me all of them."

"It was your holiday, too."

Hazel finally took a gulp of tea. She looked out over the bay, wondering exactly when their world had begun to crumble. The easy answer was with the death of their mother, but they had coped with that together. The sad fact was that, in spite of her dad's efforts, the truth about Fiona and subsequently Kate had ruptured something. It had separated Kate from her mentally, had tossed the girl into the air and failed to catch her as she had fallen. Kate was still hurt, bruised and totally out of her mind. Maybe, with patience and a little give and take, she might consider accepting that there was no possible future with David.

"Could I have one of him and me? For a frame?" Hazel saw no point in skirting the subject any longer.

"Yes. Take any you want."

"Thanks."

«●»«●»«●»

When the sun, which shone through the clouds for the whole of that Saturday, sank and the moon took over the night watch, Kate took her photos and her letter to bed with her. She read the notepaper sheets twice, before tucking them safely into her pillowcase and sliding down the bed. She had one more nighttime routine to perform, however, and she hauled both her Walkman and a single framed print from deep within the bedside cabinet. Having generously left her favourite Runrig tape with David in the hope that he might listen to it and think of her fondly, she now switched on her latest compilation. She needed to hear those words as she laid her eyes on the only photo of David where he was looking directly at her, speaking to her, smiling at her alone. He was leaning out of his truck window, his hair flattened by the hat he had hastily removed on seeing her, and his grin was one of genuine pleasure.

His rough chin was unshaved as always and she loved it. His green eyes were crinkled against the snow brightness and she loved them. His hands on the steering wheel were gloved and huge. She loved his hands. And she loved his mouth. She had kissed him only a handful of times, each one confirming that her heart was without doubt set on the right course, even though he had been incredibly cautious and had never really responded until they had said their airport goodbye. That was fine. From what she had seen, he was sensitive and moral, a man who knew that people would not view their love with an open mind, and he refused to compromise anything by rushing ahead. But he loved her. He had said so and promised her the time and backing required, even if it meant that at the end of this they could not be together.

Kate closed her eyes against that thought and instead saw David saluting her, his eyes shining, as she had disappeared through the departure gate. It had been the hardest walk Kate had ever taken, effectively removing herself from him for God knew how long. But each day had cemented her plans, and she warmed herself knowing that only David could end this, and she trusted him not to. He was, after all, not some fickle teenager who spun the same yarn to all of the females who took his fancy. David had loved only once before and that had not ended well.

Kate knew that she would never let him down, never give in to the pressure, and never love anyone but him. She could not change the fact that she was seventeen, but not one person could stop her from knowing her own mind and heart.

After all, she had witnessed for herself how a life without David had affected her mother, and had understood the depth of the woman's despair. How had Fiona stood the time away from him, her husband, with only Hazel as a reminder of their love? It was unthinkable, but one stupid, unplanned error in judgement had robbed Fiona of his trust and company. In its place, it had presented her with the product of that awful mistake, Kate.

CHAPTER 2

Saturday, 20th November 1993

David Wilder was not a vain man, but for the third morning in succession he stood before the mirrored door of his wardrobe, looking at the form before him. He had made himself look into his eyes, searching for a cut-and-dried solution to his dilemma, whether it followed his heart or not. Nothing had been forthcoming. So instead, he studied his body, an action so rarely performed that he wasn't exactly sure what he should be assessing.

He was tall, at least six-five, and during all of his forty-five years on earth, he had carried no extra weight. He knew that this was due to genetics, and his wish to remain as actively involved in the manual side of his timber business as wage-slips/contracts/meetings allowed, rather than from some fitness plan. His hair, straight and dark brown with thin silver strands appearing only at his temples, was of no particular style yet still covered his entire scalp. His chin, almost permanently graced with a bristly coat of brown and grey patches, always looked determined, although there was no earthly reason why he should remain so loathed to take a razor to it. He should actively do something about this. Apart from the odd lines around his eyes, he also had a scar which ran from one eye socket to the middle of his cheek-bone, but was noticeable only up close. Kate had seen it, of course. She had touched it and asked him to relate the full story.

David sighed, his shoulders slumping slightly as the quiver of pins and needles started yet again in his hands and feet. What on earth was he doing? Kate, young and bright, but with a soul surely forged somewhere deep in the Dark Ages, was forever on his mind. She had sat across the table from him, in a crowded diner, and sworn that she loved him and would never stop loving him. How was a man of his age supposed to react to that? He went over the conversation again in his mind, anxious to remind himself that his conscience was clear. He had not taken advantage of her feelings, he had not laughed or scorned or hurt her intentionally in any way. But neither had he brought a halt to her wishes. He had been unable to and the reason was simple enough. He loved what she was and how she made him feel.

David now wiped the mystified dampness from his brow and made himself stand tall once more. Kate had insisted that his face was perfect – 'it makes perfect sense' – a phrase he had yet to understand, but she had been smiling when she had said it, so he had not argued. He wondered, what of the rest of him? Okay, so his stomach muscles were still his friends, his collar bones were defined but not protruding, and his chest, although lean, was acceptable. Maybe he should let it see the sun more often, and instantly David was laughing at the absurdity of this last thought. When had anyone seen his body in the last seventeen years, other than Rose on laundry days, and here he was, intending to become a bronzed Adonis? Just as instantly, despair grabbed laughter by the throat, as if it had been waiting for a good excuse all morning, and finally he sank onto the bed, his face clammy as he held it cupped in his hands.

He was thankful that it was a Saturday, as there was no way he could motivate himself physically until he had untangled the electrical wiring misfiring in his head. There were so many aspects of his life which were being thrust in his face, some of them astonishing in their opportunity, yet nearly all of them with the power to cut him down. They needed to be put in order before he took another breath, and he had to start with Fiona.

"Oh, you are up," Rose's voice was relieved as she stood on the threshold of her son's bedroom, but she did not cross it.

"Yeah, couldn't seem to get going today," he replied, at last pulling on the T-shirt he had been nursing for the past ten minutes of self-reflection, and tucking it into his jeans. It was a day made for layers; but Rose, satisfied that he was still alive, did not wait to watch him button his shirt over the T-shirt or haul his jumper over his head, and instead shouted that his breakfast was on the range when he wanted it. As he pulled on a pair of socks, he thought again of Fiona.

Fiona, the estranged wife he had never divorced, had been his world; the young Scottish nanny who had caught his twenty-three-year-old eye from across a busy Duncan street, as she talked to her mesmerised charge in that matter-of-fact way youngsters loved. She had looked and sounded different from every other girl he had known, and many had been sniffing around him back then, although he had always assumed that it was because of the family business rather than his charm. In his mind, tall could be construed as lanky, and when the only people viewing your muscles were a bunch of similarly decked woodcutters, it meant nothing. Fiona had more than matched his interest, and within months they had sealed their deal.

It was irrelevant that Hazel had decided to make herself available to all before they had a chance to marry, although David always wished that he could have given Fiona the spotlight she deserved on the big day. She, on the other hand, only wanted David and the baby and insisted everything else was for show. She had completely fitted into life at The Edge, the seasoned old house which Rose and he still occupied, and it seemed incredible even after all this time that things had turned out as they had. He had long ceased to look for somewhere to lay the blame. Kate's conception had been the result of so many individually insignificant paths taken, that on any other given day, her precious life would not have come into being. That would have been a tragedy. He loved Kate.

"Oh, God in heaven," groaned David, staring at his clothed feet. He seemed incapable of thinking of Fiona and Kate in two separate compartments, and yet this was completely necessary. If he was ever going to be anything other than cruel to Kate, he must separate her from her mother. If he was ever to consider the possibility that there might be a new life ahead of him, he needed to take Fiona out of his head, and that was as inconceivable as every other part of this conundrum.

Apart from the fact that she had lived in his mind for every minute since her return to Scotland, had in fact cleared a space there and kept it tidily hers, she had given him the most incredible daughter and therefore he would never really let her go.

From the moment Hazel was born, she had squeezed his heart in the best possible way. She had evolved from a screaming pink rabbit, through a wide-eyed, giggling grabber, to a long-haired, chatty whirlwind in three years flat; and he had driven home to them, smiling, even when work had tried to break his spirit. The dark days had come like a soot-fall, uninvited and polluting everything around. The accident which had scarred David's face had also broken his leg in three places and left him a hobbling wreck for months afterwards. But this disability was insignificant when compared to the injuries caused by Fiona's downfall.

Unable to be with her for weeks, he had not understood what she was saying, as she had sobbed and clawed at her own arms. She had spoken English, had indeed looked dreadfully ill, but words such as 'pregnant', 'hurt' and 'leave' had seemed an alien language coming from her mouth.

She had been insane with remorse, but with each further attempt at an apology, he had felt only ice-cold chain mail wrapping itself tighter around him. When utter disbelief and the pain in his chest had subsided enough for him to realise that he was about to lose everything - his love, his daughter, his plans - sheer panic had set in and he had stood on his crutches, begging her over and over to stay. He would never forget those glazed, black eyes staring back at him, welling and pouring until she had physically run from his presence.

"David! Phone." It was Rose, cutting into his melancholy.

"On my way," he replied, unaware that the phone had been ringing. He took the two flights of stairs to the ground floor as he had done as a boy, three at a time, and was awarded with the same frustrated look from his mother as this had always produced.

"You'd think breaking your leg once would be enough for anybody," Rose muttered, handing him the receiver, but he took it in good part and patted her shoulder as she left.

"Hello?"

The voice on the other end of the phone was female and friendly.

"Hi David, it's Kathy. How are you?"

"Kathy," he breathed, surprised but refusing to let himself become even more burdened by complications. "Well, you know, still reeling from the last few months. How are things with you?"

The two of them exchanged niceties for another half a minute or so before Kathy suddenly suggested they meet for a drink sometime or indeed that night, if he was not busy.

"A drink?" he repeated, failing to keep the alarm out of his voice.

"Look," she encouraged, "the boys are with their dad, and I just feel like we've only been half-communicating, when there's a lot I would like to share. Maybe, something you might benefit from hearing."

"Oh, well," he replied, suddenly aware of Rose's figure in the kitchen doorway. He turned his back to her. "I may have to do some paperwork later on..."

Rose watched him pick at a piece of peeling wallpaper near the light switch, struggling with the conversation, then finally heard him agree that it might be beneficial to talk. By the time he had arranged a time, something which appeared to require an unnecessary amount of planning on both their parts, Rose had handed him a mug of coffee and gone back to her chores. When he wandered into the kitchen a few minutes later, his face still registered some confusion, an expression Rose had never been able to ignore.

"That was Kathy? How was she?"

David leaned against the sink, sipping coffee. "She sounds okay."

Rose was braising beef, watching as the onions bubbled in the meat's juices, but she had time to stir and scrape the pan three times before he spoke again.

"I'm going to meet her for a couple of hours tonight. You want any groceries brought back?"

"No, I'm good."

Rose took a plate loaded with pancakes and bacon from the warming oven and placed it on the table. David eyed it with pessimism and then closed his eyes, rubbing them absently.

"What's up, son? I've never known you to be up later than me on any day of the week. Are you missing the girls?"

"Sure," he said, taking his seat but pushing the food away from him. "It's like, there was nothing but hope for so long. And then they were here, taking over the place, making a noise and now..."

"I know," Rose sighed. "Now it's back to just you and me, and I can feel it's not enough. No offence."

"None taken," David laughed, for he had been thinking the same thoughts without having the nerve to voice them.

"Well, you have tonight to look forward to. Is Kathy going to come here first?"

"Rose, it's not a date before you go thinking—"

"Did I say any such thing?"

His coffee finished, David stood once again, sheepishly looking at the still groaning plate.

"Don't throw that away. I will eat it, just need to get an appetite first. Give me an hour at the woodpile and I'll clean it."

From the corner of her eye, Rose watched the man scratch his chin before pulling on his boots. She fought and beat down the urge to suggest he shave because, renowned as she was for her aversion to facial hair, she knew it was not the time to mention it.

Of the three men who had lived with her in this house, only her late husband Pete had shaved daily, and that had only been to please her. She had long since given up on David and his younger brother, Neil, hoping it would be a habit they would grow into. They had not.

"Won't be long," he murmured, hauling on his outer coat and hat.

The statement did not need acknowledgement, but Rose turned towards him anyway. "Oh, you could maybe wear one of those new shirts tonight. You know, one from the pile Kate picked out for you."

The door was shut before she could hear his reply, but as she looked around, Rose suddenly felt a smile tickle her face and she stood, enjoying the feeling for a few moments more.

It had been three months since David had packed himself off to Scotland for Fiona's funeral, and from that time, every day had brought some kind of revelation or memory or feeling that required addressing. At seventy-three, Rose had not only found it exhausting but unsettling in the extreme. Yet their life at The Edge had become so staid prior to the girls' visit, that she had almost welcomed the disruption as much as she had welcomed Hazel and Kate themselves. Now it seemed both David and she wanted more of something; company, challenges, prospect of change, life. And here he was, meeting up with a friend from the past. Well, whether the time was right or not, she was going to recommend that he shave before he went out.

《●》《●》《●》

David sat on a bar stool, debating the wisdom shown in his choice of footwear. Since early November it had snowed on and off, turning the roads and pavements to an icy, grey slush, and yet here he was, wearing his newest boots. Already there were matching salt lines forming between the dry and wet suede of each boot, and he stared absently at them, unaware of the song on the jukebox or the gentle milling of other patrons. He had worn those boots only once before, on the night Kate had opened her heart to him, and he liked to think of that small connection to her, especially when meeting with Kathy, whose agenda was still unclear.

"Hi, David. Goodness!" Kathy cried, assessing his frame as he stood. "You're looking very... lean."

"I think the word is skinny," he smiled, as ever deflecting anything approaching a compliment. "Involuntary stress diet."

Hesitantly, Kathy leaned forward and kissed him quickly on the cheek, then said, "Hey. You look great. Very smart."

"I have Kate to thank for that. This is the new sociable me." He smiled, shaking his head slightly, and then turned back to the bar. "What would you like?"

"Well, I'm bunking at my dad's tonight, so I am allowed a glass of red, please."

As David ordered the drinks, Kathy hovered beside him. She was trying to convey an air of complete comfort in her surroundings, but suddenly felt as if she had 'divorced-mother-of-two-out-for-a-good-time' stamped on her forehead. David looked only slightly less self-conscious, and the barman, a man she had occasionally babysat for when he was a boy, insisted on recognising both her face and her angst. He winked at her as he spoke to David about the weather so she moved quickly to the one free table while she had the chance.

"You okay?" David asked, noticing her flushed face as he joined her.

"Sure," Kathy replied, feeling no compulsion to air her insecurities, especially when there was so much to discuss. He enquired no further.

"So, Kate got back safely? That's great. I imagine it must be suddenly deathly quiet in your household."

"Rose and I were commenting on it this morning," he nodded.

"Well," Kathy rolled the stem of her wine glass between her fingers and thumb. "They are certainly a credit to Fiona. Two lovely girls."

David said nothing, but she watched him swallow as his eyes acknowledged her words and he chewed his bottom lip.

She had known David Wilder for over twenty years, had stood in as a bridesmaid at his wedding when Beth had been unable to attend and had spent many a night in his company back then. She knew that he would speak only when he had organised his thoughts, and so she waited, sipping her wine and looking around her.

"I don't know how she did it," he pondered. "I don't know how she created two people like them."

Kathy smiled but said, "Tell me what you mean."

"Well, you know what Fee was like. She was so sure she was doing everything wrong, so hard on herself, at least where Hazel was concerned. So anxious."

"But," Kathy was amazed. "She was a brilliant mother."

"Of course she was," cried David. "But she only ever believed it when I reminded her of it. She needed me for that, if nothing else."

Kathy looked at David's animated face and her stomach lurched once more with sympathy. He had not just loved Fiona for her personality or her presence, he had loved the fact that he was needed and appreciated. She marvelled that he had survived for years without acknowledgement of either.

He took a deep breath and forced himself to smile again, but was unable to stop himself from shrugging.

She touched the sleeve of his sports jacket, but said nothing.

He spread his hands in front of her. "Well, there you have it, Kathy. Without any input from me whatsoever, Fiona brought up my daughter and Kate and created two people who seem far more capable of dealing with life than any adult I've come across. Two amazingly accepting people."

"Accepting?"

"Of me. Both of them. No recriminations for keeping my distance, no questions about why I didn't tackle things differently. I love them both."

Kathy, replaying his last sentence in her head, knew that he had inadvertently opened the door on her reason for being here, and decided to cross the threshold there and then.

"The thing is, David. Beth rang me last week."

"Ah," he replied, reclining in his seat and closing his eyes for a moment. "Looks like some parts of my brain are still active. I did wonder if that's what tonight was about."

"And yet you still agreed to come?"

David took the back of his finger and wiped condensation up the brown glass of his beer bottle. He watched the trickle of cold water run down to the table before sitting forward and rubbing his chin.

"Because I need help, Kathy. I'm about as lost as I've ever been."

Kathy was a Realtor, and she had learned never to show any emotion which could be construed as vaguely negative. One wrong expression could break a deal in an instant, and she had developed the knack of smiling automatically, then following it up with a more genuine reaction. She felt her mouth sag at the edges, recognising real confusion in the man's face, which deserved more than her token smile.

"Yes, I think you may be," she agreed.

David regarded her quietly for a moment or two, trying to fathom how many defences he should raise where she was concerned. True, they had once been close. Fiona had been the link between them and they had enjoyed that easy closeness that befalls couples when the females are confidantes. Kathy had also stepped in twice when things had reached crisis point; once years ago, when Fiona had spent her last traumatic days in Canada under Kathy's roof and then again when Kate had discovered the circumstances surrounding her birth. She had removed the girl from the hell she had found herself in and looked after her until she had come through the worst. It looked as if she was still acting as a go-between, and it stood to reason that she had opinions on the matter. He was not sure how his honesty would be perceived.

But he had no choice. He needed an ear that was not his mother's or his sister-in-law's or his daughter's. Kate's views were clear, but that was of no help whatsoever. If he believed what she was saying, they were going to form some sort of magical team to take on the world. It chilled him and energised him in equal amounts, to the point where he wasn't sure what his last thought was. Another perspective was required, and he must listen to whatever Kathy had to say or live with the knowledge that he had based his decisions on his and Kate's feelings alone.

"Do you want me to start, or do you need to tell me what is happening over there first?" His voice was non-committal.

"David, I'm not here to tell you what you should do. I just want to hear that you are okay. I know you, and believe me, that works in your favour. I know what you are," Kathy paused while he digested her softly spoken words, then, "Are you okay?"

David held his head before looking at the ceiling for inspiration.

"How is Kate? I've spoken to her a couple of times and she was so ... enthusiastic that I couldn't make out what was actually going on. Beth, on the other hand, was quite a bit nearer the bone."

Kathy looked at the man before her, studying his eyes. They were green in colour, but in all the conversations they had had, she could not remember having held his gaze for longer than a second. Now, she wished that she had learned how to read them better. Clearly, he was not keen to discuss his state of mind. Nor did he like being studied as he ran his fingers through his hair and looked away.

"Are you okay?" she repeated, more forcefully.

"What do you think?" he spoke softly. "My daughter is back in my life and I couldn't ask for anything more than that. She's such a spark, loves her life, has a boyfriend. She even looks a bit like me in a certain light. And, then there's Kate."

Kathy gulped at her wine. This was unexpected. She had imagined a total shutdown or complete outraged denial where this subject was concerned. Instead, he was leaning back in his chair, his face showing mainly pained confusion and some other emotion which Kathy could not instantly name. Still she waited. A young couple walked hand in hand through the bar area, laughing at their life, and David's eyes crinkled suddenly in despair. He scooped up the bottle of beer and drank, then looked straight at her.

"You know when you live in your own world and eventually, even if you don't want to, you have to take the time to look at what you're doing, what kind of person you are?"

Kathy nodded silently, specifically not to break his train of thought.

"Well, I guessed I was an okay sort of guy. You know, nothing inspiring but good enough. I didn't steal, I liked my mom, I tried to support my daughter. Pretty ordinary, pretty safe. Now, I'm in serious danger. I feel like I'm about to press the self-destruct button, and I'm not sure that I'll be the only casualty."

His pause suggested he needed some encouragement to continue.

"In what way?" It was all she could think of to say and cursed herself for not having more imagination. This man did indeed need to talk.

"Because after Hazel left I had nearly a month with somebody I really liked, who gave me all her attention and made me feel needed. It was the most unbelievable time, and I enjoyed every second of her company. Then," he lowered his eyes, but did not alter his expression, which Kathy now recognised as hope, "she told me she loved me and it changed gears again. I felt that way, you know, when somebody thinks you're special enough to risk everything? Do you remember that? Well, unbelievably, I let her know that I ... I didn't totally dismiss the idea. Do you see? I've set us up to be obliterated, and I've almost certainly lost Hazel for good this time. I have no idea what I am doing."

He finished his speech with a wild shrug of his shoulders and drained the bottle of beer in one deep slug.

CHAPTER 3

Sunday, 21st November 1993

Dear David

How are you this week? I know I had to tell them, but I hate that it means we can't speak on the phone now. I might try to save some change and call you from a phone-box, or I might just write more letters to you. I'm now on first name terms with the Postie! One way or another, we WILL keep in touch.

Hope Beth wasn't too awful. Basically, she is tearful and worried, jumping between trying the guilt angle – what would mum say etc – to trying to be understanding and labelling me as grief-stricken and out of my mind. Kenny tends to follow her lead, which is fair enough. I'm glad he's in the house though. You don't want to know about Hazel and I mean that. I know it's selfish, but I can't risk telling you what she's like, because I know how much you love her and you might listen to her. She might be able to change your mind and I can't let that happen, because I would never forgive her.

But I'm not going to waste my letter-writing time on the negative bits. How is Rose? And Neil and Andie? I can't wait to get to know the pair of them oh so much better. I hope they're all well. But who am I trying to fool? You know and I know why I write to you. It's to remind you that I'm here, waiting, and that you never have to be alone again. Even after all the shouting and the grumpiness (which is still going on), nothing has changed at all, not for me. I think about how you look and how you smile and even how you sounded on the phone, even though we couldn't really say very much. At least, I'm hoping that's why you were so backward in coming forward! I still remember the way you kiss, my man, so don't go telling me that distance has made a difference. That's the best thing about writing, nobody else need ever know what's being said, unless you accidentally leave this lying around! Of course, I'd rather be saying it to you in person, looking up at your face and feeling your heart beating inside your jumper. I might knit you a jumper if I can find some nice wool.

What I'm saying is, I really miss you and wish you were here every single day. It's my first wish when I wake up. My second is that it won't be too long before we see each other again, although I know it could be months. It's just ridiculous. I'm here at home, not going to school and spending all my time either thinking about you or just missing mum, which then reminds me of you and it all starts again. In a strange way, mum is closer to me than she ever was, and I think, think, she's on our side. There's no way on this earth that she would stop me being happy and I'm absolutely certain that she wants you to feel loved and cared for and needed. I need you more than I've ever needed anybody, even though I've never felt stronger. But I also love you.

There, I've said it again and I'll keep saying it, so that if you still wake up and worry about what we should be doing in this situation, you'll always be able to reassure yourself that I'm not looking for anything or anyone else in this world. And the rest is up to you. I'm not going to force you and there's no rush. Well, apart from the fact that sometimes when I remember your arms around me and your hands on my face, I want to be with you so much I could scream. I ran the whole of the way down the Ben the other day, just to get rid of the adrenalin, which, if you knew how uneven the path is near the bottom, would have worried you. Only slid onto my knees once though, was quite impressed. And it was your fault. I'd been leaning against the pillar, watching the rain come in, and thinking of what it would be like if you suddenly appeared and pulled me to my feet and kissed me. I was so full of you that I couldn't sit still. You could have been the cause of serious injury!

I know I'm the lucky one. Of all of us in the house, I'm the one who has a positive set of thoughts as well as a negative set, and I find it really sad that my positives are their negatives. I don't know how to help them without giving us up and I won't ever do that, so it's really just a case of getting through the day and going to bed with your photo and my dreams. I know we can't have Christmas together, but please let me come over in the New Year, sometime, if the weather isn't too bad for you to travel to the airport. My worst moments come when I wake up and think that you might have already stopped thinking about me as anything but a pest. You need to tell me if this is the case. It would be better for me not to dream about our life together if you can't do it, but I'm really, really praying that you still want me. Oh, and I'm going to look for a job – need to make some money of my own. I'm not sure I qualify to do anything at the moment, though, apart from annoy people!

I'd better go. I want to get this to the post office so that you can be reading it as soon as possible. Please say hello to Rose and Neil and Andie, I'm hoping that you will see each other over Christmas and maybe we will be together this time next year? Remember how much I love you. And always will.

Kate xxxxxxxxxx

P.S. tell me that the Rotary Club is not having a Christmas party. Or at least if it is, tell me that you're not going. I don't want to lose you to some gorgeous executive.

CHAPTER 4
Sunday, 28th November 1993

At the age of twenty-eight, Rose Wilder's first pregnancy had resulted in the birth of David John. He had been a particularly long baby, and had refused to make his appearance until two and a half weeks past his due date; but her joy in adding a third character to the partnership of her and Pete had known no bounds. Even an infected Caesarean wound had not detracted from the event. Rose was the third of four girls, but Pete Wilder was an only child, and it was this lion of a man who had wished to fill The Edge with children since the day of their wedding. Rose had been up for it immediately.

When David was nearly two years old, Rose's second pregnancy had come to a bloody, painful conclusion in its fifth month; but in spite of the trauma of burying the tiny female infant, Rose and Pete had woven themselves another layer of comfort and support and had wrapped themselves in it. They had named their beloved departed daughter Rowan and had planted a mountain ash at the side of the house to tend and to love.

Two days before Christmas, in David's fifth year, Rose had been found sprawled, barelegged, on the bathroom floor, crying and grey-faced. Before her, wrapped in a towel, had lain a mass of clots and sinews which she had refused to hand over, even to Pete. Christmas that particular year had been something for other people to celebrate. There had not even been a burial, but in the spring, Pete had returned from Duncan with a small Amur cherry. He had let David help with the planting of it, explaining its significance to the boy in such a way that had made Rose's heart ache and sing at the same time.

Rose had been neither a frail nor frightened young woman, but Pete had refused point blank to entertain the idea of another pregnancy. So an alternative route had been sought, and in 1956, Neil Peter Wilder was brought home to The Edge, to a family as determined as they were delighted to welcome him there. David had marvelled at the prospect of a brother to follow him around, until his eight-year-old mind realised that this would not happen in the first two months of his existence. But Neil had never been anything but a bonus, somehow matching his adoptive family in height and build, and proving to Pete that a sibling was nothing short of essential to a growing boy. Neil's white-blond hair, bobbing amongst the dark heads in the house, had been the only clue to his separate origins.

Neil had taken his first adult steps as a woodcutter, becoming skilled with a chainsaw and taking pleasure in the extra cash in his pocket and the lesser responsibility afforded to the second son of the timber firm. By the time he was being eyed as a prospect by the area's young lovelies, his brother had met and married Fiona, and he had accepted the change in the little family with wide-eyed amazement. He had been able to enjoy an easy relationship with the young Scot without feeling the need to impress her, and had taken his duties as an uncle very seriously, providing the toddler Hazel with hours of attention.

Before the shock of Fiona's folly had torn all of them to pieces, he had been toying with the idea of going to college, finding great satisfaction in designing and carving wood into furniture and accessories. The family's demise had put the plan back a year or two, but now Neil spent his hours in his workshop on the outskirts of Port Alberni, lost amongst wood shavings and designs and natural dyes. His hair was more of a mid-blond these days and he wore a thin beard. He seemed a slightly less polished version of his brother, but again, he was allowed to be. He was a creative, and if he was to be completely honest, David envied him his ability to dress as he liked on any given day.

Andie, Neil's girlfriend since their final college year, was an interior designer and they lived above Neil's workshop at the end of a scrub track. They had been rebuilding the house, as money allowed, for over ten years, and the two-storey wooden structure was now fully wind- and watertight, with a beautifully hand-crafted kitchen, walls painted in deep, earthy colours and not much else. Whenever Rose asked after the general state of the house, they would cheerfully assure her that all was well and that Maslow's hierarchy of needs was being satisfied. Nowadays, Rose merely asked after Maslow.

It was the last Sunday in November and Andie was visiting her mother, leaving Neil to walk their three dogs before he settled into a day of Christmas orders. He was well on schedule to filling these and indeed would have preferred a few more to ease them through the famine that was the post-holiday winter, but Andie had a contract starting in January to create three show houses on a new estate by the airport. They would be fine and may finally be able to rip out the ancient bathroom suite, which in turn would please Rose immensely.

As Neil tramped back through the plantation which surrounded the property, whistling every time one of the dogs disappeared into a snowdrift, he heard the approach of a vehicle and looked at his watch, surprised. However, it was not Andie's car but David's dark grey SUV which came slewing towards him and he waved, grinning beneath the peak of his hat.

"Hey, Dave," he greeted, as his brother exited the truck. "You on your own? Rose okay?"

"Yeah sure, sure. She thinks I'm meeting...some... Well, I said I was taking someone to lunch. You think I could talk to you?"

Neil studied David for a moment before removing his hat and scratching his head. David seemed distracted, pale, less sure of himself than ever before. It sent a tiny tremor through Neil, but he did not allow it to show on his face.

"Anytime. Go up, I'll just feed this lot."

By the time Neil was discarding his outdoor layer, David was standing by the wood-burner, staring into the moving heat behind the glass. Neil frowned, watching the complete lack of motion involved in this activity and wondered how he would be able to help the man deal with his apparent predicament.

Before approaching him, Neil poured coffee into two mugs and took a deep breath. Whatever was coming, there was nobody else present to help absorb it, and Neil felt a very familiar tightening of his diaphragm. But he trusted David. He would never come to him with more than he could handle.

"Here you go."

David took the mug without acknowledgement, such was the depth of his preoccupation, but Neil refused to let his innards tighten any further and spoke with a firm voice.

"What's happening? You look spooked."

David shrugged. "That's not a bad way of describing it, as it happens. But if you want the truth, it's going to take a fair bit of your morning. Can you spare the time?"

"Yes," Neil answered, as if the reply surprised him. "Is it Rose? Or the girls?"

At last, David took a seat by the fire, his face showing a slight covering of moisture as he sat beneath the standard lamp. "It's all of them. It's everything, including Fiona."

"Right," Neil's voice was firm to the point of being forced and he felt his fists clench before he could stop them. He took a seat on the sofa, specifically to stop himself moving away from the situation and the tension. David immediately sat forward in his own chair.

"Hey, Neil," his voice was low and even. "Do you remember when I was teaching you to drive? You said that you would never, ever get back in the cab with me as long as you lived; and that if ever I needed to learn how to use a chainsaw properly, not to come to you for help?"

Neil was staring at him, but suddenly grinned. "Well, I was always a better cutter than you, you just couldn't see it."

"If you need that delusion to get you through the day, then so be it."

"I'm a better driver than you, too."

David sat back in his seat. "Well, I do need help now, little brother. Your help. How are you feeling?"

Neil pressed himself into the material of the sofa and took a gulp of coffee, grimacing as it burned the inside of his mouth and assaulted his gullet on the way to his stomach. He knew that his face and body language were betraying him, but he was merely on the cusp of panic and did not wish to acknowledge it.

It seemed to Neil that his relationship with David was indefinable. As boys, even with eight years between them, their bond had been strong. They had shared, they had fought, they had worked together, and they had helped each other survive black times.

But since Fiona had left all those years ago, David's presence had always been a possible trigger for Neil's anxiety and panic attacks, and this was a continual source of sadness for both men, and Rose. The consequence of it was simple. They rarely saw each other more than twice a year and almost never at The Edge. It was easier for Neil to keep his distance from the scene of so much pain and destruction because it was there that Neil had accepted responsibility for what had happened. The family had thought it ludicrous at the time, of course.

Yes, he and Fiona had gone out with friends to see a band, they had gone on to a house party and they had all had far too much to drink, but the extent of the shared knowledge ended there; at least, to the majority. When the inescapable consequences of the night's activities had eventually presented themselves, Fiona, Neil, and ultimately Rose, had painfully buried the truth. It had been a decision born out of devastation, disbelief and desperation, respectively.

Neil, however, had not been able to withstand the guilt. He had been nineteen, and his inability to cope had resulted in almost two years of withdrawal from the world, broken up only by visits to a therapist and the occasional trip out of town for wood to carve into complex and intricate pieces. He had created the two huge gateposts that marked the entrance to their estate, spending hours alone with his thoughts and designs, resulting in two unequalled works of art incorporating Celtic knots. Eventually, when life had slowed to a calmer pace for most of the family, he had forced himself to leave for college, honed his craft and had settled near Andie's hometown, which was the safest option. His last visit to The Edge had been to meet Hazel and Kate, where he had experienced a small 'episode', but everyone had appeared to deal with it.

Now here was David, acknowledging that the possibility of another was at hand, and Neil did not know how to react. With Andie he was, for the most part, a strong, steady adult. With David, he was a lost, guilty, younger brother. With no warning whatsoever, he was about to spend his day as a child when he had expected to be a creative man.

Yet, wasn't it the case that David had come asking for his help? What was it that was causing this man to sit across from him, pale and confused? Whatever it was, David had put his faith in him, spinning a story for Rose and travelling the eighty-odd miles through snow and ice to speak specifically to him.

Neil sat up straighter. "I'm fine. I'll be fine. I wish I could say the same for you, Dave. You look like you could do with a whisky."

"It's probably a very good thing that you have none in the house then," David paused, and then rubbed his eyes before speaking again. "Neil, I am this close to doing something that scares me to death. Honest to God, Mr Blend-into-the-background is under so much threat at the moment. But before we get into that, I need to tell you something."

"Right. Fine. Go ahead."

David watched as Neil began to rub his thumb under his chin. It was a classic move of his, and it brought some sense of normality to this potentially disastrous discussion. But David had had over a two-hour journey to organise his thoughts, and he liked to think that he would not have contemplated the trip had it not been absolutely necessary for his sanity.

"Okay. Well, we're all aware that Kate gave us each a farewell letter from Fee, and I really hope that yours helped you in some way."

Neil nodded, perspiration gathering on his throat, causing his thumb to slip forward from his face. He wiped it on his jeans.

"My letter," continued David, "was something I'll always keep close to me. But I can share with you that she never stopped loving me; and to see that in writing, when we couldn't actually say it over the phone, did close some really draughty doors for me."

By the end of this little introduction, Neil's head had sunk and was resting on his chest. His pained face, suddenly showing his age and isolation, did not halt David's words, but it did slow them down.

"Before Kate went back home, she left me the letter that Fiona had written to her. She wanted me to understand what happened, in her mother's own words."

During the silence that followed, logs could be heard spitting behind the glass, and one of the dogs breathed the long contented sigh of the newly fed as he lay at Neil's feet. His master did not speak to him, however, but began to massage his own forehead with the fingers of both hands. He spoke to keep the room from spinning away from him.

"Kate said she never wanted you to know. She said it wasn't fair to you, after all you'd done for them," said Neil.

"Fiona's letter didn't tell me. I knew from the minute I saw Kate's face on Skye."

Neil swore under his breath, almost intrigued that after seventeen and a half years, he was in the position which he had sweated, cursed and panicked about on an almost daily basis. Yet here he was, sitting in a warm room with his big brother, and there were no harsh words or bitter intimidation keeping them company. It had been an expletive formed from disbelief and shame, but also from relief where he had expected terror.

These overwhelming emotions which accompanied the one, quiet word also caused tears to edge down his face, and he leaned forward into his knees, his arms crossed in front of him. It was at this moment that David had to remind himself to proceed with caution. Neil very rarely welcomed physical contact.

Rose was able to comfort him, was allowed to hug him to her smaller frame and untangle his head and hands when he was suffering; but other than Andie, people were not invited into his space. David needed to keep the man safely with him, needed time to explain how much he now knew and how much of it he accepted, and so he remained seated, waiting to see how this would go. But after a minute of watching the man doubled over, his artist's hands cradling his head, David could witness his pain no longer.

As he stood, David pulled a hankie from his jeans then sat, uninvited, beside the distraught man. The dog at Neil's feet suddenly jerked up and moved away from the drips raining down onto its scalp, but not even this action halted Neil's distress. When he did not take the offered hankie, David put his arm firmly along Neil's shoulders and held him in a tight, non-negotiable grip, taking the hankie and pushing it into his hand. Together, they wiped Neil's streaked face and allowed it to dry by the heat of the fire until one of them felt it was the right time to speak. It was an incredibly calm period which followed. Minutes passed. Neil remained huddled over his knees, but the tears had stopped, and now he was staring into space, content to have David's hand still touching his shoulder. Maybe they could take the rest at a slow, safe pace.

"Do you want me to tell you now?" Neil whispered. "I can do it, I think."

David studied his brother; his face, his posture and knew what it had taken to put that offer on the table. But in truth, he did not really need to hear his version of events. Fiona's explanation to Kate had been comprehensive and designed to show how much she valued and trusted her daughter with the facts. But it had also been compassionate and honest; and while it had caused David to revisit his worst times, it had also swept up the last of the broken glass in his heart, because they had all suffered enough; he, Fiona and Neil. One mistake on one extraordinary, lonely, drunken night had caused this catastrophe. Something as fundamental as human contact had broken their lives; but it had been years ago. There had been far, far too much suffering, when neither his brother nor his wife had set out to hurt a soul. It was time to bring it to a close.

"No. It means a lot that you would try, but this has got to be put to bed, Neil. This stops now. Fiona has gone, and I can't stand the thought of us still skirting around this for years to come. We need to learn to live without it."

Neil toyed with the idea of offering one last apology, but it seemed pathetically juvenile and so horrendously inadequate a gesture that he could only unfold himself from his position and lean back against the sofa. He closed his eyes for a moment, then flexed his clenched fingers and rubbed them against his thighs.

David himself sat back, and for the shortest of moments, it felt like they had gone back to the days of arguing over which TV channel to watch, an activity which had usually ended in them rolling about the floor until one of them submitted. In those days, Neil had been half his weight and height, but they had been equally determined to come out as victor. At the end of each scuffle, they had always sat back down together and watched a bit of both programmes, but they had always needed the scrap first. It was their game.

Now David looked around him at the life Neil had created. Andie and he had no children together, and it would never occur to him in a million years to ask if this had been a conscious decision. But he did have one question.

"Does Andie know?"

Neil nodded his head. "She knew years ago. I'm sorry."

"I'm glad you've no secrets from each other," replied David. "They're poison."

They sat for another few minutes, two men lounging on a sofa with dogs lying around them, caught in their own thoughts.

David saw Fiona in his mind's eye, looking sad and ashamed, but with the slightest suggestion of hope on her face, and it caused him a small smile. Then, as ever, his mind turned to Kate, and his heart grew warm from the inside out.

Neil saw Andie, the other half to his whole, with her waist-length black hair and totally shared conviction that they needed nobody but each other in this life. She had found Kate intriguing, but in no way a theat.

When Dougal, the Bernese mountain dog of the house, finally yawned loudly enough to wake the other sleeping canines, both men shifted slightly in their seats and simultaneously took a new breath.

"You hungry, Dave?"

"Starving."

As he stood, Neil was on the point of handing David back his hankie, but then smiled slightly. "I think I'll get this washed first."

Watching Neil move confidently around the open-plan kitchen, David was momentarily mesmerised by the fact that they had survived the conversation and guessed that he would never actually get the measure of his brother until they had left this cleared hurdle miles behind them. How long would that take, and how was his own current dilemma going to compare with this in Neil's mind?

As if by some telepathic connection, Neil glanced over at David as he prised apart two defrosted steaks. His colour and original demeanour were returning, and so David slowly made his way to the kitchen table and sat, arms folded. Neil handed him a beer from the fridge then busied himself with some mushrooms. Eventually, although the atmosphere was relaxed way beyond expectation, Neil felt he had to clarify one or two more points.

"Andie told me on our second date that she would never have kids. I sometimes wonder, when the night demons force me to think, if that was one of the initial attractions, and yet that would make me a sick, sick man. She's a beautiful, complete person, and I doubt if I would be here without her. But it did allow me to tell her again and again and again that no kids suited me fine, which was a bonus."

"Why?"

"Why was it a bonus, or why did neither of us want a family?"

"Both."

Neil handed David a lettuce, a bowl of tomatoes and a knife while he chewed over the words to use in reply. "I saw how completely enchanted you were with Hazel. And how totally destroyed you were when you lost her. I knew I would never be brave enough for that and... also, I didn't deserve to have anyone in my life." He paused, then, "That would have made Kate irrelevant."

Neil took a deep breath in and leaned against the countertop for a few seconds, still amazed that he was acknowledging Kate's connection to him in his brother's presence. David thankfully allowed him his moment without commenting and continued to chop lettuce with his unpractised hand. "Maybe you'll feel differently if you keep in touch with Kate," he suggested, eventually, "Maybe you and Andie -"

"Andie was sterilised when she turned twenty-one, so no choice there. And we're happy, Dave. We don't need anything more."

David stopped chopping immediately. Instead he watched as Neil's tall figure moved back and forth between the frying pan and pile of onions and mushrooms, wondering at the reason behind so irreversible a procedure at such a young age. Eventually Neil, realising that the statement had silenced his brother, turned to face him, wiping his hands on a tea towel.

"Lots of secrets in this family, Dave. It's not good, is it?"

"Hell's teeth, Neil. We didn't know."

"Not my story to tell. But please don't ask any more. I can't tell you, it wouldn't be fair. I mean it, before you start. I've said too much already."

It was typical of Neil that he should assume this explanation would suffice, when there were dozens of questions hammering inside David's skull. "Okay. No, I understand that, but God almighty." He handed the bowl of decimated lettuce over to Neil, ignoring his brother's dismayed face at the contents. "I feel like the worst kind of big brother. We need to see each other more often."

"We can give it a go, sure." Neil grinned, never quite ready to commit to something which might prove too difficult, and instead hastily finished off David's pitiful attempt at a salad before placing two rare steaks piled with onions and mushrooms onto the table.

They ate in silence for a minute or two, both still adjusting to the knowledge each had given the other. This knowledge was still sitting on the surface and needed to be fully absorbed, but this would be easier later, when they were both alone. For now, they could go back to where they were happiest, discussing the weather or David's latest plans for the business. Suddenly, Neil frowned.

"Hey, Dave," he began, "what about Mr... what was it, Blend-into-the-background? What's up?"

David instantly laid down his cutlery, chewed for a moment more, and then shook his head in despair.

Neil look confused. "Come on. What on earth can it be that Rose and her encyclopaedic brain cannot find an answer to?"

"Rose doesn't know."

Neil now raised his eyebrows until they disappeared under his blond fringe. "Jeez, this is serious."

"Yes, it is. Serious, and no doubt highly unexpected, so don't say you haven't been warned."

CHAPTER 5

Sunday, 28th November 1993

Dear Kate,

I guess the reason for this second letter is that my first was a bit of a test for me, and it wasn't up to much. I didn't know if I could put any of this down on paper, but it looks like I can, so I'm giving it another shot.

I hope everything is calming down for you at home. I know things will be awkward and I wish I could keep you safe from it. Here, it gets a bit colder and a little bit more boring every day – as boring as this letter is compared to your page after page of tales from Skye. Yes, I can hear you speak as I read your letters and I smile for most of the time. The rest of the time, I worry. That's me being honest with you. In the past ten days, I've met with Kathy and Neil and both visits went reasonably well. Beth had contacted Kathy to tell her what had happened, but actually she was very fair about it all. She listened and she seemed to appreciate parts of our situation. Whether she really understands it, I have no clue.

Neil's visit today was my idea. I want to be his friend again, Kate. I miss him and this all seems to be urging me to do something about that. Of course he kept his distance all these years – he had a conscience – but we all still have lives ahead of us and I told him that I know everything. I'm not sure if this was your plan, I'm hoping that you will see the sense in it. Clean slate, I suppose.

I also told him about us, asked him his opinion, really. I needed to see his face, to see his actual reaction. He didn't say much at all, and I can't even tell you what that means because I don't know him these days, don't know how he works. That is not good enough, is it? Maybe we'll be able to figure him out together one day. Anyway, he knows. It was a very, very strange day and I wish I could give us both some peace of mind, but I can't yet. Rose thinks I'm interested in Kathy and I'm not putting her straight. I know, you want me to be honest, but maybe I'm not as strong as you. Not yet, anyway.

I can be honest with you, though, and truthfully, I'm still in a state of shock. Not just because you seem to have fixed your heart on mine, but because I'm not doing anything to stop this, and that might be wrong. I'm so worried that you're going to end up worse off because of me. I do want us to have a relationship, whatever shape that takes, because I think you are a remarkable person, Kate. But I also want you to know that if we can't make it to the other side together, you'll still always be welcome here, at The Edge, in my life. That will always be the case.

I don't know when we will see each other again. I think Beth and Hazel will both need to have a major change of heart before that happens. But maybe time is what we need, I don't know. Nothing in my life has ever threatened so much damage, so I don't really know how to act. I'm hoping that it will become clear sooner rather than later, because I do miss you and I do love you.

Take care, Kate. I'll be thinking of you.

David x

P.S. No plans for a Rotary Christmas party

35

CHAPTER 6

Sunday, 28th November 1993

Neil lay on his back, his body perfectly still, arms folded on top of the duvet. Even his eyes were immobile in his head, staring at the ceiling but seeing little as the sun had yet to illuminate his world. Andie's regular breathing was keeping his own heartbeat at a steady pace, and he could feel her bare upper arm against his ribs. It was a necessary and appreciated touch, which helped to maintain his sense of hope. He had to stay on the positive side of his thoughts, in light of all that he now knew.

He blinked and took in as deep a breath as he could safely do without waking Andie. David's unannounced visit had more or less thrown all normal activities out into the snow. He had not lifted a tool nor washed a dish since David's departure and had sat by the fire, Dougal's snout pinning his right foot to the floor, until Andie had come flurrying in with the dusk. He could still remember the tightness in his chest as David had confronted him and then how the blackness in his brain had finally begun to fade to grey as his brother had held him in his tight grip for as long as had been necessary. But that had only been the start of their discussions, and by the end of them he had felt, for the first time in their life together, the more able of the two men.

He remembered David's eyes, which had jumped back and forth as if trying to read the answers to his own doubts in the air in front of him. David's confessions had been so completely unexpected that Neil had simply sat, stunned, allowing his brother the chance to address every possible opinion on his own dilemma from every possible angle, without finding a solution. As his words had slowed to a few disconnected thoughts accompanied by as many sighs, David had finally looked in his direction. Neil had not been able to utter a word.

"As hopeless as that, then," David had smiled, weakly. "I thought it might be. Oh well, we don't need another catastrophe, I suppose."

As he had leaned back against the sofa, Neil had scrutinised David's face and had been appalled to see his brother's eyes brimming with acceptance. Quickly swiping at the liquid with his thumb and middle finger, David had then laid his head back and stared at the ceiling, until Neil had finally found his voice. "Dave, is this real? Can there really be enough there to even talk about it?"

David had continued his study of the ceiling. "You don't know the difference she has made to everything, every part of my day. I don't think I'll ever be able to explain that to anybody. So yes, it's real, but I don't understand it. Don't understand her. It's not just that she wants ..... me, it's that she never wants to forget Fiona, wants to talk about her. To me. I just don't know what Kate can get from it. Do you?"

It was a question which had returned again and again to Neil, since the moment he had watched David's SUV disappear at the end of the driveway. He had felt a little sad at that moment, imagining his brother's solitary drive back to The Edge with absolutely no answer to help him cover the miles. But Kate was a mystery to him, and he was as baffled as David by her motives. In the short time they had spent together, she had looked so downright lost one second and so full of fierce determination the next that it was impossible to categorise her in any way. Yet David seemed to trust her, unbelievably young though she was.

Was it up to him to try to decipher her further? David had come to him of his own free will, not because he was Kate's father. David had sought the help of his brother and Neil appreciated this trust. He sighed and immediately felt Andie's forehead connect with his own.

"Speak to me," she murmured, her breath warming the tiny pocket of air between them.

"Are you awake enough to talk? More to the point, do you really want to miss out on sleep on a cold night like this?"

Her answer was to switch on the bedside lamp and pull the mohair bed runner up and around her shoulders. She smiled at him. "Okay, what do we have? Well, we have your brother, one of the most straightforward men I have ever come across. And we have a strange young woman who happens to be the daughter of the wife he hadn't seen in years. They seem to have become attached to each other, quite strongly. It's unconventional, but it's not actually illegal, so thank God for that."

Neil's reaction to this was to raise his eyebrows for her to continue, amazed that so few words had summed up the improbable situation. She pulled a face which seemed to be a mixture of regret and empathy.

"Of course, the fact that you are her biological father makes it unbelievably complicated, but - and it's a big but, Neil - it's still not illegal. David is not related to Kate in any way. And since nobody but our little unit knows the truth anyway, the only thing that people will actually feel the need to question is the age difference. And that's only if it ever works out and they get together publicly. Who says it will?"

"They're thinking about it, though. Dave would never have told me otherwise and he looked so animated. It's so completely unlike him, the whole thing ..." Neil reached for her hand. She clasped it tightly, silently appreciating the current simplicity of their own life.

"Okay. Well, I can't help feeling a bit sorry for him. Of course he's confused. And what man isn't going to be flattered by someone who swears that they will never love anybody but them? Especially a man like David, whose emotions have been frozen since his twenties, and the person doing the swearing comes with no apparent agenda, is also very pretty and .... relatively unjaded."

Neil frowned, going along with her in principle, but not ready to commit to agreement in full. Her words were giving no credit to Kate and he felt almost defensive of her. But Andie was not finished.

"I like Kate. I think she's been dealt a rough hand, and I also think she's possibly the most serious person of her age I've ever met. I've seen the way she watches people, and when they were here that day, she never took her eyes off him unless somebody spoke to her directly. I'm not in any doubt that she believes that she and David can be happy. But you don't have to have a psychology degree to know why she's attracted to him."

"I understand all that," Neil shifted so that he could put his arm around Andie's shoulders. "Dave himself understands it, that's why he's so uptight about the whole thing. Even Kate has brought it up, they've talked about it. How she'd like to get to know me as the 'person who made her' but that all she actually wants in life is him. And apparently, she'll wait until he's ready. Can you believe that? She'll wait until he's ready."

"Wow," breathed Andie, suddenly sitting forward. "You mean, there's a chance that this might actually go further? Honestly, I thought it was all hypothetical. God almighty, who is she? Was Fiona like this?"

"Not when I knew her," Neil rubbed the stubble under his chin. "She spent most of her time questioning her own worth, which was absolutely ridiculous, or looking for reassurance from Dave. She was great with Hazel, though."

As the picture of Hazel in her brightly coloured snowsuit and pink mittens jumped into Neil's vision, Andie felt his arm tighten around her shoulders and she reached up to hold the hand that hung by her face. It was not enough.

"Jesus," he gasped suddenly as he shut his eyes and cringed against her. "Oh, Jesus. Where did that come from?"

"Hey, babe," she gripped his face between her palms. "Neil, breathe through it. It's just a thought, just a picture, it's not here with us. It can't cut you or make you bleed, it can only sting a bit. Right? Right, Neil?"

"Right. You're right, Andie. You're always right."

"I am always right. Now, tell me what you saw."

"Nothing, really. Just a snowsuit and mittens, Hazel laughing at me. She loved me so much. I called her Honey-bee."

Andie felt her throat constrict slightly, but she showed nothing on her face even though Neil's eyes were still screwed shut. She stroked his chin and kissed his knitted brow.

"It's a memory, Neil. We all have them. And the next time you remember this one, you'll smile because Hazel isn't dead. She's older and taller but she still lives on this earth with us, and you can talk to her by picking up the phone. She's fine. You're fine."

When Neil opened his eyes, the entire room was a blur, but Andie's face was the first thing to come into focus, and its familiarity allowed the sting to cool a little. The dizziness was abating, the cold sweat on his arms drying as Andie patted them with her hands. But the fear that yesterday's revelations were going to make this a more regular occurrence would not go away, and he gritted his teeth, suddenly angry. Andie sat back immediately, which made his self-disgust not only shoot faster to the surface but punch its way through it. He threw the duvet from his body and reached for a long-sleeved T-shirt which draped the arm of the nearest chair. His jaw was aching.

His jeans were shoved on and zipped before the dogs were even alerted to the movement, but by the time he had clothed himself in another two layers, the three of them were jumping at his chest in unexpected delight. Andie watched him carefully from the bed, remembering how often they had played this scene in the time they had been together, but felt no real despondency. He was doing what he always did; running from what upset him the most – his own frustration at his weakness - and she could cope with it. In their early days, she had tried to follow him to ensure that he was not putting himself in any danger, but his aggression had been alarming; and after each flare-up, he would always ask her quietly to simply let him deal with it. As the door banged, Andie slid down beneath the duvet and pulled Neil's pillow, still warm, into her arms.

Outside, Neil breathed through the tight air. There was no wind but he was breathless, and as the dogs thundered away from him along the uneven path, he tried desperately to take in sufficient oxygen. But his inhalation kept snagging midway. Mittens and a snowsuit. Huge, shining eyes and long strands of deep brown hair. The word 'Neil' preceded by the word 'Uncle'. It was all still there in his head and stamped on his heart. But what had been accepted and dealt with and locked away in the rafters was now leaking through the joists, dripping onto his life, and he didn't need it. He didn't need anybody reminding him of then and who they had been. All he needed now was Andie and the dogs. He especially did not need his niece, or even his daughter, encroaching upon it, because with them came their mother.

The image of Hazel had been clear; turquoise snowsuit with a reindeer on each knee, pink mittens with bright red woollen ties. Toothy grin. But there had been another face present. And that face had cut through the muscles in his chest and gripped his lungs without mercy. The eyes had been sparkling, the mouth grinning out words of encouragement as Hazel had tried to balance on a pair of brand new skates. There had been bare hands gripping the snowsuit around the waist, and pushing the little body gently towards him, amid many excited giggles and squeals. In another world, the overwhelming memory would have been of brightness and warmth. But in his world, Fiona's face, so full of trust and faith in him as she let her most precious burden struggle in his direction, only served as a reminder of the enormity of the family's loss.

"Uncle Neil! Catch me. Hold my hand!"

"Well, if you want me to hold it, you're going to have to reach for it!"

"I'm wobbling!"

"That's not wobbling, Honey-bee. That's skating!"

"Mom! I'm skating!"

As Neil slowed to a halt at the edge of the plantation, his breath finally evening out and allowing him to whistle for the dogs to stay close, he tried to put the memory into some context. If the ponds in the west wood had frozen enough for a toddler to skate on, then it must have been mid-winter. And if Hazel had been articulate, then it would have been the year of their last Christmas together, between her second and third birthday. The Christmas before David's accident. The Christmas before the world had juddered on its axis and everyone he knew had lost their balance. He leaned against the loose wire of the fence and looked at the sky. There were few stars, thank God; he had no need of sensory distractions.

The recent arrival of Kate had more than distracted him. He had known so little about her, but even her appearance in the room had caused his mouth to dry up. She hadn't looked particularly like Fiona, she was a little taller and a lot thinner, but that could have been grief and disbelief at their circumstances. She also smiled less, but again, that was to be expected. However, the day they had been alone at the lake, when she had handed him a letter from Fiona and had announced that the setting was the perfect place to listen to her last words, he had instantly been reminded of his sister-in-law; her absolute certainty that what she had given him was a gift and her pure joy in doing so. That was Fiona.

Kate and he had sat metres from each other, entranced by the letters; his absolving him of all guilt and insisting that the product of their union had always been cherished; hers explaining carefully and gently that this man was her father and that in some perplexing moment, her mother had loved him. After re-reading his letter twice, allowing the pain in his shoulders to recede as he read of Fiona's continued care for his well-being, he had watched Kate. Her eyes had studied the pages – and there had been many of them – without lifting her head, but occasionally she had crinkled her eyes and bitten her lip. And as she had laid aside the last page, she had glanced in his direction, and somehow he had found the strength to close the distance between them. Up close, there had been no judgement in her grey eyes, but her silent inspection of his face had brought home to him that they were indeed connected. He had gazed back at her and had glimpsed a familiar enquiring expression, like a reflection of his thoughts as well as his looks. It had been the oddest moment.

And now. Now, there was a chance she could become so much more involved with them all, and he might have to spend time in her company. He had no earthly idea what she expected of him or how she viewed him. Why did she not despise him? On top of everything – the initial betrayal, the agreeing to the secrecy and then his obvious lack of backbone in dealing with the whole thing – Kate now worshipped the man he had hurt the most. For the strongest of men, it was a situation not without problems. How was his infuriatingly unpredictable mind going to handle this? In spite of the cold, Neil's face grew hot and heavy, and he found himself folding up against the freezing wires. He hugged his knees but refused to shut his eyes, focussing instead on the tiny light still visible from the house, moving only when Dougal licked his face. He cupped the dog's wet jaw in his hand and gently eased it away from him.

His jeans were soaked, and suddenly he was in a dim sitting room, being reprimanded by Fiona for standing about in wet jeans. He could almost smell the mixture of every alcoholic drink they had tried that night, which had been the only familiar thing in the room. They had both been exhausted, out of sorts, missing their ordinary lives and trying to find the positives in their respective miserable situations. They had succeeded; he was going to go to college, where he would be a magnet for any bright young female who liked a man with skilled hands and artistic hair; and she would soon have her husband back at home, recovered, where he belonged. They were laughing, then she was crying and needing to be held. That first hug had knocked him sideways, as he held close the person who made him smile in the mornings and drove him mad with her self-analysis; the person who adored his brother and was only sad and lost now because she was drunk and insisted that every disaster in their world was her fault.

"Neil, can you lie here with me? Can you put your arms around me?" Her words had caused his head to spin and his heart to jump behind his ribs. What was she asking? Her eyes, large and pained, had appeared to need him, but perhaps he was seeing only what he longed to see. He had stepped away from her, aghast that his body might not be able to conceal anything from her if she made the simple plea again.

"It's okay," she had taken control, her voice soothing his shock. "I just needed a hug. I'm sorry. We'll put this whole thing down to too much whisky and my needy nature. Tomorrow it will seem —" and then he had kissed her and she had kissed him back until his vision had turned red and his hands had found every part of her that he had ever dreamt about. And her lips were on his face and her hands were on his waist. Then they were apart, staring and gasping and not crediting any of it. He had tried to run, the panic inside him a foretaste of how his future life would be tainted, but she had stood before him, strong and adamant.

"We will not speak of this. Not tonight, not tomorrow, not years from now when we think it doesn't matter anymore. We will never talk of this to anybody." He had agreed, without the slightest knowledge of how they would ever survive the days ahead of them. Had that been the end of it, it may have spelled weeks of awkward silences between them, the odd sheepish glance or complete and utter avoidance of each other until the treachery had been laid aside. But it had not stopped there. They had tried to repair the damage by apologising and excusing and shouldering the blame, and it had evolved into something which even now had the ability to make him sweat in his own clothes.

She had touched him. She had handed it over, her gift born out of loneliness and illness, and he had taken it with gratitude and love. It was the first and last time he had seen Fiona's true power. After that, life had turned into a collage of torn images. All the strength that he had ever known followed Fiona's out of the door.

Now Neil was shaking. Part fear, part anger, part cold. Was he to go through life depending on Andie to prop him up, watching her tackle each new challenge of his with the same patience? He was taller, stronger and older than his beautiful partner, and she deserved protection; but here he was once more, floundering, providing reasons for her to lie awake and comfort him. There was the kitchen light now glowing, as she undoubtedly re-stoked the wood-burner and filled the kettle. She would curl up on the sofa and await his return, even if it took all night.

Neil was on his feet in an instant, the frozen moisture in his jeans cracking as he pushed himself back towards the house. He whistled loudly, but did not wait to ensure the dogs followed him. They were big enough to take care of themselves. As he marched up the steps and in through the door, he found Andie still leaning by the sink, flicking through a magazine. He saw the usual look on her face, the one where she assessed him, and for once saw it alter to surprised delight.

"You okay, babe?"

He did not answer but took her hands and held them above her head, kissing her as he pushed his body against hers, and then hooking them around his own neck.

"I'm okay. I'm cold and I'm tired, but I'm where I want to be and I'm doing what I want to do. We have a good life, right?"

"We have a great life."

"Okay then. We're the lucky ones. Let everybody else do what they need to, whatever that is. I don't care anymore. Come to bed."

CHAPTER 7
Tuesday, 30th November 1993

The island that was Skye stood ever defiant against the gusting winds, which picked up powdered snow and dropped it at random over hillsides and streets alike. Its jagged mountains tried to remain hard and black against this assault, but they, too, were eventually softened into grey, and then white. Kate didn't mind; she had wisely chosen the bus over her bike and was sitting on a seat in the middle of Portree, wrapped up in the coat that David had bought her for the Canadian autumn. It would have warmed her even without the heavy-fibred layers, because he had chosen it for her. She was also wearing a woollen jumper of his, a dark brown cable knit which she had sneaked into her suitcase before leaving him behind, and she wore it whenever she was not in Hazel's company.

As she waited for the bus which would take her as far as the turn-off for Camastianavaig, she pulled the cuffs of the jumper over her knuckles for extra comfort, and told herself again that she should definitely knit him a replacement. Her gloves lay in the bottom of her bag, soaked through and of no further use. They were keeping her Walkman company, as it had slowed to a halt on the journey in and she had not bought spare batteries. Yet she refused to let her spirit falter, because she was singing inside her head, and she had David's jumper to keep her hands warm. Of course, it was too big for her, but she loved to feel the wool tickle where it made contact with her skin; and now, freezing on the bench, she closed her eyes and thought of David's face. It was all she could do on a day like this, when the world was intent on spoiling everything, and heading home had stopped being a pleasure.

"Hey, Kate Wilder! Where have you been?"

Kate was on her feet in a moment, her shoulder bag falling from her lap and spilling onto the wet pavement.

"Hellfire," was all she could manage, as she began to gather her bits and pieces, shaking the grubby water from pens, a packet of tissues and her purse. The shout had come from across the square, and she knew exactly who its owner was. It was just after 3 p.m. on the last Tuesday in November, and Kate had felt sure that all of her acquaintances would be safely confined at the high school. Yet here was Shona Syme, wrapped around her stupidly handsome boyfriend Campbell, both of them tripping their way towards her, apparently unable to let go of each other. As she straightened up, Kate managed a small wave and wrapped her scarf tighter around her mouth.

"Wow, Kate, it's been ages. What's going on?" Shona's voice was more friendly than mystified, and her face was pink with the cold. She looked stunning in fur-lined boots and leggings, Campbell obviously thinking so by the way he had her gripped against him. Kate shrugged, prompting Shona to speak again. "You look like an Eskimo!"

"You look like a model," replied Kate, wiping her wet hands on her jacket. "So nothing's changed there then."

Shona grinned and then pointed at Kate's jacket. "Thank you, miss. But honestly, where did you get that monster? I only recognised you because of your bag."

"Canada," smiled Kate, patting her coat. "Vancouver Island's best. It's actually the height of fashion over there. I am officially Canadian trendy."

"If you say so. We're going for a cuppa. Kate could come, right, Cam?"

Kate's face fell as he nodded. "I'm waiting for the bus," she faltered.

"Oh, come on. You've been AWOL for weeks and weeks. You can get the next one, or Campbell has his dad's car. He could take you as far as the road-end. Please?"

Still Kate hesitated. "The roads aren't great ..." she tried, looking from one expectant face to the other.

"They might be better in an hour?"

Kate studied her friends for one more moment before giving in. Maybe this was a good thing. It would be her first little taste of opinion and reaction from someone not so close to her; if she was brave enough to tell them anything.

"You're right," she shrugged. "You sure you don't mind, Campbell?"

"Not a problem," he said, pulling Shona tighter into him. "But let's go. I'm perishing here."

The coffee at Nicolson's was always served in unique hand-thrown mugs. A potter up by Digg offered discounted goods in exchange for free advertising, and there was one mug which Kate particularly admired, but had only been given once. It was olive green, low and bulbous, with royal blue and scarlet leaves painted beneath the glaze. She liked to cradle it in her palms and loved the colours. Maybe today she would be drinking from this mug.

With the lunch rush over, Kate secured a table by the window and watched as Shona peeled off her red Puffa, dispatching Campbell to the counter.

Then, as she slid into the seat opposite, the girl made sure her polo-neck jumper was smoothed over her frame and her hair was exactly as she liked it.

Kate gave her an uneasy smile from inside her own suit of armour.

"Are you going to sit and swelter?" Shona asked.

Kate pulled her scarf reluctantly from her face, practically igniting her hair from the static and unzipped her coat. As she hung it on the back of her chair, she heard a small intake of breath from Shona and turned back to find her staring at her.

"What?"

"Exactly. What? What in the hell are you wearing? The coat was bad enough."

Kate frowned. "You know, we're only about ten degrees south of the Arctic Circle, and the buses aren't well-known for their heating. It's a very comfy jumper and I like it."

"It's bloody enormous."

"It traps air, therefore keeps me warm, and I like the colour. Also," Kate pointed, "that's hardly a school uniform, is it?"

"Well, I haven't been there since lunch. The uniform's in my bag." Shona's grin told of unconfirmed shenanigans of which Kate required no details, and thankfully Campbell's return meant that the discussion was off the table.

"So, Kate," Campbell began, "are you ever coming back to school?"

"Nope," Kate said simply. "I've left. In fact, I'm looking for a job."

Shona's eyes widened as she looked straight at Campbell. "Well, that explains one thing."

"What's that then?" Kate asked, warily, as Campbell nodded his agreement.

"Ellis's mood," supplied Shona. "Och, he's a right crab just now. No jokes, lots of sighing. He must be so pissed off at you."

Kate shrugged her confusion.

"Oh, come on, K. You were going to be his greatest success. The rest of us might get a B if we add our marks together."

Kate sighed, wishing the coffee would arrive. But it was taking its time, so instead she found herself relating the tale of Mr Ellis's visit to the cottage. It had possibly been the most uncomfortable, surreal situation she had ever squirmed through, and it was still unclear whether it had been spontaneous on his behalf or whether Beth had set it up.

Mr Ellis had been Kate's English teacher, a man her sixteen-year-old mind had much admired, and she had taken much pride in letting her ability in the subject present itself. She had liked his humour and his praise and the man himself, even though he had an odd line in tweed ties. But her seventeen-year-old mind had altered so much in the past three months that she had barely recognised him as Beth had ushered him into the sitting room.

The meeting had been excruciating. Kate, never having seen him in any other context than his over-decorated classroom, had sat red-faced, listening to his theories on 'reactions to grief' and wondering what she would say to him if he ever stopped talking. Beth had eventually slipped from the room, perhaps hoping that it would encourage Kate to open up, but she had remained mute, while Mr Ellis voiced his further thoughts on 'wasted opportunities and regrets'.

Kate had studied him until his words had become a meaningless murmur. He had sandy hair, bordering on the ginger, and he had obviously come straight to the cottage from school, his purple tweed tie a testament to this. But he had seemed smaller than she remembered, scaled down from the norm, and it had made her smile as she realised that her norm was now David and his six-foot-plus frame. Mr Ellis seemed to have taken this smile as some sort of encouragement and had confidently played his final card about how her classmates missed her and that it didn't feel the same without her.

She had felt a bit guilty about her first words to him, in spite of his bizarre presence in her sitting room. She had asked him, in a friendly tone, if he had ever watched his mother struggle with a crippling illness while trying to stay upbeat and strong. If, in fact, he had then lost said mother and had been presented on the day of his seventeenth birthday with a father he had never met; if he had had to question his loyalties from birth when this man turned out to be a decent person who had offered a temporary existence away from all the crap. Or even, if he had then been told that this man was not his father at all and not related to him in any way.

As her teacher had sat shrinking in his seat, she had brought her own final card to the table. Could he imagine still finding Edgar Allan Poe, excellent being though he was, relevant to any of this? Mr Ellis had left soon after, and now Kate wondered if that was what was actually annoying him; the fact that he had not been able to give her an answer. Her story finished, Kate looked up triumphantly, expecting some credibility for finally having developed a spine. She found them both staring at her.

"He's not your dad?" Shona's voice was low. "That tall guy at the funeral? So, why did he come?"

"Because he's Hazel's dad," the words stuck in Kate's throat, which she found surprising. Surely she was used to this by now?

"Shit a brick," breathed Shona, leaning back against Campbell, the implications of Kate's statement writing themselves onto her face one by one.

"That's big," agreed Campbell, shifting in his seat and looking over at the counter. "How long do three coffees take?"

"Bloody hell, Kate, no wonder you've been lying low. I mean, having to cope with all of this. And neither wonder that you look like one gust of wind would blow you away. Cam, go and order some millionaire shortbread to go with the coffees. She's skin and bone."

"Thanks for that," smiled Kate. "I'm really vexed I didn't meet up with you before. This criticism, it's great fun."

"I can't believe you're still smiling."

"It's okay," replied Kate. "It's getting sorted. Things could be worse."

Shona's doubtful face made Kate's words sound implausibly optimistic, but then Shona did not have all the facts or knew how Kate's heart was packed with as many positive emotions as desperate ones. Should she share more with this person? They were close enough, although her only real confidantes had always been Hazel, Beth and her mother. But at some point along this road, public opinion was waiting to be recognised. When the time came, would it cheer and wave a flag, or would it turn its back, head hung low? Kate had no idea. Perhaps this was the time to find out.

Kate sat forward, hands on the table, daring herself to say something. Shona, still distracted, was gazing out at the grey afternoon, shaking her head at the current revelations, and so Kate faltered, suddenly unsure if her instincts to spread her better news were acting in her best interests. She could hear Campbell approaching the table, crockery clinking on the tray he carried, and instantly knew what to do. If he presented her coffee in her favourite green mug, she would tell them about her plans for the future. If not, she would nurse her secret for longer. She was not putting her faith in fate, but rather in her mother. She would make the decision for her, from wherever she was watching.

"You take sugar, Kate?" asked Campbell, handing her a pale pink mug with a pig's cheery face on it. "They only gave me two sachets."

"No thanks," Kate's voice was relieved to the point where Shona looked at her, frowning, but she felt no need to clarify it to them. Instead, she reached for a piece of shortbread and glanced over at the counter. At that moment, her favourite mug, newly dried, was being hung back on its hook. She watched it swing for a moment and then sipped her coffee.

《●》《●》《●》

Hazel's own coffee break only ever lasted as long as the lull in customers did, which could range from one to twenty minutes, and all of the staff at Mackay's bakery accepted this without complaint. They did, after all, take home with them surplus cakes and pastries on a daily basis, a perk in anybody's book; and it did mean that gossip sessions tended to be quick, intense and informative. Today, however, Hazel had nothing to offer and so had declined a break altogether. Instead, she wiped down between the keys on the till, frowning as she did so, and thought about the ridiculous situation unfolding at home.

When her dad had arrived back in her life, it had been the weirdest time. Her mother had left them, had taken her presence away at the end of their worst experiences, and they had sat, silent and stunned, trying to work out how to go forward. Within days, David Wilder had arrived and stirred some sort of excitement into all the grief. It had been the oddest concoction, sorrow and wonder, but Hazel had been eager to keep it going. David had tried so hard to fit in, and there had seemed so much about him that was endearing that it seemed easy to accept their mother's wish that they should travel to Canada to 'fill in the gaps'. Well, there had been no shortage of gaps to fill, and even those he had handled reasonably well.

"Oooooh" growled Hazel to herself, now frantically scrubbing the shelves below the till. Things had been on the cusp of brilliance when she had left Kate behind and flown home. Stuart had been waiting for her at the airport, all arms and grins and kisses; the sun had shone from Fort William to the bay, and she had been able to reassure Beth that Kate had survived. Best and most amazing of all, her dad had turned out to be a 'lovely man who just needs to get back out into the real world'. Now, it was all one big, grubby disappointment which threatened almost every relationship she had ever known.

Beth was distraught, unable to reach Kate on any level whatsoever; her mother was inadvertently to blame because of her ridiculous Grand Master Plan; Stuart had started to keep his distance from her perpetually angry face; and her dad had completely lost his mind. None of them were thinking as she was, and Hazel could not understand why this should be the case.

And Kate? Kate had turned into some sort of kamikaze pilot, ignoring anybody who tried to steer her away from her own suicide, sporting such a determined glint in her eyes that Hazel could not look at them for long. She physically choked whenever she thought of what Kate might have done to ensnare her dad, although she swore nothing had happened. However, Kate was capable of saying anything to get her own way in this, and it was possible that even their trust had become its victim.

What the hell were they thinking? How could Kate possibly be pursuing a man who had loved their mother, who had made love to their mother? As emotionally stunted as he had allowed himself to become, why was he giving credence to the feelings of a bereaved teenager, or even worse, acting on them?

It was morally unacceptable, and if Hazel attached the situation to any other forty-five-year-old man and seventeen-year-old girl, she was able to treat it with total contempt. However, she knew both of the people in question and could not help blending love, sympathy and anxiety into her disapproval, which was much harder to deal with than angry disbelief alone.

Hazel could feel a headache forming behind her ear, and she took a minute to breathe deeper and to calm herself down. It was at that moment that she saw Kate making her way across the square, two friends in tow. It seemed the most normal activity her sister had taken part in since September, and she was intrigued. She followed the little group with her eyes until they were safely inside Nicolson's, then immediately wished to know more. Had they arranged this meeting? Were they trying to persuade Kate to come back to school, like that idiot Ellis had failed to do? Fear now caused a serious shiver to run up Hazel's arms.

"Jeez, no," she moaned. Surely Kate wasn't so caught up in her fantasy that she was about to share it with others? But then, maybe Kate was tired of having no allies except a tall, absent Canadian and was touting for support.

ROAD WITHOUT SIGNPOSTS

Hazel had already lifted the counter to run out and stop this travesty when a family of four, all wearing matching yellow cagoules, came arguing into the shop. The English accents did nothing to endear themselves to her, but she switched on her best 'what-a-day-for-being-outside' smile and picked up the tongs, ready to provide. Of course, mummy cagoule wanted a takeaway soup to go with her filled roll, and by the time their order was complete, some primary school children had come in for biscuits. Finally, Hazel put her head into the back shop and asked if she could possibly knock off early.

She had never taken advantage of her recent circumstances, never cried off work, had always worked a full shift even if it meant dealing with the sympathy of half-acquaintances. But today, her pale face added weight to the pretence of a migraine, and she was instructed to get herself home as quickly as possible.

Hazel arrived outside Nicolson's window just as Kate was finishing a piece of chocolate-covered shortbread and stood watching her sister, laughing and relaxed, until her friend signalled Hazel's arrival. Instantly, Kate's face fell and she rose from the table, pulling on her coat amidst curious looks from the pair she was with. There seemed to be a short conversation about money, before Kate wrapped her scarf around her ears and trailed outside.

"Did you tell them?" Hazel accused.

"No," replied Kate, as if it had been the farthest thing from her mind. "But if I had wanted to, I would have, and I wouldn't have been ashamed of it."

"You're such a child, Kate. This isn't a game."

"I'm going to get the bus," Kate informed, but as she started back across the square, Hazel grabbed her arm.

"People would condemn him, don't you get it?"

"You would, you mean."

"I can't believe you're doing this. Is this family not complicated enough? Mum, him, Neil and now this. You couldn't make it up! Hey," Hazel frowned, "is that one of Dad's jumpers? God, Kate, you're pathetic."

Hazel, with those final two sentences, at last cracked Kate's stony expression. Tears filled her eyes as she dropped her wet shoulder bag to the pavement and took off her coat. She pulled the jumper over her head, rolled it into a bundle and handed it to Hazel.

"Here," she sniffed, "take it. It keeps me warm and makes me happy, but take it if you have to have it. Make your point. I'd rather have the man, anyway."

Kate had reached the bus stop, her coat and bag both now draped over her arm, before the tears really began to pour. She had not realised just how much comfort she had taken from the item of clothing until it was no longer wrapped around her, with no prospect of a return. It had been stripped from her for no better reason than Hazel did not want her to have any piece of him. She rubbed the heels of her hands into her eyes until they ached, ignorant of the curious looks aimed at her. You did not often see an openly distraught teenager, dressed in T-shirt and scarf, standing on a December street. Within another minute, however, Hazel had parked beside her and had opened the passenger door.

"Get in."

The main road was still reasonably clear as they travelled in silence, Kate hiding inside her coat once more, trying not to touch her burning eyes. As they began the first descent of the little road headed for the village, there was no black tarmac visible whatsoever.

"Shit," murmured Hazel. Her driving was appalling on good days. Kate sat forward in her seat, frowning at the scene before them.

"Maybe we should just leave it at the Penifiler road-end?" Kate suggested.

"Maybe. Maybe if I manage the first hill, I should just keep going."

"You're driving."

"Yes, I am."

Kate resolved to keep her mouth shut for the rest of the journey, but when Hazel slewed into the banking at the first ninety-degree turn, the left hand wheels disappearing into the ditch, both girls shouted in fright.

"Dammit!" cursed Hazel as she was thrown sideways, almost landing in Kate's lap. Kate in turn was thrown against the passenger door, her head connecting sharply with the glass, and she could do nothing but sit, eyes tightly shut, for a few moments.

"You okay?" asked Hazel, trying to push herself back into her own seat, the angle making it an almost impossible task.

"Mm-hm," replied Kate, but actually felt quite sick. "What now?"

"Well, if we're both still alive, then I suppose we're walking."

By the time they had negotiated themselves and their belongings from the tipped vehicle and were standing upright by the side of the road, the snow was not only drifting but also falling, causing a string of expletives shouted by Hazel at the weather, the road and indeed their whole life. It was a sign that her sister was close to breaking point; and

Kate, dabbing at the tiny trickle of blood on her temple, decided to simply walk away from the scene, hoping it was the least antagonistic option. But David's jumper still lay in a heap on the back seat.

Kate halted immediately. There was no way she was leaving it to freeze by the side of the road. Not in a million years. Not even if Hazel yelled in her face how 'pathetic' she thought she was. But the car was locked and her sister was at least three long strides ahead of her.

"Haze?" Kate shouted.

"What?" she answered, not turning round.

"Please, can I get... the jumper? Please."

Without even breaking her stride, Hazel threw the car keys over her head.

"Do what you like."

In spite of her relief at the lack of confrontation, it still wrung Kate's heart that their world had come to this; Hazel walking away from her, cursing and frustrated, she hunting for the car keys in a wet, snowy drift. Just for a moment, as her fingers hooked the key ring, the word 'hopeless' came marching back into Kate's head, and she sat down where she was, studying her boots. Maybe she would stay there until her face turned grey and her clothes white. It seemed easy to just sit there, the wet seeping through to her skin. She could even close her eyes and wait for David's face to make its appearance. But she couldn't risk him shaking his head at her wet, slumped figure and somehow found her feet.

"I will do what I like," Kate spoke out loud, her teeth set. "That's exactly what I'll do."

CHAPTER 8

Saturday, 4th December 1993

"Well, thanks. That's really great," Kate's voice was light with excitement. "Yes, I can get the bus in. I'll be there. Thanks again."

As she replaced the receiver in the cradle, Kate punched the air above her head with both fists, then hastily looked around to ensure she had not been seen. Thankfully, she was alone in the dim hallway, grateful that her telephone conversations were no longer under the type of scrutiny which would have impressed MI5. She could physically feel herself soaring from the news just received and hugged herself for a split second before checking the time.

It was a Saturday morning, just after nine, and Kate needed to get herself into town before 2.30 p.m. She needed to pick an outfit and she needed to have a bath. This opportunity had come her way, and it was absolutely essential that she made the best possible first impression, because she needed money. Money that nobody else had control over.

"Beth? Is there enough water for a bath?"

"Just. The immersion's been on since seven." Beth's voice was accompanied by the familiar spilling of pans onto the tiles from the pan cupboard. "Dammit! Right, we're moving. I can't stand this kitchen any longer!"

Kate froze at the bathroom door, needing to know that this was merely the usual reaction to an everyday occurrence and nothing more sinister. Since Fiona had died, anything was possible. She held her breath until her aunt appeared in the kitchen doorway at the far end of the hall. Kate gave her a smile of understanding, but waited for confirmation that all was well. Beth's face was red.

"Who was on the phone?"

"Shona Syme," Kate lied. "Met her in the square the other day and she wants to catch up a bit more. I'll take the bike to the road end and get the bus in. Maybe Hazel will give me a lift back."

Beth stood squarely in the doorway, giving her niece her full attention, and Kate's smile slid off her face.

"Don't fret. You're as bad as Hazel. I won't be telling anybody anything until there is something really positive to say."

As the bathroom door closed behind her, Kate refused to let Beth's expression bring her down. She remembered when she had first met David. It was here in this house, and each time she had walked into a room or met him in the corridor, his face had made her defensive and irritable. She had not welcomed him there, fearing he would detract from the mourning that Fiona required and upset their unit. But he had spent as much time trying to break down the barrier she had put up as he had paying attention to the much more receptive Hazel, anxious that his presence in this country would not cause even more anxiety. She saw all this now with an altered heart, but at the time the looks he had given her, full of desperate optimism, daring to hope that she would accept him, had made her fists clench. Beth's face had begun to irritate her in exactly the same way. Her aunt was closer to her than any friend, but her continual worry at the way things were developing was becoming tedious. She needed to let Kate make her own decisions.

When her reflection blurred beneath the steam from the bath water, Kate turned her back on the mirror and began to replay her telephone conversation. She was employable. Well, potentially employable, depending on how she behaved this afternoon, but it was the first interest that had been shown since she had trawled every establishment in Portree on that horrible Tuesday, and it was a job she could possibly cope with. More importantly, it was the first step to true independence. Fiona had left them some money, but it remained under Beth's care, and there was no way on this earth that the woman would hand over cash for anything she was unhappy with. In any case, making her own money seemed more in keeping with Kate's perception of herself as an adult. Legally she was not quite there, but she felt she qualified for the status nevertheless. She had lost her mother, after all.

Kate lowered herself into the near scalding water, spending only a moment on guilt at having used up the whole tank's worth on one bath, and lay looking at the ceiling. The bathroom was a riot of colour – citrus yellow, sunshine orange, pale lemon – but the ceiling remained the off-white polystyrene it had been for as long as Kate could remember. Maybe her mother had detested painting ceilings, or maybe she had just not been able to reach that far when she had tackled the bathroom with healthy vigour. Kate found herself suddenly tearful. If David had been there, he would have easily managed the job. How many times over the years had Fiona missed his practical presence as well as his other attractions? A couple of tears had plopped into the water before Kate reminded herself for the hundredth time that if any one of the circumstances which had brought them to this point had differed, she would not be so very deeply in love with David Wilder. She wiped her face quickly and stuck her big toe into the tap to stop the slow drips which fell from it. It was easier than sitting forward and turning the tap tighter.

So, the job. The hairdresser's. Not many hours to begin with, filling in for the owner's daughter who was working in some ski resort over Christmas. Mainly taking bookings, making coffee and sweeping up hair; she did not even have to make conversation if she didn't want to. It would be the start of her Canada fund, and maybe customers would be extra generous with their tips at Christmas. If nothing else, it would stop her dwelling on the many miserable hours ahead. None of the family were looking forward to their first Christmas without Fiona.

"Kate," Beth's voice was just outside the door. "Did you use the whole tank?"

"Sorry!"

"I didn't realise Shona Syme warranted such effort."

There followed a very charged silence and Kate rolled her eyes. She could practically hear Beth's thoughts, feel her hope and watch her lips turn up at the edges. Should she let her continue on her current path and lighten her mood, or tell her the truth right away and risk a helpless curse followed by a further admonishment about the hot water?

"Okay, so I'm not meeting Shona, but it's not what you're hoping for. There are no lads involved. I'm not looking. I'm never going to look."

There was a 'humph' and the retreating footsteps had a definite irritated ring. Kate held her breath. Three seconds and Beth had returned. This time her voice was genuinely puzzled.

"So, why are you going in?"

"I'll tell you when I've washed my hair," replied Kate, and ducked under the water, where there was a muffled peace of sorts.

《●》《●》《●》

Later, on the bus, Kate thought of Beth's reaction to her potential employment. On the whole, it could have been a lot worse, although six months ago if Kate had found herself to be the cause of the obvious disappointment in her aunt's eyes, she would have been miserably apologetic. The look was familiar enough to be almost ineffective, and Kate was beginning to view it as a fault on Beth's part. Had Kate really toed the line for her entire life, because their reaction to her making her own decisions seemed to be crippling each one of them, and it was becoming incredibly boring. In the end, Beth had shrugged and agreed that it was time Kate had 'something to occupy her time with'. The phrase brought a grin to Kate's face as she settled herself against the cool window glass and thought of David. What had she thought about before her mind had locked onto this man?

There had been times over the past month when she had found herself blushing at her own thoughts, and when she had gazed in the mirror, she had seen coal black eyes that shot out sparks of light. Mostly she thought of the way he had kissed her, because it was the memory which created the most heat. But she also liked to think of his hands, slim and strong, and how he might use them if they were ever together again, alone. He may trace them over her skin, following the shape of her body; and Kate knew she would watch his face as they made their journey, because apart from his hands and the beating of his heart against her ear, his face was the most magnetic thing about him. It was flawless to her. There were lines around his eyes, a faint scar on his cheek, and his jaw line was always rough to the touch; she loved every square inch of it. Kate was enjoying these shivers of remembrance when a heavy body flopped into the seat beside her.

"Hi Kate. How are the driving lessons going?"

"Grant! I didn't see you, were you at the back?"

"Aye. Heard you were in Canada, but obviously you're home. What was that like?"

The sympathy on Grant's face suggested he had thought it had been a trial, so Kate turned down her enthusiasm slightly.

"It was okay actually. It got Haze and I out of the hole we'd been in, so that was good. And it's an amazing country."

As he settled his frame squarely on the seat, apparently her companion for the remainder of the journey, he nodded his head. He was Stuart's brother's mate, not really a close acquaintance at all, but on a bus of six people had felt the necessity to make contact. They both looked ahead, not sure how to continue past these basic enquiries.

"Still playing for the first team?" Kate ventured.

"Injured at the minute," he replied, grimacing as if to prove his point. "Tendons."

Kate nodded, knowledgeably, having no compulsion to enquire after which particular tendons in case it should prove more embarrassing than interesting. She picked at a dried speck of mud on the bus window.

"I'm going to see about a job today. Just a few hours at the hairdresser's over the busy time. Fingers crossed."

"How's Hazel?" the question came out of the blue and in such an odd, concerned tone that Kate immediately sat up a bit straighter. Had her sister been talking? Did her whole circle of friends know that they were barely on speaking terms?

"She's just the same," Kate frowned. "I mean, we're still getting used to the house without Mum, but ..."

"Stu's really cut up about it."

Kate felt a sharp jab between her shoulder blades as she realised she had no idea what he was referring to, and that Grant was sure she knew exactly what he was saying. Instead of stammering some ordinary acknowledgement, Kate turned her whole body in Grant's direction.

"What do you mean?"

"You know," he replied, still staring out of the front window. "What she's doing to herself."

Kate's stomach rolled as the first pricks of sweat on her upper lip began to pool together. She swallowed and touched Grant's shoulder so that he would look in her direction. She watched his face react to hers but spoke before he could.

"I really don't know what you mean."

"Shit, Kate. You're as white as a sheet. You okay?"

"What's she doing to herself?"

Grant's eyes crinkled up as soon as he realised that he had dropped himself into an awkward little conversation and had no obvious means of getting out of it unharmed. Glancing outside once more at the journey's progress, he sighed and shrugged his shoulders.

"Stu says she's really struggling. Not sleeping, not eating at all. She was out of her head the other night, first time I've seen her touch whisky. But you know all this, right?"

Kate's tongue had stuck to the top of her mouth, and she ripped it away without grimacing. She knew nothing. She spent all of her time wrapped up in her photos, dreaming of a better time not too far down the line, ignoring everyone around her. She was removing herself from them minute by minute because it was easier to do that; it was irrelevant what they were feeling or how they were coping with it. Kate let her head dip, staring at the tartan upholstery under her thighs until the edges of her vision blurred and her stomach finally dropped into her boots. She took an uneasy breath in then exhaled an expletive that she never used. What in God's name had she become?

Grant rose from his seat, his face pink, as he spoke to her bowed head. "Hey, I've got to get off here, I said I'd meet Jamie at the petrol station. Shit, if I've said something I shouldn't have, Kate, I'm sorry. See you. Sorry."

Kate did not lift her head and knew it would be a long time before she ever looked Grant in the eye again. As the blood pounded in her ears, she palmed the sweat from her lips and chin and finally laid her head against the seat in front of her. She could not even feel sorry for Grant because her stomach was contracting out of control. But what was paining her the most? Was it that Hazel's worries were manifesting themselves in a way she had not even noticed, or was it that she had turned into some creature whose self-interest had become second nature? As the bus bounced into the square, Kate placed her hands on her clenched stomach muscles and whimpered quietly against the window.

Hope. How could a word of one syllable hold so much of her emotions within its arms? It had kept her from floundering in the last five weeks; the hope that not only would she be ecstatic in the company of the one person who had shone out of the blackness, but that she had the power to make him just as happy. It had been a sphere of sunshine within her and had helped keep at bay stubborn arguments from all and sundry. She had used it to her advantage. Now it was fading fast, as fast as her blood was pumping, and any moment it would be a cold, dead star. Because hope had no power when your particular course was causing this type of damage. When every day had brought you the joy that you were a day nearer your desire, but for others had been another bleak, sickening step into a passageway of dread. Hazel was hurting badly, and Kate was the cause.

As the bus allowed its passengers to depart, Kate levered herself out of her seat, surprised that her limbs did not snap in two as she unfroze them. She was achingly cold yet sweating within her coat, her face most probably a pale, shiny mess. At this realisation, her retreating optimism finally threw its arms in the air and ran screaming from the scene; there was no way she would survive an interrogation by a prospective employer. She needed to catch her breath and fix her face. More than that, she needed to see Hazel.

Kate's knees only just allowed her to escape the bus without giving way, but immediately she sought the nearest bench and sat, her hands trapped between said knees. She would remain there until the Square came back into focus.

"Here now, can I phone somebody for you?"

Kate had not even been aware that the bus driver had followed her departure, but there were his black DM boots and regulation uniform trousers in front of her eyes. She looked up as quickly as she dared into a vaguely familiar face and saw worry lines and a pursed mouth.

"You're a bit of a funny colour. Shall I get in touch with –"

"No thanks. Sorry, I think I'm getting the flu, and that last few yards must have turned my stomach." It was the truth, although the flu was not the cause. "But thanks for asking. I'm just going to go to Nicolson's, maybe get a cup of tea."

The driver really could not argue, as a queue was forming at the closed door of the bus and he had a schedule to keep to. But Kate thanked him again and got carefully to her feet, not exhaling until she had walked four steps and heard the suction of the bus doorway as he allowed her to go. She was in a quandary. She had twenty minutes before she was due at her interview, and that was not nearly enough time to dedicate to her sister, who would not appreciate her attempt at care and concern being interrupted by her constantly referring to her watch. Neither could she let down the one person in Portree who had taken her seriously in her quest for employment, but her legs were carrying her towards the baker's, and Hazel had seen her approach. She met her in the doorway.

"Kate? Are you feeling okay?"

Kate's eyes were wide and she glanced over Hazel's shoulder at the customer-free shop. "Can you spare a minute?"

Hazel pulled her over the threshold of the shop and pushed her gently into the corner by the drinks' cooler. Maisie behind the counter frowned once in their direction and then turned her back, surveyed the dwindling rows of rolls and pastries and began to tidy them up, whistling as she did so.

"You don't look right." Hazel's expression, which had begun as earnest, was beginning to sag back to its usual wariness, as Kate hunted for a hankie to wipe down her face. By the time she had accomplished it, Hazel's eyes had lost all real concern and she was standing awkwardly, no longer knowing how to communicate. Kate used the silence to look at Hazel up and down and felt her heart plummet once more. Her sister's eyes were rimmed with pale brown skin, and her lips were a strange lilac colour, cracked and edged by a white line. Her uniform gave nothing away, the tabard covering her body from neck to thighs, but her jeans below the hemline were crumpled and her watch hung limply on her wrist. Hazel took a step back. "What are you looking at?"

"You," Kate's voice was stronger than she imagined it would be.

"Well, don't," Hazel left her side. "You haven't even glanced in my direction for weeks; I don't need you to start now. And I'm busy."

"Oh, yes. It looks like it. But you're going to have to talk to me sometime about– "

"Oh, and you think I'm going to listen to you, when you're being a stupid, bloody-minded little idiot. You think that you still deserve to be heard when you can't see what is going on around you and what you're doing to us all."

Maisie by this time had retreated into the back shop and was met in the doorway by Janet, who had left the heat of the ovens behind to witness the drama taking place. Hazel did not even notice them.

"Alright, alright," cried Kate, shaking her head in defiance of her sister's aggression. "I'm to blame in all of this, I know that, but I'm still allowed a say in it. You can walk away from it, leave it behind if you want to, but I can't!"

As Hazel rolled her eyes at the statement, Kate felt her resentment rise again and could not keep the words from coming. "You win, Haze. Is that what you wanted to hear? Do you feel better? Let's make sure Hazel gets her own way, then maybe she'll go back to her normal, bubbly self. Don't disagree with her whatever you do, she might stop eating."

Hazel's head snapped in Kate's direction, her eyes widening and her mouth tightening into a hard line. She opened it once to speak, then closed it and marched into the back shop, dispersing her workmates as she did so. Kate breathed heavily for a second, shaking from the short confrontation and wondering what to do next, but in the next moment, Hazel had appeared once more, her tabard discarded and her coat in her hand.

"I'm not talking about this," Hazel's gritted teeth barely allowed the words out as she walked straight past Kate, who reached for Hazel's arm but missed. As she followed her out into the Square, Hazel turned on her heel and faced Kate.

"You've got one bloody big nerve, Kate, I'll give you that. You're the one who everybody is falling over to protect. It must be great to be so damaged and hard done by that nobody is allowed to argue or criticise.

But you're not dying like Mum was, so we don't have to let you get away with it!" Hazel let that sink in before continuing. "Well, I give up. Go ahead. Do it. Offer him it all, your face and your body and your never-ending supply of smart comments. And when you realise that you've got nothing in common whatsoever, that you can't be a substitute for Mum even if you think you can, and that you can't spend another minute in his company because he's boring you to tears, just leave him and watch him die, humiliated and cut to ribbons. Again. I can hardly fucking wait."

Kate screwed her eyes shut and heard rather than saw Hazel run away from her. She didn't even know if anybody else had been aware of the conversation, because opening her eyes again meant acknowledging that she was standing on the pavement alone. Her heart was fluttering and her nose prickling so violently that the tears were there on her cheeks in an instant. And still she stood petrified, not daring to do a thing. At the age of three she had fallen out of the tree beside their garage and had been winded. The pain in her chest, burning her from the inside outwards, had been the scariest, most overwhelming agony she had ever experienced. Until now.

Breathing was supposed to be involuntary, routine, without thought, but now Kate struggled with the mechanics of it. Each breath seemed to burn more than the last, but even this was not the most alarming aspect of her life at that instant. She was alone. Alone.

Her mother was dead. Not just missing or absent or nowhere near a telephone. Dead. Her sister despised what she had become, her aunt viewed her as nothing but a worry, her father was some artistic loner who didn't like to be touched. The person she loved for his strength and care was not here, not protecting her, not supporting her. He was most probably sitting somewhere, trying to think of a way of letting her down gently. She could not possibly be anything more than a distraction to him. Distraction. Had Hazel used that word in one of her rants? Of course she had. In some unbelievable paradox, Hazel had suddenly become very focussed and coherent, when she had always been prone to prattling. Kate herself had been the cause. She had altered her sister's outlook. Was there anything that she was not guilty of?

Rain tapped the back of her neck, and Kate finally raised her head and took a few steps forward, testing her ability and wiping her eyes with the back of her hand. Surprisingly, the burning in her chest still allowed her to move, and within three minutes she arrived at a picture window plastered with posters of the latest haircuts and offers.

So out of sorts was she that Kate did not even try to check her reflection in the glass before stepping over the threshold into the suffocating heat of the salon.

The shopfront was empty, but there was a black leather seat near the door; and Kate was suddenly sitting, her head in her hands, tears pouring out of her onto the cushioned vinyl between her boots. This was grief. This burning ache which would not be soothed and could not possibly be eased. Finally, after three months of coping and discovering and clinging onto any possible ray of hope, she could not keep it at bay. Nothing on this earth of hers was manageable, nothing was available to her, and there was absolutely no solution. No circular route on which her mother waited, with a cup of tea and a tale of woe-turned-triumph. Just uncertainty and despair and a long, straight road to mediocrity. No more excitement, no more desire. Her eyes stung as if they had been sprayed with onion vapour.

"Kate, is that you down there?"

Kate raised her head, but could see nothing but a round figure kneeling in front of her. She could not speak.

"Okay, honey," the voice was kind and soft. "Let's get you a nice hot drink."

CHAPTER 9

Saturday, 4th December 1993

The mist of perfume tainted the fine cotton fibres as soon as it made contact with the pillowcase, forming a pale grey circle of damp aroma on its surface. White Musk. The only perfume that Fiona had ever tolerated. Her first bottle had been a gift from Hazel, presented on her return from some archery-related school trip to Glasgow. This latest bottle was almost finished, the shoulders of it near the cap covered in a film of dust. But one spray was more than sufficient. Kate switched off her bedside lamp and pulled the pillowcase close to her face. It was cold and soft and her mother's scent was comfort itself.

"Oh Mum. Miss you."

It was a night without moon or stars, and Kate lay enveloped in black velvet, breathing in and out slowly, willing Fiona to visit her as she occasionally did. But certain criteria had to be met. Kate had to be warm enough, sleepy enough and desperate enough before she was able to conjure up the essence of her. Tonight she was all of these things. As her mind drifted, thoughts disintegrating and floating away, bumping and deflecting as they went, she could feel a light breath on her cheeks and eyelids.

"Hi Mum," she murmured, her lips the only animated part of her as her mother entered her head, bringing no vivid lights or outlandish scenery with her. Kate was not dreaming, she was simply connecting somehow with the only person who had even a vague conception of how she felt. And it was nice to hear that voice, irrespective of what it might say.

"Hi Katy. You're having a hard time of it, aren't you, babe?"

"I wasn't," Kate's lips barely moved. "I was okay. I was doing fine. Now Haze hates me. She's making herself ill and he will end up blaming me for it."

Sensing her mother's arms begin to wrap around her, Kate straightened her legs to allow her closer still. The perfume grew in intensity.

"Don't try to do so much, Kate. You don't have to do it all."

Kate inhaled again and pushed her fears away as she forced the words out of her stubbornly lethargic mouth.

"But they won't let me do anything."

"Poor baby."

Kate sighed. "I'm not a baby, Mum. I'm strong and I know I can make a difference. To David. But they won't let me."

"Kate, babe," Fiona's voice, although low, was as sweet as treacle. "You love him. Hazel loves him. He loves you both, I'm sure. Now, you have to let him decide what to do. Give him the chance to do what he needs to without clouding it. And you have to help your sister. Do you trust me?"

"I don't want– what are you going to say?"

"If you trust me, I think I can make you happy. So. Do you trust me?"

Kate nodded into the pillowcase, her eyelids brushing against the fabric but remaining closed to reality. Her mother was quiet for a moment or two, and Kate wondered if she was required to voice her agreement before they could continue. Then Fiona's lips gently touched her cheek and she was suddenly whispering in her ear.

"Take care of Hazel. Start there and the rest will work itself out. Trust me; he will love you for it. And trust him."

At once, Kate's eyes were open and she tasted the bitter, musky residue on her lips. The moon had still not appeared, but the room felt clearer, free from spirits of any kind, and Kate's chin wobbled. Her mother's visit had been pitifully short and not in any way satisfactory. Indeed, she felt as if she had been criticised and by the person whose regard she sought the most. But what had she actually said? Help Hazel and let David see it?

Kate bit her lip and let her mind run with this advice. To live without him now that she loved him did not bear considering. To live without his touch or his eyes on her face turned her heart into a lump of meteor, dead and heavy. Trust. How long could she survive on that alone? But, maybe there was some short-term solution. Maybe she could begin to crack open the door on conciliation, if her mother really thought that that was the way to go. It would solve the most urgent crisis; she might be able to appease Hazel into relaxing enough to begin her recovery.

But it seemed such a risky step in the wrong direction, one which might cause David to visit all sorts of dark areas in his head; areas she had been trying to steer him clear of for weeks. Then again, if things eased amongst them all, fear might take a back seat; and in time, they would see what she needed to be happy. What she needed to survive. She had to think about this and, for the millionth time it seemed, she longed for David to be there, running his arm along her shoulder and holding her against his side, where she felt warm and wanted and at home.

CHAPTER 10

Monday, 6th December 1993

Kate lay on the floor of her temporary bedroom, pen in hand, with absolutely no earthly idea what to put on the sheets of air mail paper before her. The new rollerball she had bought weeks ago specifically to make the task of writing to David even more special now looked depressingly ordinary as she twiddled it between her fingers. Every few moments, she laid her head back on her extended left arm and stared at the skirting board underneath the dressing table. The smell of the carpet played with her nose. It reminded her of the sitting room at The Edge when the roaring fire would warm the wool of the hearth rug and the aroma would fill the whole space. If she closed her eyes she could see the dim room, where three or four lamps and the fire complemented the flicker of the TV in the corner. She could hear Rose's knitting needles as she waited for David to answer her question or pose his own.

Kate sighed. What she had seen as David's interminably boring existence, what she had deemed her duty to change for him, was taking on the hue of extreme comfort. The atmosphere in her present surroundings did not even come close. Was she really this fickle? She liked to think that the reason she was prepared to exchange the cosy, completely familiar cottage for the lofty rooms and chilled corners of David's home was solely due to his presence. And if that was the case, then it must be love. It made sense, which made the task of writing this letter even more frustratingly ridiculous. But she had no choice.

She sat up, leaning on her elbows and wrote the date on the top of the first sheet. Initially, Kate had lain on the bed, but the temptation to just sleep the problem away was too great; and she placed the paper on an old photo album, and at last she forced herself to begin.

'Dear David'
"And that's as much as I have," she groaned, her head thumping down on top of the paper. It was the most impossible, impossible thing. This was her third letter to the man, and out of nowhere she was going to have to tell him that she was losing control. That her sister's health was being affected in a way that Kate's naivety had failed to even consider and that she was going to have to get this over to a man who loved Hazel and was connected to her by blood and not just by hope. "Get on with it!"

I've got a job. Just a few hours at the hairdressers but it's better than nothing. The snow has come and gone although I'm sure there will be more. Who knows if it will be a White Christmas? I don't really care. Whatever the weather, I'll probably go and sit halfway up the Ben and dig in somewhere for the day. It might be warmer in the house but it's not the happiest place to be.

"That's it. Ease it in gently."
Then her pen was flying across the room and she was up on her feet, pacing. Next door, Hazel would be snoring, her pale face somewhat revived since Kate had sought her company earlier. She had chosen that evening to attempt peace talks, telling Hazel that she completely understood her fears and listening to every point her sister had made in return. It had been just as difficult as she had expected, although Hazel had not been triumphant or joyful, just calmed by Kate's sudden willingness to listen.

Beth and Kenny had been witness to it all, and her aunt's face, melting into a hopeful smile, had certainly made her feel slightly better. But she knew she was being neither honest nor completely fair when she had agreed to try to move in a different direction, away from David, and was only doing so because she did indeed trust her mother. It had been the necessary first step; the rest she would argue with or defend as Hazel began to relax and calm down.

It was after midnight and she knew Beth had gone to bed, but there were still movements in the house, and Kate needed some distraction. She found Kenny in the kitchen, drying the rest of the dishes. He didn't even seem surprised that she was still fully dressed. He stepped back in order for her to fill the kettle but did not speak until she had slumped into the kitchen chair.

"What you up to, hun?"

Kate shook her head. "Not much, I'm failing anyway. How was Beth when she went to bed?"

Kenny nodded, his face optimistic. "Yeah, she seemed okay. I don't think she was expecting you to do that tonight. What," he paused, turning to look directly at her. "What brought it on?"

"Does it matter?"

"Not really. If you meant what you said, it doesn't matter at all."

Kate looked at him closely. Since her return from Canada, Kenny had almost seemed like a collaborator, but of course his loyalties had to lie with Beth. She was his love, and the rest was just part of the package. She doubted if he would ever view her and Hazel as a bonus, if the last few weeks were to be used as an example. But now, in this room, Kate tried to work out what was actually going on beneath his cropped red hair. What on earth did he make of the mess that was their family, and if she was to confide in him, would he feel obliged to share it?

"I bet in all this carry on, nobody has ever asked you if you're okay," she ventured. "So, I'll do it now and say sorry for all the shit at the same time. Sorry. Are you okay?"

Kenny smiled. After a moment, he took two bottles of lager from the fridge, eased off the tops on the side of the worktop and placed one on the table in front of her. She looked at the vapour rising from the neck of the bottle for a second and then pushed the chair opposite her out from the table with her foot. He sat immediately.

"So?"

"Kate, you're not hurting me in any way. It's difficult to see an end to it, that's all."

Kate felt her nose prickling and she lowered her eyes, because to this man and to the other members of the household, the end of it meant relief and a return to simpler, more manageable problems. To Kate, it literally meant the end. No way of going back to her plans or aspirations, no more watching the calendar and smiling that every day was a day nearer to being in David's company. Just day after day of going forward, not only without him but without the anticipation of him. At once, Kate felt the punch of resentment in her gut, and she swiped at her eyes.

"I'm trying to do what all of you want. And I'm going to keep on trying because Hazel needs to get better. But, honestly, it feels like the most ridiculous waste of feelings. And time."

Kenny sipped at his bottle, looking surprisingly comfortable and in no apparent hurry to give her advice or share any 'when I was your age' moments, for which she was grateful.

"Seventeen years Mum wasted away from him. I don't know how she did it, not if she felt half of what I do for him. But she didn't have any choice, and it looks like you've all decided that I don't, either."

The lager was bitter in her mouth, but the bubbles felt quite nice in her throat, and she matched Kenny, slug for slug. She was aware of the kitchen clock ticking and the rain showering the window every time the wind gusted, but had counted thirty-three small ticks before she spoke.

"Do you like him, Ken?"

"I don't really know him."

"Give me your very first impression, without thinking about it. Quickly."

Kenny studied her face for a second only before sitting forward. "I thought he was shell-shocked. Yes, that's how he was on the first day I met him."

Kate could feel her heart starting to race. She was being allowed to discuss David. "And after that? After the funeral when he was trying to fit in, what did you make of him then? No, please don't think about what Beth would want you to say or what effect it'll have on me. Please, for me, just tell me what you thought of him."

"Well, honestly, I thought he was a brave man coming here in the first place. I mean, you weren't exactly all sweetness and light in the beginning, but it didn't seem to put him off much. He was genuine enough. I just remember thinking he must have thought a hell of a lot of your mother to even get on the plane." Kenny stood as he drained his bottle. "I think he's probably a good guy, but he's opened a can of worms with this one."

"He loved Mum to bits and he had to let her go. That wasn't fair. None of it was fair on him, but he couldn't see past her, and it was such a waste. I can't believe how much of himself he kept away from people. Here, I don't want any more."

As Kate handed over the half-empty bottle, she also stood. It was approaching one in the morning, and she was beginning to suffer from the after-hours shivers. In Canada, it would be just before 5 p.m. on a Sunday teatime, and David would either be finishing off paperwork of some sort or planning out his coming week. She wondered if he ever stopped, mid-plan, and thought about her. Well, he probably thought she had been soundly asleep for hours, maybe even dreaming about a life in front of them both. She shivered again.

"God knows how I'm going to tell him. I swore blind that nobody would ever change my mind, and I'm having to give in at the first real test. What a coward I am."

As Kenny emptied her bottle into the sink and threw them both into the bin, he gave her a sympathetic look.

"Maybe, he'll understand completely. I wouldn't be a bit surprised. Night, Kate."

Back in her room, Kate looked at the pitifully inadequate words she had written. Four lines containing no actual information. She retrieved her pen from behind the door and gathered everything onto the bed with her. Tired though she was, she didn't like the thought of David being ignorant of the facts any longer; and within ten short, painful minutes, had completed the letter.

Dear David,

Things are changing, Dave. Not me. I'll never love you any less. That photo of you in the truck, it's the last thing I look at in bed, in the hope that you'll be in my dreams. But you don't ever seem to make it, I suppose because I think about you all day anyway, my sub-conscious feels the need to concentrate on other things. I just want you to know before I say anything else that I won't be anybody's but yours. I don't want anybody else and you have to know that. I am telling you, so that you as a person know that I love you, everything about you, and they can't make me feel any differently. I know where I want to be and that's by your side.

But, things are difficult. When you warned me that people would not accept us, I stupidly believed you meant the general public, my friends, your colleagues, and I was going to laugh in their faces. But it's Hazel. She hates me. I don't mean she has no time for me, I mean she looks at me and feels hatred. I know you warned me of this, but I really thought it would get easier, when they saw how committed I was. They can't see past the 'weirdness' of it. Do you feel weird? I don't at all. The point is that Hazel is suffering. She is making herself ill, and the guilt is sickening me. Do you know how angry it makes me to be swayed like this? But she's my sister – and your daughter, who you love – so I can't let her be hurt. And at the moment, I can't even like her, because she's making me do this. But I'll do it, because she's just as important as I am. And I'll keep doing it until she gets better or she sees that there is nothing to worry about. Maybe it will take years. Maybe you will get tired of waiting. You've waited far, far too long already, it's not fair. Maybe you need to go to some Christmas parties after all.

Just, please never stop loving me. I'm only doing this because Hazel needs me to. I'm not weak, I'm just sad and guilty. I love you and even if you doubt that it is real, like every other person seems to, believe me when I say that it is.

I love you.

Kate xxxxxxxxxxxxxxxxxxxxxxxxxxxxxx

So that was that. The deed was done, and all Kate felt was numb. Kenny had been honest, and she had appreciated him letting her talk about David for the shortest of times. But back in her bed, her letter folded and shoved in the bedside drawer, she crossed her arms over her stomach and held herself as tightly as she possibly could. Her precious photo remained in the cabinet, her Walkman lay still and silent, and the main overhead light continued to blaze. She had absolutely no will to move and alter any aspects of the situation, because things had changed so drastically. Indeed, the smile on David's face might prove too much on the night when she had allowed him to take second place to her sister. Frowning, Kate dearly hoped that she would never grow to hate Hazel for this.

«●»«●»«●»

At the instant Kate closed her eyes in the starkly illuminated bedroom, David Wilder threw his hat onto the seat of his SUV and scratched his head. It was dark, the sky was clear and the frost was already coating the windscreen, so he sat motionless in the cab with the engine running until the radiator could produce enough heat to allow him to see ahead of him. He needed to get out of the house and had concocted some unbelievably thin excuse about a hankering for salted peanuts and cringed as he replayed the conversation he had had with Rose; a conversation which his mother had allowed him to continue with, even though it was obvious to both that it was a smokescreen. He had seen the edges of her mouth go up and her eyes widen as he continued with the ruse, until she had simply waved him away and asked him to bring another dozen eggs back with him. God in heaven, was he going to be a child forever?

As he eased the truck into gear, he wasn't even sure where he was heading, but dinner was more than an hour away, and he could not sit watching time pass for one moment longer. Watching, as another sixty or seventy minutes crawled from him, waiting to share a meal with his mother, the only other human he had spent time with on this particular day. A strong, capable woman who would show concern for him until her death, but would never compensate for what he needed; to be loved by someone who was there because she craved him, not because she had created him.

A door had been opened for him, and he was still astounded by the prospect of what was being offered. It wasn't merely the company of another human, it was the particular human in question. Someone whose whole life had been spent amongst those he cherished, and who talked about them freely and with no ill-feeling towards him; someone who made his heart jump when she looked at him.

It was almost too opportune to be real, but it was far from perfect. Kate was too young. There would never be an argument against that from anybody except Kate, and that in itself was testament to the truth of it. In a million years, he would never understand her or her wishes. Why was she not content for them to be friends, when it would result in everyone treating such a friendship with nothing but unexpected delight? Surely, from the choice of roads open to them, this was the best, the most acceptable, the easiest.

David pulled the truck to a halt just as the driveway came to an end and sat, the headlights trained on the gateposts. He switched off the engine, letting the heater become still in the space he occupied and stretched his feet out as far as he could. Here, where the temperature steadily chilled around his body, he could be totally and utterly honest with himself. What in God's name did he want from his life, and what did he need? What did his heart need, what did his body need?

He swore into the frosty cab, knowing the answer to both questions and tried to think of pleasant, innocuous situations. Like the night he had attempted to explain the rules of ice hockey to Kate, who had remained resolutely uninterested and in the end had brought the conversation to a halt by sitting up from her prone position on the sofa and asking, "Does Cowichan Valley have a rugby team?"

"Rugby?"

"Rugby. I was just wondering what you thought of the change in the points. As far as I'm concerned, it'll always be four for a try and three for a conversion. Five and two is just plain wrong."

"You're a rugby fan, then?"

"Well, the internationals are more exciting than football. Rugby Union, that is. Rugby League just seems to me like a lot of stopping and starting. Although, apparently they get paid. I like the folk that do it for the love of the game. Do you get international sports here? I mean, did you see the Grand Slam in 1990? Mum nearly screamed the house down. At one point she was standing on the sofa, she could not keep still. It was great, as much for her reaction as for us winning."

From there the conversation had progressed onto how they usually spent their weekends, with Kate's main pastime being either walking any dog in the vicinity that required exercise or trying to help with the raised veggie bed project – 'a bloody disaster'. Hazel tended to go straight to Stuart's house from the baker's on a Saturday afternoon and usually stayed the night at his family's farm.

"So they're serious then? How old is he?" he had felt obliged to ask.

"Don't you mean what do his parents do and what are his prospects? I wouldn't worry. Hazel isn't anywhere near heading down that particular road. Although I think he's the only one she – em, I mean, well, she's been going out with him since she left school, so you know, and - they're both in their twenties ...."

She had ended the speech by hiding her face in the nearest cushion and shaking her head at her own embarrassment. He had laughed, silently at first until he had noticed Rose's wide-eyed amazement from across the room and the fact that Kate's toes had actually been curling inside her socks. He then chuckled into his whisky glass and assured her that he need not hear any more on the subject.

"Anyway," Kate had continued, her face gradually returning to its normal colour, "you've met him, you know he's a good lad. Hazel really needed him near the end, and he never complained. Not that I saw anyway."

That night had been one of easy conversation when all three of them had laughed together, and there had been many more of them until Kate had declared her feelings to him, and he had then approached every discussion through a terrified haze. Terrified that he would hurt her, terrified that he had accidentally encouraged something more than either of them could handle. Her last few days with him had been unbelievably intense.

On the night before she left, Kate had spent a considerable amount of time with Rose. They had settled themselves at the dining room table with a box of ancient photos, and he had retired to the sitting room, allowing them to talk freely.

For an hour or so he had stared at the TV screen and fed the fire, continually aware of the light-hearted chat and clink of coffee mugs from the next room. What should have been a few moments of relief from the responsibility of taking action of any kind, had mystifyingly made him miserable. Maybe he had grown used to her completely undivided attention, or maybe he had finally realised that she was going and that again he was going to be bereft of something. Whatever it had been, by the time Rose had announced she was bushed and had left them alone, David had been in a state of agitation. Kate had seen it immediately on entering the room.

"What's wrong, Dave?"

"This time tomorrow ...."

She had sat across from him, biting her right thumbnail, her eyes never leaving his face. He had looked at her for as long as he could manage, but when his gaze had returned to the fire, she had spoken instantly and firmly.

"It won't make any difference, you know. You think it'll work itself out if I'm not here to bug you, but I'll love you just as much over there as I do here."

"That's not what I'm saying. I'm going to miss you, and I can't hide from the fact. I'm trying and I can't do it."

She had tried to make light of it. "I'm seriously disappointed that you're trying. Seriously disappointed."

He had been unable to respond, again at a loss as to how to communicate with someone who continually made assured statements about their future, yet failed to see the gravity of their dilemma. After a few moments, Kate had crossed her legs underneath her on the sofa, and had grinned widely.

"Okay, Miserable, enough of this. This is our last night for long enough, so we're not going to sit and try to solve something that you think needs to involve the whole bloody family. Let's be cheery. Let's smile a bit more. That's better."

"It's easy to smile when you're in the room," it had also been surprisingly easy to say.

"Snap. Right, matey, tell me one thing about yourself. Something that you did when you were little, that didn't involve you being responsible or careful. There has to be something. You weren't born with the ability to look after the entire world!"

After a moment, David had shrugged. "I drove a truck into a tree when I was nine."

"Oh, my good Lord! Wait a minute. Nine? How did your feet reach the pedals?"

"They didn't, which is why I didn't see the tree."

"Well, that's half a story. So?"

"It was a long time ago, let's think. Pete was picking up a hat from the drive, so I played with the steering wheel for a while then let off the handbrake. Slid off the seat, trying to find the brake with my feet, and next thing I had smacked my head off the dashboard as it hit the trees. There's quite a camber on parts of that drive."

"Wow. You're Satan himself. And is that it? That's the worst thing you've done?"

"God, you're difficult to impress. Em, oh, this is better, I think. Maybe not."

"Out with it."

"Neil liked to set fire to things. He was always building funeral pyres for his soldiers and kept shavings and chips from the wood pile in a corner, ready for the next cremation. I soaked a load with paraffin once. He lost his eyebrows and a lot of his fringe. Sorry, that's crap even for me. I really was a totally useless prankster."

Kate had laughed. "Maybe you just liked being a protective big brother. Did you ever fight?"

"Daily, until I left school, and then it just sort of petered out. I was working. Beating up a ten-year old felt a bit weird. Funny thing is, I think we both missed it."

"Mum would never let us hit each other, which is why I think we tended to try and outsmart each other with our mouths. Hazel usually won, because, don't know if you've noticed, but you sometimes have to be telepathic to follow her argument; and usually by the time I'd understood her point, she'd already seen it as a victory. She's the babbler, so I have to try and to come up with the one-liner to kill it off."

"I'm sure you're very good at it."

"Well, I don't like to lose. At anything."

The night had culminated in Kate reaching out to him on her way to bed. He had remained motionless in his seat as she had yawned and stretched, but she would not be denied and had knelt by the side of his chair and leaned her forehead against his. His heart began to thump immediately, the pulse of it reaching up into his throat before she spoke again.

"I'm sorry if I'm making this difficult. I wish it felt as right to you as it does to me, but I'm not sure you'll ever let it. So, I'm doing the only thing I can, while I'm still here, to convince you that we'll be okay. And that I'll love you, wherever we are."

She had leaned away from him as his breath had become shallower, and he had looked at her, confused, not sure if he wanted any sort of clarification of her words. She had held his gaze, her grey eyes reflecting the moving flames of the firelight.

"I'm not forcing you. I'm leaving you alone to make up your own mind. It's the fairest thing I can think of, even though being this close to you gives me such a strange feeling, just here." She had stood and placed both her palms flat on her abdomen. "I like it."

She had then stared at him, until he too had pulled himself to his feet. He remembered it all, her fingers peeling from her own body and touching his face, making him look down at her and compelling him to appreciate what she was doing to help him. He had leaned down and tasted her lips and her cheeks and her hair, wrapping her close to his body, feeling her warmth and loving her entire being.

David sighed at the memory, even though it was the kind that heated his whole frame from within, and reached forward to switch on the engine once more. But as he pulled out onto the main road, unable to return to the house without peanuts and eggs, he felt something clear in front of his eyes that had nothing to do with the heat hitting the windscreen.

When he stripped away all the anxiety, when he took away the fear and the worry and the dread that he was contaminating another life, when he simply viewed that person as someone with feelings of their own, then he was left with a clear and simple truth. That wherever he ended up, there would be someone out there in the world who loved him with a passion, and he knew that that same passion lay beneath his own skin. It made its presence known on a daily basis, reminding him each time that he was still alive, and that he very much wanted Kate, whether it was feasible or not.

But he was sitting back, taking no action, procrastinating; and so, as he changed gears, the worst epiphany of the night whacked him on the side of the head, causing him to curse through gritted teeth.

Kate had said that she had loved him for his 'strength and care'. Even he could see that he was being neither strong nor caring at that moment. He was letting her down in a way that was unforgivable, by doing absolutely nothing, and that could threaten their foundations more than any heated words. If he was to keep Kate's love, then he had to take charge. No more wondering at the emotions of youth, no more allowing that gifted person to be hounded by her own family. It was time to start taking control; to start acting instead of reacting. Instead of trying to escape from the endless hours of waiting, from the empty spare time he had to endure, he would sit down and make decisions. He would wait until Kate told him the latest state of play, and he would then contact everybody who mattered and tell them what he wanted. The acceptance of this plan finally brought a smile to David's face.

CHAPTER 11

Sunday, 12th December 1993

"Beth, I'm nipping down to the shore before the light goes completely. You want to come?"

"I'll just get my boots."

Kate waited patiently by the back door, watching the hillside across the bay cling on to the retreating sun for as long as possible. She shivered slightly as she thought of the sheep watching it go, depressed, wondering to themselves if they would ever feel its watery heat again, not having the brainpower to realise that it would rise the next day.

"Right," sighed Kate. "They don't know the sun rises every day, but they've got the ability to be depressed and wonder if they'll ever be warm again. Get a grip."

"Who're you blethering at?" asked Beth, tying her second bootlace and looking around for her scarf simultaneously.

"The idiot that is me."

"Well," smiled Beth, taking her arm, "it's been a long time since you blethered at all, so if you don't mind blethering to this idiot, let's go."

The shoreline was greasy underfoot, which was hazardous, especially for Kate; when dusk was as clear as this, she tended to watch the hillside and sky rather than where she was putting her feet. By the time she had slid and skidded five times, the last on a plastic bottle which was totally avoidable, Beth suggested that they wander back and sit at the picnic table for the rest of the daylight. Kate did not put up a fight.

One car remained in the lay-by, its boot stuffed with duvets and blankets, but no occupants were visible. Instead of sitting opposite to each other, Beth settled herself beside Kate and put her arm around her, rubbing her shoulder. Kate wasn't sure if it was to comfort her or to share her heat, but as it did a small amount of both, she did not move away.

"Do you think she's more relaxed?" began Kate, her eyes never leaving the lights which were winking on Raasay's shore. "She had two bits of toast this morning, with nobody to impress, so ..."

"She'll be okay."

"I know that the whole thing's my fault. I'll keep at it, with her, but what about you? Have I hurt you as much as I've hurt her?"

"Well." Beth seemed to appreciate the need for candour and so took her time in answering. "I think the very worst thing was not being able to enjoy a normal conversation, or even have an ordinary debate without us always coming around to .... the problem."

"I suppose," allowed Kate, unable to feel anything but vexed that something so awe-inspiring to her was viewed as 'the problem'. "Did I say anything unforgivable? To you directly, I mean. I can't remember if I did or not. I think what I've done to Hazel might never be forgivable."

"No, you and I are fine. And Hazel, well, she'll have to get used to things not continually going her way. Your mum was the beginning; this is just another shove into reality for her. And we all have to have a dose of that at some point."

If Kate was aware of the intonation in Beth's voice, she did not show it. "She told me that nobody had to put up with my wants because I wasn't dying. Shit, Beth, I did it all wrong. I should have kept it to myself until we were all recovered, but I couldn't stand the thought of not seeing him for that long. I suppose I do look childish, trying to grab all the attention. Well, now that I've written to him, I've got to keep my word and sort this. I wonder if he's got the letter yet."

Beth turned her head at the approach of a dark figure, but what might have been Kenny turned out to be the owner of the car; and while he unburdened himself and wiped the worst of the hillside from his boots, it gave her a chance to organise her next words. When the car finally pulled away from them, the headlights now necessary in the blue gloom, she noticed that Kate was once more staring across the calm water, and took her chance.

"Kate, I'm going to ask you something, because I have to, but please, please, please understand that I'm only asking so that I can help you with Haze."

Kate's eyes remained on the sea. "Okay."

Barbara Morris

"What happened out there? How did it get to this stage? I've never seen you so adamant about anything. It's scaring me, even though I know David wouldn't..." Beth brought her speech to an end with a shrug.

Kate could see the fairness of the question. She also saw an opportunity to speak openly about her love, which she had ached to do since her return, but would that not just complicate matters? She had told them that she had written to him, effectively cutting the ties, and it was true; but she was also still completely attached to the man, and this must be hidden for the time being. Kate hesitated, thinking it through. She had to give Beth something, something to ease her fears and to give credit to David, who deserved none of the condemnation that was surely being laid at his feet. But she also had to be careful.

"I had a month with him after Hazel left. One month where all he ever did was ask me how I was feeling and what our life here had been like. We talked about Mum whenever we wanted to. That was the best time. He took me shopping, told me all about Neil. He left it up to me what I did about him. There wasn't one day when he didn't share some piece of history with me and," Kate paused, swallowing to lubricate her sandpapered throat, "and he enjoyed my company. And believe me, that was all he ever did. The rest was me."

It seemed that Beth had been holding her breath, for her words came out in one fast exhalation. "What do you mean?"

"Between the time I told him I loved him and I left Canada, we had five days together. He never touched me, Beth, he just sat around looking stunned. I kissed him a couple of times and then he started to look ... hopeful. And don't tell me that that was wrong, because I won't have it. Come on, I'm not daft. I know this is not normal, but it doesn't mean it's wrong. It feels completely right, and by the time I left, we were both much more optimistic. It looks like that's irrelevant now."

"You kissed him?" Beth's voice was low, but it had become too dark to read her expression. Thankfully, this meant it was also too dark for Kate's tears to be evident, as her response needed to be strong and convincing.

"Yes, and you won't ever get me to regret it. But you can't view him badly, Beth, because he does not deserve it. And I'll make sure Hazel knows it. She has to stay in his life, because I can't survive him blaming me for driving her away. I'm not as strong as Mum."

"Okay, Kate, okay. I just wish none of it had happened, because I don't like you being unhappy. You've been through a lot, there's no need for any more upset."

"That's fair enough, Beth. But, to me, David isn't an upset. He hasn't been an upset since you let me read Mum's diary. For me, he's not a 'problem' and he's not the cause of anything bad. He's been the most amazing outcome of the worst weeks of my life. I just wish I was allowed to enjoy even some of it."

Fiona's diary, a customised shorthand notebook, had told of her early life in Canada; and on every page, she had slowly and in great detail drawn a picture of what David Wilder had meant to her. Kate had started to view him as less of an antagonist from that moment, trusting her mother's words rather than accepting blindly Beth and Hazel's assurances that he 'wasn't all bad'. But his true worth to her was how he had helped her through the real crisis and brought her safely back to the world she had retreated from.

For the first time in what seemed like years, Beth held Kate's hand as they walked back to the cottage. It was the safest way of telling her niece that she sympathised with her, without giving her permission to freely follow her heart. The temperature was dropping by the minute, the sky no longer retaining any of its blue pigment, and Kate tried to visualise the worst of the potholes between them and the safety of the driveway. They had almost completed the task when Stuart's truck met them on the road and nicely illuminated the rest of their journey. As he jumped down to meet them, Beth made sure she thanked him with a beaming smile and a longer than necessary explanation as to why they had not taken a torch with them. Kate, on the other hand, hung back as he and Beth headed for the back door. Stuart had never tackled her directly over Hazel's decline, but she could not yet face him. There would be time enough for a proper discussion when her sister was completely back to normal. As the pair of them headed through from the kitchen to the sitting room, Kate closed the back door from the outside and leaned against it. Silence. That was what she needed at that moment. Silence and darkness.

Later, when it became 'official' that Sunday night television had taken an unbelievable turn for the worse, even with Christmas approaching, Kenny suggested a pub meal. "My treat," he announced, "and not only that, but I'll drive as well."

Kate could not think of a good enough reason to decline the offer, but it being construed the wrong way by some person. She would wed as withdrawing or trying to make a point or (the most crime of them all) planning to phone David in order to beg him ove her from all of them. Instead, Kate tried to organise her in strands of mousy hair into an acceptable shape and pulled a

Barbara Morris

cardigan on top of Fiona's ancient Big Country T-shirt. Her right desert boot seemed to be playing hide and seek with her, and, wondering if Hazel had borrowed both and returned only one, she crossed the threshold of the depressingly half-empty bedroom. As she hauled Hazel's discarded clothing from the floor, Beth shouted that she and Kenny were heading off to secure a table and that she should follow on with Hazel and Stuart. Kate frowned as she acknowledged this, but since she was not in a position to run after them, she sank onto her old bed and held her stomach to stop it dropping further within her. Sometimes, God seemed to be toying with her.

"Hey, Kath - ryn! You ready?" Hazel's voice was shouted from somewhere near the back door, and with a supreme effort, Kate made herself stand up. What were the chances that all of her shoes were missing and that she could get out of this commitment and curl up on the sofa instead? As she asked herself the question, she spotted the missing boot near the bedside cabinet and accepted that she would be spending the remainder of the evening in the company of her family. Maybe Beth would let her have a cider and she could persuade Stuart to buy her a few more on the sly. The thought of later falling onto her bed, fully clothed and incapacitated, was an acceptable one. She would neither have to think nor cry.

As she tried to unknot the laces of the located boot, which indeed bore the mark of her sister's handiwork in that they were still trussed tightly, Hazel's face appeared at the door. Glancing up, Kate saw the dull eyes actively brighten as she was spotted. Before Hazel had a chance to speak, however, Kate held up her boot and sighed.

"What do you call this? I'll tell you what I call it, Haze. A bloody impossibility."

"Give it here," grinned Hazel and began to work at the knot with her teeth.

Kate lay back on the bed, her hands linked beneath her head, like she had done for the years and years that they had shared this space, and closed her eyes. The room was too familiar to have a smell, but Kate breathed in deeply through her nose and let it out slowly. After a moment, she felt the weight of Hazel join her on the bed.

"You hungry? I think they do a carvery on a Sunday night. Stuey's high as a kite at the thought."

"Sure. I'm not having turkey though."

"Actually, I was wondering if we should ask Beth to, maybe, change the order of things a bit this year. Christmas-wise. What do you think?"

"Explain?"

"I'm not sure if there's any real point in doing exactly the same as always. Why don't we have a complete change, and do it for Mum. I know, I know, it's practically criminal, but why not?"

Kate felt, to her dismay, a hot tear roll from the corner of her eye and burn a trail across her cheek, narrowly missing her ear. She sucked her bottom lip into her mouth and clamped her teeth down onto it. Christmas without Fiona. Christmas without David.

Thankfully, Hazel was scowling at her failure to undo the lace and in the end, growled at it and threw the boot in the air.

"Why don't you wear your trainers?"

"Fine, let's go."

«•»«•»«•»

The route out of the village was reduced in width by the compacted snow on the verges, but the road itself was negotiable, and the three of them bumped along in the cab of Stuart's pickup truck. Kate's fingers pressed against the dashboard to help her counteract each bend. Hazel talked non-stop, all but drowning out the Top 40 chart countdown on the radio; although she did pause once, listened and then announced to all that if Mr Blobby was going to be the Christmas number one, then she was going to write to Parliament.

Kate could see, even in the dim light, how Hazel and Stuart's thighs bumped together occasionally, and each time her sister turned to talk to her directly, she rested her hand on his shoulder. Had she ever been aware of how often they touched each other before? It was all so calm and unobtrusive. If she had David beside her now, she knew she would not be able to stop herself from touching his chin, staring at him until he looked back at her, and the effect it would have on her would be a lot more invasive. She closed her eyes.

"What's up?"

"Nothing," she assured. "Although what happened to the suspension on this thing, Stu? My stomach is back there somewhere, and it's still complaining."

"Cheek," stated Stuart, then, "When's your driving test?"

"Second week in January."

The lights of Portree were passing them by on either side, and there were the first few flakes of fresh snow, floating down in the neon glow. A couple of the bigger bed and breakfast establishments had trees in their gardens, decked with larger-than-life bulbs; and not for the first time, Kate pondered how you could physically have electricity cables running through snow. Surely it was the most dangerous of ideas, even though it looked lovely.

"I don't mind if Christmas is different this year," Kate stated. "Well, it's going to be, anyway. But we have to have a tree. At least, I would really like one. What about you?"

"Och, yes. I didn't mean no tree, really, just ... let's change the ... expectations of it all. Let's just get up, be kind to each other and have a nice meal. Maybe go for a walk if it's a reasonable day. Get drunk."

"Sounds way better than my day," said Stuart, slowing down to look for a parking space. "Can I come over and join in?"

"You bet," breathed Hazel, near his ear. "We might even eat at night and you could have two Christmas dinners. You could stay over. I have my own room now, you know."

"I think this is my stop," groaned Kate, and was first out of the truck and across the car park, leaving them to finish their conversation in any way they felt fit.

The bar of The Isles was only half full, too early in the month for the Christmas tourists and too inclement an evening for many of the locals; but the fire blazed in the hearth, and there was Beth, stamping her feet back to life and rubbing her hands in its white-yellow light. Kenny was leaning over the bar, discussing with the barman the merits of the non-alcoholic lagers, with a look of pure distaste on his face.

Kate wandered over to his side.

"You know, I could drive home if you wanted. Nobody would care about no 'L' plates on a night like this."

Kenny regarded her carefully, his ginger eyebrows folding and unfolding, as he considered the idea. After a moment, Kate burst out laughing.

"Blimey, Ken," she grinned, "you must really hate that stuff if you're actually thinking about letting me get behind the wheel of the Defender. What was it you said? It's not a vehicle, it's a one-man machine. You're as bad as Stuart and his precious pickup."

"Kate, I've told you before, man and machine get accustomed to each other. You let other people mess with that relationship, you are asking for trouble."

"I knew it had four wheels and an engine. Didn't realise it had a soul, too."

"I'm talking about the position of the seat, the mirrors; you need to know that things are the same every time you get into it. It's essential."

Kate had walked away but was still smiling as she sat beside Beth. She could hear the man continue to justify his theories on maintaining the consistency of a vehicle's interior with the barman, who obviously understood the concept completely.

Kate grinned at her aunt.

"Where does he get half his rubbish from?"

"I have no need to know," replied Beth, picking a couple of snowflakes from Kate's ponytail. "How was the trip in?"

Kate shrugged, not wishing to talk about it and instead began to discuss the potential changes that Christmas might bring.

Half an hour later, Kate sat watching Stuart and Hazel making their way towards her, their plates piled high with food. For some reason, the sight of her sister entertaining the idea of eating everything in front of her tightened her own stomach muscles. It should have made her heart lighter and convinced her that her mother's advice had been correct, but Kate was nowhere near that stage of acceptance. Yes, she was thankful that Hazel looked so much better and felt comfortable enough to act more rationally. She was relieved that those she shared her present life with were smiling more and talking to her as they used to. It meant that day-to-day living was becoming looser, not pulled so taut in opposite directions, allowing people to breathe more easily. But Kate was also beginning to recognise things in herself that she did not particularly like. She was not, as they all thought, meek and understanding and accepting of what they were forcing upon her. She resented what they were doing to her, and this in turn told her that perhaps she was still a child at heart.

Here she was, sitting with her nearest and dearest, people who were so familiar to her that being with them held no terror or anxiety, whose company she enjoyed and whose views on life had shaped her own. But she still wanted what she had wanted all along, and so she was acting. She was spinning a yarn, allowing them to calm their nerves and to view her as mature enough to act for the greater good. She was not mature enough, not if the mature option was to give David up. All Kate really knew was that he had touched her heart so deeply that there was no way out; certainly not for her. So, did that make her too immature for him?

Kate felt herself staring at the flames in the hearth, not focussing, but aware of the movement of the light nevertheless. Her thoughts were racing. What a strange period in their lives this was. So many jumbled emotions, even amongst the five of them at this very table, and yet still they seemed to feel the need to communicate on whatever level they could. They had practically lost each other, torn at each other until they had bled; and yet, mere days later, they were sitting, laughing together, fighting to stay above the surface of the black water beneath them. Was it desperation or love that was creating this scene?

Kate shoved a forkful of chicken into her mouth and chewed it without enjoyment, thinking that perhaps it was a little of both.

"Hey! You're miles away," said Hazel, waving her hand in front of Kate's eyes.

"Sorry," replied Kate, before the significance of Hazel's words caused an awkward lull. "What's the betting that the snow will keep me from getting to work? I've only been there a week."

"It'll probably be okay," replied Hazel. "It was turning to sleet when we came in. Hey, do you get a staff discount? Those split ends could do with trimming."

"Cheers, Haze."

"What? Mine are just as bad. Maybe you could get family discount as well!"

Kate grinned into her second glass of cider, enjoying the way it made her head swim. As Hazel leaned against Stuart, fighting him for his last roast potato, an idea was taking root in Kate's head, and she felt optimism beginning to sprout from it. It was such a simple thought, but Kate viewed it as a positive one, and she had to take those where she found them. She would get her hair cut. She would ask Elspeth to shear off the long, thin strands that announced to the world that she was still a teenager, and shape it instead into a shorter, more fashionable cut. Already, she had managed to persuade herself to eat better and more regularly, to combat the gauntness resulting from Fiona's passing. It had been a challenge, but she was determined to regain the figure she had lost and to look healthy and fit. She wanted David to love what he saw as well as who she was, even if she had no idea when he would next see her.

Kate gazed at the tiny bubbles trailing up to the surface of the bright gold liquid in her glass, marvelling at the way the alcohol helped her mouth curve upwards without effort. After a moment, she noticed Hazel pointing at her and sniggering. Stuart also grinned in her direction.

"Hey, you two, stop staring. It's the height of rudeness." Kate's voice was mellow and, suddenly, that was exactly how she felt.

"Okay, well, stop smiling for absolutely no reason then. Makes you look a bit simple."

Kate grinned even wider, shrugged her shoulders and began once again to eat. The food was well cooked and tasty, but Kate would have eaten it whatever its condition, because she was on a mission. A mission to thrive; and the very best thing about this mission was that her family would only see it as beneficial. Her dearest hope was that David would benefit from it the most.

CHAPTER 12
Saturday, 18th December 1993

For the third time in an hour, the pile of glossy magazines Kate had sorted into chronological order slapped onto the tiles from their home on the coffee table. She looked at them in dismay. Not only had she ordered them by month, she had positioned them top to toe so that they lay completely flat. How was this task defeating her?

"Night, Mrs McEwen," shouted Elspeth, her last customer being the oldest and deafest of the day. "Remember to order your taxi for Friday next week. Even I need Christmas Day!"

As the bell signalled the closing door, Kate took the safest option open to her and shoved the magazines into the reception desk drawer. It was already dark outside, and if Kate wanted to catch the last bus, she would have to increase her pace. She grabbed the broom from behind the beaded curtains and began in the corner by the door.

"Hey, Kate? Did you make up your mind yet?"

Kate blushed. "I did, but I didn't want to bother you this near Christmas. You're busy enough."

"Look, you're doing me a favour. If you like, I can do it tonight, and I'll run you home after. It's Roddy's works do. I'm in no rush."

Ten minutes later, Kate was studying herself in the mirror, her newly washed and conditioned hair looking like rats' tails dripping water. Time for a change.

"So. Demi Moore in Ghost, or Melanie Griffith in Working Girl?" Elspeth's scissors were poised, glinting as enthusiastically as her grin. Kate cringed ever so slightly. "Or, we could just blow dry it?"

Kate shook her head and sat up straighter. "Definitely Demi Moore. No half measures."

"Okay then. Let's get this done."

As Elspeth assessed, snipped and told tales of her daughter's trip to Chamonix, Kate began to examine her own face further. Had there ever been enough character and beauty in those features to interest a man like David? She watched her own eyes widen as she acknowledged these doubts for the very first time. Hazel had certainly done a great job in cracking her resolve.

At The Edge Kate had been so sure of herself, determined that he had to be rescued from his life. How could someone in his position – fit, alive and just stepping into middle age – have so little to distract and amuse him? He worked hard, he attended the odd Rotary meeting and had once been seen to enjoy a game of ice hockey. Otherwise, he appeared to sit in isolation, living inside his head, and she had seen for herself that he had readily latched onto their growing friendship. Even before she hungered after him, she had hoped that he would view her as an ally, and he had certainly adapted to her presence. But then they had both been desperate. So Hazel had not been completely right; they had desperation in common.

"Do you want to keep this?" Elspeth held up a lock of deep brown hair, almost a foot in length, and Kate gasped.

"Oh, curses," she said, her voice low. "Beth is going to kill me."

Elspeth's face creased around the eyes, but she laughed. "You mean, she doesn't know this is even taking place? Oh dear. I'm beginning to fear for my own life."

"It'll be okay," Kate's reply was firmly positive. "But I will keep that. It's been part of me for years, and I might leave it with Mum, if the snow goes soon."

Kate sighed as she felt Elspeth grow tense behind her and saw her expression in the mirror, but waited until she had continued her snipping before she spoke again.

"I don't mind talking about her, you know. It's only annoying when folk look at me in a certain way. But that's happening less and less, thank goodness."

After a moment, Elspeth stood back and scratched her nose. "Fiona was a few years below me at school, so I never had a lot to do with her. Maybe if we'd got the same bus, but I was over at Carbost then. It's funny, though, I do remember her hair. Really long and thick."

"Hazel inherited that. I ended up with this nondescript mess."

"You have fine hair, but lovely hair."

"Had," smiled Kate, holding up the precious lock in her fist. "Had lovely hair."

Elspeth placed both her hands on Kate's shoulders and waited until their eyes met in the mirror. "You are going to look gorgeous. My reputation depends on it. Now, lean forward slightly."

In the one week that Kate had worked in this bright little space, where the air hung with the smell of chemicals and shampoos, she had heard every imaginable tale of family/work/holidays/relationships. The stories themselves had been less enlightening than the reaction to them, and she was, against her own wishes, truly beginning to appreciate some of Hazel's fears. It was only the juiciest, most unusual aspects to any tale which caught the imagination of the customers; and although Kate was sure she had been guilty of this herself in the past, it made her hackles rise to hear the enthusiasm in their voices as they made their opinions known.

"Hey, Elspeth," Kate spoke to her own chest as the hair at the back of her neck was trimmed into a straight line, "I bet you could write a book with all the gossip that reaches your ears in here."

Before she had a chance to confirm or deny the statement, the phone echoed through the empty shop, and Kate found herself frowning again in the mirror. As Elspeth babbled in Gaelic down the receiver, she cleared her brow immediately and tried a smile instead, again trying to see her face as an adult male might. What she saw instead was a face no longer framed by brown strands, but a more defined chin; and as she raised her eyebrows in surprise, she saw Neil's questioning look. There, for the first time, she recognised her heritage, and when Elspeth returned from the phone call, Kate's grey eyes were still staring at her own reflection.

"Hey, it's not that bad."

"I love it, Elspeth, I do," Kate's voice was on the point of cracking, but her employer was kind enough to let it go.

"Well, thank God, because that was Beth wondering where you were, and I thought I would just ease the shock by telling her you were going for a new look."

"Oh, thanks for that! This way she'll get all her ideas on 'why I did it' sorted in her head before I get home, and with any luck she won't need to let me hear them."

Elspeth smiled as she began the lengthy task of layering and feathering, and Kate realised that this was where her employer's skill lay. Not in her impressively adept way of using the scissors and her fingers to shape every hair type, but in her ability to let her clients talk without too much input from herself. Kate sat up ever so slightly as Elspeth stood back to sneeze and wipe her nose.

"Oh, excuse me. Don't know where that one came from."

"How long have you been married, Elspeth?"

"Twenty-four years in February. And the man is a saint to put up with me."

Kate laughed. "Yes, I can see how uptight and obnoxious you are, right enough. You must be an absolute nightmare."

Elspeth grinned, shrugged her shoulders, but yet again left any further conversation up to Kate.

"What's it like, being with somebody for so long? I mean, do you still smile when you see Roddy coming in the front door? Do you look at him when he's reading the paper and think wow, he's mine? Do you still get that thing where there's like something fizzing inside if you see him looking at you? I mean, I know how Hazel feels about Stuart after two and a half years, and Kenny and Beth seem to be really good ... what?"

Elspeth had stopped cutting and was staring at her in the mirror, her face arranged in a smile which could either have been of surprise or recollection, but at Kate's final question, she was immediately animated again.

"Nothing. You just ... your eyes were so bright when you were talking. Have you met somebody, miss? I know those signs, although it was, as I said, a worryingly long time ago."

Kate grinned widely. Now, this was something totally unexpected. At last she was in a position to share what she was feeling with someone who was not going to be damaged by it and who did not actually require to know every single aspect because she was not family and would not feel the need to pressurise. She might be able to get ten minutes of relief from her dark thoughts by telling this new friend about the man who had taken her heart. That would be pleasant.

"There is somebody who makes me feel really good. But he lives in Canada, and I'm not sure it'll ever be possible."

"Judging by the questions you were asking me, I think you'd very much like it to be. Am I right?"

"Yes. But apparently I'm too young to know what I want, so it's not really an option at the moment. Maybe when I'm eighteen, or when everybody I know realises that I can think for myself. Anyway, don't get me started on that. Can I tell you about him?"

"Well, you're not getting out of that chair until you do."

The thirty or so minutes that followed were the best Kate could remember since she had arrived back in Scotland, and she delighted in the way Elspeth listened to her descriptions and feelings, throwing in inquiries which showed how genuinely interested she was. What was the best thing about David? Too difficult a question to answer. How could she possibly choose between his face when she made him laugh, or his attempts to beat her in arguments or the way he looked for her on entering a room, his frown disappearing as soon as he saw her. And as enthusiastic as Elspeth's reactions were to Kate's opinions on the man, there was no way she could begin to describe his eyes or his jaw line or the way his hands crossed over her back when he kissed her.

"Oh, Kate," chuckled Elspeth, switching off the hairdryer at last and laying it aside. "You're bringing it all back. First love, what a feeling. Roddy had the curliest hair. Oh, and the muscles in his arms. Does he have muscles, your young stud?"

"Erm, well, I think he's quite fit. I haven't really seen that much -"

"That's fair enough, you've got plenty of time. Roddy didn't really lose shape till he turned fifty, then whoosh! Woke up one morning and it was like lying next to a pregnant teenager. Honestly! You could see the shape of his frame, all slim and tidy from behind, then he turned sideways and there was a baby, in a little hammock over the top of his boxers."

Kate was momentarily lost for words, thrown completely by the picture Elspeth had painted, and then they were both laughing, only the slightest guilt poking at her heart for not sharing her whole story. It didn't seem to matter. Her boss was enjoying herself, and so was Kate.

"Oh my God, if he could hear me talking, he'd remove himself - and hammock - from my bed forever. It's not fair, I've expanded just as much in the last little while, that's just how it is. Make the most of your man's young qualities, Kate, they last a pitifully short time."

"I haven't had the chance yet. And, it's not going to happen now, is it? He's on the other side of the world and things … well, I suppose it would be easier for everybody if there was a way of finding somebody as special over here."

There was a pause as Elspeth reached for the hand mirror, obviously mightily impressed by her restructuring of Kate's look, but Kate seemed to have lost her momentum. She was staring at her hands, turning them over and studying them. Before she was even aware of it, one small tear had splashed onto the skin of her right palm, and she massaged it away instantly, leaving a tiny oily residue.

"What do you think?" asked Elspeth, brightly.

Kate looked up at her own reflection, careful not to catch her employer's eye, but smiled gratefully in her general direction. The style was certainly fashionable and had achieved in no small way what Kate had set out to do. But the whole point of this transformation had been to appear older and more sophisticated to her love, and she had no clue when he would ever lay eyes on it. And there it was again, that feeling of being gutted as the core of her feelings was yanked from her; she felt her smile tremble. Was there no end to this ache? Was she going to stumble every time she thought or talked of him; was she to cave in after every little foray into the part of her mind where David still sat on the arm of a chair, waiting for her? She could see him, completely immobile, looking straight at her.

"It's brilliant," Kate replied. "It's exactly what I wanted to see."

In the next moment, Elspeth had put down the mirror, dragged a chair across to Kate's and had wrapped her up in a hug. Kate caught the faint smell of Lily of the Valley soap before she was enveloped in the thickset arms. It was an odd couple of seconds. Kate had known this woman for just over a fortnight, yet apparently she qualified as someone worth comforting. She did not shrink from the contact, but neither did she give in to the temptation to break her heart.

"You're going to be fine, you know. You're going to miss her for the rest of your life, but you're also going to have so many new things come your way, and they'll start to take up more of your time and thoughts. New people, new jobs, new places. New hairstyles."

The last few words were accompanied by an extra squeeze, which only came to an end when the phone once again screeched out to be answered. As Elspeth got up, muttering under her breath about some people's ideas of her working hours, Kate leaned forward towards the mirror and tried to remember the 'before' version, but it was long gone. As she stood, shaking the fluff of hair onto the floor and trying to untie the nylon smock, Elspeth's words suddenly started to filter through from across the room.

"... well, you're lucky, she hasn't left yet. No, I'm sure it wouldn't be a problem, but let me just check. Can you hold for a second?"

Kate raised her eyebrows as Elspeth carefully covered the mouthpiece of the receiver and jumped up and down on the spot, both her mouth and eyes impossibly wide.

"Kate! There's a David on the phone, wondering if you're able to speak to him. God, Kate, he's so polite. Is it the David? Is it? He sounds very serious."

Kate's hand went to her mouth, but she was grinning behind it and was then doubling her efforts to remove the smock, which seemed necessary in order for her to speak to him. As Elspeth hopped and fidgeted, Kate shook her hair once more in front of the mirror and tried to hold onto her excitement. Maybe the Christmas mail had delayed her letter and he would still be chatty and loving on the other end of the phone.

"Kate!" hissed Elspeth, "It's a phone, he can't see you! And he's calling long distance, for God's sake."

Kate frowned apologetically, then, "Is this going to make you late? They .... they don't like him calling the house."

Elspeth waved away her worries and handed over the phone. "I'm going to the chippy," she hissed and left, still grinning.

The receiver felt warm in her palm as she raised it to her ear. "Hello?"

"Kate. Are you okay?"

It was hard to tell if the inquiry was pre or post receipt of her awful letter, as his voice sounded more businesslike than anything else, and Kate let herself lean against the wall, wondering what answer to give him.

"I don't know. Are you?"

There was only the slightest delay as their words travelled the miles, but it was enough to make the discussion even more awkward. She heard a sigh before he cleared his throat and she answered her own question in her head as he spoke his words.

"Oh, well. I got your letter. Tell me you're surviving this."

"That's a strange word to use, but I suppose it's the right one. Did you phone the house?"

"Yes."

Kate closed her eyes, and suddenly she was sitting on the floor, the knees of her jeans brushing her chin. "Who did you speak to?"

"Beth. Hazel wasn't ready to talk. I'm not sure if she ever will be."

Kate heard the absolute defeat in his voice and immediately felt the blackness cloak her shoulders and upper arms. She almost dropped the phone as despair injected itself into her voice. "But she's getting better."

"I've messed up, Kate. Big time," David continued, not acknowledging her words. "Your last letter proved it, and Beth has filled in the details. It's no good. I was creating a dream world in my head. You were there and I was there; it meant hope and it felt ... special. But there's no room for it in reality. Reality is you and me hurting too many people, and that's not who we are. Can you accept any of that?"

Kate was breathless with emotion. His words were capable of snuffing the life out of her. She heard them, recognised the thoughts behind them and knew that she had been expecting them; they still chilled her. But she was also aware that he was speaking to her as an equal, asking her to listen to him and accept the position they were in collectively. They were in this together, for the time being. How should she handle this? Her heart was almost rattling the bars of her ribcage, desperate for her to tell him what she needed; but David was inviting her to join him in his quest to resolve the situation, and it meant that they could be allies for as long as it took. She closed her eyes.

"I hear what you're saying," she said softly, "and I'll do what you want me to do, if you'll do something for me in return."

There was a hesitation which was not solely due to distance, but eventually, as the blood sang in Kate's ears, David asked her what she needed him to do.

"Please, can we sort this together," she replied. "Please, can we do this for the best reasons and not hide from each other or stop talking. I can almost see a way through it, if you promise not to ignore me, Dave. If we can always stay close, even if we're in different places, and show them that what we feel ... isn't bad. It doesn't have to be the end, does it?"

Kate's head had dropped into her left hand where she felt the strangely soft layers of her short hair. She massaged the strands between her fingers as she waited to hear his verdict on her summation. It was a second or two before she heard his voice again, and now it was back to the tone she was used to, the depth and quality that she loved, in spite of his words.

"Aw Kate. I don't know. I was dreading that you would be unmovable on this, but I should have known better."

Kate felt her heart become a frozen fist inside her, and she sank her teeth into the bitter denim, then skin of her knees, so that she would not sob out loud. But it was her turn to speak.

"So?" she whispered.

"We can do it. Let's do it, for the best reasons."

"Together?" she urged. Surely he would give her that much.

"We'll try," he replied, "We can try to... do it together."

The reply was good not enough. Trying was not nearly good enough, and Kate felt icy fragments chip from her heart as she forced it open to the possibility of abandonment. She could already sense how it was going to be. David would perhaps ask Hazel to visit him, and they would come to some mutual understanding of what had happened. Or he would write her a letter, pages of apologies and admissions of insanity and beg her to see it as another crazy moment in their already mad world. Hazel would accept his argument and begin to look at Kate with sympathy in her eyes, or worse, contempt for her stupidity. They would cover the episode in a blanket, Hazel gradually beginning to accept it but still viewing it as a folly on Kate's part. And she would be left only to wonder what was actually said and to grieve for the alliance she had formed between them, the one that she had clung to so dearly.

"Are you still there, K?"

"Please. Please say we can do it together." Kate wasn't even sure it was fair to push him on this, but despair was already piercing her from all angles. She was forced to her feet as the pain inside became intolerable, and she stood as a stone, waiting for his reply.

"Kate, I don't see how we can. I'm not sure it would help her, to see us together, in the same room. I'm so, so sorry. No matter what I do, I'm hurting someone."

The words were honest, and Kate gripped the receiver as if it was the only barrier between her and oblivion, convinced that her heart would literally shatter if she could not be in this man's company again soon. But he was telling her that it would be better if they tackled this separately, indeed it was the only possible way of doing it without the negotiations descending into complete war. Through her bitter disappointment, Kate acknowledged to herself that the decision had been reached, and it left her with the taste of blood in her mouth. But if she began to argue against it, she might never stop, and there was the very real threat that David would walk away from the conversation greatly relieved to be rid of her. The risk was too great. So she had to trust him.

"Okay," she whispered.

"Kate?"

"Okay, do what you have to. Maybe somewhere down the road ..." Kate could not complete the sentence, because she could not bring this to an end. If he had to leave her behind, then it was up to him to finish the conversation.

She was choked. Her eyes felt like they were bleeding in her head, the liquid leaking from them too thick to be tears alone. Her throat was burning and her face was ablaze. She had no more words, and, slowly, she replaced the receiver in the cradle, aware that he had spoken her name two more times as it made its painful journey.

Once the connection had been severed, she unplugged the phone and stood, forcing herself into action. She swept the remains of her hair, sniffing continually until her face had become dry and salty.

By the time Elspeth had returned, burdened with her fish supper and three bags of groceries, Kate had loaded the washing machine with towels, switched off all the driers at the wall sockets and washed all the mugs. She did not look up as Elspeth bustled herself into the shop. She could not bear the thought of her eyes still sparkling, dying to know what had taken place. Instead, she stashed the broom back behind the curtain and reached for her coat.

"I really love my hair, Elspeth. Thanks very much for doing it." Even to her own ears her voice was like slate, hard with a sharp edge, and she concentrated on zipping up her coat. The coat David had bought for her. There was so much out there to trip her up, to remind her; but for the moment, she had to concentrate on getting home, where she could climb into bed and shut down. When she lifted her head, Elspeth was standing by the open door.

"Let's get you home then. Oh, and I got you some chips."

«•»«•»«•»

David stood on the verandah which encircled The Edge, his breath visible on the frosty air, and tried to find something in his line of vision to focus on; something which would distract him from Kate's last words and the voice which had spoken them. He had heard her distraught before, but not since she had been out of his reach, and the recognition of pure helplessness was a body blow. So many miles and so many obstacles between him and the person he wanted to be with, it was a feeling more familiar to him than any other, and he began to doubt his ability to ever leave it behind. Rose appeared at his side.

"What's going on?"

"Would you believe me if I said that you're truly better off not knowing?"

"Is it Kate?"

David's eyes turned to her immediately, not crediting the tone his mother had used. He felt his defences shoot up as soon as he saw her face.

"What did he say?" David's voice was like marble.

After a moment's hesitation, Rose stood up a little straighter and seemed to grow more inches than was actually possible. "If you mean Neil, and he's the only person I can imagine you would go to with this one, then he hasn't said a word. I heard it from Kate, before she left us, and honestly, I didn't give it any serious consideration. God, David, what is happening here?"

David closed his eyes in the vain hope that his burdens would disappear along with his sight. Every particle of frustration within him seemed to suddenly buzz in his ears, and he felt his fists grab at his own hair.

"Rose," he stated, his voice measured, fighting against the temptation to simply roar at the air around him, "I need to... walk. Don't follow me, because if I alienate you as well, then I really will have nobody. Leave me alone. For a while."

Rose let him go, watching as he marched across the frozen driveway, hands in his pockets, and disappeared into the woods beyond the lawn. The temperature was too low for him to be without a coat or hat, but Rose held her tongue. Whichever particular demons were playing with his head at that moment were his own, and even though it went against every maternal sentiment within her, she had to allow him to walk away. Rose caught a tiny sob in her throat, not only because he was hurting and worrying, even floundering, but because it was becoming clearer every day that she must stop sheltering him. Kate had been right about that if nothing else. Without a doubt, there was a man inside him who was desperate to reappear. She had seen that man years ago, when a wife and a daughter had made him shine bright. She had seen him again when both girls were here, depending on him. She had an obligation to that man; to let him choose, let him solve. To let him become himself again.

CHAPTER 13

May 1994

Port Alberni, Vancouver Island

Dearest Kate

Thanks so much for your latest letter, which I think arrived two days ago, but got lost in the pile of nonsense we seem to receive every day. It wasn't until a draught blew the whole lot on to the floor that we realised it was there! Then it was 'down tools' and all six pages were read over a cup or two. It's always a treat to hear what you're up to.

First of all, what you call an 'imposition' would most likely turn out to be the highlight of our year. So far, Neil has broken his toe and I have had to give up on the stained glass classes I was running at the high school, as I just didn't have the time. Not that I'm complaining, work is work is work and we've just ripped out the old bathroom, but I loved working with the students. Anyway, for sure it would be brilliant if you could come over and stay with us for a week or so. I can think of nothing that would be less of an imposition. We would love it.

You are very good at putting your thoughts onto paper. I wish I had that knack. I understand completely that you have had a strange time lately and if we can help in any way, we would like to take the opportunity. You must know that you are welcome here at all times. Neil was going to write this letter, although his handwriting is abysmal, but I asked him if I could instead. He gave in eventually, as long as I promised to tell you that I forced his hand and that he wasn't trying to avoid anything. (Men can be so insecure at times.) But I wanted to write to you, as I feel like we have never really communicated, and you are as dear to me as you are to Neil. Why? Because I have always known about you, and have wondered about you as much as he has. I would like to get to know you better more than anything else.

In answer to your question, we saw David when Hazel last visited and he was doing okay. You know that he and Neil are not really into sharing that much, it's all a bit new for them still, but it wasn't awkward. Hazel made sure of that. However, if you really do not want him to know that you are coming over, I'm sure we can work something out. Oh wow, I can't believe that this is going to happen, I love having things to look forward to. By the end of the summer the bathroom will be sorted, and celebrating your birthday with us is a great idea. Neil was really touched that you would want that. I hope everybody on Skye is just as okay with it?

I am not going to say Neil is a changed man since he met you, because he has always been, and is still, my absolutely favourite person, but I will say that the smiles come more easily and more often. The best thing for us is the potential of a new relationship with you. Let's see what we can make of it.

So yes! Keep saving that Canada fund and get yourself over here. I hope you don't mind, Neil wanted you to have the enclosed cheque. Hopefully, it might pay for the majority of your travel costs and I know that you are independent and capable, but this comes from us with love, so please let us give it to you. If it means you will definitely get here in September, it will be more than worth it. Call it an early birthday present. You can have your cake when you get here.

Well, my literary efforts are pathetically short in comparison to yours, but I want to post this today and this is my last piece of Air Mail paper, so I will finish.

One more thing, PLEASE, PLEASE COME AND SEE US!

All our love,

Andie, Neil and the dogs xxxxx

PART II

September 1994

CHAPTER 14

Tuesday, 13th September 1994

The pain in her ears was at the level where Kate wanted to stick a needle into both and puncture whatever she found there. She swallowed for what felt like the thousandth time and shifted in her seat, trying desperately to remember if they had ever mentioned air pressure in her third year science class and how she could possibly combat this agony. Surely there had to be a solution; there was no way seasoned travellers put up with this every time they flew. In a final attempt to ease her suffering, she screwed her eyes tight shut and forced the blood into her eardrums. She felt a movement beside her.

"You can have my last one. You look like you need it more than I do."

Kate opened her eyes and looked down at the boiled sweet being offered. Its clear wrapper showed a bright orange oval, and she wondered if it was barley sugar or some unknown Canadian equivalent. The voice of the owner suggested that it might be the latter, but the face was too sympathetic for her to refuse, and she smiled as she began to unwrap it.

"Thank you. I'm not sure if I'll ever get used to this."

"Oh, now, that is a beautiful, soft accent you have there. Which part of Scotland are you from?"

"Skye. It's an island off the west coast."

"Yes, I've heard of it, dear. Never managed to get as far north as that. My family live in the lowlands, and I've just had the most glorious month visiting them. Are you on holiday?"

Kate rolled the sweet into her cheek and looked properly at the aged face next to hers. There were white curls framing the cheeks of the lady, and her mouth and eyes were kind. Maybe if she had the sense to jettison her Walkman earlier and had not insisted on closing her eyes every time someone approached her, the hours might have sped by and she might have made a new friend. Now, with only minutes before the wheels hit the earth, she felt guilty that she had not helped this particular human being pass her own long journey in a more sociable manner.

"Sort of a holiday, yes. My dad lives here and I'm going to stay with him for a little while."

"Oh, that's nice. For you both, I imagine."

"I hope so. I haven't seen him for nearly a year. And," Kate smiled and looked out of her window as the runway appeared on the horizon, "I'm going to have my eighteenth birthday while I'm here."

"Well, I hope you have a wonderful time together. The fall can be quite spectacular."

"Yes, I saw it last year. It was special, right enough."

As Kate reclined in her seat once more, her ears gradually humming back to normality, she studied the air outside and smiled, recognising the incredible clear blue of the atmosphere. Skye had indeed been the 'misty isle' when she had waved farewell from the window of the Glasgow bus, but she had been forced to hunt out her sunglasses between Glencoe and Tyndrum, and they were still near the top of her hand luggage. Should she put them in her pocket and wear them once she was through customs? With her short hair and her eyes hidden behind shades, she might be able to spot Neil before he spotted her, giving her a chance to assess him and prepare herself for however awkward this might be. An alternative was simply to stay on the plane.

She waited until every other passenger she could see had sorted out their possessions and had headed for the doorway before she sat forward in her seat and stretched her arms far above her head. Even her fingers were delighted to be flexed. Standing, she tucked her shirt into the back of her jeans and wondered how different she looked from the last time she had stood on Canadian soil. Then, she had slid into the shadow of Hazel, and had only emerged into the light when she had become the focus of the entire visit. Since that time, she had grown up; she was no taller or older in figures, but she had grown up. Before reaching for her hand luggage, she looked down at herself for one last time. Checked shirt, black jeans, desert boots, layered dark brown hair, Indian-summer-tanned face. No make-up, Fiona's watch and a grey Icelandic jumper to keep her warm. Could she be a man's ideal daughter? She doubted she would ever hear Neil's thoughts on this subject.

There was a tiny moment of delay at passport control, as Kate's new hairstyle did not match the long, childish image on her documents, but she managed to imitate the blank expression sufficiently well for her identity to be accepted. As she headed towards Arrivals, her steps became firmer and her stride longer. The sunglasses were forgotten. Whatever reception was headed her way, it wasn't fair to try and gain an advantage on the man. He had, after all, agreed to this visit and had shelled out for some of her ticket, when he had not been obliged to do either. He was a decent man; and that was all she really knew about him.

"Kate!"

So, Neil had not come to collect her, but had chosen the much safer option of sending Andie, who was frantically waving at her, grinning and pointing at herself. Kate had to grin in return, as those people standing next to the woman cleared enough space for her to extend her arms fully.

"I wasn't sure," cried Andie, relieving Kate of her bag, "if you'd recognise me. And wow! You look incredible."

"I bet I look completely knackered."

"Not at all. Here, get that ridiculous thing off your back and give me a hug."

Kate let her military rucksack slide down to the floor and obliged, frowning slightly at the enthusiasm of the welcome. She was not on familiar terms with this woman, but after the isolation of the bus, then train, then plane, it was pleasant to feel a human body against her chest. Andie allowed the embrace to be tight but brief, and Kate smiled genuinely at her as she faced her again. Perhaps the woman was shrewder than Kate had bargained for.

"Sorry you had to drive all this way on your own," said Kate, nudging the rucksack out of the main thoroughfare with her leg.

"Oh, I'm not. Neil! Over here."

Kate turned immediately, suddenly more edgy than she had been for the whole of the day and a bit's journey, and saw him headed towards them, his hand raised in greeting. So he had made the effort after all, and it turned out to be not the only one he had made.

"Oh, Lordy," grinned Kate. "Tell me he didn't do that just for me."

The man approaching her was most definitely Neil Wilder. He was more than half a foot taller than her, had mid-blond hair and blue eyes. He was wearing a flannel shirt and jeans, but no jacket. The boots on his feet were black which had faded to grey across the toe-caps, and he had tied his jumper around his waist. He was his usual casual self, a little ragged around the edges without even being aware of it. But there was one difference. His face was completely smooth, free from growth of any description, and his hair was cut to an inch in length all over his scalp. It took about five years off the thirty-eight that he rightfully claimed as his own.

"Hi Kate. Looks like you and I had the same idea." He reached out and touched her hair quickly and gently, then withdrew his hand before either had time to worry about the feelings behind the gesture.

"Well, I was trying to look a bit different, but you've beat me by a mile in that competition."

"You look incredible," repeated Andie. "Doesn't she, babe?" She linked her arm through Neil's as he nodded, then reached up and touched his chin. "And now that she's seen the face behind the beard, maybe we can forget this slick look. I've never seen so much blood, Kate. The razor was practically an antique."

"It was an impulse," admitted Neil, scratching wildly at his jaw and cheek. "It's not one I'll be acting on again in a hurry."

"Well, thanks for the thought," Kate's voice was not as firm as she had hoped, so she cleared her throat and reached for her rucksack. "It makes you look younger, if that helps in any way with the ... itching."

"Here, I'll take that," he insisted, hauling the cumbersome rucksack onto one shoulder, and ushering her forward. His palm lightly touched her back as they moved, and both of them accepted the contact. Kate allowed herself a positive breath. There had been no awkwardness, no expectation disappointed. He had touched her hair and she had not flinched. He had smiled and she had smiled back. Andie was there to maintain a level of normality and to ensure that they managed to keep a conversation going. At least until they had spent enough time together for silence to be acceptable.

But with the first major trial that was the flight behind her, Kate suddenly saw the next week or two stretching ahead with no actual agenda, beginning with four or so hours in a vehicle. Without any warning whatsoever, she felt exhaustion hit her whole body and begin to drain the blood from her. She swayed a little as she walked. The heat in the terminal was intense, and her last thought as darkness buzzed in from the edges of her vision was that wearing your jumper around your waist was quite a sensible solution. The world echoed inside the blackness, and when she again opened her eyes, she was only aware of grey-tipped boots, hands which seemed to appear from every direction and an ache where her head had connected with something hard.

"Kate? Kate," the words sliced through the fuzz, and she tried desperately to sit up so that the acoustics, and indeed her perception of the world, would return to normal. Andie's face was the first to appear, her eyes wide, her palm resting on Kate's forehead; and as Neil knelt beside them both, Kate felt her jumper being lifted over her head. Her arms had fallen loosely back to her lap before their voices began to sound anything like their own, and slowly she began to focus on them. She frowned then shook her head slightly.

"What was that?" she asked, thankful that only a handful of the less busy travellers were slowing down to assess the situation. "What the hell was that?"

"You're very hot," replied Andie, wiping Kate's face with a tissue. "And pale. You fainted, that's all."

"Well that's a first," groaned Kate. "It would have to be in public, of course."

As she leaned on her palms and tried to lever herself off the floor, her head spun again, and so she swivelled onto her knees and stood slowly from there, Neil's hands under her armpits. He guided her to the nearest chair, Andie dragging the rucksack after them, mystified as to how Kate had ever carried this weight on her back, even for a step. Kate didn't even argue as she sat, never having fainted in her life and therefore not sure what to expect next. All she actually felt was a bit dazed and extremely embarrassed.

"I'm really sorry. I swear that's the first time..."

"You're fine. We're here and there's no rush."

Kate smiled weakly. During her journey of imagined scenarios, she had never entertained this particular one. Yet here she was, slumped in a chair with two people hovering in her eye-line, both concerned, both frowning, two individuals who seemed completely in tune with each other and both apparently only concerned for her welfare. She tried to sit forward and a yawn claimed her as its victim. She only covered her mouth at the last moment and then lay back once more, failing to find the energy required for anything else.

"Honestly," she mumbled. "I did sleep a bit. But I don't think I've ever been this wiped out. Sorry. Oh, and sorry for the embarrassment. What a carry on."

Andie's face brightened at once. "Sit there. I'll get us some tea. With sugar. Won't be more than five minutes."

Kate did not protest, but watched her hurry off, her cardigan trailing on the floor behind her, and yawned again.

"God, this is ridiculous. Sorry."

"Hey," said Neil, taking the seat beside her and stretching his legs out in front of him, "you're not causing any problem; we've got all day to get back and ... we've both been looking forward to you coming. I wanted to tell you that right away, so you didn't have to worry about it."

"Okay," Kate replied, surprised to find that she was not the only one who spoke her mind. "Thanks for letting me come."

As the conversation had taken such an odd turn so quickly, neither of them really knew how to start it up again, and Kate found herself staring down at the grey prickly wool of her jumper on her lap.

"It's Icelandic wool," she offered, without actually pointing to the crumpled item. "No wonder the heat in this place got to me. Do you like it? I could knit you one. I brought my circular needles just in case."

"I do like it," he replied, aware that the topic of discussion was so much more ordinary than the situation itself, "and if you feel the need to have a knitting project on the go, I'll happily accept any donations."

By the time Andie returned, walking slowly and methodically to ensure no spillage from the cups she was carrying, Neil and Kate were discussing the merits of trans-Atlantic food. They were both slumped in their chairs, Kate's face pinker and more mobile than before and Neil nodding in agreement, while he continually scratched at his chin. Andie was reminded of the previous night's conversation.

She had walked into the 'spare room', which had been christened thus only in the last few weeks, to find Neil squatting by a chest of drawers. The piece of furniture was only a couple of months old, fashioned from his favourite material of black walnut, and he was down on his hunkers, testing the smooth action of the middle drawer. His frown had suggested that something was not quite perfect, and she had stepped back, studying the way he ran his fingers down the runner, trying to pinpoint the source of the problem. When he had finally stood up, he had looked over at her as if she was somehow concealing the solution.

"Just a little bit tacky, half way," he had frowned, shaking his head.

"Hmm. Tough one. You know what I think? I think it's probably the most flawless piece of furniture I've ever laid eyes on."

He had chewed at a nail, looking at her through crinkled eyes and then smiled.

"You think I'm fussing."

"Actually, I think you're exceptionally handsome, in spite of the frown on your face."

"I'm fussing."

They spent the next minute or so surveying the room, both ultimately happy with the finished space yet still anxious, which seemed ridiculous for two people of their age. Andie's mother lived close enough to be able to return home after each visit, and it was more or less accepted by all that Rose and David never stayed for longer than half a day at a time. Kate would be their first actual guest. The first person permitted to live with them in their house in all the years since they had moved here and shut out the world. It had been a scary few moments, culminating in them smiling at each other in wonder.

"It'll be fine," Neil had assured. "Weird, but fine."

"Of course," she had agreed. "It'll be us, the mutts and someone who wants to get to know us. We can do it."

And here they were. Kate's dramatic arrival had apparently allowed them to transcend the initial self-consciousness, and, although they were not exactly making eye contact, she and Neil were chatting freely. Andie decided to ease her foot off on the adulation pedal; if this was going to work at all, she should let Kate see her as she was and not force the 'let-me-be-your-friend' angle. The girl would not be fooled, she was almost certain of that. So, as she handed over the cup of sweet, hot liquid, Andie merely smiled and sat beside her man. Immediately, Kate looked straight at her.

"I feel ridiculous, Andie. Can you believe it, I've never fainted in my life and I choose today to give it a go. Here, in this place, with you two. Great impression I'm making. Oh! Look, there's …"

Kate was suddenly waving and grinning at a stooped figure a few feet across the terminal. On catching her eye, the figure made her way over to the little group, hauling a suitcase on wheels behind her. At her approach, Kate tried to stand but sat again immediately, grabbing Neil's arm as she did so, closing her eyes and spilling her tea slightly.

"Easy, now," he soothed, as she tried again, this time more slowly, eventually letting go of his shirtsleeve and standing straight.

"Hello again," said Kate, then turning to her companions, continued, "This lady saved my life by giving me her last sweetie, and I don't even know her name. This is Neil and Andie. Oh, and I'm Kate."

"Jean, and I'm glad to see you all found each other. My daughter is somewhere around. You'd think I'd be quite easy to spot, but obviously not. So, this is your dad, Kate?"

"Yes," replied Kate, without hesitation, "this is him. Neil Wilder from"

"Mom!"

"–Canada," Kate finished, feeling the most foolish she had done all day. Of course he was from Canada. But she had no time to cringe as

Jean's daughter had already joined them, breathless, and wearing a long denim skirt, hooded sweatshirt and trainers. She noticed Jean assess the outfit, then shake her head slightly before turning to give Kate one last smile.

"You all have a lovely time together, and happy birthday, Kate, when it comes."

As Kate raised her hand in a final, lazy wave, she turned back and picked her jumper up from the floor. Her head was clear, and there was no dizziness left there as she gulped down the rest of her tea. Neil and Andie were still on their feet from the unexpected introductions and were watching Kate with blank faces. She looked from one to the other then smiled.

"I sat beside her on the plane but was too antisocial to speak to her until my ears nearly exploded. Then she gave me a sweetie to help. I really should have spoken to her earlier." Kate paused, then, "Are you okay?"

"Absolutely," replied Neil.

"Never been more okay," reiterated Andie.

"It's just that I'm the only one who's talking. Oh!" Kate suddenly coloured and bit her bottom lip. "Oh, curses. I never thought. It's just, I told her about you on the plane and then she did ask. But I didn't think about how you, either of you, might feel about me just coming out with ... I mean actually using the word ... Sorry."

Kate continued to miss Fiona on a daily basis, none more so than when she found herself trying to dig herself out of a pit of her own creation. Her mother would have interrupted her awkward flow of words long before she had reached the current stage and minimised the damage. But all Kate could do now was to await the reaction from the pair in front of her. She sighed and tried to recognise something like understanding in their relatively unfamiliar faces.

"Well," Neil finally swallowed and reached for Andie's hand. "I'm fine with it, and I'm pretty sure Andie is, too?"

"Completely fine. In fact," Andie stood back, her eyes glinting at the pair of them, "I'm just going to say it. Your face has all the best bits of this man in it. That makes you a very lucky lady, as far as I'm concerned."

Kate felt her face flushing. Prior to this day, Kate had spent only one intense and uncomfortable afternoon with Andie at the Port Alberni house. Rose, Neil and David himself had all been there, and the talk had drifted steadily from the state of the economy, past the most popular colours of emulsion and stains and had come to rest on the subject of Hazel and her many quirks. Each of them had sat in denial of their knowledge regarding Kate, and she had endured it because the thought of addressing the situation had seemed insane. Now Andie had put the words out into the air, information that they all accepted and understood, but that did not stop her skin reacting. She glanced at Neil, needing some direction, but all she saw was her surprise reflected back at her. Then he had visibly squeezed Andie's hand and both of them were smiling at her.

"Thanks," she stated.

"Come on, let's go home."

《●》《●》《●》《●》

When Kate opened her eyes, there was a chilly draught playing with her hair, and both of the front doors of the Dodge Caravan were open. It was dark and her neck needed careful realigning before she could sit up and focus properly. There was a light burning in the first floor windows, but before she had time to feel abandoned, Andie was heading back towards her, three huge canines jumping and rolling at her feet, threatening to trip her with every step.

"Hey, there you are," smiled Andie, sliding open Kate's door. "Bet you feel a bit better."

"I can't remember anything from the ferry onwards," yawned Kate, rubbing her neck and then staring out at the sky behind Andie's silhouette. "Aw, and now it's dark."

"Come on in. Neil has already taken your unbelievably heavy backpack upstairs. What on earth have you got in there?"

"Boots, lots of jumpers, some other things that you will just have to be patient about."

At the top of the external wooden stairway, a huge pitched pine door led into the open-plan room, and Kate's spirits soared immediately. Neil had raked through and fed the banked down wood-burner, and the whole space was cosier than she remembered. She had seen the room before, but that had been during the day when it had been achingly bright, the colours of the rug and wall-hangings and the various ceramic pots fighting each other for attention. She remembered that it had been more homely than tidy, strewn with magazines and dog toys. Now she saw the true attraction of the place.

The room spanned the width of the house, with four portrait windows on both sides. These were framed with solid oak panelling which someone had spent hours sanding and oiling; Neil, surely. And since zero neighbours dispensed with the need for curtains, their beauty was evident both day and night. The many lamps and firelight illuminated the rust-coloured walls and simultaneously softened the shades of the furniture, so that all Kate wished to do was to drop herself onto the sofa and let her eyes roam the room. But the dogs were preventing her from taking one step.

Neil whistled loudly, the sound piercing the whole room, and immediately they turned their slavering attention to him. Within a few seconds, they had been admonished, the two Labradors immediately taking themselves off to their bed, Dougal remaining unaffected. He took his time, stretched as efficiently as his bulk allowed, and lay down in front of the wood-burner, eyeing Neil with complete indifference. Kate smiled at the man.

"As you can see," sighed Neil, "this house has only one master."

"Okay. Well, it's an amazing place. I probably didn't say as much the last time I was here, but it is."

"Sit down, Kate," ushered Andie, "before Dougal decides that the sofa looks comfier than the floor."

As Kate sat, she rubbed her palms together absently, then stopped herself in case it made her look nervous or cold or both. They were all here together, and there was nothing to worry about. She watched Andie fill the kettle, then pull back her black mane and secure it with a band. It hung straight and sleek down her back, the tip brushing the waistband of her long skirt. Kate touched her own cropped hair instinctively, accepting that, had her hair been the quality of this woman's, she would never have cut it off. But it was done. When she glanced back at Neil, he was down on the floor, trying to untangle a twig from the wiry curls of Dougal's coat, murmuring to the animal continuously. Kate sat back, watching his fingers work and the concentration on his face. Just for a moment, she thought of her mother's remorse in wounding this man and his subsequent years of bewilderment. It made her face hurt. But when he finally held up the offending straggle of wood, rubbing Dougal's belly with his other hand, he grinned straight at her. She did nothing but grin back, and it felt the right thing to do.

CHAPTER 15
Wednesday, 14th September 1994

"It's not just diamonds, there are rubies, too," shouted Kate, her face turned to the deepening indigo sky. "And emeralds, if you look hard enough."

"I don't care if you can see lumps of that cheese with the blue veins; which, by the way, has got to be the smelliest substance on earth. Stars are dots of light, and that's all. In fact, they're not even that, they're -"

"Oh, Haze, give it a rest. If you're totally unable to use your imagination, just tell me and I'll bring everything back down to your level. Oh, and I could do with your torch over here." As Kate continued to dig at the raised bed with a trowel, her head-torch illuminating very little, she could hear her sister begin to giggle behind her.

"Don't laugh," she cried. "Those guinea pigs were my responsibility, they don't let just anybody keep them for the summer, and you promised you would help me with them. What am I going to tell Mrs Wilson? She'd christened them, for God's sake."

"But look who's here, Kate."

And there was David, standing a head and shoulders above his daughter. Both of them were silhouetted against the light from the kitchen window, but there was no mistaking his identity. Her heart filled up instantaneously; the feeling was overwhelming, and the next second saw the sky change again. The 'dots of light' were moving, sparkling and dropping from the now paler sky, morphing into every imaginable precious stone as they fell towards her. Beth was there, shouting at Hazel for apparently using her inheritance on a costly fireworks display, and David's illuminated face was on her own, studying her, unaware of the chaos around them.

Kate opened her eyes on an unfamiliar setting, her heart still reacting to seeing her love. He never visited her dreams, and she marvelled at the tingling in her limbs as she moved slowly onto her back. It had taken nearly ten months and a trip across the ocean in order to see his face again, and even if that had been the one and only time it happened, it had been worth it. She sat up, reaching for the discarded extra pillow and placed it between her head and the headboard, still smiling. Had she found a temporary solution to her problem? Could it possibly be the case that by shifting her attention to Neil, by choosing to come here and concentrate solely on the possibility of building a relationship with this couple, that she could allow David into her sleeping mind? Maybe the next time, his face would be directly in front of hers, or maybe he would take her hand and place it against his heart. Kate managed to enjoy two or three seconds of this prospect before she felt the inevitable pull of reality and sighed. She had ruined it already; by entertaining this option, she had inadvertently knocked it on the head.

It was light, but Kate had no conception as to the time of day or who she would find in the other room. It was the middle of the working week after all, and the pair of them had already taken the day off to meet her in Vancouver, but she could hear someone shuffling about. Before moving, however, she pulled the duvet up around her chin and looked around her. There was only one window in the room, Neil having tried to explain over dinner that until recently the room had been used for keeping his raw materials dry.

"The shed is just too damp. It leaves the wood open to warping, and my profit margin doesn't really allow wastage."

Kate had listened to the continued explanation as to why the space was so bare, not following much of it due to fatigue, which must have begun to show on her face as he eventually stopped talking. Now that she saw it in the light, it was indeed bordering on the sparse, but the walls had so obviously just been painted that it made her feel special. They had spent time coordinating the duvet cover and bedside lampshade with the colour of the rug, and even the portable clothes rail was painted the same deep blue shade. Against the wall stood a chest of drawers; each of the three drawers had two brass handles, but between these, the mid-sections had been removed and replaced with carved panels of a much lighter wood. Kate sat forward, her eyes opening wider. In the next second she had bowled herself forward out of the bed and onto the floor, giving herself a carpet burn in the process, but not even acknowledging it.

There was a letter carved out of each panel, surrounded by fine Celtic dragons, each with a gold inlay for a tail. On each drawer the letter was different. Kate, her face hot, traced the letters gently with her fingers, holding her breath as she did so, not even daring to hope that she was right in her assumptions. K, E and W. Capital letters beautifully and painstakingly etched and sculpted. Kate sat back against the bed, hugging her knees, while her eyes filled up. Had he made this for her? Kathryn Eilidh Wilder. The entire piece was so completely perfect in design that she could not take her eyes off it. Each panel was slightly different; the interconnecting loops joining the dragons at various angles, and it would have taken her days to even sketch the design, let alone create the finished article. It was one more reminder to her that the man who lived in this house was not in any way run-of-the-mill. She looked down at her hands, wondering if they had any of his talent hidden within them.

Two minutes later, Kate had donned a pair of socks, pulled her grey jumper over her pyjamas and hastily shook her head until her hair looked reasonable. There was no way she was going to waste time searching for her brush, not when her stomach was fluttering as much as it was rumbling. She didn't mind who was pottering in the kitchen, as long as they could answer her question, and she padded out into the open area. Neil was sitting at the table, coffee mug held aloft as he read a newspaper, but looked up as soon as the chocolate Lab pounced on her.

"Crisis! Get down!"

"He doesn't bother me," Kate sat hastily, not wishing the dog to get into any more trouble, and then frowned. "Did you just call him Crisis?"

As she joined Neil at the table, he could not keep the grin from his face, but then frowned, looked thoughtful for a moment and finally shrugged in defeat.

"Yes, but the reason for it is so ridiculous. Does Crisis sound at all Latin? Could I get away with that? Okay, well here's the truth then. Oh, you want some coffee?"

"Yes, please."

As he poured the drink, Neil began to talk and Kate began to relax, allowing Crisis to lay his head on her lap. It turned out that Andie's mother had been partial to the Bichon Frise breed of dog, but had been persuaded on one occasion to take home a Havanese puppy instead, the breed being its Cuban equivalent. They had named it simply Cuban, and it had proved to be the most universally loved of all the dogs they had owned before or since. Andie had therefore insisted on calling the golden Lab Cuban; and Neil, appalled that they were naming a majestic Labrador after a 'hairball', had named the chocolate Lab Crisis in response. At the end of this monologue, Kate continued to sip her coffee but had absolutely no words to say. Neil tilted his head at her for one second then said, "You've never heard of the Cuban Crisis?"

She could only shake her head.

"Well," he nodded, accepting the fact. "That's the tale, anyway. Guess I could have made up a better one. So, what would you like to eat?"

Ten minutes later, when Kate had established that it was after mid-day and that the meal on offer was lunch, she was looking at a plate of omelette with mushrooms and a basket containing more types of cracker than she had known existed. Crisis had been shooed away from the table and had left sporting a suitably offended expression, which had started another safe topic of conversation where dogs were pitted against cats in the 'which makes the best pet' competition. It was a completely one-sided and fairly short discussion, as Kate was allergic to cat hair, and she was also completely devoted to her neighbour's Jack Russell terrier. When they both fell to silent eating, Neil apparently as ravenous as she was, Kate allowed herself a moment of sheer disbelief at being there, and a further one at being quite so relaxed.

Later, when Kate had been shown the intricacies of the newly installed shower system and had washed every bit of travel grime from her body, Neil suggested they walk the dogs together so that she could get her bearings. The weather outside was on the muggy side, a layer of moisture visibly hanging just above the tree line, but many of the leaves had yet to be detached and strewn around, which allowed Kate to appreciate how enclosed the area was. It was nowhere near as secluded as The Edge, with thin paddocks on either side of the drive, but she could still see its appeal to those who wished to remain within their own safe space. She wondered if Andie had always been as reserved as Neil appeared to be, or even if it had rubbed off on her over time. Surely in her line of business, she had to be personable and outgoing, and indeed, Kate had seen nothing to suggest that this was not the case; maybe she just liked being cocooned here with the man. As they set off along the tyre tracks heading towards the plantation, Kate zipped up her coat and hid her hands in her cuffs.

"What's Andie up to today?" she asked, twitching her nose against the dampness.

"She's tied to the shop. Jayney usually looks after the shopfront, but she's on holiday this week."

"Oh, she has a shop? I thought maybe she worked here with you. Can I see it sometime?"

"Sure thing."

"So, does she have bits and pieces of yours in this shop?"

"Some. Mine's a definite style, though, and Andie doesn't like to limit her market."

They had reached the end of the drive, the main road was visible through the gap in the trees, but only one dog was by their side. Kate knelt by Cuban's head and rubbed her ears, laughing as she tried to dodge the slobbering tongue, while Neil pulled some chewing gum from his pocket and scanned the area for signs of the other canines.

"That chest of drawers in my room is amazing," Kate stood, shaking her head as he offered her the gum. "It's really beautiful; I can't imagine having the patience."

Neil held her gaze for a silent second and then looked around him once more, shoving the gum into his mouth. Finally, he smiled but began to walk along the perimeter of the wood. Kate followed, unsure what to say next.

"I'm glad you like it. It's black walnut with sugar maple panels. I thought the colours went well together."

Kate took a deep breath in, stalled, then pushed the words out, "I love the letters."

Neil's steps did not falter, but Kate dropped her pace slightly, preferring to watch the back of his padded jacket than trying to catch his eye. However, as he reached the fence, avoiding the worst of the water-logged areas, he turned and leaned against it. Kate slowed to a halt and looked back at the house and outbuildings. There was a thin trail of smoke making its way painfully into the dead atmosphere, but it was not remarkable enough to comment on, and she bit her bottom lip, wondering how to follow up her last words. Neil spoke first.

"When I started it earlier this year, I had no idea what you liked. I sort of guessed you might not be into flowers, and I'm partial to Celtic dragons, so," he shrugged, looking at the grass as he spoke, "I thought your initials would be a safe bet. It's yours, if you want it."

Before Kate could answer, there was a high-pitched yelping accompanied by multiple barks from the woods on the other side of the fence. Without a word, Neil used the nearest post to vault the wires and was tearing through the scrub in search of the source of the uproar. It took her considerably longer to clear the hurdle, and by the time she had found him and all three dogs, he was kneeling beside Dougal, whose yelping had eased to a whimper. Neil had him around the neck, supporting his weight and trying to stop the trembling in his rear leg; the other dogs were prancing around them, alternately sniffing and barking, Crisis actually yowling until Neil shouted for them all to give it up. His face was contorted as he struggled with the bulk of the frightened, injured animal, desperate to ensure that he caused him no further pain.

"What can I do?" cried Kate, over the commotion.

"I need to get him to the vet," Neil's face was shining with effort. "I've seen it before. Can you bring the truck as close to the fence as you can? The keys are on a hook by the door."

As Kate was pounding, sliding and tripping her way back through the mud, her breath becoming a rhythmic thud in her chest, she tried to remember where the gears were in the truck. If they were on the floor like the Fiesta's, then she had a chance at this. If they were on the steering wheel, there was a real possibility she would fail Neil, and she could not stand the thought of it. Cuban was running at her feet, apparently enjoying the game immensely, and Kate increased her pace until the wooden staircase reduced the momentum. There were three sets of keys on the hook behind the door, but she wasted no time in trying to choose, grabbing all three and yelling at Cuban to get out of her way.

The Dodge was unlocked, and Kate's relief at seeing the gearstick where she needed it to be was only slightly marred by the knowledge that she would have to alter her brain to use her right hand instead of her left. Cuban had to be shoved from the driver's seat onto the floor before she could gather herself and look down at the keys in her fist. As she slid the most obvious one into the transmission, knocking the stick into neutral with the sense of the recently qualified, still-following-the-rules driver, she saw Neil's figure by the fence. Dougal was lying on his side, held in position by his master, while Crisis stood immobile beside them, on guard. Kate felt a bead of sweat roll between her shoulder blades. The gearstick was solid, the Dodge roared into life under her heavy foot, and she cringed against the real possibility of stalling as she eased the vehicle away from its parked position.

Kate could not help smiling that she had gotten this far. It was only thirty yards or so to where Neil was waiting, and if she could negotiate the soft grass and manage to bring it to a halt successfully, then her job was done. She tested the brakes to see what she was up against, and in spite of the sheer weight of the machine, it obeyed all her commands without protest; this was no Ford Fiesta, but the principles were the same. Jumping from the truck, she slid open the side door.

Neil struggled back onto his feet, Dougal no longer whimpering, but licking his hand instead.

"You're going to have to keep driving, Kate. You okay with that?"

Kate stepped back in alarm, her face creasing at the prospect, but Neil missed the expression as he levered the dog onto the back seat.

"I need to keep him still, and I don't think you're strong enough," he explained.

"Okay."

As she shifted through the gears, the main road at least smoother and firmer than the driveway, Kate tried to conceal her breathing. She did not trust her reaction times in this alien vehicle, and the road was unfamiliar. She also had no real conception of how far they would have to travel, but knew that she could not possibly go above fifty. Sitting perched forward in her seat, both hands clamped to the wheel, Kate kept her eyes straight ahead while Cuban swayed on the passenger seat, tongue lolling, interested only in the shapes which sped by on her side.

"What's wrong with him?" she cried.

"It could be the ligament in his back leg. The other one went a couple of years ago," Neil's voice was now much calmer, Dougal lying panting across his knees. Kate could almost smell the dense heat and pain radiating through from the back seat, but could not look in the mirror. She had no idea where she was going.

"Is it much farther?" she asked, desperately trying to recognise anything in her surroundings. "I don't know where I am."

"You're doing great. We'll hit more houses in about a quarter of a mile and I'll direct you from there. Don't worry."

As the trees gave way to buildings, Kate slowed down further, and all at once the Dodge felt too much for her. She could not judge how far she was from the vehicles parked near the kerb, and her head was beginning to ache above her eyebrows. The tiny, frustrated noise that escaped her made her face crinkle up, and she changed to a lower gear through sheer anxiety.

"Okay, Kate." Neil spoke gently. "You can go as slowly as you like, we're nearly there. You're going to take a left turn onto the highway when I say so, and all you have to remember is to cross over to the right side. Concentrate on that."

When Kate finally brought the 'monster' to a halt in the car park, stalling only as she eased it into an empty space, she let out a laboured sigh and laid her head on her hands which still gripped the steering wheel. Relief had never tasted so sweet. It ran like honey in her mouth, and she found herself grinning against her knuckles. But Neil was already climbing out, Dougal trying but failing to lever himself up into a more comfortable position, and Kate finally put the Dodge into neutral and pulled on the handbrake. Before she could do anything else, however, Neil had opened the driver's door and was watching as she continued to grin and wipe her face. He touched her arm.

"You just sit there. I'm going to get someone to help me out, but I want you to stay here and relax, just for a minute. You come in later if you want to."

Amazingly, Kate did not even question this request; indeed she wasn't sure if her legs would still work, so she nodded and leaned back in the seat. She remained in that position, even when Neil and the veterinary nurse were carrying Dougal indoors, and it felt unbelievably good to be stationary and quiet, with only the weight of Cuban on her lap and the breath of Crisis on her neck. She felt almost sleepy.

When she opened her eyes again, the light had dimmed slightly, and Kate could hardly believe that it was already after four. She slid out from under Cuban's snout and eased herself out of the tiniest gap in the door so that both dogs would stay safely imprisoned. It was so good to stretch and take in some of the cold air; but now that she was properly aware of her surroundings, she had that strange feeling of displacement once more. It had happened a couple of times on her last visit to this country, and it was difficult to define, even to her. The buildings were big and lofty, the trees majestic and protective, and she was with people who were connected to her in the most basic of ways; but her family, the people who provided the cushion to life, were nowhere around. She was not homesick exactly. She was breathing the air of another time and place and it was weird, but not scary.

"God's sake," she murmured to herself. "Just enjoy it."

As she leaned against the Dodge, thinking how pleasant it must be to come to work every day to a place which was surrounded by trees and shrubs, with only the highway breaking the isolation, Neil came through the door carrying his jacket. He smiled as soon as he saw her.

"So, how long have you been awake?"

Kate shook her head. "Honestly, about five minutes. I never sleep this much. How is he?"

Neil's face twisted in a humourless smile. "Well, I was right. Cruciate ligament, which means it's going to be time-consuming and expensive. Thank God for insurance. Anyway, they're keeping him overnight, so we can go, and if you want to, we can drop by the shop and give Andie the 'great' news."

"Oh, I'd love that."

"You want to drive?" his grin split his face.

In response, Kate marched around to the passenger door and manoeuvred next to the golden dead weight that was Cuban. She strapped herself in and folded her arms. Neil was already in the driver's seat, his neck being licked clean by Crisis, but one word had the dog both settled and serious. As he turned the ignition, Kate recognised her overall mood as one of contentment and rubbed Cuban's head until she heard the sigh which suggested that the Lab felt the same way.

"Kate," said Neil, as he stopped at the highway junction, "you were great back there."

"I was a liability! Thank God it was a short-ish journey."

"You were great."

Kate smiled in return, but when he patted her shoulder then squeezed it, she had to turn her face away, her nose prickling dangerously. It was more than she had ever expected.

«•»«•»«•»

"I told Beth about your hair, and we thought you might like this," said Kate, timidly handing over a package to Andie. "Then I spent most of the journey praying that you hadn't cut your hair off in some mad moment of insecurity. Oh! I meant me, Neil, not you."

"None taken," replied Neil, who was lying flat out on the hearth rug, hands behind his head, as if keeping the space warm until Dougal was safely back home.

As Andie unwrapped the tissue paper, he propped himself on an elbow. He looked about twenty-five, thought Kate. Then she glanced at Andie, feeling the most self-conscious she had felt to date. The gifts she brought were spread beside her on the sofa. She lowered her head, touching them gently, hoping that they would be received in the spirit she had chosen them.

She and Beth had scoured Portree and the south of the island for anything which struck them as appropriately Scottish or relevant, without really knowing the taste of either recipient. It had taken them more than one trip. The final choices had been personal to her, and she knew she was attaching too much importance to how these people reacted to them. Kate was nervous. Her face felt prickly.

"Oh, look at that," cried Andie, holding the curved silver hairclip up to the light and turning it over in her hand. As it caught the lamplight and reflected it onto Neil's face, he sat up. On closer inspection, Andie saw that the matt finish had three highly polished thistles sitting on its surface and a smooth pine plinth to secure hair in place. She handed it to Neil, and instantly he was sitting beside her, pulling back her hair. She grinned at Kate, who in turn began to babble.

"Hope you like silver. I knew I'd never be able to find anything made out of wood that would compare to what Neil can do so.... There was one with purple jewels on it, but I thought it looked a bit tacky compared with this. Anyway, your hair doesn't need jewels."

"What does it look like, babe?" Andie asked Neil as his hands completed their work.

"Pretty. Excellent choice."

"Thanks, Kate."

Kate waved away the words and handed her a soft parcel, noticing how Neil's arm was hooked around Andie's neck and how she automatically leaned back against him. "And this is for both of you. You can use it as a... well, I'll shut up and let you open it."

Kate thought about the length of time it had taken for her to come to a decision on the colour and design of the gift. She had saved a specific amount of money, and for once had a legitimate excuse to spend it on something she could never have justified before. The designs had been many, and it had taken her over half an hour to select one. She smiled to herself, thinking that maybe her mother had been guiding her hand when she finally arrived at her choice.

"Oh, a batik!" cried Andie.

"I had to laugh," said Kate, "it took me ages to choose it and look, its the same dragons as on the chest of drawers. Couldn't believe it."

"It's a great colour. Wow, it's huge!"

Neil took the material in his hands and stood, spreading it open in the air to show off the deep red colour and the black and white creatures dancing across it. It measured about three feet by four feet. Kate found it hard to imagine the time spent on drawing and waxing and dyeing in order to produce the beautiful finished artwork.

"Hazel got one for her twenty-first, and I wondered if you would like one. She's hung hers up. I thought you'd like something from Skye. I'd love it if you got there some day."

As Andie wandered around the room, assessing the best place to hang their newest possession, Neil filled the kettle and let the water run until it was cold enough to fill the dogs' bowls. Kate followed him into the kitchen and laid a box on the table. "Don't worry," she said, "it's not an after shave set."

"You know, you didn't have to bring us anything."

"It's just a little thing, and anyway, I've decided that your real present is the jumper I'm going to knit, as soon as I've got the wool."

Neil settled himself back against the unit and rubbed his thumb under his chin, then scratched his ear. He looked at the box with as much trepidation as interest. As Kate raised her eyebrows at him, he reached forward and levered off the lid. Inside lay an innocent leather album. Neil immediately looked over at Kate, his eyes wary and his lip tucked under. Kate felt her heart tighten and her shoulders slump.

"Please," she said. "It's nothing bad, honestly. I wouldn't, I mean, I thought about it first."

"What is it?" asked Andie, joining them.

Kate looked desperately at her, the optimism she had carried with her since leaving Portree suddenly clawing its way out of her arms and hiding under the table. Neil had removed the album from its box and was holding it in both hands.

"You don't have to, honestly," Kate said bleakly, no longer able to look at the man. "I'll take them back and you can just have the album."

Neil pulled a chair out from the table and sat. As he opened the cover, Kate made her way slowly back to the sofa, not wishing to witness his reactions. She was miserable and cold and cursed herself for ever thinking that this had been a good idea. Yet she had put so much thought into it. She had chosen only a few photos of her as a child; innocent, happy, uncomplicated images that were simply meant to show her transition from baby to adult. The majority of them were of the life she led now, in the time since he had first met her, and she had guessed that they would be safe enough. But it had backfired, and she had no idea what to do next. She had made him uncomfortable, and it was only her second day here. She sighed and curled her feet up underneath her. Cuban laid her head next to her knee; one member of the family at least was unaware of her error in judgement. She was still staring at her soft brown eyes when Neil came and sat across from her on the fireside chair.

"This is special. Don't think I don't love it."

Kate lifted her head and looked straight at him, daring him to speak further or to look away. He did neither.

"It was nice to put it all together," Kate said finally. "There were loads to choose from - Mum loved taking photos. I do, too, that's why I didn't fill it."

Neil nodded his head, still holding the album, and then slowly smiled at the flames in front of his eyes. Eventually, he looked in Kate's direction.

"So, go find your camera."

CHAPTER 16

Friday, 16th September 1994

"Well, it's been four days. Maybe she's never going to mention him. Maybe she doesn't need to anymore."

Andie was leaning against her drawing board in the rear of her shop, sharpening her water colour pencils, the phone cradled under her chin. "What's she up to now?"

"Chopping wood. Says it's one of her chores at home and she likes the smell, so who am I to argue?"

"Okay," said Andie, sitting at last. "Well, I've got to finish this today, Neil, so it's up to you. Ask her, if the time feels right, otherwise just leave it. Who knows what we should be doing? I certainly don't."

"Nor me. See you later, sweetheart."

Working in the doorway of the woodshed, Kate had developed a healthy glow. The two Labradors were wandering and sniffing, unable to keep their tails from wagging whenever she spoke to them.

She had created a neat pile of split wood. At first it had been an almost impossible task. She was used to an axe, not a log splitter, and it had taken her five or six minutes to work out how to use its momentum to her advantage and another few to successfully make contact with the logs. It was miraculous she had not broken one or both of her shin bones in the process.

This had been the first full day of sunshine they had enjoyed since her arrival, and Kate needed to be outside. She liked to look at the sky above the tree line and smell the air. At home, she lived with the scent of the sea and the sound of sheep and gulls. Here, she breathed in wood and pine needles and listened to the hum of the traffic on the highway. Although it was nowhere near as familiar an environment to her, it was equally as comforting; The Edge had exactly the same air.

Kate sat on her forty-five minute offering of wood and leaned her chin on the handle of the log splitter. Her spirits were higher here, and when the sun began to turn orange and fracture behind the branches, she smiled at the clear chill it created and could not help but sigh. What would they be doing, over in that old house with the verandah? Would they be lighting the fire?

"Hey! No need to cut a whole week's supply."

Kate turned to see Neil and a strapped-up, subdued Dougal walking towards her at the dog's chosen pace. She unfolded herself to the ground and looked dubiously at the pile. "I'm pretty sure that will last about a day and a half. But I'll let you be impressed if you want to be. I'm just glad you didn't see my first few attempts at it."

Neil raised his eyebrows at her and sniggered.

"You were watching?" groaned Kate. "Did you see how Cuban kept her distance after the first swing? She's a very smart dog."

"Yeah, well, I think we'll keep the three of them shut in when you use the chainsaw." His face was perfectly serious, and he leaned down to tickle Dougal under his chin. "Eh, boy? She'll have arms like a wrestler by the time she's sawn her way through a couple of trees. Won't she, Dougal-bug?"

He rose from his squatting position to find Kate standing with her arms folded. Just for a second his face faltered and then he grinned again.

"Ready when you are," she said, standing as straight as she could, feet apart and head held high. "You don't think I can use one?"

"I know you can't," he replied. "Not my saw, anyway."

Kate began to laugh, and leaned into her knees. "Oh my God," she cried. "You're all so ... possessive. Don't tell me. Man and machine get used to each other. And you can't mess with that relationship. Heard it all before, and I don't believe a word."

Neil was looking at her, his eyes wide. Dougal had apparently hobbled far enough for one day and had sunk to the ground, where he licked at his strapping and yawned. Kate looked over at the shed door, then slyly back at the man.

"Is that where you keep it?"

"There's no way -" he began, but Kate was already surveying the musty interior of the shed. And there it lay, apparently asleep in its ancient box, on top of the workbench. It looked in good condition, the blade free from rust and the teeth gleaming with a film of oil, but a thin layer of dust on the fuel tank suggested that it hadn't been used for a week or two. She studied the saw, a little intimidated that it was almost twice the size and weight of the type that Stuart had allowed her to use once, yet anxious not to lose face at this stage. Still, maybe there was a time and place for humility.

"Okay," said Kate, as soon as he arrived at her side. "There's a chance that maybe this particular saw-"

"My saw."

"-that this saw is probably too heavy for me. But I have used one before, you know, and I know you don't play around with them. I'll let you win this one, though. There's no shame."

"Thank you. I appreciate it."

Kate wandered along the workbench. The handful of tools which lay about seemed to be old and cumbersome, the chainsaw the only contemporary thing amongst them, and Kate guessed that he kept the majority of his finer tools in the more secure workshop. In the far corner, propped against the boards of the single stall, was a push-bike. It looked as if it had been a racer in a previous life, the tyres as thin as she had ever seen. Her bike back home was a hybrid, built for road and hillside, with an exceptionally comfy seat, but the cracked plastic saddle in front of her eyes looked almost lethal in shape and texture. When she pressed her fingers onto it, there was no give whatsoever.

"Painful," she murmured.

There was a tin bath hanging from a hook near the door, but other than a coiled hose pipe covered in cobwebs and three shovels, the shed was clear of debris. When she turned back to where Neil was wiping the dust from the chainsaw with his sleeve, she saw the shed's actual use. The opposite wall seemed to be composed entirely of cut wood, fitted together specifically to maximise the use of space while allowing air between so that it would dry. She walked over to it, trying to calculate the volume of it, failing as she realised it was more than three rows deep. She glanced quickly out at her pitiful contribution then back at Neil, who had removed the chainsaw and was dusting it down properly with a cloth.

"That's some stock," she said. "Suppose winter is just around the corner."

When he did not answer, she looked at him properly, noting that his shirt seemed to be a multi-purpose piece of clothing – warm layer, dust-cloth, tool-belt, and now hankie – and waited until he was completely happy with the rehousing of the saw.

She took a deep breath in. "Was he happy the last time you saw him?" her voice was as steady as a rock, and she had to credit the man on his reaction. He did not slump, or flinch or sigh. Neither did he try to conceal that he knew exactly who she was referring to. Instead, he looked relieved.

"Let's get Dougal back inside. I think he's had his quota of fresh air, and I should have started dinner by now anyways. Cooking and talking. They go together, right?"

"Right," agreed Kate, trying to keep the anxiety out of her voice. She had to be very, very careful from this moment on.

For nine months, Kate had not spoken to David Wilder. She had written to him only twice since his phone call to Elspeth's shop, the first a desperate, incoherent mess of a letter which she had regretted posting almost from the minute it hit the bottom of the post box. The words had been scribbled at speed, when she had been beyond the point of panic, and they had been juvenile and totally unfair. She had not accused him of anything, had not criticised him for his course of action; but she had begged and offered and, worst of all, invited David to blame himself completely. Hence the second letter, sent only a week later. This one had taken her a day and a half to compose, and she had tried to apologise and show him that she appreciated his dilemma. She had written it seven times, burning each previous draft, determined to sound calm and mature. She had prayed that the final result had cancelled out the first chaotic correspondence and that the man she loved still viewed her as some sort of a future prospect and not a petulant, frantic child. He had to know that she would wait and that she was okay. He had replied almost a month later.

The letter was in her rucksack, and it remained in as pristine a condition as the day it arrived at Camastianavaig; not because she did not read it regularly, but because each time she handled it, she treated it as a piece of Egyptian parchment, more precious than gold. These days she could recite it in its entirety, but seeing his writing made him more real, and she still took it on every trip away from home. She thought of his words now as she watched Neil haul Dougal up the steps.

'When you were here, my world was better and that meant everything to me. I don't know how to explain to you what you did, I could never write letters like you or your mother. I don't know how to put these things into words and maybe that's for the best, because I can't act on them, Kate. You have so much you want to give me, but I know you can find another person who will accept it as gratefully as I would. Please could you try? If I knew you were happy, I think that maybe I could try to be ...'

Kate had pondered his letter for days. She had deconstructed each sentence, found the literal meaning then tried to find something between the lines. It was an honest enough account of his feelings, and he had not once suggested that he did not love her, but he had been clear about one thing; Hazel needed to be his priority for as long as it took. It had taken her weeks to accept that this was indeed his wish and not some submission to other people. Even after this acceptance, she had had to battle against her resentment every single waking hour. It was hideous. She wanted what she wanted and would have berated her own selfishness if she was not completely convinced that he wanted it just as much. He needed to be loved and she needed to love him. How could that be completely selfish? But there had been no direct contact since.

There was one tiny glimmer of hope, however; Kate had loaned him the letter Fiona had written to her, and he had not yet returned it. Surely this meant he still wanted to deliver it to her personally, otherwise why had he not posted it back already?

In the kitchen, Neil handed Kate four red peppers and a knife.

"Thin slices and no seeds, thank you."

Kate's mouth was bone dry, but she started to de-core the peppers without asking for a drink. Water would not help ease the fizzing inside, and suddenly she felt doubly apprehensive. This man, who could provide her with as much information as he wanted to, was also bound to have an opinion on the whole situation. She had no idea if that opinion would help or hinder her. She bit her lip in resignation, but did not want to wait another second to start the conversation.

"Have you been in touch lately?"

"Saw Rose in July and Dave about a month ago. Andie sees him more often – did you know she's involved in the chalets he's putting up?"

"Hazel said something about it. I didn't know it had gotten that far."

"Yeah, it's all good. Think I've seen more of him in the last year than I've done since I left home. Keep going with those peppers, we're way behind schedule."

As Kate tried to focus on slicing the vegetables and not her trembling fingers, Neil moved back and forth along the worktop, telling all that he imagined she was interested in. At one point he asked her if she wanted a beer, but she shook her head mutely. She learned that chalets were being built to the west of The Edge, deep in the woods and so screened from the highway. The finished constructions would share the house's main driveway for so far, before veering off, and yes, they were far enough away to protect its privacy. There were five in total, all large two-storey constructions. David was pleased with the results so far. When he turned to face her, the chicken shredded and panned, Neil found Kate sitting motionless, her eyes watching his every move. A pile of neatly sliced peppers sat bleeding their juices onto the chopping board.

"So they're both okay," it was more of a statement than a question which escaped her.

Neil sighed. Andie and he had been expecting questions since her arrival. He was glad to be able to address it all at last, to test the strategies they had agreed to. He was unprepared for Kate's own reticence, however, and had no idea what that meant in her case. Was she calm and resigned, upset and lost for words, or was she simply refusing to react until he pushed the correct buttons? The only way to solve this mystery was to keep talking.

"Rose is really excited by the project, and they've had a lot of interest in them. I think two have been sold."

Kate nodded. She knew some of this already. The previous April, Hazel had turned twenty-one, and as the date had drawn nearer and nearer, it had threatened to be even more disheartening than Christmas had been. Everything was greyer without Fiona. Then Hazel made an announcement, albeit with an admirable amount of restraint, that she and Stuart had taken David up on his offer to pay for a trip to Canada. If she couldn't be with her mother on her birthday, then she could be with her father. Kate's gut had pulled tight until it felt like the taut strapped bands inside a golf ball, but she had managed not to scream or shout or howl. Instead she had slipped outside into the dark March night, had sat down in the long grass beside the garage and stared at the moon until her eyes had stung. So many emotions she should have been able to handle, and yet they still felt icily raw, even months later.

She had been determined to label these emotions. If they had names, then maybe she had a chance of applying an antidote to each of them. Of course jealousy was there; the thought of Hazel claiming his attention and seeing his face and all of them enjoying each other's company had crippled her. Although it had been the dominant feeling, it was not the only one. She had never before tasted frustration on this level; the acrid burning that came with the knowledge that she had the power to reach out to this man, helping them both in the process, but not the freedom to do so. And finally, woven amongst them both was the only feeling that she allowed herself to feel half positive about. That Hazel visiting her dad and being made a fuss of was a good thing. It would make Hazel feel how rightly special she was, and it would warm David's heart to spend time with his precious daughter. They had deserved to be part of each other. Nevertheless, when Hazel had been away, Kate had slept very little and thought rather a lot.

On Hazel's return, Kate had decided that the time had come to talk about the man openly. If she started the conversations, showing Hazel how much she had 'grown up' and how well she could handle everything from her embarrassment to David's lack of interest in her, then it could only make things easier. Coincidentally, or perhaps telepathically, Hazel had had the same idea. It had eased things for the first day or two, when Hazel had babbled about David, Rose, the planned chalets and Stuart's complete love of all Canadian machinery. After that, he was referred to as often as any absent member of the family was, and Kate made sure she was constantly ready for it. So, she knew about the chalets being built on the estate, she knew of Andie's involvement, and she knew that Rose was healthy and enjoying the changes taking place in the woods. She had no idea what David was feeling.

"So he's busy then. And content?" Somehow, her expression was much more controlled than her voice and she frowned at the wobble which had appeared from nowhere.

At last, Neil sat at the table across from her. "Are you sure you don't want to see him? Make up your own mind?"

Kate shook her head without hesitation. "I didn't come here to see him, and that's the truth."

"That doesn't mean you can't -"

"No, I don't want to," Kate got up and finally poured herself a glass of water, but could only sip at the icy liquid. "I know you and I don't know each other at all, but I really need your help with this. I'm fine. I'm absolutely fine, but you have to tell me how he is. You're the only one I trust to be honest with me, without trying to work out what's best for me. Can you do that, or will it put you in an awkward position?"

Neil, sitting with his back to her, dropped his chin into his hand and stared at the table. Where was Andie? He needed reassurance from her, even though they had gone over this particular never-ending situation again and again, and were clear in their objectives; to bring this state of affairs to some form of conclusion. But they had been under the impression that this visit, this attempt of Kate's to build a bond of some sort, was only an excuse to remind David of what was on offer. Had they really thought her so manipulative or had they merely assumed that anyone of her age must have had an ulterior motive?

Surely teenagers became obsessed with what they thought they needed and kept going until either the obsession wore off or they grew old enough to recognise futility and its crushing blows.

Kate said she trusted him, yet he was not doing her the same honour. He had not known this person as a child, this girl who bore more than a passing resemblance to him, yet he had made assumptions about her quite freely. Here she was, trying to convince him that she only wanted to know if David was okay. He needed Andie's take on this.

"Why do you trust me?" Neil asked, turning in his seat to see her face.

He watched Kate blink and take another sip, before putting down her glass. "Because my mum did, so you must be okay. Look," she sat in the seat next to him, the closest he had ever allowed her, noticing that his beard was almost back to normal. "For nearly a year, I've listened to lots of people tell me what I need to do, all of them completely sure that they were saying the right thing, most of them ignoring what I had to say in response. I can hear Mum sometimes, when I'm nearly asleep, and she never tells me that I'm wrong. That keeps me hopeful."

Kate paused, as Neil had lowered his head slightly, but in the next moment he looked straight at her. His blue eyes, normally sparkling with some witty remark or rolling at his own folly, had never appeared so piercing, searching her face for clues. As she had nothing to hide or be coy about, Kate stared back at him, moving her eyes from his, taking in his whole expression. "What is it?" she asked.

"What makes you think I'll be different to any of the others?"

Kate shrugged and started to bite her nails. She felt Cuban, her new best friend, nudge at her knee and reached towards her soft fur without looking down at her. She was aware of her wet nose and hot breath as the dog tried to get more of her attention, but she could not afford to be distracted.

"I saved all my wages from the hairdresser's, the coffee shop and babysitting so that I could come here and get to know you and Andie. You're my dad, and it would be great if we could both feel good about that. But if you want me to be honest, I also came here to ask you about him. I can't go on not knowing. You've seen him since... then. And you grew up with him. You must be able to read him. Just tell me how he is, please."

"Oh, wow, it's so much colder today than yesterday!" Andie's light footsteps on the stairs outside had been missed by both of them, and Kate jumped at her sudden arrival on the scene. "Fall is officially here."

As Andie hung her denim jacket on the back of the door, the dogs made sufficient fuss of her to mask the sombre atmosphere, and Neil used the interruption to carry the peppers across to the cooker. Kate looked down at her hands, the tips of her fingers stained pink, and then over at Andie. The woman was always so fresh; she always breezed into a room and brightened the space. Probably what attracted Neil in the first place, thought Kate, doubting that Andie had ever hauled baggage along behind her like the rest of them had. Kate glumly laid her hands flat on the table, spreading her fingers and moving them over the grained wood. She could sense some form of communication going on between the two adults behind her and felt as if she should remind them that she was not an idiot. But the words did not come, and Andie was sitting at the table. She also traced the grain of the wood.

"It's beautiful, isn't it?" smiled Andie.

Kate nodded. "Yes."

There was a tremendous noise as the peppers hit the reheated pan, and Kate felt the familiar grind of despondency against the inside of her skull. Truly, the most upsetting thing at that moment was the realisation that this particular emotion remained within her, even in this country. She had hoped to be spared it for at least the time she was here. But she was more than despondent, she was disappointed. Even now, in this room they were still negotiating information. Why were they not being forthcoming? She felt her stomach turn and heard the chair scrape as she stood blindly. Nobody tried to stop her as she found her way to her room. Nobody tried to follow her or prevent her from closing the door. She supposed she was grateful, but really she was just numb. She lay down on top of the duvet, folding her arms across her chest, but in spite of the calming murmurs she could hear, she did not shut her eyes but lay staring out of the window at the moon.

CHAPTER 17

Friday, 16th September 1994

Hazel had every Friday afternoon off, and on this particular one, she had plans. She was determined to make the most of her positive energy because the following day was bound to be a trial. Yet it was just another day without her mum, the fact that it was the first anniversary of her leaving them was academic. However, her colleagues would be aware of it, and even if it was not mentioned, the morning at work threatened to be tense. So, today she was going to occupy her time with something only she knew about, and she wore the secrecy and anticipation around her body like a blanket. She literally ran for the car on escaping the shop.

The Fiesta needed oil, it informed her of this every time she switched on the engine; but since she could smell nothing untoward and the car itself was not juddering or coughing, she drove happily past the garage and headed south of the town. The road was almost drowning from the torrential downpour of the previous hour, but the cloud was thinning, and she was almost sure the sun would be steaming the puddles on the driveway at Camastianavaig. Usually on a Friday she dropped in on Stuart at the farm just to touch base and to cement plans for the weekend, but today she drove straight home, aquaplaning only one large wet patch along the way. She waved at her neighbour who, in the absence of Kate, was having to exercise her own dog, and smiled at the depressed look on the Jack Russell's face. Apparently, Kenny, Beth and she were not the only ones who missed Kate.

The house was silent apart from the hum of the fridge, and Hazel dropped her bag and tabard at the back door, switching on the kettle as a matter of course. It was a long time since she had been completely alone in this space, but she spent no time acknowledging what she was missing and instead went to change out of her work clothes. As she hunted through her drawers for her newest sweatshirt, her eyes rested on the plethora of photos on her dressing table. Stuart and she had such an amazing time in Canada that there was not enough room for every beloved image to be displayed. So she had been ruthless in her choices, and, now dressed, she picked up the nearest frame. It was a cracking photo by all accounts.

On one spectacular Canadian Sunday, Hazel had expressed the desire to stretch her legs and begged David to take them as far up Mount Tzouhalem as his 'old legs could carry him'. Of course, he had put her to shame, she who would rather stare appreciatively at Ben Tianavaig than ascend even ten metres of it. At one point Stuart had offered to piggyback her so far. She had declined and made herself attack the rest of the climb with as much enthusiasm and as little moaning as she could manage.

When they had stopped at a viewpoint which spread Duncan below them in the brilliant glare, Hazel had very slowly brought her camera out of her rucksack and taken three or four photos of David and Stuart without their knowledge. The one she studied showed David standing with his arms folded, tall and eyes creased against the sun, with Stuart sitting at his feet, both of them staring out over the sheer drop. The colours were stunning, David and Stuart's dark-clad figures standing out against the blue, green and gold background; but the most astounding aspect of the entire composition was that the skyline was straight and the subjects themselves were central. It had been framed as much for this success as for the image itself.

"My best men," she murmured, before letting her smile slip away. It seemed that every time she considered David, what he had become to her, she could not prevent Kate from also entering her head. The initial nausea and disbelief had faded away at some point after Christmas and had been replaced by a dull sadness; sadness that any of it had ever taken place.

Of course, Kate had changed. She walked about the house with a permanently positive expression, chatting and joking as much as she ever had, but she also spent nearly all of her spare time on the hill, in all weathers and completely alone. It may be an act, this determined optimism of hers, or it may be the only way Kate could swallow her humiliation at the idiotic mistake she had made. Whatever it was, the relationship between them was much more superficial, and she missed her. Since they had stopped sharing both a room and their confidences, it was almost like Kate had become a lodger in the house. She had separated herself from them.

'And that's where I come in', thought Hazel and headed to the hall.

The cottage never warranted a huge roof space, but Hazel knew for a fact that above the hallway, through the ridiculously tight opening in the ceiling, there was an absolute cache of nostalgia. Scrapbooks full of their history, boxes of photos and favourite books, ancient and outgrown Christmas decorations that meant nothing to anyone but them, and she was about to make use of all of them.

This was her private time, when no one else was in the house to bother her or question her motives and when she could find something special to bring her sister back to her.

As Hazel climbed the loft ladder, amazed that the mechanics of it still worked in spite of its infrequent use, she was struck by the smell coming from above her. It was a combination of sooty dust and warm mould. It was not necessarily unpleasant, but it confirmed that the best course of action was to bring the boxes down into the fresh air and bright light.

Ten minutes later Hazel was kneeling on the sitting room floor, trying not to think of what creatures might be stuck on the inside of the folded lids of each box. There were five in total, three large cardboard crates which had once brought apples to the farm shop, a shoe box and a plastic tub without a lid.

It was this tub which was making her wary of the rest; there were at least three skeletal spiders guarding their treasure, and they made her fingers itch in disgust. The tub could wait. She recognised the shoe box as the home of her mother's diary which she had read on her return from Canada the previous autumn, and so pushed it aside for the moment. That left the three large boxes, and, setting her coffee mug on the hearth, she chose the least dusty to delve into.

There was a faded piece of cloth covering the contents, and Hazel laughed out loud at the sight of it. In her childhood, the square of flannelette sheeting with teddies on it had been her constant companion. She lifted the crumpled, frayed and genuinely loved article out into the light. It was stiff with age, and she had no desire to hold it to her face, but its familiarity was a joy.

"Byes!" she cried, unaware still of how the little security blanket had come about this particular name, "you've been up in the attic all this time? Shameful."

Hazel laid it aside, intent on washing and storing it in a more appropriate place, and gingerly began to unpack the other items, careful to check the underside of each for any dead, or even worse, living organisms. She dearly hoped to find enough goods of interest before she reached the bottom of the box, because the thought of the cardboard being held together by cobwebs and bodies, as well as by tape, was making her shudder. The whole activity of removing, remembering, repacking, washing her hands and agreeing with Runrig at the top of her voice that Canada and Scotland were indisputably linked took nearly fifty minutes. Fifty minutes during which she had marvelled, laughed, slapped her head at what her mother had considered worth keeping in the first place and pondered over every photograph. At one point she had phoned the farm to tell Stuart that she had found a primary school sports day photo which showed someone like him in the background, but he had been out on the hill. She sat cross-legged, the boxes returned to the loft, and surveyed her choices. So many totally positive memories from which she would design a keepsake for Kate's birthday. It would remind her that she was still part of them all, still important, and would always be worth going that extra mile for.

"Shit," whispered Hazel, hauling herself up to turn the cassette over, unable to complete this task in the silence which had descended into the room. She frowned, desperately hoping that the first song would be upbeat, because right at that moment Hazel was admitting to herself that she had not gone anywhere near a mile, extra or otherwise, for Kate in the last year. "No! I am not getting depressed today. Come on!"

By the time Beth and Kenny came stumbling through the door at 4.45 p.m., both shouting for her assistance with the shopping, Hazel had almost completed the task to her satisfaction. All she needed was a large picture frame for the collage of photos and memorabilia, and surely there would be time to acquire this before Kate's return.

"Oh, just unpack the frozen stuff for now, please," cried Hazel, hurrying through to the kitchen and beginning to search the carrier bags for the cold items. "I want your opinion on something as soon as is physically and mentally possible! It's an extra birthday present for Kate."

"Are you not out with Stu tonight?"

"Later, but I've been toiling all afternoon with this, well, not toiling because it's been good fun, and I think it's almost definitely bound to work in our favour. Both of you, though, I need you both to see it."

On the sitting room floor, there seemed to be nothing but coloured tissue paper, old newspaper cuttings and faded photographs, and Kenny was momentarily struck by the difference between Hazel's boundless enthusiasm and the actual reason behind it. She was on the case immediately.

"Now I know it doesn't look much at the moment, but you've got to use your imagination. I'm going to get a big frame, a really huge one, maybe from the Photo Shop. Or if we all go in together, I could set it up and get them to make a frame. Maybe something in gilt. What do you think?"

Kenny nodded at the principle, then eased himself back out in the hallway. Beth, however, had sunk down amidst the chaos and was spying and retrieving and exclaiming, her voice rising in pitch at each new find. Hazel was delighted; it was exactly the reaction she had needed, and they sat together, recalling every occasion being represented in celluloid or newsprint, until Kenny inquired loudly about the chances of a decision being made on what they were to eat.

"I'll go," grinned Hazel, leaving Beth to approve the choices. There was nothing contentious amongst the pile; many photos of Fiona with both girls, portraits of them as babies sketched by their grandfather, a newspaper cutting showing Kate holding a trophy, old birthday cards, invitations and tissue paper flowers to dress them with. There was also a scarf which Hazel had knitted in Primary Three; it was one long piece of purple stocking stitch, but had been her first ever project, and Kate had liked the colour. Surely, even with all that was still going on in her head, Kate would see it as the grand gesture Hazel intended it to be; they were sisters, and that was not up for negotiation.

Beth let out a sigh, still amazed that so much could have happened in the space of a year, but she had little time to ponder it as she spotted the old shoe box poking out from under the sofa. By the time Hazel came hurrying back into the room, Beth was skimming through Fiona's diary, only appreciation showing on her face.

"I'm not taking anything out of there," stated Hazel, no longer smiling.

"Of course not, I was just revisiting."

"What's in the envelope?" asked Hazel, pointing to the buff, franked item lining the bottom of the shoe box.

"Certificates," replied Beth, oddly.

"Oh, from school? Kate had loads of -"

"No, official stuff. Papers, deeds, nothing you'd want framed with this lot. Here, shove that back on top of it."

As Beth handed her the diary, Hazel looked at her for one more moment, almost ready to accept that she had nothing to hide, but not quite. She had opened the envelope before Beth could comment further. Fiona's death certificate, Beth's birth certificate, Hazel's birth certificate.

"Where's Kate's?"

Frowning, Beth took the documents from her niece and scanned them.

"I've no idea."

CHAPTER 18

Friday, 16th September 1994

The moon was beautiful. Oddly shaped, not quite full, but still proudly showing off its grey blemishes within its silver light, and Kate for once could grasp Hazel's apparent obsession with it. It was unfussy and aloof and commanded appreciation whenever it decided to visit. Kate wondered if it was the same shape at home, not even trying to remember the rules about phases of the moon which had almost sent her to sleep in physics. It was probably obscured by cloud anyway, unable to create broken lines on Camastianavaig Bay; and before she allowed another thought of home to enter her head, she pulled herself up and forced herself over to the doorway. Why was it always so difficult to go back into a room you had walked out of? And yet, ten minutes was an acceptable period of time to be gone. She may have been simply brushing her hair, or tidying up her discarded clothes, and not, as she had been, trying to get her nerve back. She found Andie opening a bottle of lager and Neil about to plate up. There was more than a better chance that she had got away with it.

"Can I do anything?" Kate asked Andie.

"No, it's sorted. Want a beer?"

Kate shook her head and rinsed her hands at the sink, aware of music playing in the background and the lamps illuminating the living area. She could see how you could lose yourself for days in such a comfortable space, as long as you were part of the couple who had initiated it and not some awkward guest who was upsetting the rhythm and mood of the place. 'Enough!' she thought.

"Actually, could I have one? Sorry, I bet a beer would go really well with," she glanced at the dish in the middle of the table, "erm ... uh ... dinner."

Neil grinned. "Wilder-style fajitas. Isn't it obvious?"

"Help yourself," laughed Andie, as Neil continued to tease Kate with his eyes, looking down at his food and then back at her in disbelief.

"Can you teach me?" replied Kate. "I think I could manage them, although I'm not great with raw chicken. More of a mince household, ours. I can make great Yorkshires, though."

"That's it then," confirmed Andie, folding meat and vegetables into an amazingly neat wrap, "you're cooking tomorrow night. Anything you like as long as the Head Chef here says you can borrow his ingredients. He's been known to get clingy with the dried goods stock."

"And with chainsaws," offered Kate.

"You know," sighed Neil, "I knew this would happen. I knew that as soon as you two got to know each other, you would gang up on me. It's been on the cards for days now."

Kate smiled as Andie could not stop herself from reaching out and ruffling his hair. He shook his head in response. After a moment, when Kate had finally managed to seal the juicy meat into its little package, she cleared her throat. "I was wondering if you needed a hand in the shop tomorrow?"

Andie's eyes opened a little wider before she answered, "Well, that would be great, but we weren't sure if you had ... plans."

"Me? Have plans?"

"On how you wanted to spend your day," offered Neil, using his wrap to clean his plate, before laying another onto the shining surface. "Maybe a walk. Or a drive out."

Kate glanced at both of them, but before she could answer, Andie touched her shoulder. "Hey, if you want to come to the shop, that's fine by me. We're usually quite sociably busy on a Saturday morning, and I could find something to occupy you."

Kate nodded, but laid her food aside. "What did you think I might want to do?" she asked brightly.

"Well," said Neil, finally looking at her, "we're all aware of the date. I thought you might want to spend some time doing something really positive. If you wanted to, we could go to Lake Cowichan, you liked it there. Then ... we could always go have a look at the chalets."

Kate felt her shoulder blades move as she tensed inside and was surprised that Neil continued to look at her. This time last year, he would have barely been able to say the words, let alone watch her thoughts on them. Her throat caught as she tried to swallow, and she willed with all her might that the creeping hot fingers on her neck would halt of their own accord. If he could handle this, then she was determined to do likewise. She smoothed out the lines on her brow and sat upright in her chair.

"I just wanted to spend the day seeing lots of people instead of wandering about on my own. Oh shit," Kate was suddenly close to tears. "Why does everything I say sound like a criticism? I don't …. I didn't mean it like that. Sorry. Please, I need some fresh air."

Again, nobody tried to follow Kate as she made her way to the door, and it occurred to her that perhaps they were not being incredibly sympathetic or accommodating, that perhaps they just had no idea what to do or say to her. She barely knew herself where her head was, and all she really wanted to do was to find a spot away from her entire existence, some place where she could do what she had not done since the previous Christmas. Somewhere she could hold her knees to her chest and wail unrestrainedly until all of the inflexible burdens she carried on her back were cracked open and peeled from her like an eggshell. Her heart, as young and healthy as it was, could not physically keep up with the demands that were being made of it; be content, support your sister, trust your mother, show us you are okay, be the daughter he never knew, do not hurt that man any further. They followed her around continually, each of them having their own colour and smell, and she tried to treat them with respect, but they were killing her. Maybe somewhere between the house and the main road, somewhere near the plantation fence or even within the wood itself, she could find a tiny area of comfort, a place to stare as the blades of grass turned grey by the moonlight and to let her heart have its say.

Kate had no torch, but her feet could feel the ridges of the tyre tracks and the sound of the road was ahead of her; she was safe enough. Out there in the sharpness of the autumn evening, she realised that, on Skye, the day had already dawned on the anniversary they had been discussing. Beth and Hazel would surely take flowers to Fiona's grave, and here she was, not even able to call upon her mother, for her mind was too twisted and troubled. She recognised the aroma of despair in an instant and let out a whimper before she could catch it. What on God's earth was the next step? How many more moments were there ahead of her where she must act as if she were capable and thick-skinned so that everyone else could stay calm and unthreatened? It was interminable, and she felt her throat close in on the emotions stuck there.

Kate suddenly found tarmac under her feet, having walked onto the main road without a second thought. There was no traffic, but in spite of the moon, the route was black and uninviting. She hesitated. The dark held no fear for her, she had walked the road from bus stop to home on many a winter's night; but she had no idea of where a haven might be and so stood still, face raised to the stars. As she swayed on her feet, head back and mouth open, she heard footfalls from the driveway and there was Neil. She looked at his figure blankly.

"Where ...?" he breathed heavily.

"I've no idea," Kate admitted and lowered her head in submission. "I just don't want to be me tonight. I've had enough."

Without waiting for an acknowledgement, Kate moved to the grass verge and sat down.

"Kate, it's freezing."

"You know," she replied, looking at his dark boots in front of her and the lower half of his legs, "I thought you'd be one of those folk who didn't mind the cold or the dark or sitting on the ground. I thought you'd be like me. I thought that's where I got it from."

After a moment, Neil squatted in front of her and pulled her to her feet.

"You're not going to get me to do that, Kate, because I know what happens when you let those monsters on your shoulders win. When you sink down under their weight and accept defeat. So, we're going to walk, as slowly as you like, back to where the fire's burning and the dogs are waiting. Let's go."

Kate's legs did as he bade them in spite of the vacuum inside her, and she walked two steps behind him as they blindly negotiated the driveway. There was nothing to say; at least, Kate could not bring her whirling mind to a halt on any one topic, and so she shoved her hands into her cardigan pockets and followed him in silence. Once, she tripped over an unknown object and bounced her forehead off his upper arm, after which he slowed their pace further, but still he did not speak. Was he waiting until they were back at the house, where Andie would provide moral support for him? Why should he have that advantage? Kate halted, just to see what he would do. He stopped after a few more steps, but she could not see his face when he turned.

"Don't you feel the cold?" he sighed.

"Are you ever going to tell me how he is? Please just tell me, out here, where Andie and you aren't making faces at each other and where I know you're speaking to me as an ordinary human being and not some ... some moron who needs protecting from herself. Oh, I can't stand this! I can't stand it any longer!"

If there had been anywhere to hide, Kate would have taken off at a pace, but it was pointless running and far, far too dramatic a gesture.

Instead, she walked past the staircase and found herself standing under the stark electric bulb in the woodshed. From there, she forced herself into the tiny space between the workbench and the wall of wood. Less dramatic, she thought, although much more childish. But she was officially past caring and instead sat with her knees against her chest, scowling at the floorboards.

She knew she could wait all night. She had nowhere to go and no one to see, and the cold dust in the atmosphere was not scary. No doubt Andie would appear very shortly, tentatively asking her how she was and beg her to come inside, whilst Neil stood in the background, looking concerned. The very image of this made her angry. Nobody wanted to listen to her, and her father would rather hide behind his tiny partner. She put her hands over both ears to stop the certain sound of Andie's concerned voice and hid her face from the world.

However, when she felt something nudge her right boot and she opened her eyes, it was Neil who sat on the floor, legs stretched out in front of him, leaning against the split wood. He raised his eyebrows at her, and finally she lowered her own knees away from her face. He may not yet be speaking, but he had come alone to the place where she sat, and she felt her heart begin to steady its pace. She should try to explain her frustrations to him; if anybody had knowledge of anxiety, it was this man. She guessed he was also no stranger to agony.

"How old were you when you met Andie?"

Neil's fingers, pulling at a frayed hole in the knee of his jeans, stilled immediately. "About twenty-five."

"So, you didn't miss Mum for too long. I'm glad. Andie is really great."

Neil was staring at her, struck by the gentle tone she used on words that could cut him open, wondering what her motives were. Her face was nothing but grateful, as if she truly was glad that he had not suffered, but he didn't know where the conversation was headed, and he felt his heartbeat stutter once.

"I'm nearly as old as you were when you loved my mum," continued Kate, smiling slightly. "Can you remember how you felt then, how much she meant to you?"

Neil pushed himself onto his feet in one fluid movement. "Don't, please."

"I'm sorry. But I don't have anybody else I can talk to. Beth thinks I'm over it all, and Hazel goes along with that because it's what they all want to believe. Mum isn't here and David is what it's all about. You're all I have, whether you want to be or not."

He was hovering by the door by the time Kate had rushed the words out of her mouth, but she could not move. She had no feeling in her legs at all and was completely at his mercy. If he stormed off, like she had a tendency to do, it would mark the end of another painfully inadequate conversation, and suddenly Kate found herself in the skin of those who had watched her and failed to reach her for the last ten months. Shame now squeezed in amongst the rest of the emotions jostling for space inside her and, red-faced, she lowered her head against it.

Something in her demeanour must have touched him, however, because here he was, once more towering over her and reaching for her hands. She was on her feet almost instantly, surprised at the power in his thin wrists, her face still burning.

"Right," he stated with both his voice and his eyes firm. "We're going inside, and we're going to finish the dinner that we worked hard to put together. Then, we'll sit until the wee small hours themselves if necessary, until everything we ever needed to know about each other and everyone has been said and understood. How does that sound?"

Kate nodded meekly and started to move away, but he stalled her with his hand.

"But just so you know, I've never been anybody's last resort before. This could turn into a long night."

CHAPTER 19
Saturday, 17th September 1994

David Wilder's head was tucked neatly into his right shoulder, left arm resting against the headboard above him, when his alarm clock buzzed into life. As was the case almost every morning in life, he cricked his neck trying to switch the machine off and so began each new day with a pained frown on his face. This morning, however, the frown did not dissipate along with the muscle ache as he stretched both his arms out into the air in front of him. There was a hint of sunlight through the crack in the curtains, illuminating the dark boards and rug of his bedroom, but today he closed his eyes against it and covered his face with a pillow. It was going to be a day of trials, both physical and mental, and he had two choices. He could throw back the duvet and stand under the shower until his head could bear the drumming water no longer, or he could lie beneath the cool linen and think the day away. He was out of bed in a second.

He barely glanced in the mirror these days; his frame and his face were no longer relevant to anything. So, at 6.45 a.m. on a sunny September Saturday, he was towelling dry his hair and staring down at the already yellowing shrubs on the driveway instead, wondering how those he cared for were feeling. At eight hours ahead of him, they would have finished lunch, perhaps sitting at the picnic table if the temperature still allowed it. Or maybe they were already on their way to the cemetery; and, closing his eyes momentarily, he could picture the neat plots, gleaming headstones and the sea, blue and mobile in the background. Ben Tianavaig, which he had initially thought belonged to the Mackinnons, so often had they referred to it as their hill, would be there to supervise the proceedings, and he could almost taste the salt in the breeze. Would the tide be in or out? Would they visit Fiona as a family or individually? These were questions which could be answered later, when he rang them.

In the kitchen, the cold water tap was dripping steadily onto a china saucer, which sounded like a small bell chiming, and David added the replacing of a washer to his list of tasks for the day. He was a little put out by the sound, as this particular tap had only been in situ since the beginning of July, and its predecessor had never dripped in the whole of his lifetime. But this gripe notwithstanding, the room had benefitted from the refurbishment, and he was happy with the result. Rose had insisted on keeping the range, which suited him fine, as he did not want to disturb the heating system, even though Andie had hinted on an upgrade. In the end, she had managed to find some heat-resistant lacquer and given the range a black coating, so as not to limit her colour scheme. The room was painted pale blue and grey, and, with fewer wall units, was so much bigger than he had ever realised. Andie had allowed them only two solid oak units at eye level, which Rose had questioned until Neil had arrived one day with a matching dresser to line the wall next to the pantry. From then on, they accepted every idea she came up with and cooked, ate and planned in a bright and modern space. Rose had been impressed, and it had caused her to take a major interest in how the chalets were being fitted. She had rarely been at home in the last fortnight.

As the kettle began to vibrate on the pristine worktop, David scratched his ear and contemplated all of the changes that had taken place in the last year. It was almost too much to comprehend, yet here was the physical evidence in front of him. Had there been no devastating news from Scotland, there would have been no visitors bringing fresh air and vitality. Without that particular disruption to their bland little lives, he was convinced that both he and Rose would have spent their remaining years on earth amidst those dark cupboards and wallpapered walls. It would not have been disastrous had this been the case, but now that he had a taste of possibilities and alternatives, he was glad that they had taken that step forward. Even the kettle was new. He could see his face in the shining chrome and allowed himself a vague smile at the continued absurdity of his situation.

Miles away, in a country he had visited only twice, his amazingly vivacious daughter lived her daily life without his presence or his input. He had to accept this, and he felt that he probably did, except on days like today, when the only thing he wanted to do was to make sure she was as okay as circumstances permitted. The phone call would help, but it was not good enough and never would be. He wanted to see her face as well as hear her voice, to see if his words made any difference to her. He wanted to be needed again, to be of use to someone, to be necessary. He wanted to talk to people, have them listen to his thoughts and share theirs with him; thoughts which did not include health and safety checks or the price of chain oil.

He had one person to blame for this hunger of his, and it was the same individual who had caused every disturbing, unsettling, incredible awakening within him. On an impulse, David took his coffee out onto the front verandah and sat on the top step. Only when outside, where the birds alone witnessed his expressions, did he allow his mind to wind its way around to Kate. On the odd occasion when paperwork had forced him to sit upstairs of an evening, he had played her Runrig tape as a background accompaniment. But it had invariably resulted in him staring into space, applying the lyrics to their own situation like an adolescent, so he had given up on that fairly early on. He wondered how she was coping on this day. He had not spoken to her since that last awful time when she had literally cut the connection between them and forced him to acknowledge that he had hurt her beyond repair. How in God's name had he ever let it get that far? Kate was beautiful and engaging and generous with her affection, which were only three of the good reasons not to subject her to disappointment on the scale he had accomplished. Shaking his head, he closed his eyes yet again to his admission of guilt, and heard the phone ring from the hallway.

"Dad! Did I get you out of bed? Sorry it's so early, did I wake Rose?"

"Hi Hazel," he grinned into the mouthpiece. "Don't panic. I was up and I'm sure Rose is awake. How are you doing over there?"

"Oh, we're okay," Hazel's initial shouted queries answered, her voice became a little more subdued. "We've just been over to Portree. It was fine, it's exactly the same sort of day as it was last year, sunny and sticky. But at least the flowers looked good. How are you?"

"Better now that I'm talking to you. Lonely sort of a morning, if you need an honest answer," he paused, wondering if she had indeed needed to know that. He took a deep breath in. "How is everybody else?"

"Same as every other day, if you need an honest answer back. Quiet, I suppose. It's always quiet here now."

The prolonged silence which followed almost caused David's head to spin. It was so incredibly unlike Hazel to be stuck for words that he grew agitated, and before he could organise his thoughts sensibly, he had opened his mouth and asked the question.

"Is Kate okay?"

"Yes. So is Beth."

Again the conversation stalled, and David screwed up his eyes against his own awkwardness. "Well," he stumbled, "I wish I could make it easier. But it means a lot that you would phone me, sort of like you're letting me help a bit."

"Well, you're my dad, why wouldn't I want your help?" There was just a hint of sharpness to Hazel's voice, and after a tense pause, she continued, "Beth's just bringing in the washing so you could speak to her, but Kate's not here. Not sure when she'll be back. Beth! Dad's on the phone!"

"Hey Haze!" cried David, "don't rush off. It's you I want to speak to."

Whether she heard him or not she did not answer, and it was suddenly Beth's voice on the end of the phone.

"Hi, David."

He cleared his throat, a pulse in his temple beginning to throb. "Beth. Is Hazel still there?"

"Em," there was a pause, then "she's bringing the rest of the washing off the line."

"Well, I messed that one up ..."

It took three or four minutes of questions and reassurances to convince David that he had not made a bad day worse for all concerned. When Hazel came back to the phone, the remainder of the chat was surprisingly positive. Kate was reported to be fine, thriving, working three jobs and 'getting out and about more'.

It made his burden lighter when he viewed Kate in terms of Skye and her healing family. In terms of his own heart, it was one more regret; he had lost her friendship and caused a novice mind to become a degree more cynical. As the phone call came to an end, amid promises to keep in touch and to give his regards to the young cynic in question, David was aware of Rose's presence at the bottom on the stairs.

"They're all okay," he nodded, as if answering a question, and took his empty mug through to the kitchen. "What are your plans today?"

"I am aiming to make me a lampshade. The first of many if it turns out well enough. What about you?"

"I am aiming to complete the many chores on my list," he replied, in the same assured tone that his mother had used as he pulled on his boots. "And at some point, I need to go into town, so let me know if you need anything."

«●»«●»«●»

As David took the first few breaths of September morning into his lungs, Kate tried to shush the dogs one final time. She had done so well up to this point. She had rolled herself silently out of bed, dressed without one drawer squeaking or floorboard creaking and had moved slowly across the kitchen area unheard.

The Labradors were sniffing and nudging at her, Dougal was yawning loudly in anticipation of someone tending to his needs, and their enthusiasm threatened to spoil her plans. Kate moved their impatient snouts away from her as quietly as possible and made sure her scribbled note was obvious for all to see. In the next moment, she was safely at the bottom of the external stairway, had fitted her earphones over her ears and her baseball cap onto her head.

It was one of those mornings. The sun, still low, had turned everything to shades of olive and gold, and she could smell pine and sweet sap in the air. Although she had slept less than ever, she was ready to test her energy levels, and this time she was not running from the house or its occupants, she was simply giving them all some space.

Her watch read just after 7 a.m. and Kate calculated that she would reach the outskirts of town in about an hour, hopefully in time to be the first customer at The Pancake Store. This was a café like Kate had never before encountered, the choice and aromas turning her into the epitome of indecision, and she had promised herself a return visit as soon as possible. Well, what better day than on a crisp Saturday when she had walked up an appetite and had spent the three or so miles chatting with her mother?

Later she would phone Skye and have something really positive to share with whomever she found in the house. But for now, as she picked her way along the grass verge of the main road, she found herself telling Fiona about the previous night and all that she had learned and shared.

She remembered that the food had tasted great on their return from the woodshed and that Neil had waited until they were tackling the dishes before he began to talk about David and himself. Kate had listened intently, never opening her mouth, wanting to take in every tiny piece of information and purposely not asking him to skip from the past to the present. Every detail about the pair of them had been essential to her, and she doubted if there would ever be another conversation which dealt with the relationship between the man who was her father and the man she loved. Neil himself had been surprisingly eloquent and frank, and Andie had let him tell the story without input.

"He used to flick the back of my neck if he was passing or steal my spoon and hold it above his head. Of course, when I got tall enough to reach it, it wasn't half so entertaining for him. I once accidentally stabbed him in the elbow with a bread knife ..."

Although Neil had had no photographs to share with her, there had been childhood anecdotes by the truckload, and Kate recounted many of them to Fiona as she trekked towards Port Alberni. Sometime after midnight, when Andie had gone to bed and left them with a newly brewed pot of coffee and a tray of chocolate biscuits, Neil had begun to talk of David in the present tense and Kate had sat forward, eyes alert, desperate for news.

"After Hazel was here in April, he was definitely more relaxed. They had a great time. I'd like to think she came here to make him feel better."

"Things have definitely been better at home since then," Kate had agreed, and before they had retired to bed, she had felt that a strange sort of calmness had eased its way into the room with them. Arranging the duvet around her balled body, she had stared at the dark ceiling and wondered if, in the bleak light of the following morning, they would pick up from this place, or whether they would slip back to awkward avoidance. She had decided there and then to cut out this second possibility by removing herself from the morning routine altogether, and the weather had very kindly helped her out. Negotiating the verge with her long stride, she had to remove her fleece and tie it around her waist, as the sun was keen on her face and the fresh air was making her light-headed. She breathed the air in through her nose and out through her mouth, allowing herself to feel relief. David was okay. Neil had said so.

He was working hard, keeping active, not moping around the house or, her biggest fear, torturing himself with guilt. These were all positives. "Yes, you just keep telling yourself that, Kate," she growled as side one of her tape came to an end and she turned it over. "Of course that's good news. It might mean that one day you'll be able to look him in the eye again without folding with embarrassment. So, good news, and don't you forget it."

It was doubly important, whilst in this country, that Kate did not let her guard slip. She was strong, mature and out to set records straight. She had perfected this act at home, only allowing herself moments of fantasy when out on the hill or when biking through wind and rain; pockets of time when no one could interrupt her thoughts with reality. She had to paint a picture for Neil and Andie of someone who was not hurting and was not yearning, and she reckoned she was up to the task. It would ensure that David would heal, which was the best she could hope for.

Out of nowhere, a truck pulled up ahead of her and stood idling, waiting for her to walk past, its engine a strange rumble that seemed to catch after every third cycle. She felt her face become hot immediately, as her surprise turned to wariness. This was something she had not foreseen, but when she slowed to a more cautious pace and looked for the vehicle's occupant, all she could see was a large mongrel hanging out of the passenger window. Kate smiled in spite of herself, the dog's eyes too kind to be threatening, and she unhooked her earphones. There was the owner, a woman well into her seventies and wearing as much surprise on her face as Kate was.

"Oh heavens," she began, killing the engine and heaving herself further onto the passenger seat. "I thought you were Ronald, he has the same cap and you're a girl! I must have scared you to death, hanging around by the side of the road."

"No, you're fine. I'm fine."

"Are you Irish?"

"Scottish."

"Ah, yes. I always thought there was a fine line between the two. So, do you need a lift?"

Kate had taken a step back before she realised. "No thanks. I'm actually out for the fresh air. But thanks anyway."

"Okay, dearie, take care of yourself. I'm off to find Ronald. If you see him, tell him I'll be heading back home about nine-thirty, and if he knows what's good for him, he'll be ready. Bye, miss."

Kate waved as the truck chugged away, unable to understand any of the past minute's conversation, but a little aggrieved that she had been mistaken for a male. She looked down at herself and had to admit that she had done herself no favours lately: Cropped hair, cap, jeans, fleece, and boots. For the remainder of the journey, which took less than half an hour at Kate's manic pace, she tried to conjure up an image of herself based on clothes she was willing to consider buying. Maybe she should let her hair grow again. Since its first shearing the previous December, she had cut it every two months, and maybe a slightly longer style might help her cause. She sighed to herself. "And what cause would that be, then?"

There were two customers already in situ by 8.10 a.m., but Kate managed to bag a window seat at The Pancake Store, which looked directly onto the row of units where Alexander Designs was definitely the most impressive frontage and where she would be aware of Andie's arrival as soon as it took place. As she studied the menu, guessing that Neil had found her note by now and must be okay with the situation as the Dodge had not yet come screaming to a halt outside, she decided to order for Andie as well. If she did not turn up before the shop was due to open, Kate reckoned she could probably eat all of the food, anyway.

"So, what's it to be?" the waitress was no older than Kate, but seemed to radiate an authority way beyond her years.

"Em, maybe I'll try the strawberry stack, and oh, I can't remember what Andie had the last time, but I think it came with some sort of a chutney thing. Would you know what that might be?"

When Kate looked up from the menu, the waitress was smiling knowledgably and pointing her finger at Kate.

"You came in with Andie and her boyfriend the other day. Man, he's cute. Anyway, she's in here all the time, I'll do her usual. Drinks?"

"Could I have tea, please? Really weak?"

"Sure. I'll get Andie a coffee when she turns up. Be there in a sec."

Kate watched her refold the menu and stack it on the counter, wondering if she had heard the girl correctly. Had she just said that Neil was cute? She was absolutely positive that Andie was besotted by the man, they were very tactile, but she had based that on their mutual feelings, not necessarily on their looks. Yet when she really thought about it, both of them were definitely way above average in that department. Where Andie was naturally stylish, however, Neil was naturally unkempt. He was not dirty or unappealing, he simply viewed clothes as a necessary means of warmth and protection, nothing else. Kate wondered what the waitress would make of him dusting his chainsaw with his shirtsleeve. She would probably swoon at his feet.

"There you go. I've taken the bag out so it won't stew. Pancakes will be right with you."

"Thank you."

As she sipped her tea, Kate felt a familiar tingling in her fingers and she smiled, because it signalled that she was allowing herself a few moments alone with David. Daily, she put her thoughts into a boxing ring. Those thoughts she enjoyed versus those which caused the least damage to everyone she loved. Every now and again, when the pins and needles arrived beneath her fingernails, she knew there was no fight left and she could sit and think about the man unhindered.

Hazel's photos had proved that he had not changed physically in any way, and she pictured him behind her closed eyelids. There was a suggestion of a smile on his face, not enough to part his lips, but enough to put light into his green eyes and smooth his forehead of lines. Those eyes were glinting at her, and she saw her own hand reach out to touch his jaw. Wiry hair beneath her fingertips, David's eyes closing to her touch.

"You okay, there?"

"Absolutely," assured Kate, the pancakes before her not yet back in full focus. "They look amazing."

"Oh, I'll bring Andie's too. She's just pulled up."

Kate was relieved that Andie looked neither annoyed nor worried as she waved in Kate's direction. All she looked was beautiful. Her favoured combination of floor-length cotton skirt, T-shirt and long cardigan had been topped off with a bright scarf woven into her plaited hair, and Kate wondered if it was possible that even she could carry off a long skirt, if she tried. The batik shop back home had quite an array of them, all that was required was a bit of effort on her part to save the money.

"So, you're not mad at me?" smiled Kate hopefully, as Andie took her seat.

"Hey, you know I don't need an excuse to come here for breakfast."

"And Neil?"

"He had a moment or two of wondering if he had said too much last night, but I managed to bring him around."

Kate smiled her relief then grinned as the arrival of her breakfast had Andie squealing with delight. At the waitress' retreat, Kate leaned forward and whispered, "She fancies Neil, you know."

Andie nodded, smiling, "I know."

They ate for a moment or two in silence, Kate regarding the strawberry puree soaking through each pancake as if it were the food of the gods, wondering if it came sold in jars and if so, where she could buy a crate.

"Did you find out all you needed to know last night?"

Kate managed to swallow her food before answering. "Thanks for letting me take over your whole evening. I know it must be really weird having me here; if I had what you pair have, I wouldn't want anybody coming in and messing it up."

Andie was frowning. "But honestly, it's fine. I just wondered if you were any happier now."

"Neil was amazing," replied Kate. "It was great to hear about their history, and, in a way, it makes a bit more sense that Mum felt she had to be the one to leave. Plus, he said David seems to be doing okay, which is what I needed to know, so yes. I feel better for it. And I had a nice walk this morning, told Mum all about it. I'm having an okay day, thank you. And these pancakes ..."

Andie grinned in reply, and Kate was struck once more by her uncomplicated beauty. Frowning, she leaned forward.

"Andie," she began, "if you were driving along and you saw me from behind, would you think I was a male?"

And so, on her first proper trip out amongst the natives of Port Alberni and the surrounding countryside, Kate had come across Gloria Badham. Gloria and her Alsatian/wolfhound cross, JR. Andie had explained to Kate, over her second 'necessary' black coffee, that Gloria spent a regular amount of her idle time driving Milligan Road, Port Alberni Highway, and all the connecting roads in between looking for Ronald, her late husband.

"In any case," Andie had continued, "you shouldn't take it personally. Gloria sees Ronald wherever she finds the opportunity. If you walk that road on a regular basis, it'll happen more than once."

Perched behind the counter of Andie's shop, surrounded by displays of colour, fabrics and accessories, Kate thought about the lady again. She had not appeared particularly ancient, or absent, or anything other than vexed to have frightened Kate, but ultimately she must be sad. Sad and in such need to find Ronald that she spent time and money driving up and down lonely wooded roads in search of the man. Kate's lip suddenly jutted out as she realised that she must have been the cause of great hope and then disappointment when Gloria had noticed her that morning. She didn't want to be either of these things to anyone, strangers or family, and she slid off the stool and wandered through to where Andie was up to her elbows in curtain fabric.

"I should phone Neil, do you think? Make sure he's not worrying."

Andie indicated the wall extension with a nod of her head and said, "Speed dial, one."

Neil was cheerful on the end of the line, accepting her reasons behind her early morning departure and sympathising through a grin at her being mistaken for an old man. As Kate continued to chat, Andie suddenly dropped the pile of luxurious material to the floor and stood motionless, staring at the fine, expensive fabric resting on her feet. Kate frowned slightly as she continued to talk about the amazing choice of pancakes on offer; but when Andie took a seat on the floor herself and sat staring blankly at the creased pile before her, Kate put her hand over the mouthpiece and asked her if she was okay. When no reply came, Kate interrupted Neil's monologue.

"Neil, something's up. Andie looks a bit off colour. I'll ring back in a minute."

"God, I need to get this off the floor," Andie began as Kate knelt beside her. "This stuff costs a fortune, and it doesn't take kindly to mishandling."

"But are you okay?" Kate asked. "You look a bit ... out of it."

"Hey, I'll be fine, too much caffeine." Andie made it to her feet without any further problem, some light returning to her eyes. "Can you help me fold this properly?"

"Sure," replied Kate, "but maybe I should let Neil know that – "

"Oh I wouldn't bother. He'll be halfway here already."

As they stretched and smoothed out the deep coral silk, Kate continued to be confused, albeit silently inside her head. Why would Neil be on his way over? Andie had seemed pale and disorientated but only for a few moments, and she now stood determinedly upright and staunch, smiling at Kate's frown.

"It's fine, Kate. Honestly."

In the next moment, Kate's brow cleared, and as Andie blew and dusted the silk lightly with her fingertips, she turned back towards the front shop, smiling to herself. Everything was beginning to make sense. The way Neil and Andie moved around each other, continually touching arms or shoulders, smiling and looking for each other; the fact that the woman had retired to bed hours before them, and now this sudden show of vulnerability. Coupled with the fact that Neil was rushing over here to make sure she was okay, Kate was almost positive she knew what was going on. She could think of nothing more uplifting than the fact that Neil and Andie's baby would be one of the most beautiful creatures on earth and that she would be connected to it. Her nose prickled immediately and she ran to the window, awaiting Neil's arrival.

The street outside had been turned white by the strong sun, and Kate noted that there were customers sitting at tables outside The Pancake Store. It was a happy scene, and she found herself wishing Neil here so badly, just so that she could see his face. It would be so full of love but also consumed with concern for the mother of his child, and she wanted to see it for herself. Before another minute had passed, Kate had pictured the crib and high chair and chest of drawers that Neil would be making in the next few months. She wondered if they knew the gender of the child yet and if they would tell her if she asked. Of course, she wasn't going to ask any such thing, but it felt exciting to be here, to be a part of this special time. She grinned again when she thought that her sibling would be a whole generation behind her. What a strange, complex family she belonged to.

"Kate," Andie was seating herself on the stool behind the counter, sipping at a glass of water. "Do you think you could possibly go and get us three takeaway hot chocolates from the Store? I really could do with something sweeter, and, I bet, even on a hot day like this, you'd be up for one."

"Okay then," replied Kate, accepting the offer of cash from the till, yet thinking there had never been a day less like a hot chocolate day. But then, who knew what cravings visited a woman in Andie's condition?

There was a queue at the counter where only two waitresses were filling orders, and as she stood tapping her foot, watching the minutes tick away, Kate almost offered to make her own. Apparently, when you ordered a hot chocolate 'with everything' from the Pancake Store, it involved cream, marshmallows, a flake and sprinkles. Kate could not conceive how she would carry three of these dairy towers across a busy road.

"Did I say that I was taking them out? I'm not sure I can -"

"You get a tray."

Once again, Kate cursed her inability to keep her mouth shut, and now her heart was sinking because Neil's truck had pulled up across the street. She had desperately wanted to witness him kneeling beside Andie, touching her belly. She could see it all as clear as day in her head, but he was already across the threshold and she was missing it. The moulded cardboard tray allowed Kate to hurry across the road unhindered, but as she pushed open the door with her elbow, she was halted by the complete silence which met her. She stood immobile for another couple of seconds before Neil appeared in the office doorway. He looked shaken.

"She's okay, right? I brought chocolate."

"Then bring it over here, as quick as you like."

Andie was at her drawing board, smiling broadly at the arrival of the drinks which would 'cure every ailment known to mankind', but Kate remained bewildered by the variety of vibrations stirring in the room.

Neil's pale face did not relate to his joviality, and Andie's hand trembled slightly as she eased the cup out of the tray. Her mouth became a tight, white line of concentration as she placed it beside the drawing board.

"Lovely," she croaked. "Thanks, Kate."

Kate continued to look between the two adults, wondering how she had misjudged the situation. Somehow she had caused Neil to drive over here, and now no one was acknowledging that there was a problem. Well, they could all carry on ignoring that there was an issue, or Kate could step in and make them talk.

"You're wearing a cream moustache," she pointed at Neil's face.

"I could say the same thing," replied Neil, stepping forward to wipe the trail from Kate's upper lip.

She wiped her own mouth with the back of her hand before he could touch her and said, "Hey, if you've got news, I'd like to hear it." She allowed them one final glance at each other, before grinning at them both. "You're having a baby, aren't you?"

In the instant that followed, Kate was aware of just one thing; their heads moved at exactly the same time and pace, but in opposite directions. Andie's face tilted up to the ceiling, her eyebrows raised and tongue very slowly moving across her lips. Neil's head sunk onto his chest, where he screwed up his eyes at some focal point on the floor. It was not what she had expected.

"Are you? It would be amazing if -"

"No honey," Andie's eyes were as bright as buttons as she eased her way past Neil's immobile figure. "We're not having a baby. But I can see how you might think that."

"Oh. I got that completely wrong, then," admitted Kate, feeling her face burn. "What an idiot."

"No harm done," Neil spoke at last, the lines gradually evaporating from his brow.

"God, I thought I was so smart. Guess Hazel was right. I don't know everything, and I don't rule the world. But then, she has the odd funny idea herself. She's thinking of doing a catering course, wants to run a B and B. That's fair enough, but you need money behind you for that kind of thing and a bloody huge house. It's not like she's stuck at anything for very long, anyway."

«•»«•»«•»

Whatever had caused Andie's odd little episode was obviously not up for discussion as they continued to let Kate babble away her embarrassment. By the time the hot chocolate had been consumed, every mouthful producing some appreciative noise from one of them, Kate had noticed the pile of mail waiting to be posted and had planned her escape route. She was striding down the pavement, directions to the post office clutched in one hand and the pile of mail in the other. It was good to be outside in the sun, leaving Neil and Andie to get their story straight and where she could forget about the whole baby debacle.

«●»«●»«●»

"Okay, it's only late morning across there, but she knows it's Saturday night here and getting later by the second. Stu's sitting there practically expiring from lack of a pint."

"Hey, don't bring me into it," Stuart sat up in his chair, eyes never moving from the television.

"Fact remains," continued Hazel, joining Beth at the window to watch Kenny strim the front grass in the last of the grey light. "If she'd just rung first thing, we wouldn't be sitting here – oh no. Oh, that's a bugger."

"What now?" asked Stuart.

"I think Kenny might have just strimmed some dog mess. Or it could have been a mole hill. Either way, he's covered in it."

Stuart was beside her in a second and their sniggers became full-blown laughs when the man turned his body to them and held open his arms in disbelief. In the next moment, Beth was marching down the lawn, halting a good three feet from him and wearing the same incredulous expression. Hazel had time to make a guess that it was not the top of a mole hill which spattered both legs of his jeans before the phone began to ring.

"Yes, that's okay," Hazel answered the query at the end of the phone line before hearing Kate's voice at last. "Why are you reversing the charges?"

"Because I'm using a public phone and I've no change."

"Oh, right. We've been waiting all day."

"I know, sorry. I ended up at Andie's shop and didn't like to ask to use the phone there. Then time just disappeared. Anyway, how was it today?"

As Hazel began to describe the fairly reasonable morning at the baker's followed by the visit to the cemetery, and then the interminable wait for Kate to make contact, Kenny was undressing in the kitchen, being alternately laughed at and scolded by Beth. At one point he ran past Hazel in his jumper and boxers, managing a "Hi Kate," as he passed.

"He's just strimmed something unmentionable all over himself. I hope for everybody's sake that it wasn't deposited by next door's little darling. Oh, God, Beth, that stinks!"

"Well, they can't go straight in the washing machine!" the disembodied voice explained from around the sink area.

"Bet you wish you were here," Hazel sighed at her sister.

"Yip," Kate tried to keep the conversation light. "Especially since someone mistook me for a man in his seventies this morning."

By the time explanations for this travesty had been given, Beth was hovering by the phone and Stuart had pulled on his jacket.

"Sorry about the reversed charges, Beth, and the wait."

"Och, don't waste time on apologies. As long as you're coping over there, that's all I need to know. Now that her ladyship knows you're okay, she can resume her social life. All is well on this strange day. David was on the phone."

Kate opened her eyes wide, suddenly aware that she had not thought of David since breakfast, and that had been over three hours ago. Strange day indeed.

"Was he okay?" her voice took on the tone reserved for discussing David; upbeat and vaguely interested.

"Well, he accepted that you weren't in the house, which is the only thing we were worried about, right?"

Kate felt her stomach clench for a moment, still not ready to feel comfortable with the whole deception. Yet, it had made sense to everyone, including herself, when she first suggested it. Go to Canada, spend time with a man she needed to get to know better, ask him how David was and if everybody was getting over the events of the past year. In other words, find out what she needed to know, but don't risk anything by seeing David. She had struggled with the last part for a long time, not least because she felt she was changing allegiance. She wanted to be fighting the world and its pigheaded refusal to accept her wishes with David by her side, even if only metaphorically. She felt she was giving in, following the party line and deceiving the one person on earth who should never doubt her. But she had agreed to it, because the alternative was yet more time spent wondering how he was. She had needed an answer, and it would keep her going until she had enough courage to pursue him again or he let her know that he was no longer available.

"Right," Kate tried to swallow away her nausea. "Yes, well it sounds like they're all getting on with life," she paused, then, "Neil is great, Beth. We blethered for ages last night. The best bit is that he goes over to their house much more often. It must have been hard for Rose, all that time when they were avoiding each other."

"Well, that's not going to happen with you and Hazel. Do you hear?"

"Absolutely. Heard you the first six times as well. Hey, I'd better go. But I meant to say, Neil talked a lot about Mum, too. I think she might have done him a big favour, writing him that letter. I like him a lot, and I'm pretty sure she did as well."

As Beth replaced the phone in its cradle, she frowned at the sound of rain on the window. No more strimming would be done that night, and in light of this, she retired to the kitchen to put the kettle on. The face she saw in the kitchen mirror wore a frown, and, unusually, she took a moment out of time to study her own reflection. Where had that frown come from? Was it her default expression these days, or had Kate's calm voice caused the reaction? Her eyes were clear and not hooded by creased eyelids; but now the look was one of curiosity, and she began to smile, recognising that her expressions were no longer involuntary. She was controlling every movement. She could raise and lower her eyebrows, frown, grin, pout and she did all of these over and over until she felt Kenny at her shoulder.

"Why?" was the only question he could muster.

"Because I can," she laughed. "I can make my face say anything I want it to, just like Kate can try to tell us that she's finally over David Wilder. Doesn't mean either of us is being genuine."

Kenny wrapped his arms around her from behind, swaying her body against his own. "Aw Bethie. Doesn't it say a lot for her that she's still trying?"

Beth turned around, her arms slipping up to his shoulders and kissing him on the cheek. "You're as soft as butter, Kenneth. And you know what, stuff the tea. We're going out for a drink and a takeaway. I'm going to wash my hair."

As she slipped away, Kenny was left with his own reflection, and he grinned like a child. Things were very slowly, very steadily evening out, and maybe Kate deserved more than a little of the credit for it. In the past year, she had taken to confiding in him when she was at her most desperate; and he felt that, although he knew her the least, she had opened up to him the most. He knew her infatuation with David was nowhere near at an end, but she made an effort to hide it from them each and every day. That was worth applauding.

"I'll get it!" he shouted through to the bathroom as the phone rang once more. "Hello?"

"Kenny? It's David. How are you?"

"David! Hi. Again. I thought -"

"I just wondered if Kate was back yet. I didn't get a chance to speak to her earlier, and it's been awhile."

Kenny looked at his reflection in the hall mirror, and there was no longer a hint of a smile. He glanced over his shoulder, listening to the shower running and the silence growing between himself and the decent man on the other end of the phone.

"Kenny?"

"Sorry, David," Kenny watched his own lips move, aware that the box he was easing the lid from had all the lethal potential of Pandora's itself. "She's not here."

"Oh. Well, I thought I'd-"

"In fact, Dave, I can't be absolutely sure when she'll be back, I haven't seen her for a few days." Kenny could picture David's complete confusion which accompanied the following silence, and he knew it was only fair to keep talking. "The thing about Kate is, she's turned into an independent little soul lately, likes to go on trips. Transatlantic trips. She seems to have developed a taste for flying. God, I wish some of it would rub off on her aunt."

There was definite electricity in the air, but even Kenny could not continue down this road without some sign that he was doing the right thing by these people. He waited.

"So," David's voice was deep and steady. "So, Kate has ... she's gone on a trip. Overseas, did you say?"

"Well now, I know she took her passport, so that's a fair bet. Wherever it is she's gone, and again I can't really confirm where that is, she'll be there for her eighteenth birthday. That'll be nice for her and for the folks she's staying with. They're related, I hear."

"Closely related?"

"Close enough," answered Kenny, quietly. "Listen, Dave, I'm taking Beth out for a drink, so I'm going to have to ring off because I need to come up with a good story to cover this conversation. Sorry Kate wasn't here to speak to. She's something else, these days, definitely worth spending time with if you get the chance. See you, David."

"Bye, Kenny."

David's watch said just after noon. Rose was out at the chalets. The sun was glinting off the chrome taps in the kitchen. His breath was stilled inside him. He took a seat.

So, this was unexpected, disconcerting and exhilarating, but what was he going to do with the information? His mind was running away from him, he couldn't keep up with his thoughts and possible deeds, and he needed to rein them in before he did something irreversible and regrettable. Firstly, he should dissect Kenny's words and be absolutely positive about what the man had meant. Well, there could be little doubt. Kate was here in Canada, she had been here for a few days, and Kenny for some reason known only to himself, had wanted to give him this news where others had kept it from him. David studied his hands which lay on the table in front of him, marvelling that they were not slippery with nervous sweats, and continued to try to keep a tight grip on the actions he was contemplating. He had to get the facts straight in his head before he did anything.

Kate was not with Kathy, she was not related to Kathy; she had to be with Neil and Andie, and although it made sense that she should want to spend time with her father more than anybody else, the joint deception was upsetting, to say the least. Neil and he had become so much easier in each other's company, and he was working closely with Andie, but by taking part in this, they had both cut him out. For what reason? He tried to remember the last time he had mentioned Kate to either of them, but could not. Maybe that was where the problem lay. Perhaps they did not view this as keeping him in the dark so much as they saw it as not rocking a recently steady boat. No one knew what he wanted these days, not even Kate. But he knew, and suddenly there was a spark inside, a sputtering ignition of light and heat, and he had to force himself to stay seated.

"Steady," he murmured. He had all the time he could wish for. It was a Saturday lunchtime, and the obligatory call to Skye was behind him. His only remaining tasks for the day were to buy some washers, generator oil and two new snow tyres for the SUV, all of which could be purchased in Port Alberni as easily as they could in Duncan. Should he go now, leaving Rose a note saying he was unlikely to be back before morning? He could be over there, hammering on the door and demanding to be heard in less than two hours. Still he remained seated, and at that moment, his mother came whistling through the back door, glancing once in his direction.

"Well, sitting there wishing for your lunch isn't going to make it happen."

He stood and wandered over to where she had deposited three almost empty tins of paint and an old roller. Surprisingly, his head did not buzz as he moved, but he could not keep himself from rubbing his eyebrow, and immediately Rose was asking what his problem was.

"No problem here," he lied, then, "Oh, except with the sun coming out and all, I wondered if you wanted to take a trip up to see the pair of them, now that the bathroom is finished. It's been a long time coming. We could get the tyres up there just as easily."

Rose's movements did not falter, and she did not even turn her head away from him. He watched as she appeared to give the idea some serious thought and could not be absolutely sure if she was in on the ruse. Eventually, however, as he knew in his heart that she would, she frowned and shook her head. He could not keep his eyes on her face as she spoke.

"Nice idea, but I'm sure this is the weekend they're going up to Black Creek."

"Oh? First I've heard of it."

"Well, it's a surprise for Andie. She's been working way too hard. Do you want to eat here or in town?"

David found himself in the unusual position of not wanting to share another word with the woman in front of him. He watched her wipe the counter down beside the sink, silently assuming that she had managed to divert a catastrophe, and he wanted to roar at her to stand still and look at him. Instead, he felt his eyes focus in his head and he leaned against the range, trying to use the very few seconds he would have at his disposal to decide if he should play along with this. But his brain was not up for the challenge. All he actually managed to do was follow his mother's every movement with his hard, green eyes and fold his arms.

Rose wiped the remainder of the worktop, wrung out the cloth and hung it over the mixer tap. From there she filled the kettle, returned the eggs to the pantry and pulled her straying ponytail back into line. Finally, she met David's gaze, aware that this impasse between them was not about to move of its own accord.

"How old am I, Rose?" his voice was patient.

Rose found it tempting to laugh and beg him not to remind her of her own years in figures, but it was not the moment.

"You're forty-six, last time I looked."

"That's what I thought. So, middle-aged. If I was forced to fill in one of those dating agency questionnaires, what would I say? Middle-aged, runs own company, directly responsible for the jobs of seventeen men. What else? Home owner, property developer, father. Could I safely put 'successful', do you think?"

"Well, I'd say so."

"Yeah, at a push, so would I. Maybe I'll give it a go. Did you keep yesterday's paper? Pretty sure Friday has advertisements that would point me along the right path."

"Are you angry? Is it directed at me?"

David thought about the question for a second or two. "Yeah, I'm pretty annoyed. Not just at you, though. I'm pretty pissed off with everybody in my family at this moment in time."

"Does that include the people on Skye?" Rose's voice was finally resigned to the conversation.

David held up his index finger, his eyes crinkling. "With the exception of one. One man had the decency to hint at what's going on, and I daresay it'll cost him dear."

As Rose pulled out a chair and sat, her face beginning to mould itself into her usual 'well-now-let's-just-see-how-this-can-be-sorted' look, David shook his head.

"No."

She looked up at him, eyes wide.

"No. I'm way beyond the talking stage with you or anybody. So, I'm just going to say this. I'm forty-six and I'm smart. I know exactly what I want, and I deserve to have it. Whatever any of you think of my decision, there's something that you have to accept; I'm the one who lives inside my head, I'm the one who stays calm on the outside while .... while grenades are taking me apart inside. I'm the one who lies awake trying to do what is right by everyone in this fantastic freak show of a situation. But, I'm also the one who can give this person what she needs, and I'll never, ever stop doing it, because I need it just as much, and because she came to me first. She came to me."

As the door closed quietly on his retreating figure, Rose finally let out the breath she had been holding. She desperately tried to listen to his words again in her head. Did it mean he was on his way up there now? There was no engine running yet. Whatever he did, there was going to be major fall out. He was going to blame Neil, Andie, the whole world, and what further damage was that going to cause? Still, the truck did not roar into life outside.

Rose crept up to the window and found David standing by the open door of the SUV. His arms were spread, one resting on the top of the door, the other on the roof of the vehicle, head hanging between his shoulders as if he had been flogged, and Rose moved away from the window before he was aware of her.

She let her eyes wander over the gleaming new surfaces before her, looking for a familiar object to comfort herself with, something so important and nostalgic that it would let her forget the angry, indignant man outside who had every right to feel the way he did. The range was hers, as was Pete's chair by its side, but even that was covered in a new throw; and in the next moment, she was entertaining thoughts which made her shoulders weirdly warm. This warmth evolved into the flexing of her muscles, and it felt great. She began to smile. The new kitchen had not been her idea, but she had not objected to it. All she knew for certain was that her husband was no longer present in this modern space, and if he had gone, then there was no earthly reason why she should remain. The house was big and old and so full of memories laced with acid that it was capable of burning away the remainder of her years. Well, she would refuse to let that happen.

CHAPTER 21

Saturday, 17th September 1994

David could not remember the last time he had sat in this particular spot. Years before, on a snowy December morning, he had come to this place in search of surplus wooden planks to fix his daughter's sled. He had hoped to find an item of still-firm wood amongst the old steps which clung to the side of the embankment in sporadic, unsafe sections, and it had crippled him both mentally and physically. He had rarely visited the place since. Yet, it was almost the only position on the entire estate where there was an open view down to the river and across the picturesque valley through which it ran. The reason he rarely moved his boots in this direction was simple; he was not strong enough to play the 'what-if' game and never had been. He sat with his boots dangling over the edge of the rough bank, allowing himself a wry smile at how childish he must look when he had declared himself a strong, competent adult.

Across the gully, he could see the occasional vehicle crawling its way around the bends in the road and leaned back on his palms, arms straight, trying to guess the time of day by the height of the sun. He removed his watch to assess the state of the dripping tap and it must be lying somewhere near the sink, but that was a journey he was not yet prepared to make. His stomach had complained twice in the last minute or so at his total disregard for its needs, but that was as irrelevant as the time. He was not going anywhere today. Every essential thing on his list could wait another day, and he relished the freedom of having made this decision. He was sitting in shadow, the sun unable to penetrate the thick wall of trees to either side of him, but the air was sweet. Whenever the sun shone, the river gave off its summer smell, and he breathed in deeply - hot, bleached stones hiding heady fronds of vegetation beneath the surface. David smiled, leaning forward to gaze out at the scene which had not changed in the last seventeen years. He was grateful for that, because he knew that he would come here daily from now on. It was peaceful beyond belief, and he knew exactly why.

From this moment on, he could sit here at any time and appreciate the land below him, the sun above him and every positive feeling that was coming his way. It was simple enough; without the accident, without its consequences, without the unbelievably complicated path his wife had found herself stumbling along, there would be no Kate Wilder on his earth. No beautiful, trusting, undeniably thought-provoking young woman who was still causing him to shake his head in wonder. He stared down at his boots, leaning between the cross rails of the fence they had erected immediately following the accident, and grinned. She had liked these boots, and in spite of the fraying laces, they still brought to mind the night she had stood back and declared him fit for the public eye.

And here she was, a mere eighty miles to the northwest of where he now sat. It astounded him that all he had to do was to climb behind the wheel of the SUV and drive up there to see her. That in a good hour and a half, he could be listening to her voice as she sat at Neil's huge table, probably discussing the less than satisfactory year experienced by Scotland's national rugby team. Had Neil watched their progress, as he had done, just so that he could have an opinion to pit against hers the next time they met? And yet, there was no point in being envious of the man; Neil had more right, at this particular moment, to spend time with her. David hauled himself to his feet, cursing as his shin scraped the underside of the bottom cross rail and sighed. It was months since he had been obliged to put Kate into second place and it still caused him grief, but he would have to wait at least another day before he could put this right. He needed more information.

In the thirteen minutes it took for him to walk from the rear of The Edge to Chalet No 3, Peter's Lane, David had arranged and rearranged his face several times, unsure as to the attitude he wished to present to Rose. He was still offended by everyone and everything, but guessed that was now the extent of his negative feelings. However, his mind was made up. He had wasted enough time, and all he required was a tiny bit more background detail to help him with the decision he would make. He found Rose looking closely at the dimensions of the inbuilt cool cupboard and wished that he was less conspicuous in terms of height and presence as he joined her on the bare boards of the empty chalet.

"For the size of the house, this cupboard is very generous," she stated, running her fingertips over the pine of the shelves.

"Andie's worked with the guy many times. You can't beat a personal recommendation."

"Well, it's made up my mind for me, son. I'm going to buy this house, and it's going to suit me right down to the ground. What do you think of that one, Mr Smart?"

Rose made sure she had eased the cupboard door shut on its pristine hinges before she turned around to face him. His hands were tucked into the front pockets of his jeans, and his face was a picture of indecision. His eyes crinkled, then widened; he opened his mouth but ended up closing it along with his eyes, before releasing his right hand and wiping his rough chin. Finally he shook his head. "What?"

"Looks to me like we've all reached the point of action. And boy, I love this house. I've loved it since day one when it sheltered me from that downpour." She waved away his disbelieving frown. "You were at work, so don't bother trying to recall it."

"So," David's left hand was steadying himself against the empty base unit, "have you been eyeing it up since then?"

Rose shrugged. "Probably not too seriously, but it was getting to the stage where I didn't want anybody else having this view. And then, well, there's every chance that you and I have finally outgrown each other. Hmm," Rose caught her own breath. "I don't mean that in any other than a totally positive way, David. If I think about it, I've held onto you for far too long, and I'm not looking for you to argue with me, because we both know I've never been more right about anything in my life."

David began to walk around the sparse room, taking in the clean shavings which were brushed into a few soft piles every few feet or so. The windows were double-glazed, the walls panelled in pine and sealed against the Canadian winter; and even with no heating or furniture, the room was bright and attractive. He could see why she spent most of her time here. It was a compact and efficient place, qualities she had missed out on for most of her life. It would keep her cosy in the winter and surrounded by a variety of families in the summer. He could see her sitting in the window seat, telling Pete about the latest weather reports, or watching her neighbours put up their Christmas lights. It was not a ridiculous plan, but the timing of it continued to bother him.

"Is that one of the lampshades you were talking about?" he asked, pointing to where the item sat on the top of the stepladder, waiting to be attached to the pendant.

"Yes, what do you think?"

"It looks great. You could make a tidy living with those."

"Are you going up there today?"

David wandered through to the sitting room and noticed that the wood-burner had not only been delivered but installed. The glass remained covered in thick plastic, but he could see the quality. If it gave out half the heat that Neil's did, then Rose would never shiver of an evening again. He was almost envious that she got to leave behind the draughts and the heavy stairs and the verandah roof that had a tendency to leak, but only almost. He was nowhere near ready to bid a farewell to the rooms that Kate had lit up with her personality. He wanted to hear her thundering downstairs, hunting frantically through the hall desk for her Walkman and shouting out instructions about what he should be wearing. Or to find her lounging on the sofa, pointing at a Canucks game and insisting that the level of skill involved did not warrant the wages being handed over. He had seen these things briefly, and he wanted to see them again.

"Well, are you?" repeated Rose, following his tour of what she now most definitely regarded as her own.

"I should think about what I'm going to say first. I think that probably requires a bit of time on my part. Rose?"

"Son?"

"You can't move here unless it's what you truly want. I can see you here, it's true, but it would mean a lot if you could let me off the hook. You know, by telling me I didn't push you into it, even though I probably don't deserve any such consideration."

Rose was chuckling before he had finished his sentence.

He raised his eyebrows in her direction.

"Here's the deal, Davey boy. It's a quarter after three. Dinner will be on the table at six-thirty, and when we sit down to eat it, I will tell you every little plan I have for my new house. I'll tell you how much I know about Kate's visit, and I'll tell you what Neil makes of it all. In return, you can tell me what it is that makes her the reason you get up in the morning and why I should stop worrying my old bones about you both."

It seemed a reasonable trade.

《●》《●》《●》

"Now, there's a chance that you will have to trust me on this one."

Neil was standing behind the monstrous lathe in his workshop, his eyes concealed behind goggles, which suited Kate fine. It was perhaps better for all concerned that his honest expression was hidden from both of them. It was after 5 p.m., and he had made his retreat from the general mayhem that was the unloading of Kate's purchases. Considering that she had been out of their sight for one hour and forty minutes in total at lunchtime, she seemed to have been laden with half of Port Alberni on her return.

Andie had commented yet again on her disbelief at the girl's strength as she came awkwardly through the door, desperately trying not to knock over any of the displays. Kate's answer to this had been that if you wanted to climb Ben Tianavaig with a tent, you needed more than willpower. She stood in front of Neil, a tentative grin on her face, her hands behind her back.

"Before you say anything, I need to give you the reason behind my decision," she explained.

"I'm all ears."

"Okay, so, with your hair colouring, I didn't want black and grey. It would probably make you look too washed out, so the main body will be ..." she brought forward her left hand, "... pale rust!"

"Are you sure that's not orange?"

"It's pale rust. It says so on the label. Hellfire, you should have seen the choice. Loads more than at home. Purples and bluey-greens and something called hyacinth, but even I wouldn't have worn that, so I chose pale rust. What do you think?"

"Well, I was never one to blend into a crowd."

"That's what I thought. Okay, give me a minute."

Kate turned her back on the man for a moment, checking which ball of wool she should bring up next, smiling as Neil switched on the second strip light so that they could both see better. When she turned back to him, she found his eyes wide as the pale rust wool showed off its true colour.

"Right. I'll be using the same pattern as my jumper, just bigger, obviously, so where mine has the lighter grey, yours will have ... lime green."

"Excellent choice."

"And for white, I have substituted mustard."

Kate squashed the three woollen balls together for the full effect and found Neil wearing his goggles on his forehead.

"That is a winning combination. Has Andie seen the colours?"

"Well, that's the best bit, I have an interior designer's full approval on them. She said if anybody can wear these colours, you can. Here, I'm cooking, so I'd better get on. I need to get this started tonight if it's going to be finished in time."

Kate had almost reached the bottom of the exterior stairs when she hesitated and made her way back to the workshop. Neil was carefully surveying a turned spindle.

"Is Andie okay?" she asked.

"She's fine," he replied, before hiding behind his goggles once more.

Later, when dinner had been consumed, appreciated and recipes written down for future reference, Andie joined Kate on the sofa. Neil had left the dishes to drip dry and taken the Labs for a wander. Kate had managed to get the cuff of one sleeve started. Andie asked her how her day had been, and she declared that it had been exactly as she had wanted it to be; equal parts of private time and distraction.

"I'm glad you let me come. I love this place and you two are brilliant. It must be strange having a visitor, but you've never made me feel like I'm in the way. Thanks for that."

"Can I tell you what the best bit has been, Kate? For me, anyway."

"Sure," replied Kate, untwisting the balls of wool.

"Listening to you and Neil talking. Listening to a different perspective on something which has been with us since I met him and realising that he's still the best person I know and always will be."

Kate laid her knitting aside and rubbed her nose to stop the threatening prickles. She lowered her eyes for a second then said softly, "I'm sorry about this morning, it's just that you and Neil would be the best possible parents. I got carried away with the whole idea."

Andie took Kate's hand in hers. "I'll never have children, Kate, that's why seeing you and Neil together is precious."

"Hellfire," hissed Kate, turning her body towards the older woman. "I'm bloody hopeless. I think I'm so clever sometimes, and more than half the time I'm wrong. Useless."

"Look, it was a decision I made. A very long time ago, so don't go thinking you've upset me. Although, if you want the truth, there was no real choice involved."

"You don't have to tell me," assured Kate. "It's nothing to do with me. Honestly, I'm not one of those folk who needs to be in on everything."

"But that's exactly why I want to tell you," smiled Andie. "And you're part of us now."

"Really?" Kate's voice was full of awe, but she had never felt warmer inside. She grinned in gratitude.

As Andie began to talk, Kate watched her shining hair and pale hands. They were the most animated parts of her body; and by studying them, the locks that seemed to ripple whenever she moved her head and the fluidity of her fingers, she managed to stop herself from reacting inappropriately to her words.

"I had a twin brother, Dale, and although we were great buddies, I wouldn't say we were inseparable. He liked to be outside every minute of every day, and I liked to paint or read; but he was a good man to have around when the world was being unkind, and we had twenty years together and then another three apart. I lost him short of our twenty-fourth birthday."

Kate's lips were parted, but she could not think of anything to say which would sound sincere enough to convey her shock; shock at the actual words and at the candid way in which Andie spoke them. She merely stared at the woman's eyes as they roamed the room, searching for the correct phrases to use.

"Dale had Huntingdon's Disease, Kate. I don't know if you've heard of it, but it runs in families, and it's a ... well, a sufferer will only ever deteriorate and die. There is only one outcome." Andie allowed Kate a second or two for this to sink in, but still no questions or statements were forthcoming. "Our dad died when he was forty-three, and Dale and I knew that there was a chance we would develop the disease. Unfortunately, it came to Dale early. It took us by surprise, and I still find that the least fair thing about our whole situation. He didn't have the chance to live a life. We were never tested, you see. Neither of us wanted that knowledge, it was sort of a pact we had."

"Oh, Andie. No. What a ... that's unbelievably awful," Kate gasped, feeling as though someone had taken her ability to string words together. "But. You've been tested since?"

Andie shook her head. "Once you have knowledge, you can't go back, and there's nothing I can do to change it in any case; but this way, I won't be ruled by it until I have to be. If I have to be. But, I did know that I didn't want any child of mine to be in the same position, so I took action as soon as I could. I was sterilised so that I would never have to spend my life hoping and praying that my child would be free from the disease. This was my individual choice, and it has always made perfect sense to me. I've only ever seen it through my eyes, though, and many people might find that difficult to understand. Can you understand it?"

"Ye-es," stammered Kate, "I suppose, but ... but that's so shitty. I mean, that's the worst -"

She stopped speaking as the tears came, not sure how much Andie wanted to hear and confident that her own thoughts would be neither unique, nor fresh. Kate was absolutely positive that this beautiful young woman had heard every possible combination of words on the subject, just as her own closest kin had talked through every undeserved and dreadful aspect of Fiona's illness. She felt her heart was breaking all over again. Neil and Andie completely fitted together, they were only half a person on their own. For someone who hated clichés with a passion, Kate's head was spilling over with them, and she released her hand from Andie's so that she could scrabble for the hankie in her jeans pocket. As she blew her nose, one final awful notion hit her and her eyes flew wide open.

"What was this morning all about?"

"I'm not entirely sure," Andie sounded sincere. "It doesn't necessarily mean anything, Kate. Just once or twice, I've lost track of what I'm doing, but it could be down to any number of things, and I want you to listen to me. I'm not ready to entertain this yet. I'm not interested in it for the moment, so if you need to talk about it, you can ask Neil, but only if you think it's absolutely necessary. We know it's out there, but we don't let it in. We're going to keep it locked out for as long as possible, hopefully forever. One other thing. Rose and David don't know."

Kate sat back against the sofa and stared at the fire, her knitting forgotten, along with everything else in the room. What was wrong with the world? Why was every good thing she came across tainted and brushed with black, toxic oil? Neil and Andie, made specifically to partner the other, put on the earth to show the people around them what love really was, but perhaps only for a short time. Time. It ruled everything, and Kate detested its continual disregard for those it controlled. Her hands were numb, and as she tried to rub the feeling back into them, Andie levered herself off the sofa and kissed her quickly on the top of the head. The gesture almost killed Kate.

"Tea, I think," said Andie and moved away.

Instantly, Kate stood on her dazed legs and gathered up the mess of wool and needles.

"Would it be really weird for you if I went to find Neil?" Kate's voice had a dangerous tremor to it. "If I sit here, I'll end up bawling my eyes out."

"Take a torch."

Kate got no further than the foot of the stairs. Her legs took her as far as the bottom step and then declared their lack of interest. She couldn't argue with them, and there was a certain comfort in sitting under the bright security lamp, leaning against the side of the house; she was sheltered from the wind and could feel the vibration of the heating system against her shoulder. Her knees were almost touching her chin and she hugged them close, missing Fiona, the Bay and the moon in strangely equal amounts. Even her heart would not behave itself. How could the moon possibly be as important as her mother? Yet tonight it was, and she began to feel scared. Scared that her ability to handle crises was slipping so fast from her, dragging her sanity with it; and as she waited for Neil to make his appearance, the questions came at her like a steam engine. Was Andie ill? Would she ever become ill? How did she stay strong? How would Neil cope with the worst news? Where was David?

She cradled her head in her hands and wept. She didn't howl or sob, she just let the water seep from her and tried to listen to her thoughts as her head pounded at the building pressure. Not fair, not fair, not fair. Then Cuban was licking her face and Crisis was practically sitting on top of her.

"Kate?"

"It's not fair," she stood up but did not move towards Neil. She knew better than that, even on a night like this. Instead, she wiped the snot and grime from her face with the sleeve of her woollen jumper, which was not a successful move by anyone's standards, and Neil immediately handed her his hankie. "Just not fair."

Very slowly, and hindered slightly by the dogs at their feet, Neil put his hand on Kate's shoulder, and then pulled her against him. She stood in the crook of his arm; he smelled of wood shavings and frosty air and slightly of Andie's lemon skin oil. None of these things were familiar to her. She did not ease under his chin the way she did with David; instead, she hung her head against her own chest and sniffed away her misery. Once, she felt him rub his face against her hair and tighten his grip, but her sobs were preventing coherent speech, so all she could do was try to control her breathing and hope that he would take the initiative.

"She's strong. You have to be, in her position. Nothing has changed, except that now you know. I let her persuade me to answer any of your questions, but do you know what I would like more than anything, Kate?"

"For me to leave it alone?"

He did not patronise her, keeping his gratitude to himself, but said, "For the time being. We're not ready to open the door yet."

"Yes, okay," she sniffed for what she hoped would be the last time, but in the next second, her face had crumpled again. She felt him tense slightly, but his voice was light when he spoke.

"I don't know what to do with crying women, Kate. They scare me."

"Me too," she smiled weakly. "If you let me blow my nose properly on your hankie, I promise I'll stop."

"Be my guest."

Glancing at her watch, Kate understood why she had begun to shiver and immediately wanted both of them to be back with Andie. Twenty-five minutes alone in the house was long enough for the woman, and more tears were threatening, which she could not afford Neil to see. They were bringing this topic of conversation to an end for the moment, with no immediate prospect of revisiting it, and she desperately wanted to say one last piece for his ears only. He had somehow, at last, found the courage to comfort her, and this needed to be acknowledged.

She looked at him, his face the most strained she had seen on this visit. "It's just that," her voice was tinged with grief as she handed him back the hankie, "I think you would have made a great dad. You're doing right by me, if you need proof of that."

She did not remain to witness his reaction to this, because she had not said it for effect, and thankfully his boots followed hers up the steps. He was okay.

Andie was not curled by the fire as Kate had supposed, but was in the kitchen, elbow deep in cake batter, and singing to an unimpressed Dougal, who had collapsed near the cooker.

Kate hung back for a moment, but when Neil took off his boots and disappeared into his bedroom, she wandered over to the kitchen.

"Okay, Kate," Andie stated, seriously. "Decision time. Lemon sponge, carrot cake or chocolate."

"I've never had carrot cake in my life."

"Then it's time you had."

Neil reappeared, wearing a thicker flannelette shirt and gilet. He hung a cardigan of Andie's over a kitchen chair until she was free enough from flour to put it on, and then folded his arms and rubbed his chin, content just to be beside her.

Kate gazed at the pair of them, feeling that maybe she was, on this occasion, not required on the scene. "Well," she smiled as she retreated to the heat of the wood-burner, "that jumper is not going to knit itself."

CHAPTER 22

Sunday, 18th September 1994

"Ka – ty," her mother's voice sang at her through the shaft of bright sun on her face, and Kate lay perfectly still so as not to shoo her away. She could not prevent the smile curling at her lips, however.

"Hey, Mum. That was some day yesterday. Mum?"

Reluctantly, Kate opened her eyes, ready to be vexed that she had missed out on an opportunity for discussion, but surprised instead at finding her bedroom so very bright.

"Curses," she murmured as her watch confirmed that it was approaching ten-thirty. There was no possible excuse for sleeping so late and preventing the rest of the household from getting on with their Sunday. She pulled herself together enough to stand up. As she did so, the phone rang a couple of times before halting in the middle of its third ring. Kate smiled, relieved. It meant that Neil had answered the extension in his workshop, and so she was not guilty of keeping him from his day. She reached for her towel and headed to the shower, determined to talk to her mother, even if on a one-sided basis.

By the time Kate's hair had been dried upside down to see if it would appear longer and fuller and failing on both counts, the clock above the wood-burner was past eleven and the house had been returned to its peaceful state. No Andie, no dogs, no radio and, surprisingly, no sound of machinery downstairs. There was no way he could still be on the phone, and right on cue, Neil came steadily across the threshold, carefully watching Dougal's progress as he did so.

Kate was delighted to see them. "Morning. Where's Andie?" she called out, still trying to find some volume in her hair with her fingertips.

"Hey! She walks the earth again! Sleep well?"

"You know, officially," Kate replied, pulling on her socks, "at a push, I could still get away with the time difference excuse. It's only been five days."

Neil grinned, but did not take up the bait. "Andie's at her mom's, same as every Sunday. Have you eaten yet?"

"No, but don't bother about me. I can wait until you're ready."

Again, Neil did not argue but instead leaned against the window which looked down onto the woodshed. Sighing, he rubbed his chin, but did not look particularly worried.

Kate joined him, wondering if the Labs were still outside, but there was nothing to see. She looked up at him, questioningly.

"Hmm," he pondered, "time I took down another tree, I think. Would you be up to some splitting before lunch?"

"Yeah, okay. I like to earn my keep, and I'll do anything you want. With the exception of driving."

"Great. Let's go."

To the right of the woodshed stood a trailer which had no right to look so pristine, considering it spent all of its life at the mercy of the weather. The only nod to it having been used at all was a pile of needles blown into one corner and a very few loose twigs and pieces of bark lining the base.

Kate looked at it, impressed. "So, what's the plan?"

"There's an old white oak near where Dougal floundered. You can come and help me load a couple of sections to bring back here, and I'll cut them up so you can start splitting. We'll do as many as our stomachs will allow."

It was after mid-day before there were any cross-sections of wood for Kate to attack, and yet again it took her a couple of minutes to get her swing correct.

Neil watched her for a second or two, his face purposely neutral, just observing her complete determination to get it right.

"What time is it?" he asked, as she tried to line up a piece of wood that was heavily knotted and probably beyond her capabilities.

"Ten past twelve, and no, I'm not hungry yet. If you want to get another load, that's fine by me."

"Right," but as he turned to go, there was sufficient hesitation to his step for her to pick up on it. He was practically dancing, his feet were so undecided on their path. She stopped herself from lifting the splitter into the air. Eventually, he eased himself back around, where he was sporting an unusual expression.

She thought it looked vaguely like the face he had worn last year, on the day of their first meeting, a mixture of nervous uncertainty and hope; but it seemed such an odd day for it to reappear that she wasted no time in trying to second guess its meaning.

"What's wrong?"

"These last few days, Kate. They've been amazing. Andie loves you being here, and for me, it's been a complete pleasure."

Kate let the log splitter fall to the ground. "Are you sending me home early?"

"What? Jeez, no."

"Okay," breathed Kate, "it's just, what you were saying, it sounded sort of ... final."

"No, no. I just wanted to say that, whatever your actual reasons for this visit, it's meant a lot that you would stay with us."

"Well," smiled Kate, "I've still got a week here, and okay, so I feel like I've packed a lifetime into five days already, but it's been the biggest help. Made things a bit clearer."

Neil was leaning against the tailboard of the trailer, giving her a chance to say more, and she knew that she had given him little to work with to date. They had talked about Fiona, the different versions each of them had known; they had gone over Hazel's reactions to everything; his brother's well-being and Neil's own recurring self-doubt. But not once had she told him of the depth of her feelings towards David.

She had asked him to open up to her, and she had given nothing in return. Now she was party to a secret so upsetting in its possibilities that it practically rendered every other problem insignificant, and still she had not dared to risk his condemnation by talking about the man she loved. Instantly her mind was quoting from David's letter, months before '... He didn't say much at all, and I can't even tell you what that means because I don't know him these days ...' Yet, the man in question was now right in front of her, and she felt sure he would be sympathetic, but it was Neil who spoke first.

"Will you come see us again, Kate?"

Kate swallowed as she looked at him. This was not what she had expected at all, on this Sunday morning when the prospect of swinging the log splitter until her arms ached and her belly rumbled had seemed both satisfying and worthwhile. He was confusing her. She had thought his reason for hanging around was to get the measure of her, but it appeared that it was far more fundamental. He was looking for assurance that their developing relationship meant something to her.

"Don't move from that spot," she pointed her finger in his direction, not allowing him a moment to argue, before she was pounding up the steps to the house, two at a time. As she hurried through to her room, she could almost hear Fiona's laugh of encouragement and smiled in return. The piece of paper she required was in the side pocket of her rucksack, folded neatly inside her passport, and the sight of it increased her pace.

She found Neil exactly where she had left him, attempting to remain in a completely frozen position.

"Am I allowed to breathe?" he asked, through gritted teeth.

"You know, Hazel and you could be a double act. You're as funny as each other."

He grinned down at her, and Kate found herself taking her own new breath. "Neil, I've got something to show you. I brought it from home, and when I packed it, it was for a totally different reason."

Neil shook his head, intrigued.

"I know, I'm rubbish at explaining things," admitted Kate, "so just look at it."

The sheet of paper was crisply creased where it had been folded neatly and hidden away for years. Kate watched his face as he took in the official stamp and details recorded at the time of her birth, noting the gradual pink tinge appearing on his cheeks and the crinkling of his eyes. He leaned further back against the trailer, reading the words again and failing to hide his surprise.

"Well," he whispered. "I'd no idea she'd actually ..."

"I didn't think you had, which is why I brought it."

Neil still could not take his eyes off the document. Kate eventually stood beside him, her face hopeful, as she also read what her mother had committed to paper almost eighteen years earlier. Sitting in some bare office, possibly with herself asleep in her arms, Fiona had decided that the truth should be put onto paper and filed, even if it was never acknowledged amongst her closest family. Kate felt a strange satisfaction at seeing both her mother's full name and that of Neil on the same certificate as her own. It felt good. It felt right.

"I found it about six months ago, and when I tackled Beth, she was as surprised as I was. Mum had never showed it to anybody, you see, and we had never bothered ourselves with it. When she got us our passports for a school trip to France, we weren't interested in what was involved, we just wanted to see how bad our photos were."

"I'm astounded," his voice had increased in depth slightly. "It's the last thing ..."

Kate found her hand on his shoulder and lips on his cheek before he could say another word. He remained in such a state of disbelief that he did not even flinch.

"When I packed it, I wanted you to see that you meant enough to her for her to do this. But actually, I'm showing it to you now because it makes me really happy. Really happy to know that you're my dad, even if I never get around to calling you that." She ran her fingers over the words as still he held the paper tightly. "Look, Neil Peter Wilder, Kathryn Eilidh Wilder. No denying it now."

"No denying it now," he repeated, finally folding it up and handing it back. "Keep that somewhere safe. You never know when you might need it."

"Okay, boss," she said, heading for the house once more. "But when I come back, you'd better have brought me another load. We'll be doing this all day at this rate."

Standing motionless in the yard, Neil felt the breeze part his short hair, and he caught some of that fresh air in his nose and inhaled deeply. He had experienced many an odd day in his lifetime, days which forced him to retreat along his dark corridor alone, or days when the sun shone so brightly that it almost singed the hairs on his head. Today, in the four hours he had been free from sleep, he had experienced a remarkable number of emotional punches which, amazingly, had not yet succeeded in knocking him out. The day, cool and sharp for all its brightness, had begun with Andie's hand roaming across his stomach and her lips kissing his eyes open. Neither of them would ever acknowledge the reason behind the feverish, chaotic love they had made the night before. It had been mutual and necessary; but just as necessary had been the sweet, controlled follow-up in the light of day, where their eyes had locked and life had been reaffirmed. They had lain motionless and at peace for the longest time, until Andie's sigh had brought them back to the routine that was a Sunday morning, and they had gone their separate ways.

As he bumped the Dodge and trailer up to the plantation fence, his mind moved onto the second incident, when his search for the missing spoon chisel had been interrupted by the telephone. He remembered the instant when his surprise at hearing David's steady monologue had turned to anxiety. He had been in the process of gathering his thoughts to represent himself as a busy man with an ordinary Sunday ahead of him, when the words had reached his ears and he had closed his eyes against them.

"I want to see her, Neil. How would that sit with everybody?"

The anxiety was mild, he was more disappointed than anything else; disappointed that he had been exposed for his part in this, but more than that, disappointed that he was no longer in charge of the situation. Having begun this journey thinking that meeting David was Kate's only motive, he had moved on to accepting that her goal had been merely a little guidance. He had been placed back in a position which had always been a possibility, but suddenly had appeared badly timed. He had heard himself exhale before replying.

"I did this because it was necessary -"

"You're right. It was," interrupted David, "and I'm grateful that somebody had the guts to act. It should have been me."

"Dave, she's only been here five days, and it's been a remarkable time. We've talked about the most incredible things, but," Neil hesitated, then, "in all honesty, I don't know where she wants to go from here. She keeps pretty buttoned up about you."

There had been too long a silence at this juncture, and Neil had frowned into the mouthpiece, praying that he was not causing damage where it was not required. He had felt the need, at least, to explain his part in the deception.

"She needed to know you were okay and happy. That's what she wanted to know. That's why she came to see us."

"What did you tell her?" David's voice was pure fear.

"I said you were busy and healthy and that since Hazel had visited, you seemed more content. I told her the truth as I saw it, and I think it's what she wanted to hear."

Neil rested his chin on the steering wheel, recalling David's pained reaction to this. There had been no shouting, they had not accused or defended; but to hear the man trying to justify every move he had made since the previous Christmas had been distressing, especially since both subjects were so much better known to him now. What had started off as a plea for understanding on David's part had grown into a declaration that from that moment on, Kate alone would have the final word on his future.

"That's why I'm coming over there. Kate hated people not talking, so God knows what damage I've done by cutting her out. That stops as of now. If it's too late for me, it's too late, but I'm going to find out today."

And so, Neil had tried to prepare himself for the visit. This had taken the form of ten minutes devoid of any movement whatsoever, as he addressed the dilemma of whether to warn Kate or not. Then, on entering the house, she had been dressed and grinning, ready to greet the coming day. He had decided to try to gauge some of Kate's feelings before he told her anything else, but she had misunderstood his subtle comments about her visit, and then the discussion had taken the weirdest turn. She had managed to give him yet another gift, and his heart had been subjected to the third test of the day; her birth certificate.

As Neil jumped from the Dodge, he thought once more of that piece of paper and how Kate had stood beside him, loving her mother for being true to herself when the very act must have brought every painful memory to the forefront of her mind. He thought of Fiona, remembering her inability to look him in the eye as she had sat isolated in Kathy's car, a wide-eyed Hazel on her knee. He had wondered that day if he would ever take another innocent breath. Yet she had absolved him of everything in her last letter, and, much more than that, she had made sure the world knew that Kate was his child. He knew of only one other person on earth who possessed such generosity of heart, and he woke up with her each day. For someone who had made such devastating errors as a young man, he found himself astounded at the calibre of women who had made him an integral part of their lives; Fiona, Andie and now Kate. It was time to look at repaying some of his debts.

"Hey!" Kate's voice was softened a little by the distance, but there was no mistaking her tone, and when he turned in her direction, he saw her flapping her arms at him, impatiently. "Get on with it!"

Neil smiled as he vaulted the fence, but he did not hurry to where the chainsaw lay awaiting his return. David was almost certainly only minutes away, and if he was to be of any use to either of them, now or in some devastated future, he needed to be on hand as a witness. He stole a glance at Kate, wondering how David truly saw her. Of course, she was attractive, but if you noticed her in the street, you would view her as pensive more than anything else. She always seemed totally occupied by thoughts, which could make her smile for no reason or frown just as easily. What was she doing on these occasions when her feelings spilled out into the public eye? Was she talking to her mother, or was she following her heart on some fantastic journey where those closest to her understood her perfectly? Neil did not know her well enough to answer this. Perhaps David did.

Perhaps she had shared everything in her heart with him already. Perhaps he was the only person she ever would confide in. Well, everybody was permitted one such individual in their life, why should a decent man more than twice her age not be hers? It was true that in the time she had been in their company, Kate's age had seemed irrelevant. She had talked from the heart, she had said what needed to be said, and she had asked only one question of him; was David okay. His reluctance to give away any information immediately had been the only thing to crack her protective shield. Perhaps this was testament to her feelings. Who knew?

"Bloody knots," cursed Kate, throwing away the first truly awkward piece of wood she had encountered and choosing the smoothest section available to her instead. Her efforts with the splitter were warming her whole body, and she was forced to get rid of her cardigan in response. The breeze felt wonderful as it fluttered her loose shirt, and so she pulled this free from her jeans for extra impact and took up her stance once more. Maybe she would have wrestler's arms without going anywhere near Neil's precious saw. He was returning with the next load already.

As the splitter sent the wood in three separate directions simultaneously, Kate stood back with a flourish and gave a low bow to the vehicle pulling up a few feet away. But it was not a Dodge Caravan she was grinning at as she stood, and it was not Neil behind the wheel. Her smile left her immediately. She was staring at a dark grey SUV, and the sole occupant was staring straight back at her.

CHAPTER 23

Sunday, 18th September 1994

"I'm not well, you know," moaned Hazel, shifting onto her stomach. "Folk might think it's Sunday night-itis, but it's something much worse. My throat's on fire and my ears itch. Here, Beth, look at my throat."

"I'll look at your throat if you can make the journey from the sofa to this chair."

"Hmm," Hazel's answer was to turn her back on Beth and hide her head under a cushion. It was not so much the three feet she would have to negotiate, it was the almost certain fact that her throat would look absolutely fine to her aunt, which rendered the journey pointless. She sighed.

"If you're bored, Haze, the Sunday Post is lying crumpled under your feet."

"Beth," Hazel sat upright, clearing her throat and grimacing to prove a point, "the last time the Sunday Post was interesting was when Kate got her letter printed. Now how long ago was that?"

"Oh, aye," laughed Beth. "Imagine having the nerve to say that 'Eastenders' should have Gaelic subtitles. She was only about ten."

"Imagine printing it! Must have been a quiet week for the letters page. Anyway, where's Ken?"

"Mrs Bryant phoned about that bloody guttering again. I don't know why he doesn't sell up and be done with it."

Hazel sat up. "Would he give the Bryants first refusal?"

"Who knows? I'm sure there are tenants' rights, but, thank God, I've never had to get involved."

Hazel remained upright and thought about Kenny's neat little terraced house on the north side of the town. It was a property his parents had persuaded him to buy when he had made the permanent move north from the Borders, and its size and location reflected the amount of money a newly graduated marine biologist had at his disposal. It was now a steady little money-maker, but unfortunately neither big enough nor blessed with a good enough aspect to act as a bed and breakfast establishment. Screwing up her nose in acceptance of the fact, Hazel reached for the remote control and began to flick through the channels on offer. In the end, she switched the set off in disgust.

"Argh. There is literally nothing on."

"What's the matter with you? You've been in a mood since Stuart left. You had another argument?"

Hazel scowled. "What do you mean another? Which ones have you been aware of before now?"

"Forget it. But it would make life a lot easier if you would stop waltzing around what's on your mind and just say it. That way the rest of us might have a chance of keeping our heads on our shoulders."

As Beth left, Hazel at last made the effort to move her legs and walked over to the window. It was already black dark; and out there, somewhere on the hill across the bay, Stuart was probably out with his rifle, imagining that each rabbit had her face. Well, if he could be pigheaded, then so could she. She wasn't even sure how the argument had started. One minute he had been laughing at the old photos she had found, and the next they were debating how Kate would be on her return. Hazel, in her blithely determined manner, was positive that she would be cheerier and more focussed. Spending time with Neil would be exciting and show her that you could be friends with a man of that age, without throwing yourself at their feet, declaring undying love. Stuart had not completely agreed.

"You ever thought that being in a country that speaks with the same accent as your dad might make her even more ...," he had shrugged, "... unsettled?"

"No," she had frowned, because she had not, although it had suddenly seemed a real possibility. "No, it'll be fine. Won't it?"

Stuart had maintained his doubt on this point, and this had led to them discussing David instead. They had still been reasonably on the same path at this point, recalling their holiday and experiences.

Then suddenly they were not smiling. Stuart seemed to think that David had not been 'insane' or 'ridiculous' in his admiration of Kate and that 'at the end of the day' where would the harm be in two people that Hazel herself loved being together? This had gone back and forth for a few minutes, both of them gradually edging away from each other on top of Hazel's bed as they became more animated. One phrase was still clear, and she was pretty sure it was the one which had resulted in her asking him to leave.

He had twisted his face and, rolling away from her, had said, "Haze, I hope you're right about it. I do. Because if you're wrong, you'll be a person neither of them wants to know."

Well, that was rubbish. Her dad always wanted to speak to her, to make sure she was okay. They had spent two brilliant weeks with him, drank champagne on her twenty-first birthday; he had even let Stuart and her share a room. Hazel cringed slightly at the memory of the needlessly awkward conversation she had brought about on that occasion, when David had taken their bags and deposited them both in the room she had shared with Kate, and she for some reason had felt it necessary to ask him if he was definitely okay with this. He had actually taken a step back from the question, mumbled something about assumptions and left them with the reminder that there were other free rooms if required. She had found Stuart cowering in the window recess, in pain from suppressed laughter. No, her dad would always put her first, yet there it was again, that dull ache where she imagined her stomach to be. Maybe it was time to address this feeling with somebody other than Stuart. Beth was in the kitchen, staring at the kettle.

"Okay?" Hazel asked.

"Absolutely. Thought he'd be back by now. Are there any tea bags left?"

Hazel found both bags and teapot while Beth brought some stewing steak from the freezer to defrost overnight. She looked a bit tired and Hazel was surprised that the clock read no later than 8.30 p.m., but still she needed to talk.

"Kate is bound to like her present, isn't she? I mean, I really want it to help. She never talks to me about anything important any more. I want her back. Properly back."

Beth shrugged, her face still preoccupied.

"So you agree it might make a difference," pressed Hazel, "if she remembers all the good times?"

"I'm sure she'll love it. She'll certainly appreciate the time you took."

It was so unlike Beth to be this reserved that Hazel began to give in to her fears. Stuart was presently her enemy, and if she was completely honest with herself, it was because some of his words had sounded feasible. Kenny, the arbiter of the house, was not here, and Beth was too lost in her own mysterious situation to engage in anything.

Fiona's absence, still a painful, silent cavity amongst them, allowed these fears to begin their domination, and Hazel found herself trailing back to the sitting room with her mug, her eyes downcast. Here it was, the guilt she absolutely refused to entertain, which somehow seemed to be stronger each time it resumed its attack against her. What did she have to feel guilty about? She had helped to prevent a disaster. She had saved her dad from making a total laughingstock of himself and spared Kate a lifetime of remorse from when it all fell apart. More than that, she had allowed David to keep the memory of Fiona safe. He would thank her one day for not letting that be tarnished by a ludicrous infatuation which had made him feel special for a while.

"Oh shit," groaned Hazel. What had he said to her again, when she had finally let him talk to her about the whole sorry mess? Something about not being able to explain it to anybody. Something about feeling wanted again. She remembered that she had accepted none of it in her enraged state, and he had not tried to justify anything further.

Kate had gone underground with her thoughts and feelings, not sharing anything beyond work-related incidents and the state of the weather. Only after her birthday trip, when both Kate and she had begun to drop David's name into the conversation, had it altered for the better. Even then only marginally. What was preventing the return of the Kate she had grown up with? The unabridged version that had been her best friend?

Hazel's thoughts were interrupted by the sound of the back door opening and closing, and she waited to hear if Beth had gone out or if Kenny had returned. A few mumbled words and footsteps in the hallway signalled the latter option, and Hazel wondered if a fresh pair of ears would help her out. She was on the point of shouting out his name when both Kenny and Beth marched into the room. Nobody marched anywhere in this cottage unless there was a situation unfolding, and this, coupled with Beth's straight-mouthed scowl, had Hazel almost spilling her tea.

"Think about it, Ken," Beth's statement was a warning.

"Do you think I've been fixing guttering all this time, like? It's dark, Beth. I've been thinking about nothing else since this morning, when you let me have your many opinions on my 'mistake'."

"What the hell is going on?" asked Hazel, totally mystified. "Or should I -"

"Em, no, Haze," replied Kenny, "you need to hear this. You need to know what's happening so you can tell me what you think of me, as well. Then I can tell you what I told Beth. We can all discuss it together and either fall out completely, or try to fix bits of it. It is called communication."

Hazel remained mute. It was the first time she had witnessed Kenny's face corresponding with his fiery red hair, and she peered over his shoulder at Beth. Her expression was less adamant, more resigned.

"So here goes," Kenny sighed. "David phoned last night after you'd gone out. He wanted to speak to Kate because he cares about her. So I told him where she was because I have my own ideas on this and because I think he's a good man. This morning I told Beth all about it, and now I'm telling you. I know what she thinks about the whole thing, let's hear your reaction."

"But why?" whined Hazel. "Why would you think that it was a good idea? Even Kate didn't want to see him."

"Kate didn't want to see him!" scorned Kenny. "Kate might have agreed with the majority decision of the supposed 'democracy' that is this house, but she did it because she needed to find out how he was, from people who would talk to her about him. It's time we all faced something. Kate's not going to give him up. You two can believe what you want, but I know better. So. It's done. I made a spur-of-the-moment decision, and I don't regret it. The question is, how are we going to tackle it from here?"

"You mean you haven't got a solution for that one?" cried Hazel, as much dismayed as angry, because someone had the nerve to articulate what she had always refused to admit. "Have you been in cahoots with Stuart about this?"

"What?" hissed Kenny. "For God's sake, Hazel, just because I'm still trying to find my place in this house doesn't mean I can't see for myself what's happening! At least Beth is prepared to entertain the idea that I might be right, even if she doesn't like it."

Hazel noted that Beth had not followed her usual route of sitting with her head in her hands and was merely frowning at the standoff between them. This was ridiculous. Had they all travelled back in time?

"You're telling me that Kate has never even tried to get over him?"

"That's what I'm telling you. She made a bloody good effort to please folk, make sure everybody calmed down a bit and now, because I thought I should, I gave David the option to take part. I know you two are mightily pissed off, but I'll just remind you of one more thing. In two days' time, Kate can do what she likes. Maybe that means she'll stay there and damn the lot of us. Maybe David will decide that he needs to sort this out himself, who knows? It's not up to us. It's up to them now."

Hazel was fuming. Fuming and cold and absolutely convinced that this was the last time she would have a conversation with this man about anything. He wanted to discuss it. It was called communication. Well, he could want until his fortieth birthday, she needed to get out of this room and out of the house. She did not flounce or stamp her feet, she just stood and walked past him, through the hall and out of the back door, the keys to the Fiesta in her hand.

If he wanted to communicate, then he could talk to Beth, although she had appeared just as unimpressed with his antics. She was going to the only place left to her, even though it was dark and would prove a little odd if she were to be spotted by a member of the public. She was going to sit with her mother and tell her the whole sorry tale.

The Fiesta was a reliable car when treated with respect. It did not seem to worry about the rain, the undercarriage had suffered bumps and scratches and been healed in the past, and the heater had never refused to work.

However, oil truly was essential to the continued well-being of the engine, and at the end of the driveway, as Hazel accelerated with the foot of a madman, it simply bumped itself halfway onto the road amidst the most unnerving, juddering knocking sound she had encountered. It was accompanied by an appalling smell, and it was this which had her switching off the engine in panic and scrambling back out into the fresh air.

She took a couple of steps backwards, her heart fluttering, wondering if she had in fact killed the vehicle. As this possibility dawned, she felt another burden start to make its weary journey to the summit of her mountain of problems, where it would sit down heavily on top of the rest of them. Her chin trembled, but she refused to give in to such a pathetic emotion when she wanted to remain furious, and assessed the practicalities of the situation instead.

Not heading into Portree to talk to Fiona was one thing, but leaving the car stranded diagonally across a road which boasted precious little leeway on either side was another entirely and just not feasible. Callum in the next house might be able to help push it onto the verge while she steered, but it meant explaining why neither Kenny nor Beth were available, and that would prove too juicy a detail for his wife to ignore. If only she had turned left downhill and not right uphill, then she might have had a chance of sorting it herself, but now it was beyond her.

"Sit in it and put it in neutral," Kenny commanded, appearing at her shoulder. "Try not to lock the steering and avoid the ditch if at all possible."

So, on top of everything else, he was criticising her driving. It was Hazel's dearest wish to tell Kenny to take himself back to his leaky guttering, but in the absence of Stuart, she needed his help. Silently, she climbed back behind the wheel and did as he had asked. She even managed a terse 'thanks' when he finally eased the vehicle off the road, but it was not acknowledged as he made his way back to the house. Locking the car door and pocketing the keys, Hazel began to trail her way down to the shoreline, the salty air on her face the only thing to be really thankful for.

When she had let herself think about this particular weekend, when it had still been a future time to worry about, she had supposed that the Saturday would be the worst day, with the Sunday being a relief of some sort. Sunday meant that their first year was behind them and it was a day nearer to Kate's return. This day had proved to be one of the worst so far; a day when the building blocks seemed to have been bulldozed. If Kenny and even Stuart were to be believed, nothing at all had been accomplished in the David-Kate scenario. Worse than that, Kenny was suggesting that it was not just Kate who had been stringing them along all this time, but there was a chance she had also been duped by her dad. What was even more unusual was that Kenny and Beth were experiencing what it was like to sit on different sides of the fence. How had that happened? A truly weird day all round, it seemed.

In the lay-by stood one stray sheep. It seemed mesmerised by Hazel's approaching figure and only tripped off down the middle of the road when she shouted at it to leave her alone. She let her eyes roam from bungalow to cottage, all along the bay wherever a light shone, and wondered how many of her neighbours were in the middle of an argument. Maybe they were all simply existing in their own individual worlds, waiting for the news, doing their homework or ironing their work clothes for the coming week. She would bet every penny she owned that not one of them was nursing as many afflictions as she was. In the distance, she heard the odd pop as somebody took out another rabbit, and she wondered if it was Stu or his brother. She wondered when Stu would decide to come over and make up with her. She made her way back to the picnic table and burst into tears.

CHAPTER 24
Sunday, 18th September 1994

Kate gently let go of the log splitter and watched the handle make its way to earth, coming to rest on the result of her efforts with a satisfactory wood-on-wood clatter. Before she was even aware of it, her hands were pulling self-consciously at her hair, and it appeared they were the only part of her body she was able to move. As the door opened and David stepped out, she was struck with one thought only; perhaps time was her friend after all. The man had not changed, and his face, serious though it was at that moment, was no less perfect than it had been ten months before.

What on earth did she look like to him? In her fear, she made herself leave her hair alone and instead reached for her cardigan, pulling it on and hugging it close. Her smile may have disappeared, but her expression did not turn to anger or sadness. How could it be either of those things when she was looking at the face and body of the person who meant everything to her? She was vaguely aware of Neil in the background, making his way towards them, and she wondered who had taken the initiative to set this up. It was irrelevant. David had come to see her, had made the decision and made the journey. She could stand for hours, just looking at him if she wanted to, the logs no longer of any importance, the weather itself redundant to the scene.

Only when he started to walk carefully towards her did her smile return. He was wearing a shirt that she had picked from the peg of a department store in Victoria and which had graced his body on the night he had first kissed her. It was her favourite shirt without question.

"Kate?" his voice was unmistakable, and suddenly she was so full. Full of billowing, amplifying emotions, and she began her own journey, blindly clambering over split wood and debris, to meet him.

Up close, Kate began to examine the man. She scanned his face, the pale scar running from eye to cheek, the dark brown hair, straight and short with a few unruly wisps lying against the back of his neck. Her heart had not hammered like this in months, and she was almost glad he had not spoken again, as she doubted she would have heard his words. She could not look at him enough. His green eyes were shining, watching her face as she continued her study of him. Boots, jeans, belt, shirt, hands, wrists, shoulders, jaw line; and in all this time, she had not acknowledged his actual height. The very best thing of all was seeing his appreciative eyes as he looked down at her. Instead of speaking, Kate took her hand and brushed the man's hair back from his forehead then allowed her hand to rest on his shoulder. One more second and her face was against his chest, buried deep in the cotton of his shirt, simply breathing him in. His heart matched her own in pace, and all she could do was wrap her free arm around his waist.

"I never gave up," he whispered into her hair. "I know it must have seemed like it at times."

Kate could not even reassure him for the moment. She had no desire to do anything but hold onto the man, and she knew that if she were to stand there until her legs lost their ability to support her, he would simply lift her off her feet. In a sudden desperate movement, she linked both of her arms around his neck, still hiding her face until she was ready to open her eyes again. He was shaking, she could feel it, and it signified one thing to her; this moment meant just as much to him as it did to her. Then his arms folded across her back and she was being held. Held by David. She screwed her eyes even tighter and finally spoke.

"They made me hard-faced, Dave," her words were slow and deliberate. "It was the only way I could do it. But I'm not. I'm not. No, don't let me go!"

"I want to see this face of yours," he replied, gently easing her away, and finally she opened her eyes, allowing them to focus on the brown/grey patches of hair on his throat before looking up at him. The smile that he wore was classic David. His mouth was turned up slightly more on the right side, his teeth not on show, but his eyes throwing out more joy than the widest grin could do justice to. "Nothing hard on this face," he soothed. "It's just as I remember it."

Kate smiled at last. "Snap. Yours still makes perfect sense after nearly a year."

David cupped her chin in his hands, but for one second only, before turning the pair of them to where Neil stood. The man was about fifteen feet away, and straightened his slouched back as soon as they looked at him. He raised his hand and waved in an attempt to cut through the awkwardness. "Okay?"

Kate was suddenly torn. She wanted to run to Neil and say, 'Do you see now? There's nothing to worry about here'. She owed it to him, he had spent time with her, no doubt forming his own anxious views on all of it, and had made the effort to help. There was no possible way that she was leaving David's side, not when the heat from his body was still present and his arm was voluntarily resting along her shoulder. In the next moment, however, David had taken her hand in his and was walking both of them towards the man. It did not even feel strange.

Neil's face was unreadable. It could not seem to decide on an expression; and Kate guessed that even now, after all he had been told by David and all that Kate had tried to conceal from him, the sight of them together was proving unsettling.

As they crossed the last of the distance between them, she wondered what David would say, and then she was smiling and walking with a purpose. At the last moment, Neil managed to find a look of optimism, but before he opened his mouth, Kate had pulled her hand away from David's and was standing alone by Neil's side. His eyes were wide, but not concerned.

"I didn't want to lie," said Kate, softly. "So I didn't. But I could have told you more. Sorry."

"Hey," he shrugged, "we do what we have to."

"Okay. But you and Andie deserved more." She exhaled quickly to prevent the onset of tears. "Do you see it, Neil? Do you see how it is for Dave and me?"

Neil looked over at David, the man he had tried to impress his whole life, to find him also looking to him for some acknowledgement that the situation was possible. It was a look he had seen before, on a dark December afternoon, when he had been unable to give him any assurances whatsoever. Now the man was waiting for his answer; Kate may have asked the question, but it came from both of them. Finally he smiled, although he gazed back down the driveway as he spoke.

"I see two people here who need each other. That's what I see. Nothing wrong with that."

It was enough for Kate, but not for David. He stepped forward.

"I do need her. But I also love her."

Kate slipped her hand back into his, aching inside from adrenalin and passion, and looked at Neil for his opinion on this. He answered immediately.

"Then you'll make it work. You have to." He did not add that they were choosing a difficult road. Why point out something so very clear? The fact remained that their particular family had never managed to find a smooth route through life to date. Perhaps they were indeed made of a strong enough fabric to go ahead with this.

"I'm going to give you a minute. Go inside, Dougal could do with the company."

"Don't you want to eat?" Kate felt strangely disloyal, allowing him to go back to work, but he was smiling as he walked towards the plantation.

"Oh, I'll be with you shortly."

The sitting room was fresh, the far window open to allow the mid-September air to circulate and stir the furnishings. Kate closed the door behind her and leaned against it, still astounded that she was staring at David's frame in front of her. He must be cold, no wool upon his back to trap the air between it and his shirt, and with a draught fanning his face. She toyed with the idea of lighting the fire, until she remembered how totally useless she was at such a task and instead remained by the door. Would time help them again? Would it slow down sufficiently for her to truly enjoy this level of feeling? Just to be alone with him after all this time, with only an apathetic dog to pass judgement on them. David must have sensed something similar, because he walked no further into the room.

"I can't believe you're here," he said, looking at her from the safety of four feet away.

"I cut my hair," she replied, then shook her head, "obviously. But I wanted to look … more; I wanted you to see me as a fair enough prospect. Do you like it?"

"Yes," he replied easily, then held out his hand to her. "Come here a minute."

David's skin was warm as he took her by the wrist and led her to the sofa. She relished the fact that he wanted to touch her, something he had always been a little fearful of doing, and it felt as if he was pulling every part of her to him. When they were seated, he put her small hand between both of his. He cleared his throat.

"I had a speech, but it's gone. I think it went as soon as I saw you."

"We've got plenty of time. Haven't we?"

He nodded, and then grinned. "How long have you been swinging a log splitter like Paul Bunyan?"

"I have a style of my own," she laughed. "I like the smell of the wood. Reminds me of you."

He smiled. "Still saying exactly what you think. I've missed you."

"I've thought about you every day. There's even a spot on the Ben which is just yours and mine."

During the moment's silence that followed, they heard Dougal yelp in his sleep as he dreamed of a time when both of his back legs worked efficiently and he could chase whatever took his fancy. When he did not stir further, David put his arm around her shoulder.

"It's so long since we talked. I came here today to find out if anything has changed. I know I've let you down."

"Do you feel the same?" Kate needed the question to be answered by the man himself.

"When you were last here, when you told me how you felt and made me listen to what you were saying," he began, "it was the most incredible news to me. We had just made it through some shattering times, and I'll admit, I tried to slow it all down. I tried to be really careful with it because it scared me out of my mind."

"Why?" said Kate, her face vexed.

"Because I didn't know how it was possible that you were thinking rationally. You were hurting. You might have been reacting to my attempts to help. But you know this already. You know why I was scared. What I want to do now is make sure you know how sorry I am for the way I had to handle it. I did nothing but hurt you more."

Kate released her hand from his and shrugged. "Like Neil said, we do what we have to. I had to do it, too, and it's worked, hasn't it?"

"I hope so. We had to help Hazel, and I think we're more than halfway there with that one. Every time I felt like I'd done something positive and good for her, I thought of who I was ignoring, who I was missing, and who I was still hurting. You were clinging to my side the whole time, Kate, and there had to be some reason why you wouldn't let go of me, so I let myself think about us. It made me happy, and still does, even if it only ever turns out to be a fantasy."

Kate thought about his words for a moment before she stood up. "You know, I told you over and over that they wouldn't break me or change my mind. If you had more faith, you might have spared yourself some grief."

She allowed him a minute to acknowledge this, and he nodded his acceptance of both the point and the admonishment. "So," she continued, "do you feel the same as you did on the day you put me on the plane?"

Kate could see the moment in question. It was her favourite mental picture, when she had stood on a bench and looked straight into his eyes. It was the first time neither of them had risked neck injury, and she remembered his arms around her waist as they kissed for the longest time to date.

"I'll tell you exactly how I feel. If you still want me after that, I'll show everyone who thinks they have a right to an opinion on this that some things are not up for discussion."

Kate folded her arms, the draught from the open window beginning to chill her slightly. "So, tell me."

Before he began to speak, David took it upon himself to shut the window. Perhaps he, too, felt the cold air, or perhaps he simply needed a minute or two to recall his thoughts. Either way, she was grateful.

"It's like this, Kate. I used to look at photos of your mother and Hazel, and they filled a gap for about thirty seconds in each day. Then you came into my life, and photos were a poor substitute. I began to rely instead on replaying conversations and situations to help me get to sleep at night. Then I had you, and you were great to have around. When you left, when the house went back to that mausoleum of a place, and it looked like you would never be able to come back, I couldn't stomach it. I needed more. I wanted more, and that was the first time I had wanted anything in a long, long time."

His words had been spoken during his tour of the room, and now he was back beside her. "I guess I wanted what you were prepared to give me, and that still scares me, but not as much as it did."

Kate grabbed both of his hands and shook them impatiently. "Look what we've been through in the last year, look what we've managed to survive. How can you still be scared for us?"

"Because I have to be!" he cried. "You don't have any fear at all and … and everyone else you know cannot fathom what you see here."

"Does that include you?" Kate was in her element. She was on home ground. There was no argument in this vein which she could not blow to smithereens.

Her question seemed to throw him momentarily. "Do you know what I do when I'm not working or sleeping or acting normal in front of people? In all the hours I spend on my own, every single time I take the dog for a walk or bike over to see Mum, do you know what I'm doing?"

David was looking at her through narrowing eyes. He shook his head.

"I'm thinking of every imaginable opinion on why we will never work. At first, I worked with the obvious ones, and then, over the months, I started to take bits of one and attach it to bits of another and make sure there was a solution to all of them. Math was never my best subject, but do you know how many possible combinations there are in this? I can argue with every one of them and win. The only person who can beat me down is you. Please, please don't do it."

Kate found herself breathing heavily into the air between them, watching as David digested her words.

Eventually he smiled. "You too, huh? Maybe we should get around to comparing notes. Sooner the better."

It was the least expected, most hopeful set of words she could have wished him to say, and he was not nearly finished.

"I'll tell you what I feel now, even after all this time. I want you to be with me for every day I live. I want you to scream at me when you're mad; I want you to laugh at me when I don't follow your argument. I want you to look at me like you are now, like we're allies and can do anything together. But do me a favour, please?"

"What?"

"Throw this old man a bone and reassure him that he's not asking too much."

"Oh, for heaven's sake."

Kate knew that there would be many days of talk still to come on the subject; she hoped to sit with David's face close to hers so that she could open up completely and liaise with him on how to handle every situation. But now was not the time. Neil would be arriving shortly, no doubt nervous as to what was taking place in his safe haven, and Kate did not wish to waste another minute on this strange, non-contact sport they were playing. She placed both of David's hands on her waist and pulled his face gently down to hers.

"I love you," she said. "And even if you had just said that we were never going to be together, I would still love you. True, I would have had to spend my life loving you from a distance, which would have been ridiculously cruel, but I would have done it, because I'll only ever love you. It's a life with you, or no life at all."

David's kiss could not be equalled. Kate's hands went from his face to his hair and threaded her fingers through the brown strands, simply to ensure he did not stop. Ten months of dreaming of what his kiss did to her, and dreading that he would never touch her again. She had felt every minute of those months acutely. She heard a strange noise in the back of her throat as his arms wrapped around her. She wanted his hands to be hers, to go where she bade them. She wanted his whole body against hers, wanted to be crushed so that she would still feel him when he finally had to let go. He was lean, he was strong, she could not stop herself moving forward, every part of her pushing against him. Then he was pulling away.

"Kate," he rasped, holding her at arm's length. "God, Kate."

"I know, I'm sorry, I just wanted you to know that it's all for you. You can have anything you want."

David closed his eyes but moved her back to the sofa. "Not here. Not in this house. It wouldn't be fair to anybody."

"You're right," Kate squeaked, but in truth she wanted to howl in despair. Instead, she got up and knelt by Dougal, who stretched out at her arrival and nudged her knee with his snout. She covered her growing embarrassment by placing his head in her lap and tickling him under the chin. She could not even look at David's face until Neil's boots could be heard on the steps outside, when she found him staring at her with a baffled smile.

"I love you." It was all he had time to say.

So Kate was grinning as Neil crossed the threshold and was even more delighted to see that her father's face was less strained than when they had left him.

"You're ruining that dog," he stated, pulling off his gloves. "He'll expect the same treatment long after you're gone."

"Sorry." She did not even have a smart retort as she jumped to her feet. "I'll make lunch. Way past my turn."

As Kate began to reheat the monstrous pan of broth from the day before, she thanked God that the two men in the next room had a permanent stock of subjects to discuss. In all the times she had been in their company, there had never been a shortage of safe topics, which was more than likely a legacy from the time Fiona had left. Topics gleaned from the news, or the sports channels or, more recently, the chalets on the estate; easy discussions for two men with complicated lives.

She began to see how lunch would stretch interminably, with her simply slurping soup and looking from one speaker to the other. Perhaps she should add a little spice to the proceedings, get them talking about the reason they were all here. It was as good a time as any.

"Hey, Dave," she called out at the first lull in voices, "how did you know I was in Canada?"

She smiled as she heard the predictable pause, but was then taken by surprise when he appeared at her shoulder, Neil following close behind. She blushed immediately and concentrated desperately on stirring the soup.

"That would be Kenny," David sighed, leaning against the worktop.

"Really?" Kate's face fell at the implication. "Aw, poor Ken. He's going to be in so much trouble."

"Did you think it was me, Kate?" Neil's voice was merely curious.

"No. Okay, maybe. But I wouldn't have blamed you. I've been a bit psycho in the last couple of days, must be the Canadian air. Seriously, though, poor Kenneth. I'll have to make it up to him. Maybe I could knit him a jumper."

As Kate hunted through the cupboards for 'the best crackers on earth', Andie appeared in the doorway, Cuban and Crisis almost bowling her over in their desire to reunite with Neil. Kate noted David's genuine smile at her entrance. She walked towards him with her arms extended.

"Hey, you," she hugged him. "How are you doing?"

"Well," he replied, "I feel better than yesterday, when I found out that there are some seriously tight-lipped people in my family."

Andie shook her head, smiling. "Okay, but look at the positives, Dave. You haven't beaten up your brother, you're still talking to me, and you and Kate are not standing at opposite ends of the room, ignoring each other. It feels pretty good in here just now. Or am I completely on the wrong track?"

"I'm pretty good," agreed David, smiling at Kate who paused in serving the soup to make sure the whole room knew that she was, too.

"You're early," Neil spoke to Andie as they took their seats at the table. "Iris okay?"

"Oh, yes. But when you phoned, she wanted to know what was happening. So, I told her, and she was desperate for me to come and … make sure all was well."

Kate looked intently from David to Neil, then back to Andie, who seemed to be taking the still atmosphere as their acceptance that she had not committed a crime in sharing this information. Neil continued to eat, his face neutral, and so Kate stared at David. He paused for the shortest time and then reached for another cracker.

"What did she say?" Kate asked.

"The thing about my mom," Andie was almost chuckling, "is that partial stories are not an option; and let's be honest, it takes more than five minutes to give this the attention it deserves, so it was quite a lengthy chat. But she's a wise old bird, really. She just wants to know if there's going to be a happy outcome. Enough sadness in the world without inviting more. I think those were her exact words."

When she looked into Andie's eyes, Kate saw her meaning instantly, and she had to curl her toes inside her socks to ensure that she did not acknowledge it with words. Instead, she turned her face to David, and again, his eyes were determined and calm.

"Wise old bird indeed," he stated, looking straight at Kate.

"Jeez, Dave," said Neil, "never let Iris hear you call her old. She'll take you out with one punch."

《●》《●》《●》

It was dark by the time David and Kate next had a moment truly alone. They had spent an easy afternoon, talking, splitting logs, catching up on the things which had upset them and pardoning each other, with Neil and Andie dropping in and out of each scene whenever they were called upon. David felt he should go. It was too much for them to be under the same roof, after all that had been acknowledged; but standing beside the SUV with only the security lamp for light, Kate had never been so intensely terrified. She had been wringing her hands since David had said his farewells to the others, and at last he was aware of it.

"What is it, sweetheart?"

"I'm scared, Dave," her teeth chattering in spite of her jumper and coat. "You can't leave me now. What if you have an accident? It's a long drive and it's late. Please don't go. Or, take me with you! You said Rose was coming round to it all. Curses, I feel sick."

"Hey there," he sounded surprised, and Kate's stomach rolled again. Maybe he thought she should be handling this better.

"Sorry," she hung her head. "I just feel better when you are here. I won't survive if you don't come back to me."

"Kate," David made her look up at him. She could see his eyes even in the dim light. "Do you want me to be honest with you?"

"Depends on what you're going to say," she wavered.

"That's more or less permission," he nodded, and then took her trembling hands. "You need to know something, so I'm going to be frank. I'm finding it really difficult to keep myself from going too far. You're so lovely and … vital to me. You're standing here next to me, shining so brightly, and I can't get enough of it. But when you say you want me, I nearly lose it. If we're going to do this properly, now is not the time for me to lose it."

Kate could not take her eyes off his mouth as he spoke. Now that he was silent, she didn't know how to add any words to his. Apparently she had actually lost the ability to think, along with the ability to speak, and could only stare up at him. She watched him raise his eyebrows, hoping for some sign of understanding from her, and her thought processes helpfully kicked back in. Did he really lose his head over her?

David, in the time she had loved him, had created many weird and wonderful feelings within her, and here he was introducing yet one more; power.

"When?" It was an ambiguous enough question for him to crease his eyes slightly.

"When?" he repeated.

"When are we going to see each other again?"

He seemed relieved. "Rose and I will be here on your birthday. Is that okay?"

Two whole nights and a whole day without this man beside her or in her eye-line or even in the next room. Kate swallowed the water forming in her mouth and nodded, wishing more than anything that she could hold him for another minute or two, but apparently it was too dangerous. He kissed her lips, cradling her head in his hands for a mere moment and then climbed into the SUV. As he opened the driver's window, she massaged her lips together, desperate to retain something of him. She stood so that her face was close to his, but did not speak. She could hold his gaze until the end of time if necessary.

"What is it, Kate?"

Her fingers rested on the metal door between them.

"I'm just dreaming, Dave," she said and touched his face. "Dreaming of when we can both lose it. Together."

PART III

November 1994

CHAPTER 25

Friday, 25th November 1994

Kate had been to a wedding once at the Skeabost Hotel, where she had been intrigued by the fact that the chairs were wearing clothes of their own. They had been fitted with royal blue covers and trimmed with navy bows. She remembered her mum's face as it turned from surprise to amusement at such a sight, but Hazel had clapped her seven-year-old hands, and naturally Kate had done the same. She had no memory of the bride but had an inkling that, no matter how beautifully she had been kitted out, she could not have felt as high as Kate felt this day. The Registry Office had been a place to conduct business. It was a room Kate would probably never set foot in again, but it was already committed to her memory; the flowers, the curtains, the polished wood, the Registrar.

Kate had worn a lilac silk blouse, bought for a school party eons ago which had never been attended, and a pair of white linen trousers. Neither particularly suited the day's weather of biting wind and sleet, but they had both been brand new, and Hazel had loaned her a pair of white ankle boots, whose inch heels just kept the hems from dragging through the puddles. There had been David, dressed in a black suit, tall and handsome, taking her hand as soon as they were in the same room and looking down at her, not one doubt evident on his face.

Their vows had been straightforward, penned by some anonymous official years before, but they had been easy to say with David squeezing her hand; and when he had kissed her, their first public kiss amongst people who had the power to destroy such a moment, she had let it linger long enough to send a message out to all. They were in love and that needed to be appreciated. After reflecting David's grin back at him, Kate had looked straight at Hazel and found her cuddled into

Stuart, eyes damp but soft enough. It had been a positive picture, noticed by both her and David; and amidst the subsequent congratulations and hand-shaking, he had taken Hazel aside and spoken quietly to her. Kate would never ask him what he had said, but it had culminated in Hazel straightening his tie and him handing her a hankie. It had been a beginning.

Outside, the sleet had turned plumper and whiter and Kate had stood, her face raised to the sky, hypnotised by the flakes. It had been a tiny, quiet moment before Beth was throwing a heavy coat around her, kissing her cheek and asking if she was okay. Then Kenny had hugged her against him, his red hair already covered in white droplets, and Stuart had fumbled in his jacket for confetti. He had been beaten to it, however, by Shona Syme who had appeared from nowhere, squealing, and had dumped nearly her entire box of paper shapes on David's head.

"Kate! First one to tie the knot! Can you believe it?"

When David, laughing, had tried to shake the rubbish from his hair, Shona had mouthed 'wow' at Kate and hugged her quickly. "Hellfire, Kate," she had mumbled, "does he have a brother?"

The real reason behind Kate's sudden burst of laughter would forever remain a mystery to her friend.

Kate gazed out at the falling snow from the comfort of their room and thanked God they had reached the hotel before the driveway, which fell away from the main road in a steep and winding trail, became non-negotiable. She did not attempt to imagine how she would have handled her first night with David, stuck in a lay-by as the weather closed in around them. Even worse was the thought of staying together in the cottage, something she had been dreading until the very moment Hazel had stood beside her on the snowy Registry Office pavement, and offered her own olive branch in the shape of two nights at The Flodigarry Hotel. It had been a warm moment, but now Kate shivered and closed her eyes, touching the cold glass to ease the tingling in her fingertips. In her mind's eye, she saw David's face, and suddenly she was grinning because she no longer had to play this game. He was with her, here in reality, and he was here to stay.

Kate looked at the pristinely groomed bed. The duvet, the plumpest she had ever encountered, was a duck egg blue and was topped off with an obscene amount of pillows. Well, they would have to go. Kate required only one pillow to sleep, and that had to be pretty thin or she woke up with a crick in her neck. Immediately, she felt the nervous rash pricking at her throat. She headed straight for the en suite.

"No, no, no," groaned Kate. Was this a joke? So, after weeks of dreaming and longing and denying, David's first glimpse of her body was going to reveal a blotchy mess. The cold flannel she applied to her neck did nothing but become a warm damp rag in her burning hand, and she dropped it hopelessly into the sink. Grey eyes stared back at her in desperation as she tried to mentally calm herself, but after a few moments, she straightened up and watched herself shrug.

The world was not perfect. The weather was taking a turn for the worse, only four guests had been present on her happiest day, and Hazel's boot had blistered one of her little toes. But, she was in a warm, private space, waiting for a man who loved her, and she was prepared to show him how nervous and excited he made her. It was not a perfect world, but it was an honest one.

"Kate?"

As she came out of the bathroom, Kate smiled openly. David was standing by the open door, but closed it gently, his own face clearing as he accepted that she had not in fact run away from him but was still here and apparently still happy.

"Look at this," she grinned, pulling the collar of her blouse apart. "That's your fault, Wilder. You do that to me. Attractive, isn't it?"

David, taking off his jacket, beckoned her across the room. "Come here."

Whenever Kate stood in front of this man, her eye level lay somewhere just below his collarbone. Usually, she would spend her time looking at a frayed button hole on a checked shirt or the loose-knitted cable of a jumper. Today was different. He had on a brand new shirt of white cotton and a bottle-green tie. Without his jacket, he looked incredibly lean. Kate felt a strange thudding inside, somewhere between her heart and belly, and marvelled at the effect different clothes on his familiar frame were having on her. Boys at school wore shirts and ties, and she had on a couple of occasions been pulled into a jokey bear hug. But all she could think about was how David's skin and muscles would feel beneath the fine material. She smiled up at his clean-shaven face, which was almost as unfamiliar as the shirt and newly trimmed hair, and turned her head slightly to show him her glowing skin.

"This," said David, tracing his finger from her throat to earlobe, "is indeed very attractive. Always was, always will be."

Kate placed her ear against his shirt front and felt his hands skim through her hair before he rested them diagonally across her back. He laid his chin on the top of her head and hugged her close.

"Are you happy?" he voiced the question which had sat poised on her own lips all day, and she lifted her face from the steady thump of his heart so that he could read her eyes.

"Yes. I've been happy before and it was nothing compared to this, so I think we'll have to find a better word. How do you feel?"

"Stunned."

"Stunned? That's not half bad. What about hopeful? As in full of hope?"

"Excellent choice. Happy, stunned and hopeful."

"And in love," concluded Kate.

David looked down at her shining face and closed his eyes. "And so much in love. Far too much in love."

"There's no such thing," grinned Kate, unfolding herself from his grip and crossing over to the watch the pale drapes of water sweeping in from the sea. "Did you manage to get through to Beth?"

"Yes, she knows we're safely here."

"Great. And what time is dinner?"

"We get to choose, as long as it's between seven and nine."

The sea was a deep lead grey as Kate looked at it for one last time before closing the curtains. The next time she viewed it, it would be morning, and it might be blue or green or silver. Whatever its colour, Kate guessed that it would be spectacular.

David remained where she had left him, standing on the Oriental rug, arms folded and head tilted slightly as he watched her every move.

Kate's heart threw in a couple of extra beats as she realised that they were not only completely alone, but that they were allowed to be; and from this moment on, they could follow any road they wished.

"David?"

"Yes?"

"Please, can I take off your tie?"

If Kate had any self-knowledge, it was that she could surprise people with her words. It was a relatively new skill, born around the time she had learned of her parentage and had decided to say exactly what she was thinking at any given time. She watched David's eyebrows lift, but he also unfolded his arms and smiled.

"I'm all yours," he replied, his voice at such a low pitch that her legs threatened to let her down suddenly. To steady herself, she unzipped her ankle boots and slipped them off before walking towards him, forcing herself to concentrate on the knot of material at his neck.

"This is a nice tie," she eased the words past the lump in her throat as her fingers loosened and pulled until she had worked the tie free.

"We should keep it safe." Kate took her time rolling up the length of silk and placing it on the dressing table. "Maybe I should undo your top button because it looks a bit weird without the tie."

David had the greenest eyes she had ever seen, but now his irises seemed to be disappearing as she struggled with the stiff buttons. By the time she had managed to undo both the top and second button, she was also sure he had stopped breathing. Before she had time to ask after him, he smiled down at her and cupped her face in his hands.

"Have you any idea what you've given me already?" he asked.

"No. I don't know anything much at all. Only that this is the best thing I've ever done. The best I've ever felt."

"Me too, Kate. Me too."

As Kate leaned into his chest once more, she caught a glimpse of his collarbone and suddenly hid her face, embarrassed, laughter jumping out before she could stop it.

"Oh, Dave. I've just thought of something, and it seems a ridiculously long time ago."

"What is it?"

Grinning, Kate took a step back to watch his reaction. "Remember the night at The Edge when you were trying on your new clothes for that Rotary dinner? The one that never happened? You were taking your shirt off, cool as a cucumber, and I had to run to the loo because, because I saw your collarbone and I wanted to touch it so much."

This time, David could not hide his amazement. "Really? As long ago as that? God, my radar really was busted back then."

"Well, I tried really hard to hide it. But in the end, you needed to be told what you were doing to me." Kate paused, then, "What you're still doing to me."

He looked at her grey eyes, no longer sad, but wide and bright. "Thank God for you and your straight talking. It's brought us all the way here."

Kate felt her face grow pink and wondered if it now matched her throat and neck. David took her hand and seated her on the bed. She felt almost enveloped by the duvet, which was even softer than it had looked, but managed to stay upright and alert.

"I love you, David," she whispered into their clasped hands, seconds before he moved away from her.

When he turned back to face her, he had effortlessly unbuttoned his shirt, eased it out of his waistband and pulled it from his body.

Kate gasped at the sight of him and made a mental note to practice unbuttoning shirts before she grew a day older.

"Oh, God," she said, looking at his face, "you're so ... completely ..."

"Yours," he finished. "I'm yours and that's all I'll ever need to be."

Kate stood, suddenly feeling that crazy power of her own, and walked towards him, her hand outstretched.

"I was going to say amazing," she stated, placing her fingers on David's shoulder. She could sense the tension beneath his skin, feel the heat from his chest fanning her face, and at last looked up at him. Since the day they had said their first farewells at Vancouver International Airport, there had never been anything timid about their kisses, and Kate was grateful that this was one area she was confident in. As she hooked her wrists behind David's neck, his hands rested on her waist, pulling her farther into his kiss. She moved against him, but as sweet as it was, Kate wanted to be able to keep her eyes open and drink in his looks and his frame and his own obvious desire.

She eased a small space between them and placed the palm of her hand on his taut stomach. It tensed as she did so, and she saw David lift his eyes to the ceiling, the tendons on his neck screaming for attention. She placed her other hand on his throat and eased his chin back to its rightful place. His eyes were blazing, and Kate felt that whatever she did next could only be the right thing. Never before had he allowed her to stand on this platform, controlling him to this extent; yet she felt absolutely no fear and instead began to act on the ache spreading through her, filling all the voids within her with rolling lava.

"I want you," she croaked, taking his wrists in her hands. "But I'm not really sure ... don't let me spoil this."

"Not a chance," murmured David, moving to the head of the bed he switched on the lamp. In the light, Kate saw the sheen on his face and marvelled that she had caused this reaction. It seemed that their bodies were unable to conceal anything from each other. Kate liked that.

David kissed her lightly on the lips then looked her straight in the eye, an action which caused a sudden sob of pure joy to escape her. She was going to be able to look into those eyes whenever she wanted. David, mistaking her sob for nerves, touched her hair.

"Trust me?" he asked.

"Every day of my life."

When Kate opened her eyes after his final kiss, she found him untying his bootlaces. His fingers were as adept at this as they were with buttons, and when he was barefoot, he pulled Kate towards him. He kissed her slowly, and then, his eyes never leaving hers, he began to unbutton Kate's blouse. She thought she may keel over as her head grew lighter and lighter. So, this was true anticipation; this constricting of every organ, this inability to reach the desired point quickly enough. As he peeled the material from her shoulders, his fingers brushing her skin, Kate could not stand still for one moment more. Before he had placed the blouse on the dressing table, she had unhooked her bra and discarded it.

Kate knew, without the aid of a mirror, that her eyes now matched his. She felt her pupils expand as clearly as she saw David's do it, and it was she who moved nearer to him, taking his hands. Still, he hesitated.

"Kate," he whispered, "I don't deserve you."

She placed his hands on her breasts, gasping in air as she did so, and hoping that the spontaneous reaction showed him at last that he was mistaken. He deserved everything, simply because he was sure he did not. There was no arrogance in him, he had kept his desires at bay to protect them from the worst of the flack; and now, the entire world must surrender and admit that they both deserved to be happy.

Kate put her arms around David's neck, delighting in the way that their bare skin made contact. He in turn lifted her up to his eye level. She buried her face in his neck, finding the tiny areas of facial growth which refused to be tamed beneath her lips, kissing them again and again and again. She felt her toes bump against his shins, his arms effortlessly holding her aloft so that he could breathe in the fragrant skin beneath her earlobe.

"I think," she whispered in his ear, "we still have too many clothes."

As he lowered her to the ground, she did not trust herself to look at him and scurried to the other side of the bed, removing her remaining clothing with her back firmly turned to him. She may be almost exploding with need, but this was still a huge deal, and she worried that at any moment her inexperience might make itself evident in some devastating way. It was safer that he did not see her face.

By the time she had eased herself beneath the duvet, her teeth chattering wildly, David was already there. She breathed with relief and put her finger between her teeth to stop them giving away her fears, but with one movement David took her hand from her mouth and pulled her into the crook of his arm.

"Hello, Kathryn Eilidh," he whispered, stroking her shoulder. "That's an impressively beautiful name. But I think from now on, when it's just the two of us alone, I'm going to call you Kitty. Kit for short. A name only I get to use. What do you say?"

"Well, David John," Kate replied, "I've got no problem with that." She propped herself up on one elbow, loving the way he smiled over at

Barbara Morris

her, still amazed that she had managed this much without making an idiot of herself. "What do I get to call you, though? Neil calls you Dave, Rose calls you Davey-boy. What do I get? I think you'd better kiss me again while I think about it."

David, in response, placed his lips on Kate's shoulder, and as he moved it slowly over this area, her elbow lost its ability to support her, and she fell back upon the multitude of pillows. Before he reached her lips, David himself stopped, opened his burning eyes and whispered, "Let me look at you again, Kit."

Kate pushed the duvet down to her waist, her eyes locking onto his face and loving his appreciation of her, appendix scar and all. He traced his fingers between her breasts and then drew them back and forth, giving each individual rib the attention it deserved. Kate became aware that her legs were trembling, quite obviously quivering, completely of their own accord, and she grew terrified that it would halt his journey. She sat up and wrapped his head in her arms.

"I'm not ... scared," she faltered. "I can't control it. Don't stop, please. Don't ever stop."

He eased her back against the pillows and placed her hand on his chest, where the familiar thump was stronger and much faster than she remembered it.

"This is what you do to me, Kitty. We're in this together."

"Yes," she agreed, kissing his mouth because she could. "I want it all."

When David's answer to her trembling thighs was to peel the duvet from them and kiss them, Kate's hands shot above her head and she pressed them against the oak panelling of the headboard. But she could get no grip and her palms slid from position, leaving small temporary handprints there. She heard a tiny panicked noise come from deep within her, and instantly David's face was next to hers, kissing her cheeks and eyelids.

"Sshh," he soothed, "we don't have -"

Kate grabbed his face, his eyes widening at her grip.

"David," she cried, "if you stop, I'll die. Simple as that."

"Okay, sweetheart, okay. I love you."

"I love you more."

David shook his head at the absurdity of her statement then placed his hand on her lower belly. He looked at her with raised eyebrows. In response, she took his hand and slid it between her legs. She had no time to wonder at her own bravado or even acknowledge David's eyes closing as he caught his own breath, because the blood was already

212

thumping in her ears, the beat of which seemed to be echoing beneath David's beautiful fingers. Was her chest supposed to be this tight? Were hot tears supposed to be running sideways into her hair and ears? Ultimately, how long could an ordinary human withstand this intensity?

These questions suddenly evaporated as Kate's hips trembled, her skin peeling away from the bedding beneath her as her body did what it liked without conscious thought. It stayed suspended in mid-air for an unknown period of time, while Kate's eyes remained screwed shut against each swell of pleasure as if opening them might diminish this whole thing. Kate felt David's hand lower her back onto the damp sheet. Quickly her arms were around his neck, and she was sobbing against his face. Her arms were slippery, her chest a landscape of hills and streams and they slid against each other until David locked her tightly and kissed her salty shoulder.

"Oh, Dave," Kate cried. "I didn't know. Nobody ever said ..."

"I'm glad," he murmured. "Some things are best just discovered."

Kate's heart was hammering, her inner thighs quaking, a further river damming up inside her as she sat back and looked at her love's face.

"Why didn't you ...?" she asked, genuinely mystified. He stroked her chin, then brushed beads of sweat from her fringe.

"Because I wasn't sure if I could ... hold on long enough. You're not just the person I love, you're also very beautiful and unique, and I don't do this every day. There was a real danger it wouldn't have been very special for you."

"Well," breathed Kate, lacing her fingers through his. "It was astoundingly incredible, and I love you, love you, love you. But now, it's my turn."

"Your turn?"

"My turn to make you feel like I just did. Please, let me."

David's expression was enough to restart the drumbeat within her. She threw the surplus pillows across the room and settled herself beneath his gaze. He kissed her, she kissed him and then pulled him on top of her. As his arms held his weight away from her, Kate touched his warm stomach and moved her legs apart. She wanted the connection, body and soul, more than she had words to describe how much and knew that, as David eased himself inside her, he was taking the greatest care.

In turn, she accepted the pressure, her eyes focussed on David's flushed face and understood at last the power she had within her; she had the ability to give pleasure whenever she wanted to. She gasped as this acknowledgement itself allowed David to sink himself deeper still, and she watched him give in to long-forgotten sensations.

Kate felt no great pain, just complete wonder that she could make this man react in such a way. She touched his face so that he would open his eyes again and confirm what she already knew; she was an equal partner in this.

He had created earthquakes and avalanches within her; and now, minutes later, she felt herself rising to meet him again. His hair was damp, his eyes black, and as much as she wanted to watch him till the end, her neck arched as she felt him thicken still further and tense inside her.

He moved his head away from her, anxious not to let any sweat fall upon her, but she took his face in her hands and brought it down to hers, where she cried against his hair until he kissed her eyes dry.

CHAPTER 26

Saturday, 26th November 1994

"I hate cliches. And look at us. Newlyweds who didn't make dinner. It's a disgrace."

Kate was standing in front of the mirror of their en suite, concentrating on the task in hand, yet talking loud enough for David to hear.

"A disgrace," he called back, stretching his entire body so that his feet hung over the end of the bed. "We should be ashamed of ourselves."

"And yet, I'm not. Although, it has to be said, I am bloody starving this morning." Kate moved to the doorway and peered round it, catching David with his hands still above his head. "You know something else? I'm not even going to look embarrassed at breakfast. I'm just going to smile and eat."

David grinned at her from the bed, then hauled himself up into seating position, his head tilted in her direction. It looked as if she was wearing his good shirt. "What exactly are you up to?"

"You'll find out when the time is right," cried Kate, immediately closing the door between them. "Until then, there is no need for you to know everything about me."

The light in the bedroom was dim, although David could see a brilliant white aura surrounding the curtains and guessed that a stunning winter landscape would greet whoever decided to open them. Should that be down to him, he pondered, before rubbing his damp hair back into its normal shape. No, he was sure Kate would take greater delight in the activity, and her wide-eyed grin would make him smile in return. He glanced over at the suitcase, still packed apart from the toilet bag, and tried to persuade himself to do something with that instead. They would be here for one more night, so really there was no need to unpack it, but his stomach was also beginning to protest at its neglect, and so he pushed himself out of bed.

As he hunted through the case, he heard the shower being turned on, followed by a tiny yelp then a few notes of some melody he could not quite identify. Kate's singing voice was unnaturally low for someone of her age and gender, and although he guessed it was a popular tune, it remained beyond his recognition. Still, she was singing. She was smiling. She was happy.

David switched on the dresser lamp and looked around him. The extra pillows remained where Kate had thrown them the night before, and he felt the hairs stand up on his arms as he remembered her burning eyes at that moment. It was a feeling he hoped he would never take for granted. And she was there, a few feet from him, warbling in the shower. Her body would be covered in soap behind the steam, and he imagined her face beneath the cascading water as she massaged her short hair. He had stood there himself, just fifteen minutes earlier, wondering if he should wake her and invite her to join him. But he must not smother her. At this early stage, when her body was still adjusting to what they both wanted so much, he had to let her come to him. She would, because she loved him; and when she understood completely how he made her feel, then he would give in to everything.

By the time David was dressed in jeans, shirt and had just tied his second bootlace, Kate strolled over to the window, wrapped in a bath towel. Her hair had been hand-dried into a set of wild spiky peaks, but she was anxious to see the weather before attacking it with a brush.

"Oh, yes! Dave, look at this!"

The sea was silver grey, but the land before it, the small island and the mainland beyond were various shades of white, violet and black. No snow was falling. The sky, while heavy in parts, also allowed patches of electric blue to cut its way through. The sun shone on the mainland hills, suggesting that perhaps it might make the journey across the strait before the morning was over. Kate laughed at the possibility. David stood behind her and wrapped his arms around her waist, gripping the towel tightly in place and burying his chin in her gradually subsiding hair. She felt warm and damp and fresh. Kate put her hands on his wrists to ensure he held onto her for as long as possible.

"Isn't it beautiful?" she murmured, tingling inside at being hugged so close. "Imagine if we get snowed in. That was one thing I never thought of. I mean, I know it's November, but it hasn't been that cold."

"Well, I could probably cope with being snowed in, for a week, anyway. After that, I might struggle."

When she turned her inquisitive face up to him, daring him to explain the meaning behind the remark, he laughed and kissed her. "I only meant I didn't bring enough to wear. Oh, and talking of clothes," he said as Kate started to sort through the unpacked goods, "that is my jumper. I'd be prepared to bet on it."

Kate had the presence of mind to look a little sheepish as she hooked up her bra and glanced at the brown cable knit.

"Em, the thing is," she began, trusting that it had not been too heinous a crime, "I needed it."

"I needed it," he laughed. "I hunted the house for it."

"Okay," she accepted his argument, pulling on her one pair of jeans. "But my need was sooo much greater. I needed it to survive." She paused as she picked it up and held it to her face. "My very survival depended on it."

David folded his arms and raised his eyebrows at her semi-apologetic expression. "Is that your best argument?"

"Two seconds," she replied, handing him the jumper. As he watched, Kate gave her hair a couple of quick swipes with her brush then blasted it into shape with the hair dryer. As she did this, David held the jumper to his own face and smelled her fragrance amongst the prickly strands of wool. When he caught her eye, she grinned a 'see?' grin and he nodded back, understanding her completely. When her hair was tamed and she had donned a black polo-neck sweater, Kate held out her hand, and he gave her back the disputed jumper.

"I took it," her voice muffled as she pulled it over her head, "because it was yours and because it felt like you were snuggled against me." As if to clarify, she wrapped her arms around herself, her hands hidden in the oversized sleeves. "Also, it traps warm air and covers my bum, but they were just the practical bits. Really, it was because I couldn't fit you in the suitcase."

"Well," David felt his throat constrict at her continual honesty. "It suits you. It's yours."

"Tell you what, we could have a week each because," Kate held open her arms as if the thought had just occurred to her, "we are going to be in the same house!"

"Sounds like a plan," he agreed. "And it looks like it's your week."

"Och no," she laughed, pulling it back over her head. "Not today. Not in public. Today, I am sophisticated."

"Today, you are gorgeous."

CHAPTER 27
Saturday, 26th November 1994

As they made their way down the wide oak staircase to the dining room beyond, David made a point of taking Kate's hand, and she squeezed his in return; but the room was not busy, and they only drew the gaze of a pre-teen girl and her toddler brother. Their parents seemed too intent on arguing in terse, overly-emphasised whispers to notice the unusual couple who sat at the only table for two in the window. Kate smiled at the girl, who surprisingly grinned back, before trying to get her brother to continue eating. Within seconds, Kate had forgotten everything but the view before them, and she turned her shining face to David.

"Aw Dave, look at it!" She took his hand across the table. "Was there ever anything so special? I think we just about have to wrap up and get out there. You up for it?"

It was agreed, over the porridge and fruit, that the light and landscape needed exploring. It was further suggested, as Kate watched David empty his plateful of sausages, black pudding and eggs, wondering where his frame stored all of it, that if the snow stayed away, a drive up to the foot of the Quiraing would be worthwhile. It would be spectacular if the road was passable and would be dependent on what the weather threw at them. If that was out, then they would have to come up with a contingency. David, without any form of cunning whatsoever, challenged her to think of an alternative plan. Kate spent the remaining two minutes or so distracted, her mind running with so obvious and attractive a solution that she could not think of a clever enough way of expressing it. Instead, she forced herself to eat, her tingling ideas suddenly diminishing her appetite for food in the nicest possible way.

As David rolled up his napkin and patted his imaginary belly, Kate reached out and touched his chin. He didn't flinch, but seemed to take in a deep breath. "You're so handsome," she sighed. "I can't decide if I like the smooth chin or the rough chin the best. I suppose you'll just have to keep surprising me with that. Can't wait."

"And I know you'll surprise me every time you speak to me. But it's kind of exciting."

"I think we'll get on just fine. Ready?"

David let her lead the way from the dining room, thanking the waiter as he left as much for not raising his eyebrows at them as for his service at their table. At the foot of the staircase, Kate put her hand on David's arm, halting him immediately.

"Dave," she whispered, moving her face as near to his as his height allowed, "I'm going to wait for you by the front door. Please, could you bring our jumper with my coat and gloves?"

His eyes creased slightly before he smiled and turned his whole body towards her.

"Sure, sweetheart. You feeling okay?"

Kate slipped her hand into his and hid her face against his shirt for a moment before looking helplessly at him. "It's just that," she swallowed, her neck prickling, "if we both go up there now ... well, I won't be able to ... not ... and probably they'll come to make the bed or something, and the whole thing will be mortifying. It's safer if I stay here."

The last part of this speech was directed at David's feet as the blood spread from her neck up to her face, and she couldn't help noticing that one of his bootlaces was double-knotted while its mate was on the verge of coming undone. Imagine if he tripped and injured himself before he could once again hoist her up into his arms? She felt his hand under her chin and then he was grinning down at her, his green eyes as full of humour as they were of heat.

"You are remarkable, Kate Wilder. I'm not going to argue, because you have a point. It's one thing to miss dinner, but to hang the 'Do Not Disturb' sign on the door all day is just too predictable."

Kate's face fell. "We have a 'Do Not Disturb' sign?"

"Enough!" David laughed, kissing her quickly and turning her away from him. "Go and see what is happening with the weather before you begin to scare me with your expectations."

As Kate marched towards the front door, listening to his boots scale the stairs three at a time, she found herself grinning, blessing the hotelier who first thought of the notice which kept the unwanted at bay. A movement from behind the Reception desk caught her eye, and she was still smiling as she looked straight at a familiar face.

"Kate? Hello!" the voice was loaded with surprise as its owner hurried out into the hallway, and here was Ailsa Macdonald, her blond hair in a bun and her eyes almost popping in her head.

"Hi Ailsa," Kate could not take her eyes off the bun, a feature which made her ex-classmate from Biology look about thirty. 'A bun would have been less drastic than an elf cut, right enough,' thought Kate as she pulled a stray strand of fringe from her face.

Ailsa snapped her fingers in sudden realisation. "Right! Shona phoned me last night with the unbelievable news, but I never guessed you would be staying here. You look great, by the way. Your hair's fantastic!"

"It was a lot shorter at first. It could do with another trim."

"Well," Ailsa hesitantly patted Kate's arm, awkwardly. Their relationship had never really progressed further than sharing a Bunsen burner. "Congratulations. I suppose, like they say, if you find the right one, you'll know ..."

"Oh, you definitely know, Ails. Never doubt that one," said Kate, aware of David's boots on the stairs behind her. "You want to meet him?"

Ailsa's eyes widened and her mouth opened slightly, confirming that Shona Syme had also conveyed, by means of the telephone, all the unusual aspects of her new husband. "Erm, I'm supposed to be -"

"Dave, this is Ailsa. We used to fight over equipment in Biology. Ailsa, this is David."

David handed Kate her outdoor clothing as he offered his hand to Ailsa with a smile. As Kate shoved her arms and head into her jumper, she could hear David asking how long she had worked there and her friend attempting to put a sentence together in spite of her awkwardness.

That would have been Kate herself a year ago, intimidated by a tall stranger showing an interest. Not now. Ailsa's face was pink by the time Kate had pulled on her second glove, and in spite of David's friendly chatter, she felt she should let the girl get back to work, where she could recover in peace.

"So, we're going for a walk. That breakfast was huge."

"Well," Ailsa almost squeaked in relief, "it was gorgeous out there just after eight, and I don't think it's snowed again."

"Great, because we're only here for one more night, so we need to make the most of every minute, right Dave?"

The implications in the statement proving too much for Ailsa, she turned from them, waving as she retreated to safety. "Take care," was all she could manage.

The air was sharp on their faces as they stepped out into the brilliant glare, but already the trees were dripping, and Kate pouted dramatically. David rubbed her lower lip back into a smile.

"Don't worry, Kit. I'm sure we'll get snowed in at some point in our lives."

"Oh, so much to look forward to," she laughed back, slipping her gloved hand into his bare palm. Just as quickly, she took it away, removed its woollen protection and wove her unclothed fingers into his.

"Skin to skin is much nicer," she explained, hunting through her expression drawer for her most innocent look. He saw right through it, however, and made sure she knew it with a glint of his eyes.

"Come on, Wilder."

By the time they had toured the grounds and negotiated the minor hairpins of the driveway, the road was a wet, black tarmac again. There was still no traffic on the Staffin road, and they put up a good pace, covering the ground by revisiting the small reception of the previous day in its entirety, followed by the tediously bumpy drive through the snow to where they had both wanted to be. However, as they wandered past a tiny lochan wrapped in miniature hills, with even the sheep regarding them with little interest, they had fallen into a contented silence. It was weird to be so quiet in the still air. Kate sneezed once, then, "Do you like lochs - lakes in your case - or the sea best?"

David scratched his chin where bristles were already appearing. "Well, I never really had much to do with the sea. I guess rivers are more my thing. I'd put money on your preference."

"It's that obvious? I can't help it. It's not just the sound, but the smell I love. We should see it again around the next corner."

The land was dropping away from the roadside, and they were once again blessed with a winter seascape that took Kate's breath from her. She ran from the edge of the road and stood down by the fence, her arms wide as if to gather all the sights and feelings nearer to where she could enjoy them more. She breathed in deeply, and as the cold air reached down into her lungs, it brought with it the taste of salt and the scent of seaweed. All she needed to complete her rapture was for David to put his arms around her waist; but when she looked back at him, he was standing a few feet away, his face showing more concern than glee. In an instant she was by his side.

"What is it?"

"Hey," he soothed, forgetting how quickly she could read his face. "Don't look so scared. I'm fine."

But there was no mistaking the subdued tone, and Kate felt a frown appear. He knew better than to try and hide things from her, so whatever had caused his sudden dip must be significant. She blinked once, but otherwise waited for him to speak. His eyes were clear, and he held her gaze, the smile slowly turning into something more resigned than happy. He raised his eyebrows in submission.

"Is Mum with us, Dave? You know I don't mind if she is."

His arms were around her instantly.

"And you know I'll always tell you if she is. So I swear to you that she's not. That's not the problem."

"Then what?"

David put his arm around her shoulder and walked her back to the fence as she hooked her arm around his waist, wishing that his coat was thin enough for her to feel the heat from his skin. "This," he said, quietly. "This place you love. I'm taking you away from it."

They both stared out at the scene. It was in Kate's power to put him at ease immediately, but the point he had raised was valid, and it deserved to have time spent on it. He knew what the island meant to her, she had talked of it in every letter she had sent him, and home was home. That feeling when you walked along a street or track which was so beyond familiar that you did not even acknowledge it. The features in your eye-line that rarely required attention because they never changed, even when they were all you wanted to see. It did not mean you did not appreciate them, it meant they were your best friends. Surely he knew this? Perhaps not. Maybe even now he wondered if she had doubts about leaving.

She raised her hand towards Staffin Bay, which was hidden around the next headland.

"There's a great-looking beach up ahead, especially on a blue sky day. Not as special as our little bay, mind. And if we ever do walk the Quiraing, you'll see shapes you'll never see again. I can show you lots of really special places, Dave. Thing is, it's only grass and rock and water if I'm there without you."

Kate left it at that, but her left hand gripped his waist. She felt him tense slightly, but still his eyes never left the lines of the land before him, less defined now as a snow cloud began to envelope the nearest hill, and Kate finally let go. Instead of retreating, however, she unzipped her coat, spread it on the grass and settled herself onto it, knees bent and her elbows resting on them. When she sensed David's intrigued expression, she took her time looking up at him.

"Well, you needn't think I'm moving till we've talked about this."

"Is that right, miss?"

"It is indeed right. Although I'd hate to catch pneumonia in the meantime, and we'll get some very odd looks from the postie if he hasn't already been past."

David, sighing, eased himself onto the half of her coat she had left for him and put his arm around her shoulder. She allowed him to pull her against him, but she didn't look at him until he spoke.

"You think you've got this all sorted, don't you honey? All worked out, neat and tidy."

Kate nodded, wide-eyed, grateful that his tone was softer than his actual words.

"I wonder if you'll ever let me point things out to you, things you're not necessarily going to agree with, things that worry me. God knows, I'm not smarter than you, Kit, but I've seen some things before, avoidable things. Do you understand what I'm saying?"

Kate tried to nod again but felt suddenly desolate and completely out of her depth; so much for assuming that she was invincible. She tried to wipe away a tear before it spilled onto her cheek, but failed. David used his thumb to dry the dampness from her icy skin.

She swallowed and sucked in her bottom lip before putting her hand on his knee and scratching at a non-existent blemish on the dark denim.

She had become used to saying her piece, denying everybody who stood in her way that this admonishment was suddenly devastating. She blew air out of her mouth and shook her head slowly.

"Sorry," her voice was a tiny, isolated noise.

"There's absolutely nothing to be sorry about. I am asking you to trust me; trust me like you did last night. Trust that I'm as much in the dark as you are when it comes to what we have, but I can try to steer us away from some potential problems. It's the only advantage I can think of that comes with my age."

Kate thought again of how many times those who truly loved her had tried to get her to see their point of view and how hardened against them she had let herself become. Lately, she seemed to disregard their opinions on the most unimportant of things, purely out of habit. It was the least fair she had ever treated anyone, and it caused one more tear to trickle down her cheek.

David kissed the tears away, but thankfully said nothing else.

"Well, okay," Kate smiled at last, trying to sniff up the last of her wobbles. "We can take advantage of your age. It's just that people question me so often. Do I know what I really want; do I know what I'm doing, what I'm giving up? I just didn't expect it to come from you, too. You're my ally. You're the one."

"Then, I'm sorry, too. I just want you to be happy. We've such a lot to face yet, and if you regretted anything down the line ..."

"Please believe me. I've no choice in this. There is nothing, nothing that will ever come close to the way I feel now. Don't take it away from me. I'll beg, if I need to."

"You won't need to. You're mine, I'm yours."

Kate breathed again, smiling at the sea, the face of the man she loved and then down at the ring on her finger. She had once worn a plastic square emerald on that finger, bought from the newsagents on a whim instead of her usual packet of crisps, and she had worn it until the band had split and even Sellotape could not prevent it from falling apart. Now the band was shinier and more solid, with no stone at all, and still felt a little alien as it gripped her skin. But she tingled when she looked at it and could not stop herself from kissing the side of David's neck. "I love you."

Within another few seconds, the air was filled with tiny droplets of water, not quite snow but more than mist, and both of them glanced southwards. Amid mild curses from Kate and much scrambling, they managed to get her wrapped into her coat and had reached the road just as the colours around them became duller. Heads down, they began the hike back to the hotel at a businesslike march. Not much was said, the sudden dampness cutting back on the need for chat, but Kate could not help laughing out loud at the sheep, who were huddled in a foursome, their backs to the road as if determined to snub the driving sleet. The sound of her giggling in the rising wind made David's heart thump harder, and he slowed his pace, pulling her back in line with him as he did so. She was still laughing as he held her face in one hand and tilted her chin upwards. He had time to only stroke her cheek, however, before she had glanced over his shoulder and stepped out into the middle of the road.

The scarlet postal van looked like it had been superimposed onto the black and white scene as Kate, jumping on the spot, waved it down. She leaned into the driver's window and then beckoned to David, grinning from ear to ear. As he followed her, raising his hand in gratitude to the man behind the wheel, Kate stood waiting by the passenger door. She beamed up at him.

"This way our hands will thaw out before we get back, which is good news, because after last night's practice session, I am now much faster at undoing buttons."

CHAPTER 28

Friday, 2nd December 1994

There was a spot, probably not even a quarter of the way up Ben Tianavaig, where a lone tree clung to the very edge of the escarpment and where you could view the crags and gullies of the east side in relative safety. Kate had always known this place as simply one of the many markers on the way to the top, but in the last year, had laid claim to it and labelled any other person found there a trespasser. It now belonged to Kate and David, and on this bitterly cold Friday afternoon, they were perched against the nearest crag, laughing at the wind. There had been no fresh snow since the previous weekend, but neither had it thawed; and at the current altitude, the ground remained blue-white in the low sunshine. It was literally breathtaking as the wind continually took their words and threw them across the Sound to Raasay.

"It's a lot easier to sit here in the summer," yelled Kate across the space between them.

"I bet," he shouted back, "but I wouldn't have missed it."

It was true; a person would rarely forget the sky reflected off the water and the mountains to the south and west tipped in gold. Even so, Kate had brought her camera. She moved the scarf from her lips, kissed David and then tried to get him to pose. As ever, this was easier said than done. For a good-looking man, he was surprisingly awkward when it came to committing his image to photograph. Amid the usual groans, which she claimed to be unable to hear, she finally got him to stand with his back to the distant Cuillins, allowing him to keep his arms folded as a sweetener. She could not help grinning at his reluctance, since he was recognisable only by his eyes and nose, the rest of him completely covered in waterproofs and wool.

He had seemed reasonably comfortable when Kenny had taken photos on their wedding day, but only a handful of those had been set up specifically, the rest having been taken unobtrusively across the reception dinner table. And in the last few days, when Kate had declared that everybody should have a worthy set of honeymoon photos, he had preferred to be the photographer rather than the subject. She had wondered at one point if he was embarrassed to be photographed with her, but since he was just as ill at ease when they were alone as he was when she asked passers-by to snap them together, she had dismissed this.

Beth had also reassured her with one sentence; 'all men hate getting their photograph taken, unless they're on the telly.' It was just one more piece of knowledge that a male-free childhood had deprived her of, but she was learning every day.

"Hey!" David cried, as she tried to shove the camera back into her pocket. "Hand it over!"

"But the film's nearly finished!"

"Nearly will do."

"Okay," she smiled, "but give me a second."

David watched as she pulled herself up to the first platform available on the crags, her gloves and boots moving in unison. Once, near the top, her right foot slipped beneath her and she found herself on her knees instead, dearly hoping that there was nobody on Raasay's shore catching her curses.

"Kate!"

"I'm fine!" she yelled and stood with only the sky behind her and brushed the slush from her knees and shins. She spread both her arms wide and grinned down at him. "This one's for you!"

Later, as the temperature dropped and their single-filed descent became more urgent, Kate watched the man in front of her and realised with amazement that she had never seen David in a summer light. She was married to a man that she had only ever seen during the winds and rains of autumn and the snow of winter.

Neither of them could speak again until they were within the heated confines of the cottage, so Kate allowed herself to think of David wandering around in a T-shirt or even chopping wood in only a pair of jeans and boots. There was absolutely nothing wrong with these images and, she reminded herself, nothing wrong with her picturing them. Just as she was about to reach out to tap him on the shoulder, she spotted Stuart's pickup below them, silently pulling itself onto the driveway. David must also have recognised both the vehicle and the implications behind it, because he turned back to her and pointed, his eyes alert. She shrugged in response, but instantly felt colder than she had done all afternoon.

When Kate had returned from Canada two months ago, Hazel had refused to enter into any discussion whatsoever on the subject of her little sister's life choices or David's part in them, and Kate had accepted this with little debate. Beth, with Kenny's help, had at least tried to be more understanding and eventually saw the situation for what it was; something she could try to feel positive about or something she could completely deny. Either way, Kate was going to marry David Wilder. Kate had talked it through with her whenever Hazel was out of the way, not just how she felt or what they had gone through the previous year, but also the legalities and how Neil, David and Rose were all working together to make it possible. There had been paperwork and blood-tests and lawyer's fees, but the three of them had gone through it because they had believed David and she deserved to be happy.

Beth by this stage had been philosophical enough. "Well, you don't have to get married, if it's going to prove that complicated. Just live together."

"But we want to be married," Kate had frowned. "It's okay for you. Kenny and you are a relatively normal couple. The world apparently sees us as ridiculous. I'm damaged and obsessed and he's out to take advantage. Well, the world needs to mind its own business and look after itself a bit better. It can start by watching us commit ourselves for life and then by leaving us alone."

David had arrived on Skye in the middle of November, all good news and impatience, and Hazel had promptly moved in with Stuart's family. It had proved both a burden and a relief for the rest of them until, two nights before the big day, Kenny and Stuart had taken David out for a drink, and they had ended up back at the farm. Kate still did not know the details and had no heart to ask, but the next evening when David had gone for a walk with Beth, Hazel had arrived at the cottage with a pair of white boots in her hand. She had lingered on the back doorstep for about twenty seconds in total and had spoken in a matter-of-fact manner.

"Thought these might go with your trousers, although I'll need them back. Stu's mum wishes you luck and hopes that the rain stays off." She had scratched her upper lip and looked around at the garden, before turning back. "Stuart and I will both be there. Try not to fluff your lines."

"Thanks."

That had been it. No reconciliation as such, but no condemnation, either; and now, after another seven days with only a minimal amount of contact, here was Stuart's truck arriving at the cottage, and the occupant was Hazel. She had made an effort, for whatever reason, and she was about to find the house empty. Kate could not bear this thought.

"Dave! Let me go first, I know this path, I can run!"

His eyes had creased. "It's nothing but ice!"

"Trust me!"

She had dodged past him before he was able to support his argument further and could only watch her steadily increasing speed as she picked her way efficiently over boulders and flattened bracken. She was jumping rather than running, but was certainly covering more ground than he was, the unfamiliar, half-buried path requiring all of his concentration. For a couple of seconds near the foot of the hill, Kate's head bobbed out of sight and then she was at the gate, safe. She turned to wave once before tearing off in the direction of the house.

Relieved, David slowed his own pace, and felt the weight of Kate's camera in his pocket. In spite of the constant wind which blasted his face, David found an area of flat ground which allowed him to assess the scenery on offer. She might have referred to it as grass and rock and water, but he knew how much it meant to her and, in the dying light, found a composition of bay, hill, house and sky that might well end up framed and cherished. It seemed an incredibly simple gesture in comparison to what Kate had given him, but he was prepared to bet that she would love it.

Before he tried to imagine what Hazel's visit might mean, David allowed himself to take one more still moment to think about his new wife. The term still astounded him, as he guessed it would astound many, many more people in the coming weeks; and twice now he had woken in the dreaded minutes before dawn and felt the weight of fear on his chest. Fear that he would be far too over-protective towards her. Fear that he would stifle her in his attempt to block out the world's reaction to their union. Apart from those closest to her, Kate had appeared unmoved by all of her acquaintances' wide-eyed responses, citing that they were about to leave them behind, anyway.

But at home, he could almost see himself standing in front of her, or steering her away, or speaking on her behalf, and he absolutely must not do this. He did not have to put her on show, but equally, he must not hide her away. She was far too much of an individual for him to repress.

Perhaps if he made himself think along these lines every day in life, if he opened his eyes to each new morning and thought 'let her shine', he might do her the justice she deserved. Somehow, Fiona, with all of her insecurities, had helped shape Kate into someone with drive and spirit, and he could not do anything to jeopardise this. He imagined that Kate's first sixteen years on earth had thrown very little poison at her, which had thankfully allowed her to survive the past two; and whoever had taken part in forming the person he now knew – family, teachers, islanders – deserved a commendation from God. She had built her own unique Kate on top of their foundations, where she did indeed shine. And she wanted him to be there with her.

By the time he had reached the gate, David was smiling, the memory of that morning's conversation making a welcome return. Kate, as always, had been awake before him, propped on her elbow and grinning when he opened his eyes.

"Sshh," she had whispered, touching his lips. "Listen."

Just above the noise of the shower running, David had heard the wind howling outside, but nothing else. When he had turned back to her in the navy light, his face puzzled, she had lain back on her pillow and stared at the ceiling.

"Listen to the wind, Dave. It's moaning its way around the house, and we're here, under the duvet. I love it when you know it's absolutely freezing out there and dark and miserable, and you're tucked up and cosy. What you have to do is lie still and imagine you're outside in it, and all of sudden you start to shiver from the inside out. Your whole body ends up quivering. Try it. Feels lovely."

After convincing her that he had indeed experienced her 'morning shivers', she had sighed and switched on the bedside lamp.

"Okay. Question," her voice had remained low and intriguing as she leaned her head against his shoulder, "and you have to say exactly what comes into your mind without delay. I'll know, mind, if you're trying to say what you think I want to hear."

"Nope, you've lost me already. It's too early -"

"Just this. Would you object to us not sleeping in your bedroom when we get home?"

"Tell me more."

"Well. Och, here goes. I don't mind Mum being anywhere in the house with us, but I think that maybe, if we're going to be honest about what might or might not feel ... strange, I don't think we should be in that room. This last week has been okay, because it's been temporary. But I would like somewhere of our own. Also, and probably this is the actual problem, Rose sleeps right underneath us. Do you get my drift?"

He had tried desperately hard not to grin at her and had somehow managed to show her an understanding smile instead, as she had searched his face for his answer.

"Good point. Points, in fact. Yeah, that's fair. Why don't we get home and you can choose which one we want. How's that?"

She had sighed contentedly but in the next second had sat upright, letting every inch of heat escape from the duvet.

"Oh, but Rose will think I'm coming in and taking over. Why wouldn't she? I would in her shoes."

"Hey Kit," he had pulled her back, settling her against his side. "Allies, remember? I think we can bring Rose around."

It had been enough to allow Kate to drop off to sleep against his shoulder and he had lain back and enjoyed the knowledge that she had nothing to worry about where Rose and the house were concerned. But there were still obstacles to clear, and some threatened his heart more than others.

The kitchen light was burning, and David could hear a conversation taking place in the sitting room as he rid himself of the outdoor layers. The discussion did not appear to be heated, just a little stilted and he hesitated, anxious not to halt negotiations in case they were at a critical stage.

He filled the kettle and hunted for mugs, flexing his dead fingers as he did so. When he re-closed the fridge door, Hazel was leaning against the doorjamb. She was cracking her knuckles so loudly that he found himself raising his eyebrows and gritting his teeth. She stopped immediately and instead rubbed her lip with her finger.

"Bet it was cold up there," she ventured.

"It was freezing. Would you like some tea?"

She nodded mutely, pulling out a chair. It appeared that they would be staying in the kitchen and that Kate would not be joining them. It was probably time. His heart stumbled slightly because Hazel looked peaky, worried and more childlike than at any other time on this visit. It was up to her to set the tone of the discussion, and so he concentrated on brewing tea.

"I'm not really sure what to say, Dad." Her voice had altered, the fast-paced, ramble having apparently been replaced by a quieter, more defeated relation.

He placed a mug in front of her face, but did not sit at the table.

"I can't believe she's leaving us for good."

"It's hard," he agreed, "when someone you're close to needs to go their own way."

"Are the pair of you really going to be able to do this?" she was staring at him over the rim of her mug. "I mean, actually go out there and be … ordinary?"

"Yes."

"You're brave, both of you. But what about Mum? How are you going to fit yourselves around her?" If Hazel had imagined that this would shock David, she had misjudged him badly.

"Neither of us has a problem with Fiona. She knew us both very well."

Hazel shook her head, unwilling to accept this and disappointed that he would try to use these words so flippantly. He picked up on this immediately and finally took a seat.

"I want to tell you something, Haze."

"Okay, I'll listen, but first, hear this. If this goes wrong for you both, who do I help? Kate will be lost and she'll need me, but that means I lose you for good. I don't want to be cut off from you again!"

David's throat had begun to ache. He swallowed before taking Hazel's hand. "It won't happen. I'll always be there, available, at the end of a phone, waiting for your next visit. I swear it to you, Hazel. You're part of me. You're what I gave to the world to enjoy, and it owes me for that. It can't keep us apart."

"Do you love her more than Mum?"

David had once imagined, in his more heartsick, bleak moments, that this question would be put to him by Kate herself, and he had tried to construct some kind of explanation which would not alienate her in any way. He knew that she would never ask it, because it was not what was important to her; but Hazel had almost as much right to an answer, and he had to consider his words carefully. He scratched his head and thought of Fiona.

"Your mom stood out from the crowd. Totally different to anybody around her, and she was interested in me. It was simple. We were both ready for life and amazed that we'd found each other. So when I think of her, even now, I remember that we were uncomplicated and happy, depending on each other to live. That's how I loved your mother. I loved her for being my partner at the beginning of my life."

Hazel's eyes were forlorn, but she did not shed a tear. Instead, she stared straight at her father and pursed her lips. "And what about Kate?"

"Kate is in the next room. It's not really fair –"

"Please explain it to me. Please."

David hesitated. Was it fair to do this, when Kate herself had not heard this account of his feelings? But his daughter was sitting across the table from him, asking something of him, and it would be the last time in God knew how long that he would be in such a position.

"With Kate, it's anything but simple. She began as a puzzle, but then she was a puzzle with Neil's face, and I wanted to make sure she made it through the bad times, for your Mom and Neil, as well as for the pair of you." He paused, trawling back through the denser of his thoughts. "It was as if one day our roles just swapped. She was the one looking out for me, asking me questions and dragging a personality out of me. She was helping me, and then she was telling me how she felt and what she wanted. But she knew you were hurting, and she let me do what I needed to do. So, when I think of Kate, it's not a clear picture, it's a jumble of the strongest feelings I've ever had mixed up with what she said and how she handled this last year. I love her totally."

Hazel was looking around the room for inspiration, but when nothing came to her aid, she cupped her chin in her hands and sighed. David could not afford to let the opportunity pass them by, however, not when there was so little animosity evident, and so he touched her hand.

"Somebody we both love has made me very happy. If you can take that at face value someday, then you might feel better. I hope you can."

"I hope so too," she frowned, gently moving her hand away. "But I'm not there yet. Do you hate me for that?"

David shook his head and could not hold her gaze. "You know," he spoke as steadily as he could manage, "two years ago I had nothing inside me. Not even the ability to react, really. Meeting up with you again, Hazel, meant more than just the chance to share in your world. It meant I started to feel again. You won't know what I mean, because I doubt you've ever been numbed by life."

"Mum dying was awful," she offered, but she was not stupid. Hazel knew that he was talking about years of lonely, grieving inactivity, rather than the intense raw shock that she and Kate had experienced.

"Well, you need to know that I'll never hate you," stated David. "It's a physical impossibility for me. All I can wish for is that you come to understand me sooner rather than later. But if it has to be later, Hazel, I'll still wait for it to happen."

Hazel inhaled deeply, and in that moment David longed for the days when she had made it her enthusiastic business to try and sort his life, when her flow of words had ended in some outlandish statement regarding his prospects and lack of cooperation. Her advice and opinions had rarely been realistic, but they had always been unpredictable and full of good intention. It seemed an age since she had looked at him with any real connection, and it made the misery he had shouldered in the last few months feel more pointless than ever. But he should be thankful; she was here and they were not cutting each other with their words. He wondered if she had made a similar sort of peace with her sister.

"Do you know why I married Kate?"

Instantly Hazel was massaging her hot brow, staring straight at the table in front of her. Her right foot began to shuffle from side to side, as if it was preparing itself to flee the room, but her father was not going to give her any relief until she responded to his question.

She shrugged her shoulders.

"I married her because she proved something to me. She proved that she loved you as much as I did, and I knew it made her matchless. She took a back seat so you would feel better, even though it hurt her, and that's when the doubts left me. She's worth anything that comes our way. When you eventually get used to us, Haze, you'll start to remember who and what she is."

It would have been very easy for David to end on this note and leave his daughter alone to digest his words, but he was not prepared to do it. The hours he had left in this country were too few for him to remove himself from her company, and instead, he sipped his tea and sat back in his chair. Hazel viewed him across the table, her eyes returning to his after each sweep of the room and each crack of her knuckles. She appeared unable to form her thoughts into words, and it was one more needle of sorrow piercing his skin; he had taken the sparkle from her, and he feared it would only return when he had gone. He felt his eyes sting a little.

"Are you and Kate anywhere near okay?" he asked.

Hazel stood and poured her tepid tea into the sink. "She has the same face as she's always had, and she's still trying to have the last word on everything; but since everything else about her has changed, I've no idea if we're okay or not."

CHAPTER 29

Monday, 5th December 1994

It was dusk by the time David had negotiated the frozen driveway and pulled up at the back door of The Edge. In spite of the enchanting blue twilight and clear sky, Kate was a little concerned. The windows were black against the clapboard walls, no light showing on the ground floor, and even the thin trail of smoke from the chimney did not combat the chilly atmosphere. Yet David was whistling and less tired than he had seemed for the whole journey, completely unaffected by the empty building. He practically jumped from the vehicle and was opening her door before she had the chance to mention her unease.

"Got a surprise for you, Kit," he grinned, reaching for her hand.

"Is that the reason you've been trying to whistle for the last two miles, because you've got something up your sleeve? I still don't know what the tune was."

"Well, in my head it was 'Scotland the Brave'," he smiled, unlocking the door. "Now, before we go in, just please tell me you weren't in love with the kitchen wallpaper."

Kate stepped across the threshold and dropped her coat in amazement. Gone were the dark units, the two ceiling pendants with red shades and the famous wallpaper which felt the need to show the same bowl of cherries every half a metre. The replacements were almost blinding her by their sheer novelty and number, and as she moved further into the room, she could feel David's silent grin follow her progress.

"Andie," she breathed.

"Andie, indeed, although I did choose the grey to go with the blue. Do you like it?"

"I've never seen a kitchen like this," she nodded. "No formica anywhere! And it's so huge. Oh, Dave, Rose needs to put her good plates on the dresser. It would be perfect for them."

Kate felt his arms go around her waist, and she turned to face him, mirroring his grin. "I thought that maybe you could choose what should go there. It's Neil's handiwork, so you get to deck it out."

"Thank you," she kissed him, then frowned. "Where do you suppose she is?"

"Rose? I've got a good idea. I'm going to check on the fire, and then we'll go find her. You've got about twenty seconds to get layered up, gloves, hat, the lot."

"We're going out again?"

"We are, but we're walking."

《●》《●》《●》

David's long stride was more confident than Kate's as they walked back up the driveway through the rutted slush. He had the most massive torch she had ever seen in one hand - 'it's like a spotlight' - and her hand in the other, and she found herself out of breath within twenty metres. In spite of this, the night was not bitter, just a little tingly to the fingers and toes, and Kate was happy not to speak, but to watch the trees in the beam of light. After five minutes or so of bumping along beside David, he suddenly took a path to the right; and in front of them, winking through the branches, she could make out a cluster of lights.

"Shortcut to Peter's Lane," David stated through the wool of his scarf.

"Right."

On arrival, Kate noticed that the five buildings formed a cul-de-sac, each with short lamps illuminating their individual gardens. Two of the chalets were dark, but the remainder already had an air of community about them, with parked cars, and potted outdoor plants; one had erected a Christmas tree on the porch, and as they marched towards the central chalet, the lights were suddenly switched on. Kate squeezed David's hand, delighted, and then there was Rose ahead of them, standing in the doorway of Number Three. She was rubbing her hands.

"You're here!" Rose shouted beckoning them wildly. "Come in, come in. I saw the truck lights, so I've been waiting."

Kate watched as David unwrapped his face and bent to kiss his mother's offered cheek before she began to take in her surroundings. Her eyes were even wider than when she had first glimpsed The Edge's pristine kitchen, but she managed to hug Rose before she started to remove her hat and gloves and tour the room. There, on the shelves above the worktop, were Rose's good plates for all to see. Kate could feel her face flushing in the quiet room.

"What's going on?" she asked both of them, as she pulled her coat from her back.

"Rose?" David offered.

"Well now," began his mother, "let's go through to the real heat. My hands are frozen."

The sitting room carried an aroma of burnt wood with an undercurrent of new pine and paint. Behind the wood-burner was a chimney breast consisting of panels of circular cross-sections of wood strapped to the pine wall, which ran from floor to ceiling and which concealed the cast iron flue. The two exterior walls were oiled to protect the pine, but the remainder were painted pale yellow, and it was so very bright in comparison to the sitting room which Rose had inhabited for most of her life. The curtains, window cushion and even the lampshades matched, and Kate was warmed that Andie had obviously been consulted on so much of the interior; there had barely been one item at The Edge which had coordinated.

In spite of her confusion, Kate asked no further questions and seated herself on the familiar brown sofa and looked around, pleased that Rose had positioned her family photographs on the walls for maximum effect. Rose herself sat in Pete's old kitchen chair, which had been positioned at a comfortable distance from the raging heat of the burner, and which now wore its more contemporary throw.

David sat beside Kate and put his arm along her shoulder. Automatically, she fitted herself under his arm. Rose did not even blink.

"I am so in love with this house," Rose began. "You can feel the heat in every part of the room! And only one flight of stairs. It's like being on permanent vacation. What do you think, Kate?"

"I think it's beautiful. I'm a bit lost for words actually, but," she bit her lip, "please tell me this wasn't down to me. To us."

Rose sat back in the chair and laughed heartily. "Oh, Kate. Davey said exactly the same. I think you two will fit together nicely. No, honey, I'll tell you exactly why I wanted this house. It's cosy and comfortable, and I wanted to be alone with Pete again after all this time. I potter about a few small rooms, pleasing myself and chatting with the neighbours. I'm having a ball. Selfish, maybe, but it's so enjoyable, I can forgive myself."

"Nothing selfish there, Rose," the statement came from David, and Kate found herself agreeing immediately.

"But," Rose continued, "If I'm allowed to say so, I think it will suit everybody, not just me." In the amiable moments of silence that followed, each of them envisaged their own version of what this would mean, and eventually Rose laughed out loud once more. "Exactly. Now, Dave, give me a hand with the coffee. Kate, take yourself off and explore the rest of the kingdom. Queendom. Queendom? I would like to hear your opinion on the bathroom. I'm wondering if maybe I went too far."

The stairs to the second floor began in the far corner of the sitting room, turning at a ninety degree angle after four pine steps, and as Kate placed her foot on the first of these, she realised that she was trembling. David and Rose had retreated into the kitchen, completely unaware of her utter shock at this state of affairs, and she was a little unnerved herself by her reaction. It was, as Rose had pointed out, to everybody's advantage. However, whereas Rose and David had planned this out together and probably explored every potential eventuality connected with it, she was being presented with it here, tonight, and it had caused her hands to shake. She forced her legs up all twelve stairs, bypassing pictures which had hung in another house for an eternity, and was presented with four doors; two bedrooms, one laundry cupboard and finally the large bathroom at the end of the carpeted corridor.

"Mercy," was Kate's first reaction as she pulled the cord for the light switch and then she was laughing. The turquoise walls were bright, but the colour was not the most remarkable aspect of the room. With just the white bathroom suite, the room would have qualified as spacious, but somebody had installed shelving on two of the walls, probably for toiletries, trinkets etc, and Rose had chosen a better use for them. On every inch of those shelves, on top of the mirrored cabinet and on the majority of the floor space, were potted plants. There were spider plants and various types of ivy trailing their foliage down the walls, and three ornamental ferns and two yuccas on the floor, all housed in navy ceramic pots. There were even three cacti on top of the cistern. It looked fresh and alive at that moment, although Kate guessed that a steamy bath would make the place feel like a rainforest. She smiled as she pictured Rose touring the garden centre, unable to stop herself filling her trolley. Perhaps it had been a long time since she had done anything quite so carefree, buying goods simply because she wanted them.

As Kate wandered back along the corridor, she paused by an oak bookcase, and on its polished surface found a photo of Neil and Andie, standing arm and arm outside Andie's shop. There was a banner across the doorway which read 'Grand Opening', and she found herself grinning; of course, there had to be a good reason her father was in a jacket and tie. He was looking down at his partner while she waved at the camera, and Kate was immediately warm inside. These special people were her family, and she was delighted to have that link. Staring at their now familiar faces, she could hear David and Rose's voices and marvelled that from now on, she would be the only person in her everyday life who would speak in a Scottish tongue. If she wanted to speak Gaelic, she would have to do it over the phone, and even that would have to be with Beth, as Hazel and she rarely used it with each other. She must make a conscious effort with this. And there would be no end of a carry on if, somewhere down the line, she were to sit in Nicolson's coffee shop sporting a Canadian accent.

At the top of the stairs, Kate positioned herself on the spongy carpet and laid her head against the wall, the shaking at last subsiding. Just a few moments, sitting here in comfort and thinking no thoughts would put her right. 'Have you ever tried to think of no thoughts' she thought and then suppressed the laughter bubbling inside her. So, maybe she would close her eyes for a second and think of how her solitary existence was no longer necessary. With David, it had been an intense three weeks of excitement, organisation and unbelievable exposure; and even she, who had been so adamant that they would work, had been surprised that there had been no real issues between them. She had opened up to him instantly, because he was her ally. Now, her real task was to open up to other people who were important, and Kate screwed her eyes tighter, unsure if she had the ability.

As she placed her fingertips on the carpet and felt the brand new woollen fibres scratch her, Kate could smell White Musk on the air, and instantly she froze, even her breath held tight by hope.

"Kate, my love," the words were no more than a whisper in the atmosphere, but they were like manna to the starving. "I'm so proud of you. So, so proud."

Kate felt herself loosening, her facial muscles relaxing. "Thanks, Mum," she murmured, finally letting her breath go. It was Fiona's first communication in over two months, and it was this which proved to her more than anything that she was facing another crisis of confidence. "How do I do this properly?"

"With help. Let them all help."

"You don't think I can do it on my own?" the soft words were accompanied by one tear.

"I'm saying you don't have to. I love you."

"Love you, Mum."

Kate's eyes remained closed, her heart breaking at the incredible briefness of the visit. She wanted to see her mother, to touch her and to hug her. Yet none of these things were possible, and opening her eyes was a further testament to it. But there was time enough to accept this fully, she did not have to do it right this second. Then Kate felt a gentle hand on her shoulder, and her eyelids slowly parted. David's face was close to hers.

"Tears, Kit?" his voice was a quiet question as he touched her cheek.

Kate put her arms around his neck. "Just one tear," she snuggled her face against his throat. "I'm really, really tired, that's all. I think coffee is what is needed."

He smiled at her attempt at reassurance and helped her to her feet. Coffee was a short-term solution to a short-term problem, and they would deal with the next one when it came along. After all, long-term situations were just a bunch of short-termers, as long as you kept a tight rein on your imagination. Rose was seated next to the coffee table, which was groaning with sandwiches and biscuits, mug already in hand.

"Well?" she eyed Kate. "Too much?"

"It looks quite," Kate paused, then "tropical. But don't plants remove oxygen, or do they provide it? Biology and I were never great pals, but you'll either be full of energy after your bath or a bit breathless!"

"Guess I'll find out soon enough," chuckled Rose. "Now, I'm sorry, but I need to hear all about this wedding."

In spite of the coffee, within half an hour of chat Kate had dozed off against David's shoulder. When he suggested to Rose that they make a move, his mother stayed him with her hand.

"One more minute," she spoke quietly, studying the pair on the sofa in front of her. David's hand was linked with Kate's, no space visible between them whatsoever, and as he raised his eyebrows in enquiry, Rose shook her head in wonder at his expression.

"What?"

"You look so different, Davey boy," her voice was lower than ever, and he had to watch her mouth as she spoke to catch her words. "Whatever happens, try to stay as strong as you are now. Nobody deserves happiness more than you do."

"Well," David was hesitant. In all of their years of cohabitation, David had rarely spoken to this woman about his feelings, and it made the whole evening a little bit more surreal that she assumed he would do so now. "All I can hope for is that anybody who knows me will eventually see us as ordinary. If they can't, then so be it. She's mine and she's worth it."

Rose nodded, and then smiled widely.

"Neil and Andie are coming over on Friday night. Don't worry, they're staying here. My first visitors. I daresay I'll have to fight Dougal for Pete's chair. That okay with you?"

"I was going to suggest Kate and I go up there, but that's fine. It'll be a nice end to our first week of normality."

By the time Kate had stopped apologising for falling asleep and they had layered themselves against the December night, there were tiny flickers of snow visible in the air, and this time Kate matched David's pace back through the woods with ease. She stopped once to re-tie her bootlace, and as he moved slowly ahead of her, he was smacked on the back of the head by a ball of slush and ice. Turning his torch on Kate, David found her standing with both hands over her mouth, eyes wide.

"Oh, God," she snorted, "I never hit my target, I swear it. Ask Hazel the archer, I am completely rubbish at aiming. I thought it would just fly past your ear, honest!"

David could feel a couple of thin trails of ice begin their descent down his spine. Time seemed to stand still in the silent dark, until Kate sensed exactly what he had in mind, and in the next second she had somehow dodged past him, and they were both tearing back up the driveway, the slippery road not hindering their progress in any way. The torchlight was ineffective, its beam merely flicking through the trees to either side of David as he ran, so Kate concentrated on the porch light ahead of her and had managed to scale the steps before he caught her. By then, she could do nothing but laugh and breathe. Within moments she was in his arms, the momentum of their run pinning them against the front of the house.

"What was that in aid of, Mrs Wilder?" he cried, his shallow breath thawing the frost on her fringe, "And more to the point. How did you think you were going to get away with it?"

"I should never have admitted it was a fluke, should I?" laughed Kate, trying to see his eyes beneath the wool of his hat. "You might have been more impressed and less offended. Anyway, you should know that just because I get to wear this ring and call you my husband, doesn't mean I'm ever going to stop trying to hit you with a snowball. Oh, and take that as a compliment. It means you're the One."

David rolled his eyes and took off his gloves. "Okay, then, here's the thing. Just because you get to wear that ring and I get to call you my wife, doesn't mean I'm ever going to stop chasing you and trying to get my own back. Like this, maybe?"

Kate watched, a confused smile never leaving her face, as he placed his left hand onto the freezing door handle for a couple of seconds, then in one quick movement had unzipped her coat and had found the bare skin just above the waist of her jeans. She shrieked in surprise as at the iciness of his fingers, but in the next second he was kissing her, and his hand seemed to be in its proper place. Within a second of responding to him, however, he had stopped, reached for his discarded gloves and was pulling her towards the back door.

She squeezed his hand. "Okay, it's a deal."

Kate stood in the middle of the kitchen and did a complete rotation, seeing the space in a different light to before. This was no longer Rose's kitchen, this area belonged to David and her, and she began to wonder what the cupboards actually contained and indeed whether there was any furniture left elsewhere. She made a 'hope-I-don't-let-this-house-down' face at him, and then gasped, "Here, Dave! Does the no boots in the house rule still apply?"

"S'up to you, boss."

She thought about it for a second then nodded. "It's a fair enough rule. Let's stick with it."

As she sat at the table and bent to untie her boots, a wave of fatigue almost drowned her, and she grabbed the table edge, determined not to faint for a second time in her life. She could hear David bringing in the rest of their luggage but could do nothing but lay her head on the table and pretend to hunt for her laces with her fingers. Even that was too tiring, and eventually she simply let her arms swing at her sides and her eyes close. The next movement she was aware of was a tugging at her feet and there was David, rolling his eyes at her and helping her out of her chair.

"Can't I sleep under the table?" Kate slurred. "Too many stairs."

"No you can't," he replied, but when her boots and socks had been removed, he hoisted her onto his back. After her initial surprise, Kate leaned her face against his neck and sighed contentedly.

"You need to eat more," David stated as they reached the first floor. "You weigh nothing."

"You mean I'm not perfect? Thought you said I was perfect."

"Who am I kidding? You're perfect."

Kate managed to hold her head upright as they crossed the doorway of Neil's old room, where his bed had been made up with fresh linen and where at last both windows had curtains.

"It's only temporary, but Rose reckoned it was the safest place to put us until we know where we're going."

"Rose is great," yawned Kate as she slid to the floor, eyeing the soft duvet and wanting nothing more than to fall face first onto it. She shook herself instead. "I can't remember where the toothbrushes are."

As David went to retrieve the luggage, Kate hauled off her coat and hung it on the back of the door. In the harsh overhead light, she reacquainted herself with the room simply to keep herself awake. The bed was still missing a headboard, and the wallpaper remained the pale blue of a young boy's bedroom, but it felt as if it had been recently swept and dusted. On the chest of drawers, which was a pitifully ordinary piece of furniture compared to Neil's creations, the stereo, old albums and hairbrush set remained. Kate frowned. On her previous visit, there had been a beautifully carved set of bookends, and now there was no sign of them. They had, in fact, been the only interesting item in the whole room, and they were most definitely absent.

"Here you go," said David, handing over the smallest case. "I'm going to lock up and bank the fire, then I'll be straight back. What's up?"

"I can't see Neil's bookends anywhere. Has he got them at his house now?"

Kate saw the light of understanding dawn, and then David grinning as he retreated to the door. "Actually, they belong to me. He made them for me a long time ago, so don't worry, they're safe. Two minutes."

It was more like six minutes by the time he walked back through the door, and Kate had somehow forced herself to clean her teeth and find a concoction of nightwear which was more practical for the icy bed than her usual T-shirt. She sat up in bed, her arms folded across an inherited 'Portree High School Archery Club' sweatshirt, rubbing her feet together in an effort to create heat. Before David could comment, she held out her arms and laughed. "Well, looks like the honeymoon is officially over, my man. I am wearing three layers."

"Right," acknowledged David, pulling jumper and shirt over his head in one movement, leaving only his T-shirt on his back. "But don't you realise that the more clothes you wear, the less your body heat makes contact with the duvet? It renders it practically useless."

"Hah! That's a man's line if ever I heard one," Kate smiled as he went to clean his teeth. Still, it made a sort of sense, and by the time David had returned she had not only taken off the sweatshirt and jogging bottoms, but was rolled up in a ball, asleep.

As David eased himself under the duvet, he was reminded of one of the more basic joys of sharing your life and bed with another; the extreme comfort of finding that space already warmed by the person you needed the most. He lay for a moment, hands behind his head, allowing relief to wash over him; relief that they were home at last.

The journey had been long and demanding, more mentally so than physically. Farewells under tense, emotional conditions, hours of sitting together on the plane, trying to marry together what they had left behind and what they were heading into in the most positive way, and yet always returning to how they felt about each other. No wonder she was out of it. He thought briefly of finding her sitting on the stairs at Rose's house, and what that tear might have meant; but then he thought of the snowball and her hysterical laughter after the chase. Short-termers, he reminded himself, and listened to Kate's steady, contented breathing instead.

CHAPTER 30

Tuesday, 6th December 1994

The sitting room did not look sparse, even though the sofa had disappeared along with the coffee table, an occasional table and most of the wall of photographs. Kate stood in the doorway, cinder bucket in one hand and a stash of papers in the other, taking it all in. The countless glass paperweights had also been removed from the perimeter shelf, which actually was a blessing in Kate's book; but the rug remained, and she smiled at the fireside chairs facing each other. One of those chairs was now officially hers.

She had been gently shaken awake just after 7 a.m. by David turning on the bedside lamp. He was fully dressed, and Kate could not sort out the images in her head; David, woollen hat, Neil's room, floral duvet cover.

"Honey, I have to get to the yard. Are you awake yet?"

"Mm-mm."

"I didn't plan to go in today, but it almost had to happen after three weeks away. Anyway, its early, you sleep all day if you want to. Otherwise, call Rose or me at any time. You got that? Numbers are by the phone."

Her eyes unstuck at last, Kate had sat up and put her arms around his head, almost suffocating him. She had pulled his hat off, kissed his hair and mouth, then replaced the hat and slid down the bed.

"You owe me so many kisses I can't even think of the number," she informed him, her eyes closing as she spoke.

"Okay," he agreed. "Don't be alone today. Go see Rose. I'll be back as soon as I can."

Kate had flapped him away. "See you then, then."

It was 11.45 a.m., the house warmed by the central heating alone, and Kate was ready for action. Waking for the second time, she had not wasted one sigh on the depressingly empty space beside her, for the simple reason that she would see David again that day and the day after that, and then again the next day. This was a luxury to her mind, and, besides, the house was awaiting her inspection.

She showered, ate, set the fire and then carried out a recce of the rooms, listing their pros and cons. Maybe by then Dave would be home, and if not, she would walk over to Rose's house and show her every honeymoon photo she had developed.

The ash in the fireplace seemed to be finer than she was used to, and Kate wondered if it was due to their habit of burning logs only. On Skye, Beth insisted on using as much coal as possible, adamant that it heated the water better, but it was a devil to clean out. When the shovelling, sweeping and constructing of paper and kindling had been carried out to her own satisfaction, Kate sat back on her heels, knowing her limitations. The rest was up to David.

Her hands washed, Kate went to the sitting room with a duster, aware of what disturbed ashes did to a mantelpiece and its surroundings. By the window seat, she found a brand new three-deck music system. It looked complicated and still had a thin plastic film over some of the buttons, but it was plugged in, its standby light a steadily flashing blue. Kate picked up a stack of nearby tapes.

"Oh!" squealed Kate, "I have missed you!"

She held in her hand a Runrig tape, the precious item she had loaned to David over a year ago and had never replaced. Buying a replacement would have been as good as losing faith in the pair of them, and instead, she had sung the memorised songs in her head whenever it had been necessary. Now she could listen to the superior original version, and she could play it as loudly as she liked.

It made the remainder of the dusting, the rearranging of furniture and the removing of all the randomly spaced pictures infinitely more enjoyable. She stacked these pictures by the doorway, to be rearranged and re-hung later, and wandered through to the dining room. This room appeared less disturbed, the large mahogany dining table and chairs still in situ, with only Rose's precious china cabinet missing, and Kate reckoned it would be one of the last places they would touch. As she stood on the first stair, the phone began to ring.

By the time she had sprinted through to the sitting room, turned down the music and skidded back into the hall in her socks, there had been three long rings. "Hello?"

There was a slight hesitation, then, "Who am I'm speaking to?"

Kate gaped at the phone, not recognising the voice and suddenly unprepared to speak to anyone but family. She cleared her throat.

"This is Kate Wilder. Can I help you?"

"Kate, you say? I was looking for a Mrs D. Wilder. I have a trunk ready for collection at her convenience."

Kate let our her breath, annoyed with herself for being so easily unnerved. A year of answering the phone at Elspeth's Salon should have made her more than comfortable with the piece of equipment, but she still hated it.

"Well, that's me. Where do I, I mean how do I collect it exactly? Hang on, I'll get a pen."

As she wrote down the details, she tried to sound knowledgeable concerning the directions and prayed that David knew exactly where to go. The man ended the call on a friendlier tone, having established her origins before hanging up, and Kate let out a relieved sigh.

When she was nervous, Kate tended to provide too much detail. She replaced the receiver, amazed yet thankful that she had not blurted out her age or lineage to a being that had no need to know. She tidied up and rewrote her notes while the conversation was still in her head and then phoned David. He was out.

Kate made tea and took it up to the first floor. She was about to enter Rose's abandoned room when the phone began to summon her once more. She answered on the fourth ring.

"Kate. You're awake, great. I wasn't sure if you were busy, but if you're up for it, my scones will be out of the oven and cooled by about two o'clock. What do you say?"

"I'll be there, Rose. I'm going to have a look upstairs, but by then I'll be ready to eat about seven of them."

Rose's old room was bleak. The curtains hung limply against the wall, and every piece of furniture was gone. And yet it was a great size, with a view of the front driveway and, unusual for The Edge, a fitted carpet. It was exactly the same size and composition of David's room above and so technically might suit them very well. With new curtains it was definitely a possibility. However, when Kate climbed the final flight up to David's office, her face broke into a wide grin. She could hear Hazel's initial reaction to the space in her head at that very minute – 'Oh, wow. Now I'd give my right arm to have this as a bedroom' – and instantly began to plan.

Not only did the office have a shower room and toilet built into the back corner, it also had a fireplace hidden behind a table and double aspect windows. With a little imaginative storage, they could swap over David's bedroom and office and create a spectacular space with the best of views. All she needed now was his cooperation and intended to have the rooms mapped out in her head before spilling her ideas.

She was on the point of crossing the threshold when the phone downstairs rang for the third time.

Kate refused to hurry down the two flights, preferring instead to curse mildly at the continual imposition on her time.

"Hello," this time the word was a guarded statement.

"You're back, Kate. Thank God."

"Neil! Hello. Yes, we got back -"

"Kate," his voice was distant and dull, "I need your help."

As Kate began to listen to the words being spoken, Rose was settling into the window seat of Number Three, enjoying the grand aspect of her particular house. They were two buildings to either side of her, all four of them slightly different in design, but none of them with her view of the driveway, and she loved the feeling of sitting in court amongst her subjects.

As she nursed her mug of beef soup, she watched the cat from next door toying with a low branch. Every few seconds, its ginger paw pulled the frond of needles to the ground then let it go, for some reason enjoying the regular shower of powdery snow it brought down upon itself. Maybe she should get a cat.

Even when her neighbours were out at work, Rose still felt surrounded and comforted by the presence of their garden furniture and curtained windows. She had never known so much natural light and space, and surprisingly it did not make her feel exposed or vulnerable, but rather appreciated. How strange and exciting to be here at the dawning of a brand new neighbourhood, amongst people who seemed determined to enjoy their beautiful if sheltered surroundings. The Morgans in Number One had already begun to construct a little play park in their backyard, the remaining two chalets were being sought by more than a dozen prospective buyers, and only a few minutes away lived a man and his new wife whom she hoped to watch grow and prosper.

Rose glanced at her watch. Ten more minutes and she would put the scones in the oven, maybe offer some to Jessie Morgan who had three children under five and who was intrigued and desperate to meet Kate. Rose remembered the conversation of the previous week word for word.

"Hey Rose, Bill says David missed the game on Saturday. Is he ill?"

"No, he's not ill. David is actually in Scotland, and, hold onto your hat, the next time you see him, he'll be a married man."

"What? Oh my God! David? How wonderful. Oh, tell me everything. Bill is going to need many more details."

"Okay. Well, here it is then. Her name's Kate and she's quite lovely. She's also a lot younger than Dave, but they're really ... together. I hope you'll see her for what she is."

"Goodness, Rose, you're painting a fascinating picture! And David! Bill won't believe it."

Rose remained convinced that few people would, but that would be only one of the trials in the days ahead, and now she stood, thinking instead of how positive the last two months had been for all of them. Just as she was retreating from the window, she caught a flash of bright red emerging from the rear of Number Five.

The coat belonged to Kate, and her figure was very definitely running towards her, head down against the wind. By the time she had opened the front door, Kate was on the porch, breathless and bent over. There were dusty streaks on her pained face and she held her side, trying to ease her breathing. Rose reached for her shoulders, at which point Kate burst into fresh tears, and then the chill really took hold of Rose. Kate's tears seemed to be laced with terror, her broken features a testament to this.

"What's happened?" Rose knew better than to assume this was a minor glitch in Kate's day; the girl rarely cried, which made the situation even more frightening for both of them. Kate caught her own breath and spoke.

"Andie's in hospital."

"Where and how bad is it?" Rose was reaching for her coat as she spoke, but Kate stepped over the doorway and closed the door behind them.

"I need to tell you what's going on before we do anything. Neil asked me to."

"Oh no. Neil," groaned Rose. "How did he sound?"

"Quiet. Blank, sort of. Here, I need to sit down."

«•»«•»«•»

David brought the SUV to a halt just inside the gateposts and pulled on his gloves before jumping into the slush of the drive. Against the background of snow, the posts' reddish-brown tinge emphasised their carvings, and they remained impressive in spite of the excavating and repositioning which had taken place earlier in the year. The constant traffic of timber trucks, contractors' vehicles and finally removal vans had been the reason behind their relocation, but it still felt strange to see them situated differently. David was intent on checking for evidence of untoward movement. They had taken a full year and a half of Neil's time and inspiration to complete and were as much part of this estate as the woodland and even the house itself.

As he leaned his entire body weight against each post in turn, he wondered what his wife's morning had consisted of. In the last three weeks she had barely been out of his sight, but this morning's urgent task of deciding on the fate of the timber yard's oldest but most valued forwarder had meant time away from her. Not just that, but it had meant solitary time for her, when she may begin to wonder at the path her life had taken. She had berated him in the past for doubting her, but now, alone in a big shell of a home, surrounded only by trees and ice, she might begin to dwell on what she had left behind.

He and his foreman Rob had stood about beside the dejected hulk of a machine, kicking stones and scratching heads, debating whether or not it might even qualify as an exhibit at the nearby Forest Museum. Once they had regretfully agreed that retirement was its only option, they had moved onto the more mundane and unremarkable aspects of his elected absence, until they were both outside the log cabin which had been the yard's office for as long as David had been alive. When his boss had asked him to give him a further minute of his time, Rob had followed David inside, unconcerned.

"I just wanted to let you know how much I appreciate you holding the fort, Rob. I mean, in the last year or so I know you've shouldered more than your fair share. Even when I've been here physically, well, you know what it's been like. Thanks for helping. Sincerely, thanks."

"Heavens, Dave, you've no need to thank me. You were in the middle of a crisis, we all knew that. And here we are, still alive, still solvent!"

Handing Rob a mug of coffee, David had indicated that he should sit, before he had begun to try to explain how his life had altered in the most dramatic of ways. A handful of the crew had met Kate on her initial trip to the country, each of them understanding the situation without acknowledging it and most viewing it only in terms of David's integrity; she had been incidental to the visit, someone who had been brought along for her sister's sake. Hazel had been their focus, his sparky daughter whom some of them remembered and who had taken over every conversation. Now Kate was about to become more central to their lives, and David had needed to pass on this information. It had been unexpectedly easy to say the words, less so to wait in the silence for Rob's reaction. The man had sat motionless for about three seconds, before his coffee mug had slowly moved from his lips back to the desk.

"You're married. To Kate," Rob had stated. "You went across to Skye to get married."

"I did, Rob. I got married to someone who is extraordinary and wants nothing else than to be with me. Tell me what you think and what other people will think. It will help me in the days to come."

"Did you just go there and ask her and that was it? Is she here with you now?

"No and yes. I knew how she felt before she left last year. To say I was surprised would be a pitifully simple way of putting it, but it was also so easy to start to think about everything I could have, and she is … remarkable. To me. The time we spent apart was not a good time." David had paused, trying to be concise with the man who had never in all their years as colleagues asked him how his personal life was faring. "I didn't want to be alone anymore, and she waited until I'd realised this. That's the top and bottom of it, and now I have to protect her from what's coming."

Rob had sat forward in his chair, rubbing his forehead.

"And what do you think is coming, Dave?"

"Judgement, I suppose. Ridicule, probably, at least until the shock wears off. I just don't want Kate hurt. She's the most important person in my life. She wasn't always, but she is now, and she's young enough to think herself invincible. I don't want strangers knocking that out of her, not on my account."

"Well. I would say, honestly, that people will need some time. Although I think the biggest surprise will be that you have finally let someone in there, man. You've been out of the game for so long."

The remainder of the conversation had consisted of David continually asking Rob for his thoughts on the reaction of others and Rob asking question after question of his own. Would he be letting the general public know that she was Fiona's daughter? Did he intend to tell them Kate's actual age? Did he want him to spread the word, sympathetically of course? Could he tell his wife? David had suggested that Rob simply tell the men that he had taken the plunge, and he would fill in the details himself. He had felt, and still did, that this should be a step-by-step education. Whether or not he would succeed at any part of this remained unclear, but it was the best he could do. And now, he thought again of his wife and grinned widely, remembering that at the end of each day, however much criticism or opinion he should be party to, she would still be gracing the rooms of his home.

Kate was not anywhere in the house. As he dialled Rose's number he glanced down at his still boot-clad feet, then back at the wet footprints on the oak floor. Yes, some rules made sense.

"Hi Rose. Kate with you?"

"She is, son. I'm glad you're home. Can you bring the truck over? Andie's had an accident. Come quick, David."

Kate met him at the door, white-faced and anxious. She had obviously been crying. "Thank God you're here."

Rose ushered him to a seat as Kate wandered around the kitchen.

"How bad is she?" he could not believe he was asking the question. And here was Kate answering him instead of Rose.

"She drove through a red light, and she's in intensive care. Neil phoned. I think we need to get up there. I think we need to go now."

David looked from Kate to his mother, who was now sitting opposite him, her head in her hands. She was whispering Neil's name, her voice desperate. Kate had started to pace, looking for a reaction from him.

"Do you know what else he said to her?" he asked Kate, nodding in Rose's direction.

"He didn't call Rose, he called me," replied Kate, narrowing her eyes at his perfectly fair misunderstanding. "He called me because I need to tell you something else before we go up there."

David sat back in his chair, non-plussed. Whatever was coming had apparently already been shared between the two women, yet Kate's obvious distress and tear-stained cheeks did not tally with the fierce determination in her voice. Why would Neil burden her instead of Rose?

"What is it?"

"It's total crap, that's what it is. Even more crap in a world overflowing with it already." Kate also seated herself next to him. "When I stayed with them, they told me that Andie had been a twin. Did you know about her brother?"

David shook his head, amazed. He was almost as close to Andie as he was to Neil, and was on first name terms with her mother. Yet in the dozen or so years of their acquaintance there had been no mention of a brother or any other siblings. He had always thought that she had been brought up single-handedly by Iris, hence their incredibly close relationship, and nobody had put him right on this.

"What's the story?" David asked, handing Rose his hankie.

"He died when he was twenty-three. He had Huntington's Disease, and so did their dad. I looked it up in the library at home. It's grim," she paused, aching at the sight of David's crestfallen expression. He ran his right hand through his hair and let it come to rest on his chin. "There's no cure, Dave."

He nodded. "I saw a programme on it once. What are you saying, exactly?"

"Andie was never tested, she has no idea if she ... has it inside her. They wouldn't have told me anything, I'm sure, except that I jumped to the wrong conclusion and they sort of had to."

David shook his head confused.

"It doesn't matter," sighed Kate. "But when I was there, she had a bit of a turn. Nothing much at all, but Neil reacted so oddly that it all came out. Now, she's ended up in hospital, and they're not sure how it happened."

Kate began to twiddle her thumbs, not out of boredom, but to stop herself from wringing her hands and to try to rid her head of the sound of Neil's voice. In the past she had heard him laugh at her thoughts on homemade chilli paste, croon at the dogs and sing quite melodically in the shower. What she had heard today would agitate her for days to come. His completely dead monotone edged with anguish, words and phrases which had sounded wrong coming from his mouth and which she was unable to picture him saying. On one occasion only, she had witnessed him succumb to his demons, and it had not been easy to watch; but the time she had spent with him in September had been so very positive that she felt physically gutted by the latest development. David and Rose seemed similarly affected. She watched David roll this information around in his head, understanding the implications if not quite accepting them, while Rose worried the hankie in her hands. The silence was broken momentarily by a fall of snow from the roof, and this in turn saw David take Kate's hand.

"Are you okay?" he asked, her fingers so cold in his grasp.

"We need to go and be with him. Right, Rose? He's on his own up there."

Rose scraped her chair back noisily. "Yes, we need to go. I'll throw some things in a bag in case he wants me to stay."

David was still watching Kate's face, assessing her capability to deal with yet another potentially dreadful situation, but on sensing this, she gave him a warning look and stood. "I didn't lock the door when I came out. Do we need anything while I'm there?"

David was on the point of offering to go, but Kate was already at the door and focussed on leaving, her mind only on beginning the journey. He shook his head and fitted the chair neatly under the table. His legs felt hollow and chilled in spite of the heat in the room, and he forced himself to stand straight, stretching his spine in preparation for two more hours folded into the truck. Despite her eagerness to leave, Kate had not yet opened the door. They stood looking at each other. They were both shocked and upset, but neither of them seemed willing to crumble. It was almost as if they were testing the air, daring each other to be the one to crack, the one to show the other the level of their dependence. This was a new game.

They heard the bathroom door creak above them, and David raised his eyebrows at Kate. She took one step towards him and halted. He wiped his chin. She stared at him and finally said, "Partners?"

"Partners," he agreed and covered the distance between them. It was just a hug, but it was a hug involving desperate arms and bowed heads and it lasted more than ten seconds. Kate suddenly looked up at him, her eyes creased.

"There's one more thing. Don't tell Rose."

"What is it?"

"Neil was really ... well, he's not entirely sure that she didn't do it deliberately."

CHAPTER 31

Tuesday, 6th December 1994

The tiles on the floor of the family room adjacent to the ICU were made of a thick vinyl. Neil had been staring at the same four of these for some time, trying to work out if there was indeed a pattern or if they were completely random. Pale blue swirls on a beige background, and he could not imagine why the administrators would lay individual tiles instead of rolled vinyl. The patterns would blur and sharpen, depending on his concentration level, and sometimes he would move his eyes to his boots, where the soles were still damp even after all this time. He could feel his diaphragm moving up and down, and grew amazed that his body, on every other day of his life, had managed to do this without his conscious knowledge. At that moment, he could picture his entire working mechanism, hear his own blood pumping, and grew terrified as he thought of Andie, lying in a bed alone, allowing her body to fight its injuries without her active help. Was it capable of doing so?

With his head resting on his knees, Neil placed his palms flat on the tiles and felt the cold sweat trickle from the base of his back towards his neck and into his hair. At that moment, the tingling began in his fingers. He needed to stand up and conquer this, but even as he acknowledged it, he was reminded that his strength had been based on Andie's ever steady presence. And she was wounded and bloodied next door, being tended to by people who had no claim to her. How long did it take for them to assess her for a third time, and why had he been removed from the room? He must stand up.

The wall clock said 2.05 p.m., and so Neil began to walk very slowly around the room. The three remaining members of his family would be well on their way, and if Kate had done as he had asked, there would be many, many questions. His ears hummed with the thought of all the words that were coming his way, and he leaned heavily against the wall, determined to stay on his feet. Another minute passed, with his face against the cold plaster, before he was once more allowed to sit at Andie's bedside. He could not look at her face, but concentrated instead on her pale right hand. The car which had careered into the driver's door could not have been doing more than the permitted thirty miles per hour, but it had managed to injure her entire left side, limbs, extremities and face. She had not been conscious in the whole of the four hours since his arrival.

"There's no harm in touching her free hand," stated the nurse, kindly. "As long as you don't dislodge the drip, you can do no damage."

Neil did not answer, but took Andie's hand into his and tried to entwine their fingers so that it would feel as if she were taking part. Her palm was warm but a dead weight, and he studied her fingernails. Each and every one of them was bitten well past the fingertips, the silver band on her thumb still in situ. He remembered asking her on one occasion if he made her permanently nervous, so little nail had she left on either of her hands; but she claimed that short nails stopped the snagging of expensive material, and he had allowed the ridiculous explanation to be acceptable. Now, her hand was as it always was; small and perfect and his to caress and kiss as he wished. He laid his forehead softly on the bed, his face against this beautiful hand and his head resting against her thigh. She was warm and still beside him, and as that was the only comfort available to him, he closed his eyes and sighed. He remained in this position until Rose appeared in the doorway and said his name.

David stared out of the family room window as Kate hovered by the door, watching Rose cross the threshold of the ICU. Hospitals held no fear for her, her mother never spent more than the minimum amount of time inside one; and, on Fiona's orders, Kate had never once visited her there. So, there was no painful association linked to the smells and the sounds of the area they now occupied. David, on the other hand, had spent weeks laid up after his life-changing accident and was probably reeling at the remembrance of it all. Weeks when he had missed her mother and watched the woman deteriorate with each visit. And now, there was the real possibility that this situation might prove even more devastating than his broken bones had done. Did this accident signify the beginning of another black time?

Kate frowned as she sat in the nearest leather seat. Where did these come from, these insignificant errors in timing that caused so much carnage? Obviously, there was no answer to the question, and she began to think instead that she should go and comfort David. But truthfully, it felt easier to remain in her seat and not ask her legs to do anything further.

"What are you thinking?" David's voice was raw and curious.

"I was just wondering why accidents happen. Not how they happen, but why. Do they have a point? Are they trying to teach us something?"

It appeared that David's legs had also given up the fight, as he merely turned his back on her again and spoke to the window and scenery outside. "I had years with those questions, Kate. It got to the stage where I was scaring myself stupid, asking why more accidents did not happen. So many people in the world doing their own thing, focussed on their own paths, how did we get through most days without killing each other? You've just got to accept that it's all down to luck."

"But, that's ... terrifying."

"Yeah," David agreed. "It is. So try not to think about it."

As she stared at her feet stretched out in front of her, Kate was aware of her husband moving at last, and she heard him gently close the door before taking up the seat opposite her. His face was drawn and thoughtful.

"But you're saying that this might not have been accidental?"

Kate shrugged and pushed herself upright in the chair. "That's what he said. He wasn't very calm, mind, he was just thinking out loud. I said something like, was she ill. You know, I meant was she having more 'turns'. I was trying to be subtle, but I'm useless at it. Anyway, he said nobody could give a reason for what happened, and then he said 'she promised she would tell me when she was ready', I think. Oh, God, David. This is bona fide shit, isn't it?"

"Bona fide shit, Kate." They looked at each other in silence for a second or two, before David's face twisted into a humourless smile. "The sort of shit I was hoping to steer you clear of."

"Snap," she said, watching as he rubbed his forehead then gazed back at her. "If we're going to help Neil, I think we need to concentrate on him. So, you stop worrying about me, and I'll stop worrying about you; I'm okay if you are. All I need is you and me together in the same place. Honestly, that's all."

Neil appeared in the doorway before they could say another word, and both were on their feet in a second. As always, even after the progress they had made in September, they waited to see if Neil was up for any physical contact, or if it would break him in two. He managed a strained smile when he saw Kate and put his arms around her, but could not speak immediately. David found himself holding his breath, his chest suddenly tight.

"Welcome home," Neil finally whispered into Kate's hair then looked over at his brother. His face was pure distress. "Dave, I need some fresh air. Could you maybe come with me?"

"Sure, buddy."

Kate remained where she was, suddenly alone in the space and found herself, in spite of her recent words, bleakly out of sorts. The room felt cold and without hope. She sat once more.

Out in the freezing air, Neil lowered himself onto the nearest bench, too distracted to do anything but sit and stare ahead. David unzipped his coat and wrapped it around Neil's thin shirt, then watched as he blew his breath out into the chill. His brother's eyes were empty as he searched for words which would remove him from both the place and the circumstances. Nothing seemed to be forthcoming, and David remained on his feet, trying to judge the best line to open with.

"Have they given you any idea how bad it is?"

Neil began to speak, his voice low and factual, as if repeating a speech regarding a stranger and not his reason for living. "Her pelvis is still aligned, no breaks. Two fractures below the elbow and the femur has a crack in it. The rest are abrasions to the skin. She's pretty stable, but they were scared of internal bleeding, and so they brought her here. They'll move her once she's able to talk to them."

"So," breathed David, "she's out of danger."

Neil looked up at him, his bottom lip safely tucked out of sight as the water in his eyes began to pool and trickle. David was struck by the fact that the last time Neil had cried in front of him, he had had the power to make the situation better. There was no such luxury available to him now.

"You know the whole story?" Neil asked, wiping his entire face with his shirtsleeve, his voice as yet to find any expression. David nodded, to which Neil closed his eyes and leaned forward on the bench, wishing with his entire being that the concrete beneath his feet could be dry and warm and that he could curl up in a ball and sleep the pain away. He wanted to be part of the earth so much; he needed to melt into the ground and hide from every one of the 'monsters on his shoulders' who were suddenly making themselves known again. He folded himself into his own lap.

"Neil!" David squatted beside him, grabbing his arm and hauling him up against the back of the bench, "Come on, man. You're okay. We can deal with this."

"No, I can't deal with this. I've learned to bury a lot, I've learned to face up to things I never wanted to even admit to, but this is something I can't do."

David was confused. "You're making no sense. Andie is going to recover from this, and we're going to sort ... the rest together."

Neil stood, his face suddenly furious and watched as his brother took a step away from him. "You're not listening," he hissed. "Three hours ago you didn't even know about the rest. I've lived with it for the last dozen or so years, and Andie for the whole of her life. Do you think you can make it better by feeding me a few stock phrases, Dave? Nothing is going to make this better. Nothing is going to make this negotiable."

"What do you mean?" The chill was not merely sitting on David's unclothed back, it was running in his veins.

"I'm not discussing this with you," Neil stated, standing straighter and folding his arms. "But it doesn't mean I don't need your help. I'm really, really scared, Dave. I'm scared of what's coming, and I'm scared she's going to be disappointed in me."

"Look, come back inside. We can sit inside the door and calm down. We don't have to see anybody else for the moment."

Neil's face betrayed the utter hopelessness that he was feeling, but he let himself be led back into the heated foyer. As he sat, he wondered how many people, in all the years the hospital had been open, had sat in this space, their hearts breaking and guts ripped out. He was obviously not the first, and yet the place was not tinged with misery or regret, it was warm and bright and stung the eyes with its optimism. It made Neil nauseous.

David pulled a chair directly in front of him and sat, mere feet apart, not allowing his brother to look anywhere else but at his face.

"Just please give me something to go on, Neil. Why would Andie ever be disappointed in you?"

"Because she's going to need me to be stronger than she is, and we both know that's not the case. I'm not scared of going ahead with it; I'm scared I'm going to do it in the least helpful, most pathetic of ways, which will end up being unbearable for her."

David felt his fists clench and his jaw become rigid. "Neil. Whatever it is that you two have planned, it's not going to happen. You're scared? I'm sitting here beyond petrified. Talk to me. You're not moving from here until you do."

Neil's smile was cold. "You still think you can take me down, brother?"

"The way I'm feeling, I could bulldoze you through that plate glass."

Neil shook his head and closed his eyes on his brother's animated face. Running his fingers through his hair, he laid his head back against the spongy material of the chair and let out a long sigh. His hands were shaking, but he pressed them against his thighs and began to grind his teeth quietly. Where to begin?

"In the last couple of months, Andie's been a bit low. She was losing minutes in her day, or sitting for too long trying to work out what she should be doing. Sometimes, there would be shaking. I think she was probably hiding most of it, denying a lot, but then suddenly we were discussing the possibility of our worst nightmare paying us a visit. It's something we had never done, it wasn't part of us and there we were, talking to each other about how our lives were about to be … terminated."

"God help us," breathed David. "How long were you going to keep us shut out of this?"

Neil looked confused and defensive. "Hey! It's like this. If Andie wasn't lying unconscious upstairs, we would not be having this conversation."

"You were never going to tell us?"

"It's ours!" Neil cried. "It belongs to us, nobody else!"

"David?" Kate was standing six feet from the where the men sat. At her voice, David turned his head towards her, and for a split second, Kate saw absolutely no recognition on his face. Then he was on his feet, torn between the need to reassure Kate and the desire to shake Neil until he saw sense. "I just came to tell you she's awake."

Neil was past them and headed for the stairs before either of them had the chance to address him again, and Kate stood, bewildered. Clearly, her father was out of his mind, even though his partner was in no danger. Her husband was white and angry, exhibiting a level of frustration that she had never before witnessed, and she had no clever comments with which to lighten the mood. So she remained motionless, staring at the floor beneath her feet, completely and utterly lost. How very odd and unexpected this was.

"Hey, you," David's voice was soft as his boots appeared next to hers. "Let me see your face."

Kate lifted her head, but could not persuade her frown to leave. "I thought I could do anything, Dave. Thought I was so bloody smart and grown up and capable. I'm no use to any of you, because I don't have a clue what's going on."

"You're of use to me, my love," said David. "You remind me what life is, and in this case, that's worth more than gold. Come on."

Rose met the pair of them at the top of the stairs, showing a little more colour in her cheeks, and looked hopefully in their direction.

"Thank God," she beamed. "Andie's talking. She's coping with the pain and she's talking, well, trying to talk." Although both of them nodded, neither of them smiled. Rose's face fell. "What?"

David felt Kate's fingers lace through his. Some things had to remain undisclosed. "Neil is worried about her condition," said Kate. "They both think it's time to face up to it."

Rose took a step backwards. Of course, they had talked of little else on the journey over, Kate informing them of every fact she had gleaned from the medical dictionary she had read, and David adding his snippets of retained information. They were not specialists, they were quoting recorded statistics and ideas and attempting to apply it to a person they loved.

Rose had no desire to act on assumptions of ordinary people. They needed to address this, but they needed to do it with clear facts and with expert opinion. There had to be a way of making this better. Rose looked at both of the concerned faces in front of her. "Yes," she agreed. "I think it's time they did."

«•»«•»«•»

To Andie, it appeared that her jawbone had swollen to the size and density of a breeze block, and the gauze on the side of her face further restricted any real movement. She was aware of both of these things before she had even opened her eyes. Then as she had focussed on Rose, watching as the woman fled the room, she had stopped trying to form words and had relaxed her head back against the pillow until Neil's face was in front of hers. She managed to raise her right hand in his direction, dread beginning to fill her heart. She must not let another second pass without letting this man know that this had been a complete accident. She remembered approaching the junction, trying to sing along to the radio and nothing else, but what was Neil thinking? How was he regarding what had happened? Did he imagine that she had stuck her feet over the bed that morning with the sole intention of leaving him behind? She needed to speak, for both of their sanities. She moved her head steadily from side to side, lowering her eyes and gripping his hand in hers. "No," she whispered. "Didn't mean ... babe."

Neil put his face so close to hers that she could not focus properly, yet there were his eyes, blue and frantic, enclosed in worry lines and pierced with fear. "We haven't talked enough yet, Andie. I didn't know it was so bad."

"No, babe ... swear ... didn't mean ..."

Neil cleared his throat and stared.

It felt to Andie as if he were reading her thoughts through her eyes, looking for proof that she was telling him the truth, and in response, she felt the tears forming and clearing the way for him to do just that. Slowly, he sat back in his chair, his breath not yet even, but ragged and wheezy. "Thank God," he uttered, then, "Oh Andie, look at you. I'm supposed to shield you from this. It's my job and you're … in pieces, hurt. I'm so –"

"Right, Mr Wilder," the voice of the nurse matched her footfalls; firm and masculine. "If you could just give us a bit -"

"Jesus!" cried Neil, "Can you just give me one minute to speak to the person that I live my life with. I thought I'd lost her!"

"I'll give you two minutes if you like," replied the nurse, not in the least bit surprised or put off by Neil's tone. "Then after that, you'll let us do our job so that we can get this patient of ours on the road to recovery. Okay?"

"Thank you," breathed Neil, watching her retreat. Andie was gripping his hand tighter than ever, and he brought her fingers to his lips, watching as she tried to loosen her jaw to an acceptable level. There was so much she had to say to him, but every movement caused discomfort in at least one part of her abused frame.

"Driver?" she asked, looking straight at Neil.

"Shocked," replied Neil. "He may have broken a wrist. He's going to be fine, and he was alone in the car."

"Didn't mean to. Believe that?"

"Yes," assured Neil. "I do, because I know you couldn't; not yet, not to me. And not to a stranger in a car."

"Thank … you."

He still trusted her, and now she watched as he assessed her again, this time with an air of resignation rather than pure terror. She guessed he was trying to put the coming weeks into some sort of workable timetable, and she ached to stroke his chin and tell him to relax. But there was no energy or ability remaining within her to do this, and so she let him take his personal thoughts and play with them without joining in.

Back in the family room, Kate had never left the doorway. While Rose and David discussed the logistics of staying over and providing the best level of support for Neil, she leaned against the doorjamb. She could add nothing to their discussion; they were in a far better position than she to know how much help he could stomach, so she stood watching the comings and goings of the staff instead. She heard Neil's indignant demand to be left alone and expected the banished nurse to return at any moment, to a hopefully more respectful welcome. She longed to see Andie, no matter how depressingly damaged she looked.

There was a water cooler in the family room, but no cups, and so Kate wandered along to the far end of the corridor and collected four from the dispenser at the top of the stairs. It seemed like days since she had been assessing rooms and making plans with which to surprise David, although it had been a matter of hours. It seemed even longer since they had spent a silent minute or two, holding each other, with no other thought than how monumentally amazing it was that they had found this love. Now, they were back to the place they had been forced to inhabit for the last year, that darker place where others were in deadly danger and they had obligatory duties to perform. At least this time, they were acting together. As Kate retraced her steps, trying to stop her boots from squeaking quite so loudly, she wondered if David would ever draw her into serious conversations, ask her opinions on everyday problems, or whether he would continue to try to steer her through situations he deemed too dangerous. She hoped not. She loved the man more than any other being on earth, but he still had a lot to learn about her.

Kate suddenly wanted to see Andie more than anything else. Neil was her father and Andie was his life; there was surely no harm in creeping into the unit and seeing them together for a moment or two, before Nurse Adamant and probably a crew of cronies came in to bodily remove Neil from the scene. Without giving it any more thought than that, Kate had opened the door and was heading towards the sound of low voices. She began to smile as she pictured the pair of them, sitting close to each other, as they were meant to be. Perhaps she would try to sneak a look at them without showing herself. She really did not want to disturb their precious few peaceful moments.

"... just promise me," Neil's voice was a whispered demand. "We'll make watertight plans. No, don't try to speak. I know what you're thinking, but you have to accept something, babe. You've made your choice, and now I'm making mine. You can go ahead of me if you insist, but I'll be following you within the hour. Wouldn't you rather walk down that particular road with me holding your hand?"

Kate was standing perfectly still, desperate to hear Andie's reply, but even more anxious to understand what was being said.

"You know," mumbled Andie, "... want."

"We've been lucky, Andreana. We've had years of each other, the only years that ever made sense to me. More of them would have made us greedy, don't you think? Look, we'll talk again. Don't look at me like that, babe, it won't alter the facts. It doesn't matter when we go, as long as we head in the same direction when that time comes."

When the nurse finally returned to shoo Neil from her patient's bedside, she found Kate sitting on a chair by the ICU entrance, four plastic cups rolling back and forth between her feet.

CHAPTER 32

Thursday, 8th December 1994

It was approaching four in the afternoon, and the blue dusk had persuaded Kate to switch on the overhead light in the sitting room. It sent out a quality of light she detested, cold and severe, but she was determined to get to the bottom of the trunk and tidy it away before David returned from work. She needed as many familiar and treasured items in her sight as possible. Thank God David lit the fire before he disappeared. Warmth and comfort and her own familiar belongings, it was these things which were keeping her mind in a safe enough place; for the time being. Her legs had pins and needles from kneeling too long, and for one moment she thought she would scream in agitation. God was sending her too much at once. She threw some more logs onto the flames and stood by the heat, stamping out the pain.

In some remarkable feat of restraint, she had kept Neil's words to Andie locked away for two nights now. Two nights of lying beside David's restless form, praying that Neil had temporarily lost his sanity or that she had completely misunderstood his grotesque intentions. She was permanently on fire inside, swinging between utter disbelief to a kind of sick fury. How dare her father think about removing himself from all of them, when her mother had endured months of agony, wishing with all her strength to stay on this green earth? On the other hand, she had seen what Neil and Andie were to each other, and, even to Kate, his world without his partner in it seemed bleak. Their house would be a barn of an empty space which not even two wood-burners would be able to heat. She had to be mistaken. This was nonsensical and she must have misunderstood him.

《●》《●》《●》

Kate dragged the empty trunk next to the bureau and shighed. It could be moved elsewhere later. Once in situ, she placed some of her photos and a stack of cassette tapes on top of it for convenience, but apart from the three ceramic hedgehogs for the mantelpiece and the pile of paperbacks stashed on the window seat, the remainder of her goods needed to be housed in a less public place; photos of Fiona, letters, keepsakes and, of course, her framed birthday present which would be positioned in their new bedroom, wherever that might be. Kate held up the object, marvelling at its composition.

Her favourite item of the many was tucked into the right hand corner. It was a photo of her and Hazel dressed as Jekyll and Hyde and had been taken just before her sister had given up on the 'institution' that was school. In spite of the hideous make-up and tattered clothes that Kate had adopted, both of them were laughing straight at the camera, arm in arm. She remembered a particular conversation prior to that night for two reasons; firstly, it had been the one true victory she had ever had over Hazel; and secondly, her mother had, for the first time in their living memory, uttered an unbelievable string of oaths at the pair of them which had left them wide-eyed and smirking as she had departed the room.

When presented with the idea of attending the school Halloween party as the infamous doctor and his other half, Hazel had grabbed the bag of ancient dressing-up clothing and announced that she would be the 'bad one'.

"Why?" Kate had asked. "The idea was mine, so I get first choice. If it was up to you we'd be going as Dracula and his victim, again. Oh, I found the plastic fangs down the side of the bed, by the way."

Hazel had shaken her head. "But I'm older, that makes me the obvious choice for the shabby, evil-looking … one."

"Bloody hell, Haze, you don't even know his name! Which one is the rough one, then?"

Hazel had rolled the names around for a moment then, "Well obviously, it's the mister one. Doctors are always smartly dressed."

"Okay, but you had to think about it!"

Their mother's voice had drifted in through the open bedroom door. "What's the fuss?"

There had then followed a three-way spat, growing louder and less refined with every second. Acting abilities and looks had been questioned, with Fiona growing increasingly frustrated at the level of acrimony being thrown around, and Kate winding Hazel up further by continually referring back to whose idea it had been. Finally, when both girls had been bellowing opinions at each other without waiting for breath, their mother had stamped into the room, issued orders about mess and noise and carry on, without censoring her language, and had then left, slamming the door for greater effect as she had retreated. In the screaming silence which had followed, Kate had stared at her sister until neither could hold back their laughter for another second. The battle had finally been won by Kate, who had persuaded her sister that she would have a far better chance of attracting a mate if she was immaculately dressed with shiny hair, than if she looked like she had been dragged through a rubbish tip.

Kate looked forlornly at the photo, and in the next second was dialling the international code number which was permanently in her head. Only when the tone began to ring in the earpiece, did she look at the time and regret being quite so impulsive.

"Hello?" the voice was surprisingly alert for the hour. "Kate?"

"How did you know?" laughed Kate, pleased that it was Hazel.

"Well," replied her sister, "it was a pretty safe bet, it's nearly midnight. You missing us already?"

Kate hesitated. "Are you on your own? I mean, is Beth still up?"

There was an audible yawn before the reply reached Kate. "Nah, she went to bed about eightish. Migraine. Kenny's out at a darts match. Sorry, it's me or nobody."

Kate sat heavily on the hall chair. "It was you I wanted to speak to. I do miss you. You, especially. We were good mates, remember?"

"Yeah, I remember. Listen, if this is going to be a long, nostalgic one, can I go and get my jumper and bed socks? I'm shivering in a T-shirt here."

As Kate sat cradling the phone to her ear, she checked her watch. David was due back at any moment, but as she had been trying to keep her brain from crashing by filling her day with mundane and exhausting activities since he had crawled from their bed at dawn, she supposed that she could afford the luxury of one phone call. The meal merely needed reheating, and the house was warm and lit. More than anything else, she needed to speak to Hazel. Not Beth, who she was sure would have very definite opinions but not necessarily applicable solutions, but to Hazel. Hazel was nearest her age and would say exactly what she thought without choosing an immediate angle. She needed to talk this through, not be fed the line 'you'll understand when you're older'. Kate doubted that anybody would ever understand this particular situation, irrespective of their age.

"Okay, Kathryn, what is happening with you and how is my dad?"

Hazel's voice was not exactly flippant, but if Kate had been in anything other than a perplexed state of mind, this might have led to an argument. As it was, Kate squeezed her eyes shut against the majority of her anxiety and answered plainly enough. "Something pretty major has happened, actually, but David is fine. I need to tell you this because I think I might actually start throwing things at walls shortly."

"God's sake," sighed Hazel. "Could you not have got all of these nitty gritty things sorted before?"

"Hazel! Andie's been in a car accident and she's in hospital. But if you really want me to give you the details about how fine Dave and I are, I'll do it," Kate paused, but there was no reply. "This is serious, Haze, and I'm telling you because you're my best friend. Please help me."

"Okay, okay, calm it."

Hazel was using a voice Kate had heard on countless occasions, one which hung heavy with genuine shame but which would never actually be persuaded to form words of an apology. It did, however, mean that she was ready to listen; and by the time Kate had explained about the illness, the accident and the shockingly unambiguous nature of Neil's promise to Andie, Hazel had begun to sound more like the collaborator Kate had made use of her whole life. She was also determined to find an alternative meaning to Neil's words. Nobody could really plan such a final and unnecessary course of action, surely.

"What if he meant that, maybe, if the time came for her," Hazel was obviously starting to struggle with the composition of her thoughts and words, "that he would, be with her, you know, help her to ..."

Kate held her forehead. "I thought about that too, and I really want to believe it. But what if I go along with that in my head and, and, and then it's too late? What if I should be trying to talk to him about it, because of what I heard, and I don't and then ... Tell me what you would do, Haze. I've got to do this right."

"Well, you've got to tell Dad, then. If you don't and the worst happens, you'll end up admitting you knew and, well shit, none of this bears thinking about. I should get Beth."

"No, no, don't! It was your opinion that I needed, it's the only one I want, and you're right. This is too big for me to do on my own. Wish you were here, that's the only thing. Wish we were friends like we used to be."

"Well, we're probably getting there ..."

"Hey, Haze, I think I heard the truck. He'll kill me if he doesn't get to speak to you, too. Don't say anything to him, but can I give him a shout?"

"Sure, why not? It's not as if I'd like to get to sleep or anything."

"Right, two secs. Thanks for being nice to me, Haze."

Kate laid the phone next to the Christmas cactus on the hall table and ran to the back door. The face that David wore as he came stomping into the kitchen was strained and tired, but she watched it evolve into a smile and thanked God above that she had the ability to do that for this man. She hooked her hands around his neck and kissed him slowly before she beamed up at him. "Hey, Dave, Hazel's on the phone."

"Really?" he replied. "This late?"

"I phoned her. Go and talk to her, I'll get the food."

The baked potatoes were still steaming nicely as Kate took them out of the warming oven, and she made a note to herself to let Beth know that ranges were the best invention in history. The stewing steak she had found at the back of the freezer had been supplemented with onions, mushroom and a bottle of beer and smelled reasonably edible, although Kate would have preferred her first show of cooking to have been something she had more faith in. A year of part-time jobs had at least allowed her to attempt to learn to shop and cook for others. She wondered if David would take her to Duncan and let her buy a serious amount of food, as the past day or two had seen their meagre supply dwindle amid the drama. But as she piled the meat swimming in thick gravy onto two plates, she felt her heart dropping. What was she doing? Why had she spent the entire day sorting and scrubbing and cooking when something so potentially destructive was being planned less than one hundred miles from her door? How was she possibly going to justify eating a normal meal with a man she trusted completely, when she was keeping something so monstrous from him? Well, it was simple, and Hazel was right. She had to tell him.

"She sounded in good spirits," David said as he took a seat at the table. "How was she with you?"

Kate shrugged. "Better. I just thought they should know about Andie. Have you heard from anybody today?"

He shook his head as he loaded his first fork. "I'll ring the house after dinner. Rose is bound to be there, if Neil isn't."

At the thought of what Neil might be doing, Kate's stomach rolled a little, but before she could speak, David was pointing at his food with a look of confused admiration. She folded her arms and said, "Something you want to say?"

He shook his head, his mouth still full of food, and gave her the thumbs up. Kate tasted the meat and found it surprisingly tender.

Ranges really were a remarkable necessity. As she reached for the pepper, David caught her hand and held it across the table.

"Aw Kit," he sighed. "I wish you knew how much it means to me that you're here, because I don't have the words to tell you." He took another mouthful before continuing. "Some of the men came to offer their congratulations today."

"And what did you say?" Kate was genuinely intrigued.

"I said that I'd introduce you properly as soon as this Neil and Andie thing was more settled. They seemed fine," he paused then squeezed her hand. "I said you'd saved my life just by being here, and it's true. Coming home to your positive face makes everything easier."

Kate held her breath, trying to choose the right path to follow. Should she tell him everything and risk a sleepless night for both of them, or should she allow him one more evening of positive gratitude and keep her secret for a little while longer? The moment passed and she held her tongue, because tomorrow would come soon enough. She concentrated on eating instead. "So," she said, "I was thinking about the bedrooms and I might have an idea, or two."

Later, as David spoke to Rose over the phone regarding the latest state of play, Kate fed the fire and tried to find a news channel for a weather report. The last thing they needed was for a winter storm to keep them from travelling back to Port Alberni the following afternoon. By the time David walked back into the sitting room, Kate had pulled her armchair next to his so that they could both see the television. The fire was nicely belting out heat, and the curtains were closed against the frosty night. She was studying the map of the area on the screen, tapping her fingers on her knee; but when he settled himself into the chair beside her, it was not nearly intimate enough, and suddenly she was sitting in his lap, her head nuzzled into his neck. As ever, all he could do was breathe her in and marvel.

"You've had a busy day, sweetheart," he murmured. "Was it a lonely day?"

Kate shifted herself slightly so that they were both more comfortable, shook her head and yawned. "No, there's nothing lonely about this house. Still, it was nice to speak to Hazel. For once, she had some half sensible things to say. How are things up there?"

"Oh, they've moved Andie to a ward. Her lungs are fine, and the fractures don't seem to be causing any further chaos. She's quite coherent now. According to Rose, she and Neil spend most of their time within a foot of each other's faces. That's when she's been with them. She's mostly been looking after the dogs and house."

Kate's skin had begun to prickle under her collar, and she dreaded that he would pick up on this. In the last month, they had become so finely attuned to each other that she was amazed that he had not sensed her unease before now; she was sure that if work had not removed him from the house, then they would have already discussed the situation.

She lay completely motionless against him, trying to imagine how their week would have taken shape had Andie managed to stop at that red light, her fingers drumming on the steering wheel impatiently as the bright morning had carried on its business around her. Perhaps they would already have chosen a bedroom and begun to make lists of requirements. Andie herself might have been asked to wander from room to room with a notepad, moving swiftly from window to window, assessing the light and listening to Kate's inane patter. Instead, they had blundered from day to day, David desperately trying to regain a handle on work and her trying to make sense of what she knew. Kate sighed, acknowledging how selfish it was to be wishing for a simpler, more positive period.

"What time is it?" she asked.

"Getting on for eight, I guess."

It was the most relaxed either of them had been for days, and Kate could feel her eyelids beginning to droop. "I love you," she whispered.

As he repeated the sentiment quietly into her hair she smelled White Musk, but instead of allowing her mother to wash over her, she forced herself to open her eyes and pushed the warm nugget of gold to the side. She wanted only David. She wanted a simple, straightforward night, talking about their future. Whatever had still be faced in terms of Neil could not be addressed until tomorrow, and tonight, she wanted some peace.

"What are the chances of you dropping me off in Duncan in the morning? We need food."

"Well, you could always take Rose's car."

"Eh, no I couldn't."

"One of these days you'll have -"

"But not yet," finished Kate, firmly.

David smiled. His wife's hair was soft against his chin. He wrapped her hand in his. There was an incredibe calm inside him, and it seemed to intensify in the best possible way with each quiet moment they allowed themselves. Since his arrival on Skye for the wedding, the only periods of solitude they had enjoyed had been behind their bedroom door. Even the days at the Flodigarry, their 'official honeymoon', had seen them sit at the bar chatting to other customers or out for bracing walks. Only here, at home, had they spent time just being together. He loved her heat against him, she liked the way his fingers entwined her own and how they could study their combined hands for minutes at a time, as if never having seen them before.

In her previous home, nobody simply sat. There was always some activity being discussed or planned or argued over, and Kate had only noticed this as she had begun to withdraw from it. Now, the silence they sat within was the norm, but with an added bonus which was priceless. She was in the company of a man who thought she was special and deserving enough to have him. He was engulfed by the presence of someone who breathed and whose palms were real when they pressed against him.

"I've never seen you in this seat without a whisky in your hand. Shall I get you one?"

"I'm quite enjoying just sitting here with you."

Kate looked around the room, the television a mere flicker in the background, and wondered if she truly was all that he needed. She was harbouring knowledge which he was almost bound to think she was too young to handle. But she would level with him as soon as she had tackled Neil, and even if she made an incredibly childish mess of that job, David would at least see that she had been trying to help without burdening him.

"Am I enough for you?" Kate's words were not fearful or melancholy. They were matter-of-fact and curious. When she glanced at him, she saw his intrigued face and hurried to qualify the question. "At times like this, do you wish you had someone with more ... know-how? You know, maybe someone who's had experiences which might be a help? I'm never going to be in that position."

"Sweetheart," he smiled as she finally moved from his knee and faced him from her own, cold chair. "I stopped looking for help years ago. All you really end up with is a load of different ideas, pointing you in every direction. I need something more indispensable than ideas; I need somebody who loves me. It's as basic as that, and I'll take it for as long as it's on offer."

Kate sat forward and stared into his green eyes, daring him to doubt her ability to love him for the rest of her life, yet again. She suspected there was nothing more she could do to prove this to him, other than to still be at his side years from now. This thought had her suddenly grinning.

"What?" he mirrored her expression.

"I was thinking of all the years stretching ahead of us, when it will always be on offer. But what I'm really looking forward to is the day when you actually believe it. My, we'll be celebrating when that day comes, big style."

David had the presence of mind to hang his head a little; this was the only thing she ever admonished him for, and it suggested that she had no intention of changing the way she felt. Although he would never say anything so negative to her, he had been in this situation before. He would always be a little wary of the future.

The present was enough for the moment. The present meant an end to loneliness, it meant two-way conversations, sharing memories and making this precious person smile. He had forgotten the joy of making a difference to someone's day. How could he have forgotten that part?

Then there was Kate herself, with her exploring hands and eyes that set him alight. This would remain the biggest, most amazingly beautiful mystery of them all; that she wanted him.

"I don't think that day is far away," said David and kissed her hand before standing and reaching for one of the ceramic hedgehogs. "Where's the rest of your stuff, honey?"

"My books are over by the window, I'm going to find homes for the photos later, and everything else is waiting to take up residence in our new room. I suppose I must be a light traveller."

Whenever David stood at full height, Kate found herself unable to keep any suitable form of distance between them, and she was beginning to wonder if she would be able to stop herself from literally attaching to his body in public. She had one absurd image which was becoming clearer and more highly defined every time she pictured it. She saw David struggling to talk on the phone to a client while she hid her head under his arm and clung like a limpet to his side, her legs wrapped around his thighs. As he moved across the room, hindered yet patient, she remained mute and happy.

She had to get a grip on her yearnings, because there would be just as many public occasions as private; and, apparently, David had no problem with her being clingy or demanding when they were alone. She could be sensible and appropriate when required. Yet, this was not one of those times, and now her arms were around his waist and her ear was against his chest, where it had waited to be its entire life.

"You okay, Kitty? What's this weird little anxiety I see tonight?"

Kate rubbed her forehead against his beating heart and screwed up her face. "I was just thinking about Neil. He loves Andie like I love you, and now he might have to say goodbye. I'd be so completely ruined, if it was you."

David did not reply, the thought of losing her too painful even to agree about. He simply allowed her to stand against him, the back of his jumper clenched in her fists, until the clock began to chime the arrival of 8 p.m.

"I'll take you shopping tomorrow, Mrs Wilder. We can call in at the yard first, to show everybody how lucky I am, and then we can get food and look at some furniture, if you like. A new bed, a new sofa and whatever else you want."

"Oh Lordy! That's a scary one. Not the sofa obviously, the yard bit. I'm going to have to be really strict with myself. No clever remarks or trying to hold your hand. I can see it now. You're going to be standing there, all tall and important and ... boss-like, and I'm going to be this little insignificant being in a woolly hat, trying to look like I fit in. Jeez, Dave, I'm not going to sleep a wink tonight. Where are you going?"

Throughout her rant, David had managed to settle the fire into a non-movable lump, switch off three lamps and the television and move himself across the dark room to the hallway. "I'm going to bed. I feel the need to be lying with you tucked into me, and since we are lacking a sofa, then bed it is."

"Righto," agreed Kate, thankful that her blushes were hidden as he dealt with lights and locks, and watched as he took the phone off the hook. She grinned her understanding as he raised his eyebrows; they would have tonight to themselves and deal with the rest the following day.

CHAPTER 33

Friday, 9th December 1994

Kate was buzzing inside from the day she had put in, and it was still only mid-afternoon. She had been fed, but her stomach felt as if a pint of liver salts was simmering on its surface; and at one point, she wondered how much fizzing and popping could take place before her skin split open and she sprayed the dashboard with effervescent liquid. Rather than lean against the window as normal, she was sitting upright, trying to make sense of the radio news programme and failing. So she let her mind replay the most memorable bits of the morning, beginning with David's advice with regard to her grand 'introduction'.

"They'll see what they want to see and have probably made up their minds already. So all you can really do is turn up and -"

"Don't say 'be yourself'," cried Kate, "because there's more than one version! I suppose I could go with the coffee shop waitress one, but honestly, that would probably be too smiley and enthusiastic."

David had stood, watching her hunt madly for an appropriate item of clothing, and had kindly not pointed out that she was much more decisive when it came to what he should wear. He had then made the expected noises about the opinions of others being unimportant, which, whilst nice to hear, had been believed by neither of them. She had finally picked up the cleanest pair of jeans, a shirt and a V-necked jumper. "Well, it's what they'll see me in every other day, so ..."

Rob had been the first to shake her hand, and apparently his nerves had matched hers. He was a short man, about her height and almost as round as he was tall, but he had been so taken aback by her unannounced appearance that he had physically backed away from her after being introduced.

She had smiled and had begun to babble. It had been almost half a minute before she had noticed David's eyebrows disappearing almost into his hairline and had finally brought her monologue to a conclusion. Rob had followed them into the office, managing to look more relaxed, until she had picked out an ancient framed photo of Fiona with Hazel on the wall behind the desk and had squealed in delight. This had proved too much for his sensibilities, and he had shaken her hand again and retreated outside.

However, he had obviously spread the word, as two cutters and a young apprentice had appeared at the door within ten minutes. This time, Kate had managed to stand with her arms folded and let David do the majority of the talking. She had answered specific questions and explained which part of the world Skye occupied, before David had ushered her back into the truck and declared the whole thing an unqualified success. She loved him for having said it.

The food shopping had proved a less fraught/entertaining experience, which had taken far longer than it should have done due to Kate's inability to recognise alien packaging. 'Yes, but how do you cook it? Do you have to add water?' However, the subsequent choosing of a new sofa had cheered the pair of them immensely. Not only had they found an end-of-stock item whose colour offended neither of them, but if they agreed to take the one in store, the very one that they had both sunk happily into, then it could be at The Edge by close of business, December 23rd. They had been eating lunch by 12.30 p.m., pleased with themselves.

Agitated and within twenty miles of Port Alberni, Kate was becoming less and less vocal. David himself was concentrating on the road, which had a covering of fresh snow and remained a bright glare in the low afternoon sun. She reached into the glove compartment, handed over his sunglasses and was rewarded with a smile which brought him back into the cab for a few moments at least. She sighed quietly. How long would it take them to travel twenty miles? Long enough to start regaling her fears to the man? David's arms had soothed her to sleep the night before, but she had promised herself that today she would tackle the problem.

"David, I'm worried," she looked directly at him, almost twisting her neck with the sudden movement.

"Tell me," he glanced in her direction in acknowledgement, but could not look at her for long.

"What do you think will happen when Andie gets really ill? How is Neil going to be?"

David's face was bleak behind his sunglasses. He said nothing for a moment or two, then thumped the steering wheel with both hands.

"God knows," he growled. "It's so typical of the man to keep this to himself. So, it comes at us out of the blue, and none of us have the ability to help him. He's done this for years now."

Kate watched David's body movements, feeling suddenly a little strange. She had been on the point of sharing something appallingly scary with him, but now began to doubt that they would even be on the same side if she did. "Are you mad at Neil?"

"I'll tell you the truth, Kate. I'm scared to death for him and mad at him. I don't know why he doesn't trust us with these things. He has Andie and he has us, and that's about all he has."

Kate was staring desolately at the highway in front of her, completely stalled in her mission. Where did she go from here? David's words were surely born out of the cold frustration and worry they were all feeling, but he seemed less sympathetic and more irritated than was necessary.

Neil was in yet another space that no one should ever be asked to occupy, but David appeared to be concentrating on only one aspect of it. Kate, on the other hand, had begun to think of Neil's plight as something more fundamental, and a familiar knot of fibres was forming in her heart. What if this truly was the price you paid in life for genuine, complete happiness? You could have a taste of perfection as long as you handed yourself over to total desolation after a painfully short time. If this was the case, what did that mean for David and her?

Kate folded her arms and bit her lip, as she began to study the countryside, looking for colours and objects to distract her. Snow stacked at the side of the road, the highway black with grey streaks, the sun turning everything from turquoise to lilac as it hid itself behind the trees, with headlights approaching on the opposite side of the road. It was an ordinary day in somebody else's life. Friday night was on its way, people were relaxing and planning the next couple of days. Andie and Neil should have been on their way to visit them, with excited questions and congratulatory smiles. Kate could not prevent the one tear from making an appearance and so continued to point her face safely out of the window.

"D'you think that was harsh?" David said, his tone climbing down from aggression.

Kate shrugged, unable to speak, but did not object to him taking her hand. Eventually, when the tear had dried itself invisible, she looked in his direction. He squeezed her palm in his and let it go.

"Okay, I'm terrified," he continued. "I can't see how he's going to be able to deal with this at all."

Kate looked back out at the cold blue light. It was beautiful, but even so it seemed incapable of providing her with inspirational words. She had knowledge that he did not have, and this fact would not stop gnawing at her.

"So am I," she suddenly found herself speaking, and with each word out in the open, she felt a kind of release. "I think he's planning something, something that isn't going to have a happy ending for anybody."

David was silent for a moment.

She guessed he was about to ask her what she meant, but instead he removed his sunglasses and rubbed his forehead as if it pained him. When he turned to look in her direction, she saw no real surprise, more resignation. He twisted his mouth in acknowledgement and asked quietly, "What did he say to you?"

Kate cringed at the level of blackness in David's words, and she knew that there was no choice now about what to share with him. But her brain would not instantly give her permission.

"He didn't say anything to me. I overheard them, and that's the only reason I haven't told you before. I might be totally, completely wrong, and I really hope I am."

"What?" David continued to press.

"I don't think they're going to wait for the illness to appear. I think that they are going to decide when. When she goes."

In the next moment, David had changed down a gear and was pulling into a lay-by in the last light of the day. The space was no more than an area of cleared scrub carved out of the roadside trees; but as soon as they were stationary, he turned his whole body towards her, his face showing the expression belonging to their raw, early days of grieving. It was the one expression which took away her optimism every time she witnessed it. She had to force her hands not to reach out to him. The moment was far too critical to be diminished.

"When I spoke to him at the hospital," sighed David, "he was more or less rambling, but I didn't like it one bit. Talked about ... termination and letting her down. So, Kate, if we're going to do something about this, I need you to remember exactly what he said."

Kate nodded but had never felt less like speaking. Neil's words had not been for her. She had managed to persuade herself in the last few days that they had been said only to make Andie feel better, to make her feel less alone in the time when she was broken and bleeding. It had seemed clear to her at the time what he was saying, but really it could have been a reaction to the whole shocking business. She was being asked to repeat his private promises, and she was still unsure that she should. She licked her lips, watching David's eyes begin to disappear in the semi-darkness.

"Kate?"

Kate shook her head. "I wasn't meant to hear it. It was private."

She heard David exhale into the gloom. "I understand that, but this is as serious as it gets. Please tell me what he said."

Again Kate hesitated. She could feel herself blushing, embarrassed to be denying David anything, but instinct was holding her tongue. Why, when she had spent days planning a way of instigating the conversation? She laid her face against the glass and stared at the snow now beginning to flicker against the black trees. David took her hand and pulled her quite firmly back into a seating position.

"No you don't, Kit," he said. "Stop thinking about the pros and cons and just tell me. He's my brother, and I won't let him do this to any of us."

"But I don't know really what he was saying."

"Then let's talk about it together. That's how this works."

Kate could no longer read his expression in the murky dusk, but as his face was caught in the lights of a passing vehicle, she saw determination tinged with patience. Really, it was one more instance of her floundering with his expectations of her as an adult, but they were partners. And if that partnership was to survive its first month, she had to trust him yet again.

Kate hung her head before speaking, "It was nothing straightforward, it wasn't like 'right, we're going to do this and this at this time'. I thought he was just comforting her, really, although I remember being really shocked at the time. Now, I'm not sure what he was thinking. What did he say to you?"

"That he wasn't scared to go ahead with whatever it is, but he didn't want to do it badly."

They mulled this over in the cold silence, both desperate to find a simple, uncomplicated meaning to Neil's words without success. Kate chewed her thumbnail in the dark and felt chilled to the bone. The heat was escaping the cab at a steady pace, and she began to feel pressure building in her forehead. Surely they were both overreacting. Surely Neil had meant he would be there for Andie. It was not possible that he would be contemplating anything so drastic.

"Oh, shit, no." Kate breathed, finally recognising that there was no uncertainty. "No."

"What is it?"

There was a danger that the cab was about to engulf her in its black fist, and Kate suddenly put her hand across the void between them, searching for his. He grabbed it and moved towards her. "What, honey?"

"We're sitting here wondering if he's going to help her die, right?" she gasped, "Which is something that is completely beyond me. But Dave, it might be worse than that. I think it might be much worse, and I've just been deliberately shutting it out, making myself think about anything and everything but it."

"Tell me," David's voice was rough, and she knew that he was as frantic as she was.

"I'm sure he asked her if she wouldn't rather they walked down that road together. That was it."

David's hand and hers felt clammy together and she pulled away, and desperate for fresh air, she opened the door. Out in the dark, she leaned against the closed door of the SUV and took as many deep breaths in as her lungs allowed. Her head hammered at the change of temperature, and she stood cradling her forehead, willing the ache to subside. Rather than listen to her, it seemed to intensify and thud against her skull. She felt sick to the stomach and could not comprehend how she had managed to bury this enormous fear for more than two days and how it was only making itself felt now. Since mentioning it to Hazel, she had covered it with excuses and purposely refused to string his words together in those particular phrases. And how the hell was David now viewing her? Bile was in her throat before she knew where she was, and she grabbed her own knees as her lunch came splattering onto the frozen soil. She retched twice more before she managed to feel her way down to the rear of the truck and sit on the ground. Another second and David was there.

"I'm sorry," she whispered, relieved at least that the headache had gone. "I'm sorry, Dave."

Kate felt David's hand on her shoulder, his hankie making a gentle tour of her face, but she could barely keep her head upright, she was so shaken and ashamed. What on earth had she been doing for the last few days, keeping busy and pretending to David that all was well? She had even crawled all over his body in the night, loving him, whilst concealing something hideously dangerous, and that made her imperfect and deceptive. She could have huddled herself into a ball and rolled away from him, she was so mortified. She was indeed a child, and it was not what he needed. She swore wildly to herself and pulled her knees up to her face.

"Hey," David's voice was a whisper in her ear, as if he knew she could not handle any more volume than that. "Come back to me. It's okay. We're going to make this okay, but I need you to help me. It's you and me now, honey. Neither of us can do this without the other, remember that."

"Don't let him do it, please. He can't. It's too ... too ... there's no coming back."

"Come on, my love," his ability to haul her body to his always amazed her, and as she leaned into his heat and fragrance, she began to feel so sleepy and light. He had remained in spite of her betrayal, and she felt some of the concrete in her heart shatter open and fall in a dusty lump to the earth. But only some. She could not keep her eyes open, and she felt herself begin to drift away on an ocean of consolation; and then, suddenly, she was frowning and holding her head aloft once more. No. She was here to support David, not to be a drain on his soul. She put her hands on his rough face and kissed him. It was true, neither of them knew how they were going to tackle this problem, but two fighting together was surely better than two uncertain, lost loners. She kissed his cheeks, his eyes, and his chin.

"I'm going to help you, Dave. We can do it. But," she loved the way he held her face in his hands. "This is one of those times, I think, where we have to take advantage of your age. I'll do whatever you say."

"Okay," his voice was assured enough, but in truth, David had no conception of what to do next.

«●»«●»«●»

The painkillers were doing their job, and Andie eased herself up the bed enough to reach her watch on the bedside cabinet. It was approaching six in the evening, and tonight Neil would come striding into the ward with David and Kate at his side. She was delighted at the prospect.

Iris had sat with her for over an hour that afternoon until the pain in her left thigh had brought on the sweats, and she had been even less inclined to talk. And what had they really discussed? With their worst fears now in the room with them, the two women had been calm and observant; watching each other for signs of panic or overwhelming grief, neither of which had made themselves known. At least with her mother, there was no need to discuss the decision itself. Since Dale had left them of his own accord all those years ago, mother and daughter had carefully boxed up and stored away this current possibility, accepting the way it would be handled should they ever need to unpack it. Lying in a bed of drug-aided comfort, Andie allowed herself to delve into the memories of her brother.

For fraternal twins, they had shared only two things; their black hair and their strength of character. Well, thought Andie, now three things if you included their genetic make-up. When his symptoms had come on at an unprecedentedly fast rate years before they had even begun to watch for them, Dale had told no one and hidden himself away at college until he was unable to conceal it further.

It had been only three years since their dad had passed away. They had lived in the same house, watching him deteriorate for nine years prior to that. That particular Christmas Dale had arrived in a taxi, all his worldly goods filling its interior, still able to walk up to the house, but not without obvious tremor. Andie could smell the snow in the air now, remembering how she had stood, frozen to the spot, watching him make his painful progress as their mother had marched up to him and held him close. She remembered two other things from that day; how his face had been more energetic than resigned, and the horrific howl which had escaped her as she had sprinted from the scene, her heart disintegrating as she had fled.

His test results had not altered his face; a face which had been as familiar as her own, a face which had shared the same cot for the first year of their lives. And when they had finally held each other at the end of that day and she had taken in his purely personal thoughts, she had come to appreciate that, for him, his wishes were less cruel and more productive than any other option. Iris had remained in the room with them, albeit at a distance, listening to him speak and plan with the persistent presence of a wounded collaborator.

Iris had loved that face even more than Andie had done, and as his eyes had stayed shining on them, they had shown only one emotion; complete control. He had decided on how, when and where. He had thought he deserved this, and so had they.

Andie sighed, thinking of another day which had somehow, remarkably, been the most fulfilling, touching day of her life to date. A day when Dale, Iris and she had sat in a dim sitting room, the sun shining behind the drawn curtains, and had shared every thought and emotion as it had entered their heads, uncensored and without restraint. There had been much more laughter than there had been tears, simply because they had chosen to make it a special day. As the sun had disappeared, Iris had drawn her son a bath and had washed his hair and his back, while Andie had sat on the floor and sang every song he had requested. They had not questioned his decision once.

Dale had no desire to subject his family to any more than was required, not on that day or in the years to come. The last thing Andie had done for him was to bring him a bag of ice, and Dale had insisted on numbing his arm and opening his skin unaided. He had been shockingly able and precise in the few seconds it had taken, and in spite of his pained and sweat-ridden face, had managed to thank them both over and over.

Stroking his hands, Iris and Andie had continued to murmur words as they had done all day, as the bubbles had turned pink before them and Dale had gradually ceased to respond. When he had gone, they had mutely tidied up around them and left the room. Suicide it may have been, but Dale had not been alone, and for that, they had all been thankful.

A sob cut into Andie's thoughts as she remembered the horrendous journey she had made from the bathroom to the sofa on that day; dizzy, breathless, blind. She had taken her seat, truly believing that her heart was about to sever the veins and arteries which allowed it to function. Never again would her brother speak to her, never again would he call her Warhol or ring her in the middle of the night to ask her how to make potato cakes. He would never see another birthday, and she had never celebrated even one without him.

She had sat on the sofa in the black dark, bent double to ease the pain which was cutting her in two, until Iris had lit a lamp and rang the police. From that moment, Andie had sat upright, ensuring that her face showed shock and disbelief as well as total grief, which actually had required no effort whatsoever.

《•》《•》《•》

It was well after six, and still there was no sign of her family. She lay, frustrated and shaken to the core by her recollections. Andie thought of her mother and her ability to withstand what life had given her. She was a woman who had taken more than one risk in life in the name of love, and she was about to have someone else removed from her, after an almost cruel respite from it all.

Her mother was not a saint. She could be distant and ruthlessly independent, yet she had viewed each of her family as precious and understood every aspect of their fears. Like every other unit on earth, they had been susceptible to accidents and experiences and worries, but they had been part of something which included more knowledge and bitter awareness of time.

This knowledge had allowed Andie to make a decision about children, which she had never debated with anyone including herself, because she knew she was no Iris. It had not, however, stopped her from pining for that particular link with another being.

Now, on this night, she was desperate to see Neil and Kate together. She hoped that they would both be upbeat and smiling, because it was then that she could see their connection; and she loved to move her eyes from one face to the other, finding similarities and noticing their expressions when they talked directly to each other. She had no clue how much longer she would be given to watch them grow together. It was the only obscure area of their whole, crystal clear plan and had yet to be discussed.

Where were they?

CHAPTER 34

Friday, 9th December 1994

"Do you think we should eat before or after, son? David reckoned he would be here by now."

Neil was working on the leather of his belt with an ancient awl, making an extra two holes to accommodate his shrinking waist. It did not seem to matter how much Rose forced him to eat, he was burning off the calories faster than ever. He spent every moment when he was not at Andie's bedside in his workshop, flitting from project to project, unable to commit more than ten minutes to a single piece of wood. Even the dogs felt the tension, and Rose was ever thankful that David and Kate were about to provide her with a little respite.

"I don't mind," replied Neil, "let them decide, as long as we're at the hospital by six. She's started to watch the clock."

"Okay. Well, the food won't spoil either way. Want some coffee cake, while we wait?"

Neil shook his head and, threading his belt through his jeans, whistled the dogs to heel. The four of them were out of the door before she could say another word, and in response, Rose lifted the already cut slice of cake to her own lips and took a huge, comforting bite. The flavour was most definitely coffee, but there was nothing remotely satisfying about the taste or texture, and Rose continued to eat it simply to avoid the guilt of throwing good food in the bin.

Neil could feel his heart fluttering in his chest. It had been intermittently quivering, jumping and missing beats for days now, but he had put each occasion aside because it was not life-threatening or even unexpected. Still, it remained annoyingly unpleasant, and he hated the fact that his state of mind could affect his whole constitution like this. He had work to do, he had dogs to look after, and all he could think of was Andie lying in a bed that was not their own, taking stock of every passing minute. Each dusk and dawn marked time, and he knew that his love had begun studying the movement of the sun. He needed to be with her. He needed his world to be made up of their shared moments, not these allotted times when he could pick up where he had left off the previous day. Had those in authority no idea about what was acceptable in these circumstances? Well, of course they hadn't. They had no idea what the circumstances entailed.

The wind chill was fierce, and Neil realised too late that his padded jacket was required. This thought was quickly tossed onto the irrelevant pile, and he wandered on through the dark, listening for the dogs and trying to pick out the reflection of their eyes in the house lights. Since the beginning of this horrendous week, he had begun to take note of every visual and audible experience. Ice on the windscreen turning to water and running into the radiator grid, the thud and roar as the central heating boiler fired up without warning, the thickening, then crisping, and then burning of eggs in a pan, the tick of the clock. His senses seemed to be hypersensitive, stinging him with their continual assault on his mind. He was on the edge of reality and constantly amazed that he had not been found curled in a catatonic state somewhere on the highway.

Tonight, David and Kate were on their way, with their ever present optimism and determination to find a solution to every blessed thing in life. Sometimes, there was no solution, had neither of them learned that by now? At least, no solution they would view as appropriate. His eyebrows itched with the aggravation of it all. Kate remained an enigma to him even after all this time; she was too understanding and too blindly positive for her own good. David was a reliably constant character, who had accepted every piece of crap ever launched at him with the sort of tolerance that made you doubt his wisdom. They seemed to be happy, which he could not bring himself to condemn, but they had no real idea of what represented a decision or a choice. He growled, his breath shallow and laboured as he scolded himself for his bitter judgements. A week ago, he had been cheerfully awaiting their arrival. Now this brought coldness to his heart which had nothing to do with the temperature.

Neil had made a frantic-paced tour of the plantation and was almost back at the house when David's vehicle pulled onto the drive. He had time to fill the dogs' bowls with kibble before they pulled to a halt, the headlights trained on where he stood. He did not smile as he glanced in their direction and, unexpectedly, they remained seated in the cab, studying him. Only when he began to frown and rub his thumb under his chin, did David slowly open the door and step out into the cold air. Shifting his eyes to his daughter, Neil noticed that Kate's face was peaky. She remained where she was.

"Dave," Neil spoke without feeling. "What's happening?"

"You tell me."

Neil felt his eyebrows knot even further. This tone of David's was new, so unlike him that Neil was about to comment on it, but was stalled as the man stepped into the light of the security lamp. Neil tilted his head slightly as his brother walked straight to him. On this night, none of David's stoic acceptance was even remotely evident, and his eyes seemed dead. He glanced back at Kate once, flicked his head in the direction of the house and watched her carefully as she left the truck and disappeared quickly up the stairs. Something was not right.

"So," stated Neil, his tongue hot and dry in his mouth. "You've obviously got an opinion on something. Let's hear it."

David's eyes remained blank as he walked past Neil and made his way to the woodshed. In spite of his earlier ideas, Neil followed his brother, intrigued. He had rarely seen him so imposing, and in truth, he hoped that whatever was coming was going to be more than a minor, insipid set of statements. Neil was ready for battle.

Rose was stirring the fire when Kate came hurrying in through the door.

"Here she is!" cried Rose, but immediately lowered her voice. "Kate, you're very pale. You feel ok?"

Kate shook her head, unable to put on an act for Rose as she had been asked to do. "No, not really. But I think a cup of tea would help."

"Sure," frowned Rose, then, "Car journeys sometimes get me like that, especially if the radiator has been blowing in your face. Where's David?"

"He's talking to Neil. They're feeding the dogs." All of this had been said while Kate removed her hat and gloves and so had sounded reasonably bland and ordinary, which was the most she could hope for considering she was worried to death. Up until that point, she would have allowed herself to think that she had seen most sides of the men downstairs, but not now. Both of their faces had belonged to strangers. "Have you seen Andie today?"

"No, Iris was there this afternoon."

Kate had not yet met the woman, but wondered how much she was privy to. Well, it stood to reason that she was aware of everything; and since she doubted that she would be on their side, Kate withdrew her from the equation. As Rose handed over a cup of tea to her daughter-in-law, they both sat on the sofa and stared at the fire. Kate's fingers were white, blood-free and could not seem to hold the mug properly. She laid it at her feet.

"You know what I was thinking the other day," Rose mused, "and I'm sure you'll appreciate the sentiment. I was thinking that for someone who has spent most of my adult existence amongst a surprisingly few number of people, luck has been on my side."

Kate shook her head, "How?"

Rose smiled and looked around her. "Well, I mean those people who have joined my life along the way have been amongst the best people on earth. First there were my boys, a joy, the pair of them. Then your mom. Kate, she was one of the loveliest girls I've ever met, and possibly the most resilient. I don't think you and I ever talked enough on that particular subject. I look forward to when we can give that the time it deserves."

Kate's eyes were growing wider by the second. The fire was beautifully comforting, and this woman's words were kind. Without warning, her chin gave the tiniest wobble.

"Then Andie came out of nowhere," continued Rose, purposely not acknowledging Kate's frame of mind. "She was like a mountain sprite, black hair and bright colours, and she pieced Neil back together. She was always completely intrigued by him, and, I'll admit it, I wondered if she would lose interest, once she had cracked his shell. Then suddenly he was living again, taking on this place and building them a home. I wish they had visited us more, but it was understandable, and in a way we just got on without each other. But we're so much better now. This is not going to be an easy time for any of us, Kate."

"I wonder if they have any paracetamol," murmured Kate, heading quickly across the open space and into the bathroom. Her nausea had returned, but she was damned if she was going to be sick again. She grinned wryly to herself, recognising that in a matter of days she had been shoved back into the position of the last year; 'show them your strength, don't buckle, don't make things any harder for those around you'. How foolish she had been to think that David's constant presence would allow her to relax a bit more. Had she really thought that life from now on would be a simple case of wandering the rooms of The Edge, doing a bit of cleaning, planning meals whilst listening to the radio, greeting David with a kiss? What about the rest?

The cabinet containing the few essential painkillers and cold remedies was positioned immediately next to the bathroom window.

Kate could see the light on in the woodshed; and with a minimal effort, she eased the sash window open a couple of inches, gasping as the icy blast flowed over her hands. There was a murmur of voices, not raised, but quick and unstilted, and she hovered in indecision. To hear their discussion meant being a witness to potentially harsh words. To not hear it meant an agony of curiosity. She watched her own reflection in the glass, interested to see what her intentions were, and all she saw was a pair of confused eyes in an incredibly juvenile face. She closed her eyes on the image and gritted her teeth.

"Right," she said, taking a slow steady breath in through her nose. "Here we go then."

As Kate marched back into the main room, she found Rose laying the table, but wasted no time on hesitation or explanation. "I'll get them," she stated over her shoulder. Her steps did not falter on their dark journey to the woodshed. They did not falter when she recognised that the exchanges taking place inside were cold and hard. She cleared her expression and stepped into the glare of the light. She stopped only when both pairs of eyes turned to her.

"I need to know what you want me to say to Rose," Kate barely recognised her own voice. It was as unyielding as a rock face, and she glared at each of them through narrowed eyes. She saw David turn his whole body towards her. His face was flushed, but it did not alter her stance or tone. "If you're going to make me stay up there, I want you to tell me what to say. I'm not lying for either of you. She doesn't deserve that."

She watched Neil fold his arms and look to his brother, who had somehow lost his grip on the conversation.

"We've just got to sort a few things, Kate. If you could -"

"No, I'm not going to. I know I said I'd do whatever you wanted me to, but I'm not taking part in this. I'll be in the car."

As Kate departed the woodshed, David began to rub his forehead, struck by the absurdity of this particular evening; the surreal topic of conversation with his brother, the obvious anger of his love, the fact that he had to decide which situation to deal with first. Neil seemed to have made the decision for both of them, however, as he unfolded his arms and moved towards the door.

"Well?" spat David.

"She's right. Rose needs to know."

David grabbed his arm and for a couple of seconds, they were stationary, before Neil shoved him back against the wall of wood. Neither of them was surprised. This had been on the cards for the past ten minutes. David could feel the logs digging into the base of his spine as he looked at the face mere inches from his own.

Neil's eyes were bright, antagonistic, and desperate to be allowed to carry this to its physical conclusion. He held David's wrists against his chest.

"Hey, Neil," David snarled, "what do you see when you look at yourself?"

In an instant, Neil released him and stood back, his eyes narrowing to venomous slits and his fists clenching in fury. David was nowhere near backing down from this particular challenge, not when the stakes were so very high.

"Do you see a strong man, Neil? A worthy man?"

"What, you're kidding, right, Dave?" Neil's laugh appeared genuine until his eyes were added to the mix. They were black and lifeless. "How could I possibly see any such thing when I have your shining example to compare myself to?"

"Well, I'll tell you what I see when I look at you. I see a boy who has played with the same toys for too long, but doesn't have the sense to go and look for new ones."

"Jesus," scorned Neil, "that's an unbelievably crass analogy. In fact, it makes you look lazy. Your arguments are feeble, you know that?"

David smiled. "And yet you still feel the need to top them, so they must have some worth."

There was a long pause, during which neither man looked at the other. David cracked his knuckles until the unbearable sound had Neil moving again, but he had not taken four long strides across the yard before David grabbed his shoulder and hauled him backwards. For a moment, Neil's face crumpled into an agonised mask.

Kate, watching from behind the car's windscreen, winced in sympathy. Too late David thought about Neil's imperfectly positioned vertebrae, and the resulting pain he inflicted saw his brother finally swinging the first fist. As it connected with David's temple, Kate screamed his name and hastily struggled to open the car door.

David did not lose his footing and in turn grabbed Neil's shirt and pushed him forcefully away from him. Neil fell hard, allowing David a moment's grace to shake his brain back into position before both of them were once more upright, alert and facing each other.

Neil's face still betrayed some degree of pain, David's spoke only of purpose. Kate feared that neither of them would be prepared to submit. She stood by the side of the SUV, so shaken that she could not even screech at them to stop.

"What the hell?" shouted Rose, her appearance on the scene having no effect whatsoever.

David tackled his brother at waist level, determined to floor him and therefore have the greater physical advantage. In doing so, they both ended up crashing into the trailer, David glancing his thigh off the metal rim and letting out an outraged curse as the pair of them lost their footing and ended up head first on the trailer's gritty base.

It was too much for Kate. This was not a Hollywood fight; there was no perfectly timed, choreographed connecting of fists with skin, accompanied by masculine grunts. It was awkward and angry, the two men in front of her grappling and tearing and wounding, and she could not see how it was going to end.

Rose's mouth was a tight line as she stood as close as possible, waiting for the tiniest lull so that her words would have the most impact.

Still they continued to swear and throw as many unmasked grudges as they did clumsy punches. Only when Kate heard her own name mentioned in some unknown, incoherent context did she turn and leave.

Rose, still awaiting her opportunity, did not even notice Kate's departure. Kate didn't run. Running would have made the panic she felt even more acute, and instead, she marched away from the scuffling noises and the bitter words and began to hum to herself instead. The tune was unimportant, all she required it to do was to block out the melee of sounds behind her; and by the time she had reached the end of the drive, all she felt inside was the rhythm of the folk song, and she started to sing the words out loud. It made sense, on that dark, cold road, when the only thing she had left now to keep her company was a set of Scottish words in a lilting melody.

Time was unimportant, and she only realised that minutes had passed when she reached the first road junction. Thankfully, there was enough early evening traffic for the road to have a regular source of light, and when Kate's song eventually dried up and the sweat gathering seemed to be less of panic and more of physical exertion, she allowed herself a still moment to decide what to do. She could hide in the wood, forcing these people to come looking for her, like a child who needed to be the centre of attention; or she could head off in the direction of the town and get a taxi back to The Edge. She was relatively happy to settle for the latter option, and if nothing else, it would prove to David that she would never be prepared to witness the likes of their fight again.

As she assessed, in the intermittent headlights, which side of the road had the most verge, she heard the sound of a truck slowing down behind her. The red tail lights as they trailed past her made her angry all over again. Just for once, she didn't want to be rescued from anything. She wanted to walk off her fears and shock in her own company, but as the truck pulled to a stop, Kate saw neither the Dodge nor the SUV, but an ancient vehicle whose engine sounded strangely familiar; as if it was not quite in full health, hiccupping every third rumble. And there was the silhouette of a large dog appearing out of the opening window. "Is that you, Ronald? Do you know how late it is?"

In spite of her amazement, Kate walked up to the truck, prepared to have exactly the same conversation as she had had over a year ago and smiled at the passive, uninterested eyes of the animal on her. "Hello, JR."

"Oh, you're ... Wait a minute, how do you know my dog?" Gloria Badham was wrapped up for the winter and barely recognisable apart from her low, cigarette-fuelled rasp.

"We've met once before, on a better day than this."

"Of course we have, dearie. You're that Irish girl who didn't want a lift. I bet you'd like one tonight."

Kate did not even hesitate. "I would indeed, if you're going into town?"

Without ceremony, Gloria hauled JR over into the middle of the front seat by the neck and waited for Kate to climb aboard. The heat inside the truck was stifling, and Kate began unwrapping her scarf immediately, incredulous that the woman beside her had not expired beneath her many layers.

"Well, let's go. Hey, this is great, isn't it, JR?"

JR was almost as big as Dougal, but smelled a little riper, for which his eyes seemed to be permanently apologetic. But sitting up high, perched on the cracked leather seat, at least covered the road quicker, and Kate forced herself to focus on how to get from Port Alberni to The Edge with the least possible trauma. She was on the point of asking Gloria where she could locate a taxi rank, when the woman slowed her driving down to a minimum, peering along the verge, her nose pressed against the windscreen.

"Thought I saw a black jacket there," she murmured, then accelerated again. "Nope, not this time."

Just like that, Kate remembered the reason for this lady's journeys and felt herself sink further into the seat. It was one thing to trawl through the autumn landscape in the low morning sun, but to wrap up against the elements and head out into the freezing night in constant search of her love was just too sad. Yet Gloria appeared more happy than worried, patting JR's head regularly and grinning over at Kate. Perhaps each journey filled her with hope, an emotion which was sufficient to lighten her heart and kill more lonely minutes. Perhaps she returned to a cosy, bright house after each outing, contented that she had made the effort to look for the subject of every photo on view. Kate had no judgement for this woman. Hope was better than nothing, and as the streetlights took the place of the deep blackness, she suddenly wanted to see Andie again.

"Mrs Badham, isn't it?" Kate enquired quietly, mindful that she was actually superfluous to the journey. "My name's Kate Wilder, and I wonder if you could point me in the direction of the hospital when we hit the town. I really need to visit a friend of mine."

"Oh, gracious, I'll take you right there! Lord, I worked my entire career at the place. Radiographer, you know. Ran the department before they retired me. I'll drop you at the door. It would be my pleasure, dearie."

For the remainder of the journey, JR rested his head on Kate's lap. After all, it was his seat, and Kate was glad of fur beneath her hands. The heat from the radiator was pleasant, but as she stared out at the passing buildings and Christmas lights, her mind insisted on returning to the horrific scene she had left behind. In all her life, Kate had never witnessed truly passionate aggression, had never seen men trying to hurt each other simply because they were angry or frustrated or scared to death. What made it far, far worse was that both of them were so dear to her. Neil was central to her existence; David was the person she would trip along beside, to the brink of oblivion itself. Somehow they imagined that by breaking their bodies they would alter each other's perspectives. How on earth did two intelligent men reach that conclusion?

"Actually, Kate, I love this spot," sighed Gloria, contentedly, almost blinded by the glare of the hospital spotlights. "The last time I spoke to Ronald was in this very place, and the staff are very good here. Your friend is definitely in the best place."

Kate gently eased JR's head back onto the seat as she departed the truck, but instantly he was back into his upright, regular position. Kate's visit had been unusual and reasonably enjoyable, but his job was to look after Gloria, as she found her weary road back to their home. He licked Kate's hand once and then stared once more straight ahead of him.

"I really appreciate the lift, Mrs Badham. It saved me a lot of time."

"Not a problem, dearie. See you again, I hope."

Kate glanced at her watch after waving the truck on its way, amazed that it was not yet six-thirty, and pointed her boots in the direction of the entrance. She had no idea what explanation she would give to Andie, but she was here, and she needed to see a face she loved. By the time her new ward was located, Kate felt grimy, salty and too tired to attempt the stairs. She stood with three other women in the gigantic lift and marvelled that less than six hours ago she had been standing, laughing with the crew at the timber yard, relatively unaffected by their curiosity. She guessed her appearance was causing more than one raised eyebrow, but did not lift her head to confirm this. In fact, she studied her boots for most of the length of the corridor, and by the time she had been ushered to Andie's room, she could feel how bleak her face was, but the muscles involved refused to tighten into a smile. Andie's relief at her arrival disappeared almost immediately.

"Kate?" the bruised mouth spoke the word easily, Andie's battered face free from gauze. "You're on your own? Did you drive? Wow."

None of the words were registering with Kate as she took off her coat in the overpowering heat, and by the time she sat in the chair, she was past the point of talking. But she owed an explanation, and this woman had been waiting for a visitor for over half an hour. How much should she share? Finally, Kate reached out and touched Andie's wrist as it looked the least painful area on offer. "I didn't drive. I got a lift with Gloria Badham. Ronald died here, you know."

Andie was obviously completely thrown and glanced over at the open doorway. "You got a lift? Where's David? Where's Neil?"

Kate scratched at her ear. "I think they might be on their way. They were taking too long."

As Kate's idiotic attempt at delaying the truth came to an end, there was a brisk knock at the door, and a young male face appeared to be surveying the occupants before he came marching in.

"Well, Andie," he began, "I know you'll be inundated with family at any moment, but is it okay to have a quick word?"

Kate by this time was not even aware that perhaps the 'word' was of a private nature and slid down a little in her seat. She sat chewing her thumbnail.

"Fire away," stated Andie, frowning once more in Kate's direction before turning her attention to the doctor by her side.

"Okay, well, just to let you know, that the blood we took earlier has confirmed our suspicions. It's a condition that you'll need to learn to manage; but believe me, if you take it seriously, diabetes will soon become part of your everyday life."

There was a moment or two of complete silence, the doctor's optimistic words not quite having the effect he had hoped for. Andie was gaping at him, her eyes completely mystified, and her young visitor seemed completely frozen to her seat.

"I have diabetes?" asked Andie.

"Indeed," the man replied, although their reactions were beginning to spread doubts through his own mind. He held up a chart as if to prove he was not lying. "Surprisingly, considering your age, it's Type 1. Sorry, I thought this possibility had already been mentioned. Blood sugar can cause all sorts of complications; I'd put money on it causing your concentration lapse. Anyway, I thought you might like to share your news with your family. We can start to discuss your treatment later tonight."

Kate's lungs felt as if they were on the point of bursting. God had finally pushed her over the edge. Her hands were throbbing and she put her head on her knees, which somehow signified to the bringer of the news that his work was complete. He retreated two steps before waving to his patient. "I'll be back later. Or ring for me if anybody needs clarification on anything."

Kate only raised her head when she heard Andie's breath being exhaled. In all of the trials Kate had encountered, this was the least comprehensible of them all. How was there any justification whatsoever in giving this beautiful person in front of her yet another burden? But Andie's face was not closed and lost, it was clear and serene. It was just like her to cope.

"You can't have," whispered Kate.

"Sorry, honey?"

"Your... condition and now this. It's not fair. You can't have both of them, you just can't."

Andie put her hand to her mouth and swallowed. She seemed to be massaging her upper lip with her tongue and then she was looking down at her strapped arm and rubbing her grazed face. Kate watched her, awaiting some sort of acknowledgement of this dreadful news. She seemed agitated more than anything else. Then she laid her head back against the pillow and blew her breath out slowly into the air.

"Kate," she said, a strange vibrato present in her voice. "Do you ever want kids?"

It seemed easier just to answer the odd question. "Well, yes. Someday."

"Do one thing for me," continued Andie, still staring at the ceiling. "If you have a little girl, think about calling her Hope. I love that name."

«•»«•»«•»

"Kate?"

In spite of being the only two visitors gracing the hospital coffee lounge, Kate did not raise her head at the sound of David's voice. She did not want to see him or talk to him until she had put her thoughts into an acceptable order in her head, so she stared instead at the foam on the top of her milky coffee, noticing that one of her thumbnails was much shorter than the other, and ignored the man who sat opposite her.

"I didn't know where you were, Kitty."

Kate shrugged her reply, but as she lifted the mug to her mouth, she caught a glimpse of his face, and immediately put it back onto the table. She stared at him, sitting back and hugging her arms around her. His face, usually so familiar that it was like looking in a mirror, was expressing equal amounts of accusation and worry, and it annoyed her. It annoyed her more than the cut to his head and the swelling of his lip. She knew that look. He had permanently made use of it in their early days on Skye, when he had been trying to break down barriers and continually accepting her reluctance to let him. Well, even after all they had been through, this expression still had the ability to irritate her and she did not yield, not even a fraction.

"Don't look at me like that," she said quietly, her eyes never leaving his. "You don't have a right to worry about me now, not after that back there. That was the time to worry about me, to wonder how I was feeling, when you were beating the crap out of each other. Did you think I was just going to stand around and watch it?"

David clasped his hands in front of him, and looked at her through narrowed eyes. He needed to justify himself sooner rather than later and sat in silence for a moment or two, trying to think of the words to put things right. As always with Kate, the best thing was to open his heart and tell her exactly as it was.

"He wouldn't listen," he began and thought how petty that sounded. "I was panicking. I couldn't make him appreciate that his words were one thing, but to plan what he was planning and then to physically count down the days until ... I'm sorry, Kate. But he would have done it. He would have left us. I couldn't stand by." He held his hands up, literally, and dropped them back into his lap. "I don't know if it's made a difference, even now."

"Is Rose here?" asked Kate, her voice still unable to excuse him.

"No. She's as mad as hell and doesn't know the half of it. She can't ever know."

Kate felt herself slide down her chair a little and her boot accidentally made contact with David's under the table. He moved it away instinctively, and that, more than any other horrific occurrence of the evening, made the walls around her crumble as easily as Edinburgh rock beneath a toffee hammer. David and she were one person, they shared the one personal space. They did not need to treat each other as they treated the public; there was no need for politeness or reverence because they were each other. Kate stood and moved to where he still sat, lost and thoughtful. She sat on his knee, squeezing herself between his body and the table without invitation, but to her eternal gratitude, he simply put his arms around her waist and held her tight.

"Don't scare me like that again," he said, his tone not open to negotiation.

"Snap," she replied and laid her sternest, firmest glare on his face. "I've never actually hit anybody in my life, but it looked painful. Let me see your hands."

He held them up in front of her. They were not cut open, but seemed to have raw burns along the digits and knuckles, and just for a moment, Kate wanted to kiss them better; but he did not yet deserve the reprieve. So she sighed instead and shook her head at him. "You know, and I know, that these hands have to be taken care of. Why would you want to put these hands out of action, Dave? Really, why would you?"

"Because I was desperate, Kate. I'm still desperate."

As they sat and pondered this state of affairs, Kate's head against David's cheek and her hands gently holding his, a couple in their twenties wandered in from the corridor and joined the waitress at the counter. All three of them allowed themselves a moment or two of curiosity at the sight of such an unusual and intimate pair, but Kate could not be bothered to respond in any way. There were thousands of oddities in the world; she and her husband were nothing in the scheme of things.

"Did Neil phone you?" whispered Kate.

"Yes, as soon as he knew you were here."

"So," Kate nodded, "you're speaking to each other again."

"Well, that might be stretching it ..." David's voice trailed off at the sight of Neil. The man was walking towards them both, his face strangely set and his gait betraying the extent of his aching spine. Kate, as a matter of course, moved back to her own chair but kept one of David's hands in hers. Solidarity.

"What is she saying now?" Kate asked, apparently not prepared to reprimand him to the extent she had her husband.

"I'm lost," announced David, frowning, to which Neil looked straight at him.

"Me too," he replied. He was a dishevelled mess of a man, his eyes as wildly unsettled as his clothes and hair, his skin shining beneath his shirt. He sat for a moment, unable to qualify his thoughts, his bent knee reverting to its uneasy tapping rhythm. As Kate watched him, there seemed to be an energy returning to his body, which David also picked up on. She felt him squeeze her hand and with that encouragement, she touched Neil's wrist.

"I haven't told Dave," she said gently, "because I don't really know what it means. Can you tell him for me?"

Neil took out his hankie and wiped the sweat from his face. He seemed to be alternating between anxiety and possibility, and once his fists clenched while he hid his head and breathed deeply. Kate felt David tense beside her, but she gripped his hand and they let the man be. Finally, he looked at his brother.

"She's been diagnosed with diabetes." Neil shook his head as he spoke, apparently as confused as Kate was. Then he laughed at the absurdity of his life, and through tears, he finally spoke. "I think I might be losing my mind."

CHAPTER 35

Saturday, 24th December 1994

It was almost midnight when Stuart MacIntyre switched off the pickup's engine at the bottom of the driveway. As always, when he was acting on impulse, he could feel electric currents pulsing through him and forced himself to take one last look at his situation before he moved.

He was twenty-three and fit. His father would continue to farm until old age and lack of inclination decreased his hours, at which time Stuart and his brother would take over completely. He was set up for life, as long as the economy and the weather remained reasonably consistent, and this was a positive thing. Stuart sighed, prepared to acknowledge the rest of it. He had spent the last two years living on the edge of a storm of grief and animosity, where his role had consisted mainly of support and light relief. Now, when it seemed to be abating at last, he found himself assessing what he was left with. It vexed him that David and Kate, in spite of all the prejudice they had risked and still might encounter, were in a happier situation than he was. Yet the sight of Hazel still made him sit up and take notice, and tonight he had had some sort of epiphany.

Their chosen Christmas Eve disco had been overwhelmed with teenagers, and Hazel had decided to supplement her vodkas by toasting absent friends with tequila shots. They had left just after eleven, the Square yielding no more Christmas spirit than a dark night in February, and she had clung fiercely to his arm all the way home, humming 'O Holy Night' in an attempt to stay awake in the heat of the pickup's cab. Suddenly she had kissed him hard on the cheek.

"I love you," she had stated. "I know folk think that because we've been together for ages that we've just turned into a habit, but I love you, Stuart. Thanks for not dumping me when I've been a crabby bitch."

"You're welcome," he had replied, changing gears and allowing her to dose against him. They had arranged, between long, wet kisses, to meet up at the cottage in the morning and exchange presents; then he had simply left her at the doorway and headed back up the hill. Now he was back, staring at the dark cottage, watching light rain in the headlights. He switched them off.

Stuart knew the reason behind her thoughts, her anxieties and even her sadness. Still she remained the person he wanted to see on a daily basis. He knew her self-doubt and envy where David was concerned, and still she was the girl he wanted to hold close and cheer up. He knew that she missed her mother and her sister in equal amounts and found it difficult to look ahead sometimes, and still she was the one he wanted to smother him with her needs. He was out of the vehicle and knocking on the back door in less than twenty seconds. It took two attempts to rouse the household from the sitting room.

"What did you forget?" asked Kenny on opening the door, coffee mug in hand.

"Hazel. Forgot to ask her about her plans." As Stuart wandered through to the sitting room, he smiled at his own ambiguous and innocent reply. Sometimes, he could be as sharp as Hazel. There she was, flat out on the sofa, hand trailing on the floor, head pointed in the direction of the TV but seeing nothing. Beth welcomed him in as he knelt beside the sleeping form and gently shook her awake.

"Hi babe," she yawned, "what did you forget?"

He waited until she had propped herself up on an elbow and her eyes were focussed. "I forgot to say that I think it's about time you married me. I haven't got a ring, and it'll take me a year or two to fix up a cottage, but I think we should be making plans and getting things sorted. What do you think?"

By the time he had ended his speech, his words remarkably articulate considering he had never rehearsed them, Hazel's face was pink. Beth was sitting upright, rigid, holding her breath while Kenny stood grinning by the door.

"Em ... erm," Hazel closed her eyes, bit her lip, and then opened them almost immediately to find his questioning face surprisingly determined. "I think ... I agree. Making plans and getting things sorted sounds good to me."

"Right then," Stuart stood up. "It's official. We won't wait for years and years to get together, and we won't be getting married at the

Registry Office, either. You're going to be the star of a proper big wedding, no offence intended to anybody. Okay, well, I'd better go. Got a phone call to make. See you in the morning."

Beth did not sit back in her chair until Hazel had jumped up and followed Stuart's retreating figure out of the door. From her more relaxed position, Beth was suddenly chuckling, and before another second passed, Kenny had seated himself opposite her and had joined in. "Merry Christmas," he toasted her with the last of his coffee.

So, at approximately eight minutes past four in the afternoon, the phone began its long shrill note to the packed house which was The Edge. As Kate was lounging between Andie and Kathy on the new sofa and could not be inclined to move to answer it, Rose did the honours. Only when the woman came looking for David with the news that Stuart was on the phone, did Kate sit upright. David, trying to persuade Kathy's oldest son that ice hockey was better than soccer, glanced once at Kate as he moved towards the hall, as mystified as she was. She followed him immediately. The hall was chilly and Kate stood as close to David as possible, shivering. She watched his face as he made general enquiries, returned the season's greetings and then began to smile. He put his arm around her and held her against him.

"Stuart," she heard him say, "that would be perfectly fine with me. In fact, it has made my day." There was a pause and then he laughed and said, "Okay then. We'll speak to her tomorrow. Thanks. Bye, Stu."

Kate frowned up at her husband. "Is she okay? Why didn't you speak to her?"

David, unaware of Rose hovering by the door, tilted Kate's chin and kissed her softly before answering, "Because she wasn't there. She was at home in bed, I daresay dreaming about the engagement ring she's just been promised."

"Oh, yes!" shouted Kate and punched David on the shoulder. "Oh, Stuart's so lovely, isn't he? I bet he's been planning and rehearsing it for days! But she hasn't got the ring yet? Well, who needs an engagement ring, anyway?" she grinned wickedly and put her arms around David's neck. "I'm so happy. Only one more mystery to solve, and this day would be perfect, but I guess we're going to have to be patient. Kiss me again, please."

Rose moved away and stared at the sitting room before her. The Christmas tree took up the majority of the window space, but the fading blue light enhanced the lights and baubles, making it radiate as much heat as the fire. Joey, Kathy's youngest and shiest boy, was sitting on a footstool beside it, alternating between reading a storybook to a young Morgan and gazing up at the colours. He seemed happy enough. His brother Keith, in David's absence, was sharing his opinions with Neil and Rob's wife, who was from the North of England and seemed to know an inordinate amount about 'football'. Neil was happily accepting their arguments, with only Rose aware that he had lost interest. He grinned at his mother now and finally moved off to sit beside Andie, who looked as fresh as she ever had. Her arm was in plaster, but her face was clear of bruising, and she was chatty and festive in her red velvet dress.

'Only one more mystery to solve and this day would be perfect'. Rose repeated Kate's words in her head. She was right, of course. There were so many positives to this day; Kathy had accepted their Christmas Eve/wedding celebration invitation with delight, a genuine emotion directed straight at David and Kate through a haze of her own memories. Rob and Eileen, the Morgans and the Weatherstones from Peter's Lane, and Iris; each one of them was happy to be here and show their support, because they could recognise the obvious; that the newlyweds deserved to be together and, in particular, the chance to stay together. Neil and Andie were there because there were serious bridges in need of rebuilding. Rose could still hear the horrendous sounds as her sons attacked each other with words and fists. At the time, she had feared that each subsequent wound was a step nearer severing their relationship altogether, but rather than feeling desperate, her anger had erupted in front of them. She stood between them, a tiny bulldog between two greyhounds, and roared at them to give it up.

"What in the name of all that is holy is this?" she had raged. "We're none of us in a good frame of mind at the moment, but to throw each other around the yard like teenagers is beyond my level of understanding. It stops right now. You're both bleeding, for God's sake."

Since that unspeakable day, the two men had tried to face the damage they had caused and were attempting to cancel their regretted words by spending more time in each other's company. Kate had remained quite cool with the pair of them, at least in public, and Rose had found that commendable. In spite of Andie's gradual recovery from broken bones, there remained a question mark in all of their lives; a question mark which Andie had finally acknowledged head on.

Rose remembered Neil returning from the hospital, agitated and alone and needing her comfort. The revelation of Andie's new diagnosis had proved incredibly positive to their particular situation, casting welcome doubt on what they had been so sure of. But it had reduced

Neil to a hyperactive ball of scepticism, whose nerves had finally admitted defeat. He had, in front of her, opened a newly purchased bottle of Jack Daniels and drank half a glass before the shakes came.

"Don't misunderstand me," he had cried, pointing his glass at her, "it's the only way forward. We nearly did something ... well, we ... and now what we were so sure of might not ... We just need to find out, one way or the other. We've faced it once, we can do it again." He took in a pained breath. "But, I'm not sure I can put in the time needed, Rose. This blood test could take weeks to come back. How am I going to deal sensibly with this? How am I going to do this right, for her, until we have the result?"

Yet he was managing. They were two weeks into that restless period of time, the end of which would provide Neil and Andie with either a total reprieve or a suspended sentence. Yet if the horror was destined to come to them again, then each member of this family would be on hand. Perhaps they would even regard having to share the burden as a sort of blessing, as Andie's brother had surely done. In truth, it was all part of someone else's blueprint and out of their hands. Rose watched Neil trying to undo the top button of his shirt beneath his tie, while Andie laughed at his poor attempt, unable to help because of her own handicap. He began to match her chuckle and winked at her, just as Kate dragged David back into the room. He was clutching a bottle of champagne.

"Hazel's engaged!" she shouted, giving a little jump of excitement and hugging Rose. "Can you imagine the level of noise in that house at this moment?"

As Neil made his way to congratulate David, Kate sat once more between Kathy and Andie, sighing happily. What a great day it was turning out to be. She was spending her first Christmas with David in her new home, and her sister was at last going to have something other than them to occupy her mind. There was a fifty-fifty chance that Andie may be totally free from her father's affliction, which was so much more than they could have imagined three weeks ago; and Neil and David were at last treating each other as equals in this game of life. Whatever was coming was coming, but today, there was something to smile about, and it was time to relax.

As Kate stretched her feet out in front of her, aware for the first time that day of the tiny hole in her sock, she smelled White Musk. Startled, she sat forward slowly, just in time to see Kathy put a tiny bottle of perfume back into her handbag. At Kate's enquiring look, she looked slightly ashamed.

"A single woman still likes to smell nice," Kathy explained, and raised her glass as David toured the room, offering all those who cared to the chance to celebrate Hazel's news.

PART IV

June 1997

CHAPTER 36
Sunday, 15th June 1997

The sun was a stubborn, blazing ball of fire above The Edge, and both front and back doors were wide to the world, trying to rid the hallway of the smell of emulsion paint. It was a momentous day. The last coat of paint had been applied to the final piece of new plasterwork, and at last The Edge was totally theirs. David stood sipping at a bottle of lager, his jeans and T-shirt both as much white with paint as with age. He had taken a week off work to complete the task, and, in spite of the heat of the Canadian summer, he now sported a full beard.

"Do you think it makes you look younger, because it doesn't, matey," Kate stated, her eyes glinting. "If you're having a crisis, please stop. Why can't you understand that I'm the insecure, dramatic one? You're the tall, strong, handsome one. Crises are my department, so stop stealing my lines, Dave."

There was no answer to her nonsense, and so he settled himself on to the rail of the verandah and gently rocked her in the porch swing with his bare foot. It was a hazy Sunday afternoon and they were to eat with Rose later, but that was still an hour or two away. Their chore completed, it seemed ridiculous not to simply sit and enjoy the heat and the colours, especially since Hazel's phone call of a few hours earlier. Apparently, Stuart had finally decided that the near dilapidated cottage he had taken on had reached the standard required for them to live in, and they had set a date for their wedding. She had expressed her hope that both of them would be available on 7th February 1998, because if she had to go back to the drawing board on the date, there would very likely be a divorce before there was even a wedding.

Neither David nor Kate could see a problem with this arrangement and had spent the last hour or so discussing the future nuptials and admitting that perhaps they were in the best place from where to watch the proceedings unfold.

Kate was happy. When she was happy, she found it hard to sit still and so, while David took his tall, strong, handsome body off to the shower, Kate climbed the final flight to the top of the house and grinned at the room, contentedly. They had transformed the old office into their bedroom in their first year, yet the place still had the ability to impress her as she turned at the top of the stairs. Today, the sun was creating shafts of bright dust particles which moved constantly in the breeze from the windows and washed the dark boards under her feet with light and heat. Gone were the gigantic maps of plantations, the incidental tables, filing cabinets and desk. In their place were pale green walls, new bed and rugs, David's massive wardrobe and Kate's handmade chest of drawers. This last piece of furniture was as dear to her as the framed set of artefacts put together by Hazel which hung above it. Neil had made it for her. His personality was carved into it, and it was precious and permanent. However, Kate had no time for sentiment. She was on a mission.

Tucked into the far corner of David's new office was her trunk. Regrettably, David had used it as a table and positioned a kettle, some box files and a printer on top of it, all of which Kate had to heave onto the floor before she could open the lid. But that done, she was soon humming to herself, and after a moment or two of hunting and parting and piling, she spied the objects she required; two ordinary yellow envelopes snapped together with an elastic band and hidden beneath an old baby's bonnet. Kate sighed. She really had no sense of pride. If she had, those envelopes would be tied with a satin ribbon and placed in a box of sandalwood, perhaps gracing the top of her chest of drawers and somehow tying her, David, Neil and her mother together. But here they were at the bottom of a trunk which was being used as a makeshift table. Tutting, she moved back through to the brighter bedroom, leaving the office disturbed and abandoned.

She lay flat on her back, the duvet rising like dough around her, and held one envelope in each hand. She knew both equally well, and it seemed like today was the perfect day to revisit them, when the house was humming in the heat and David had declared that The Edge was entering yet another era. Fiona's letter to David always made her feel lucky; lucky that she had known someone as incredibly strong as her mother. That in all the years she had hungered for the love of David,

Fiona had never once hinted that her life was miserable or lonely. She had asked him to look kindly on Kate, which had turned out rather well in the end. Kate missed her and would always miss her, in spite of the miraculous road her life had taken and how contented she now felt. She lifted the letter marked with her name from its pale yellow home and immediately was smiling. She only needed to view her mother's unique handwriting to instantly hear her voice.

Kate was halfway down her third page when David arrived at the top of the stairs. Even her mother's words were not enough to prevent Kate sitting up and watching him cross the room. The sight of David in a towel and not much else could not be ignored, no matter how often she was permitted to view it. And, of course, his face was now completely clean shaven. She laughed out loud and fell back against the pillows.

"For a grown man, you are far too easily swayed by the words of a mere female," she chuckled.

"You've never been 'mere' in your life," he replied, glancing in the mirror and flattening his mess of hair before joining her on the bed. "Also, it was too hot. Maybe come the winter. Pass them over then."

There were many different aspects to David which Kate loved, but one of the most endearing was his continued delight in sharing Fiona with her. It made sense. Both of them had adored her, and the mention of her name had caused no problems to date. What others made of this state of affairs was irrelevant, and now, as Kate read of her mother's feelings and her connection to Neil, she handed them to David as if they were nothing more than a dinner menu to be viewed and appreciated. It was a moment of calm after a busy week; it was an activity which allowed them both to relax beside each other on a balmy summer's day. It made them both happy. After a moment, David closed his eyes and let his hand and the page it contained fall to his side. "Read the final bits to me," he murmured. "You always say them just right."

"Okay," replied Kate, "I will. But here's the deal. I read the rest of this and in return, you run me a bath. A shower is just not going to cut it today. What do you say?"

"I say that, considering what your usual demands are, I'm getting off lightly."

"Well, I didn't say I was going for a bath on my own," she replied, kissing his stomach. "So. Here we go." She cleared her throat.

'Don't think for one minute, Kate, that Neil was what you would call a lover. I loved David. I always loved David, but on that night, Neil was so good to me. He listened. He always listened, even when I was being my usual ridiculous self and I loved him for that. I wanted him to hold me and he did. Sometimes emotions run so fast that you end up running with them and you get to the point where you stop thinking. And then you force yourself to think again, and you worry that you've been so very unfair to the person you're with, a person who deserves more consideration, that all you can do is to keep running. And then, dear Kate, you are in the middle of something you can't stop. This won't make sense to you, not at this moment, but one day you'll understand everything. Please, please don't hate me. Please don't think badly of Neil. I took advantage of a younger man's feelings. I didn't intend to, but that doesn't mean it wasn't wrong. And don't despise David. David was my love and he is a special, unique man. I loved David as a husband and on one night, I loved Neil in a strange, unexpected way. But never forget, I loved you equally as much as either of them, and made sure that nobody ever doubted that. I love you, Katy. Be happy and forgive me if you can. Mum.'

Kate moved her head closer to David's and heard the slow deep breathing of a man who had drifted away, contented and satisfied with his lot in life. She propped herself onto one elbow and let her eyes wander over him. His body looked no older than when she had first viewed it, and still she marvelled that he was hers. His face, free from hair and sporting only one tiny, accidental spot of blood, remained perfect in spite of its characteristic pale pink scar; and up close, she smelled soap and warm skin. She had, as a child, once pondered which one of her five senses she could give up if forced to, and had always assumed that smell would be the least useful to her. But not to be aware of the aroma of David's skin, now that she had experienced it, would be a tragedy. She gazed at the far more prominent scars on his ankle and calf, markers of the accident which had set their entire lives in motion, and had the urge to touch both; but as she moved in the direction of his legs, she felt his hand take hold of her elbow.

"Where are you going?" he whispered. "Stay just a bit longer."

«●»«●»«●»

Later, when both letters had been stored carefully, Kate heard the phone ring and, picking up the bedroom extension, was pleased to hear Rose on the other end of the line. David, dressed and whistling something reasonably like the theme from Local Hero was running water into the bath, when he heard Kate's frantic call from the floor above. He turned off the tap and stood at the door.

"What was that, honey?"

"Hospital! Now! Rose will meet us there."

By the time they had tended to the housekeeping, shutting all the open doors and windows and asking each other a plethora of questions which contained no immediate solutions, Kate's face was a livid red.

"How many beers did you have, Dave? Are you okay to drive?"

"I didn't even finish one. It's fine. What did Rose say exactly?"

"Just that she would meet us there and not to rush. Oh God, Dave. I'm really scared."

"Don't worry, Kitty. It'll be fine. He'll be fine ..."

In spite of the anxiety involved in most of her recent visits, Rose was reasonably content to sit in the hospital waiting room and await instructions from an official in a white coat. When it appeared that she could offer no further help for the moment, she had wandered down to the nearest refreshment booth and ordered her tea, thick and strong. In fact, the tables and chairs, arranged as they were, gave the place an almost continental café feel; and in spite of her hammering heart, she had forced herself to sit and watch groups of family members wander around aimlessly, like herself, waiting to be called.

So, here was her entire family, at last in the position they had always considered possible but had never really pursued; one precious son and daughter-in-law rushing to her side while the other two occupied a side-ward upstairs, frightened and indisposed, about to accept their fate. Her tea tasted like liquid iron, and she could not stomach it. She tried to recline in the chair, but the hard plastic was almost as inflexible as God's plan for her children, and instead she sat forward, her elbows resting on her knees and thought of the faces of those dearest to her.

There was David, a year short of his fiftieth birthday, his frame and outlook kept young by the complete adoration and constant teasing of his wife. The man had not smiled so much in years, and he seemed content to feed his wife's mild eccentricity by accepting that she would always be around to shake him up whenever he was in danger of growing old gracefully. His face had laughter lines of its own, and, best of all, she no longer lay awake wondering if he was curled into a cold, isolated ball of grief. He was fine.

Kate herself made no attempt to hide her commitment to the man and refused to be judged or intimidated by anyone. Her husband was twenty-eight years older than she, this was a fact. Although Rose guessed that Kate's soul had toured this earth many times before, the girl took delight in sharing her youthful enthusiasm with anyone who crossed her path, sometimes to an alarming degree. She did not try to be perfect, her housekeeping skills were basic, and she preferred letter-writing to any other activity. What she did with her time was a mystery to most, but she shared that time as if each minute were precious. To somebody who had lost her mother too early, it obviously was.

What of Neil? It was almost two and a half years since Andie's accident had scared them all to death, and in that time there had been both physical and mental changes. His body had at last regained some definition, which suited him better than the emaciated frame produced by the trauma. He had also become so much calmer, approaching every potential crisis with less apprehension and more tolerance. Kate had persuaded him that his fortieth birthday required a ceilidh and had spent weeks working with Jessie Morgan on the dances and how to teach them on the night. The result had been a mixed success but hilarious nevertheless, and Kate now had a fiddler, a whistler and a drummer added to her list of friends.

Rose had watched Neil as he had followed his daughter's progress around the dance hall, and she hoped he had allowed himself a nugget of pride. Since that awful fight, when he and David had dealt with more than one outstanding debt, he had finally become an adult. He may no longer be quite so boyish or quick to tease people, but he had developed a smile which at last reached his eyes.

Andie, exquisite Andie, whose face had gradually begun to betray her emotions after a lifetime of masking them. This had not made her features less enchanting, it had merely added complex layers, and it was difficult these days to remember how she had been prior to this. Rose dared not admit, even to herself, that this woman touched her heart the most out of all of them, and thinking of her now brought a tiny hint of a tear glinting onto her cheek.

In the next second, Rose was on her feet. At the far end of the corridor, Neil was jogging towards her, his open checked shirt flying behind him, T-shirt untucked from his jeans. Rose swallowed to moisten her dry mouth and waved at him.

"Neil! Over here."

He diverted his course immediately, and following behind him, less out of breath but just as excited, was Andie. Her hair was in two long pigtails, which Kate had likened to Pippi Longstocking's, but which she loved to braid through with purple ribbons. She looked about fifteen.

"Any news?" she breathed, kissing Rose's cheek.

"Well, her water broke when she was on the phone to me, so she's definitely in labour, but they reckon the little one might not be 'little' by any measure. If he's anything like his dad, we could be here all night. So, I hope you didn't drive like a maniac, Neil."

Neil sat heavily on a plastic chair and shook his head. "I was very restrained, but I could murder a coffee, and it's time Andie ate, right?"

Andie threw a look of minor exasperation in his direction, but did not argue and headed off to the counter to view what was on offer. Neil was nothing if not conscientiously rigorous in his care of Andie, but she could not fault him for this. They had sat together in an austere consulting room, as one person, listening to traffic on the street, the shuffling of papers, the breathing of the man with the answers. It had been dense in that room, thick with all of their memories swirling down to those last few seconds free from knowledge. And then the sun had shone, dispersing the fog, and Neil had stood tall, his hands shaking by his side. As her heart had floated to the ceiling and the sobs had gathered in her throat, she had watched his hands and was suddenly so grateful. Thankful that those hands which had reached for her would be creating masterpieces for years to come, and that she would still be there to apply the Band-Aids. No, he could fuss all he liked, it was his privilege.

"How's Dave doing?"

Rose screwed up her face. "He was absolutely fine until they started talking size. You know how tiny Kate is. Now, of course, the world is about to end. You might be able to talk to him. Ring the ward from over there."

Five minutes later and Neil was looking at David's rigidly straight back. He was staring out of the landing window, rubbing the back of his neck, completely unaware of his brother's approach.

"Hey, Dave. You taking a break?"

"Neil. Buddy. They're talking about maybe a section. He's curled up ... awkwardly."

"Well then, no worries. He'll be out in minutes, and Kate will have some story to tell somewhere down the line. You're not going in there?"

"Depends on what staff they have, they might have to put her under. God in heaven, this hurts. Why am I in pain?"

"Let's take a seat, Dave. Hey mate, you do know you're going grey, right?"

«•»«•»«•»

It was about 11.30 p.m. when Kate finally began to emerge from the blackness and started to string images together into a moving scene. Her eyes were being incredibly uncooperative, and her throat seemed to have closed up completely. When she tried to ask David a question, the words came out in Gaelic, and she had to look away before their horrified faces made her laugh. Everything, inside and outside of her body, ached at its mistreatment, and she feared that any muscular movement might prove beyond her endurance. She saw David's face near to hers and felt his lips on her forehead, then a blur of other faces in the background. But she needed to see one face more than any other.

"Where is he?" she croaked.

Rose emerged into focus, and there he was in her arms; a not-so-tiny bundle with incredibly long fingers and no hair whatsoever. Rose tried to fit him neatly into Kate's arms, but his legs were too long, so she lay with him against her chest, her arms not yet capable of cradling him, until David sat up close and held him safe against her.

"I'll hold him until you can."

"He's sleeping? Thought he might be crying for me."

"They say he might be sleepy for a while, just like you. But don't worry, we'll stay right here. He's fine. He's perfect."

Kate felt herself slipping back into the velvet casing of a dream world, but just as she reached the point of falling, her hand moved itself to her baby's foot and she held it in her palm. It was warm and soft, and hers.

When Kate awoke again, it was light, and the crack in the ceiling above her head was almost the exact shape of a treble clef. She gazed at it, mesmerised, for two or three seconds then tried to move up the bed a little. It took a monumental effort on her part to progress even a couple of inches, but she was rewarded with the view of David asleep on the chair in the corner. He had one leg hooked over the wooden armrest, and his head was crooked into his folded arms. Kate frowned in sympathy; his neck would regret that unfortunate position. She noted the crib had been wheeled from the room, and now that she was fully alert, she needed to look on her son properly for the first time.

"Dave," she called gently, then, "David!"

It took him only a second to stand, and he did not even grimace until the act was completed. Then he was at her side, grinning and subsequently yawning. She held out her hand for his.

"Where did they take him?" she asked.

"Only to the nursery. Honestly, Kit, he's fine. How do you feel?"

"Amazed," she smiled. "Amazed that it's over and I'm still in one piece. Well, mostly still in one piece, we can compare scars later. I'm also amazed that he's bald. Oh, and amazed that that crack looks like a treble clef. Can you go get him?"

"Yes, I think so. I'll see what I can do."

When finally Kate got to study her son, she declared herself amazed once more, and then entered into a semi-rant on how much her vocabulary had deteriorated; almost from the day she had discovered she was pregnant. "It's just laziness on my part," she crooned, noticing the minute white spots on the infant's silky nose. "I shall, from now on, endeavour to astound the pair of you with my inspiring turn of phrase. Oh, Dave, look at his lashes!"

"Your lashes and my chin, I think. Not a horrific combination. What's the final decision on the name then?"

Kate settled back and took hold of David's hand. "If you really want me to choose, then I do have an idea."

"Let me have it."

"What about ..." Kate meandered around the words, "... Alasdair Neil. For my granddad and for this little one's granddad. Because there will only ever be one David to me. What do you think?"

"Alasdair Neil Wilder," David touched his son's head with his fingertips. The child's brow creased for a moment, and then his fists punched the air as if he, too, was in agreement at the chosen name. "You know, he's not actually bald, the hair is just very, very fine."

David's face was close enough to Kate's for her to kiss his chin, and still he could not take his eyes away from the tiny, immaculate person. Kate felt heat spreading up her spine and onto her scalp as she witnessed his adoration. No doubt he had felt the same on the day Hazel had been born, and Kate was instantly in need of his face in her hands, but before she could speak, he was flashing his eyes wickedly at her.

"Jeez," he grinned. "Neil a granddad. Aw Kit, my darling. I hope this little guy's got your sense of humour, because one day he's going to have to try to understand his unusual ancestry. I think I'll leave the talking to you."

"Take him a minute, Dave," she said, and as he settled him into his own arms, Kate leaned over and cupped David's smooth chin. This man was her whole world. "I love you," she said. "I love this wee man. I love you together. I love being me, but you know all that already. So I'll just say this. I will never, ever take him away from you, David. We belong to you."

«•»«•»«•»

16477090R00181

Printed in Great Britain
by Amazon